PRAISE FOR *T*

"Families, like ships at sea, some   .nd begin to break apart. Which is exactly what happens to the Vergennes family in Sonja Yoerg's luminous *The Family Ship*. Only a heart of stone would be immune to the charm of the Vergennes children, all nine of them. Yoerg offers this large, disparate crew to the reader with the wisdom and compassion of a consummate storyteller. And she tops off the tale with one of the most exciting finales I've read in years. I recommend this book with my whole heart."

—William Kent Krueger, *New York* Times bestselling author of *This Tender Land*

"With both wit and wonder, Sonja Yoerg navigates *The Family Ship* through choppy waters. This novel is completely immersive and highlights the enduring power of story in both our lives and our families. Yoerg's prose and imagination are the strong currents that bring this fabulous tale to life."

—Patti Callahan, *New York Times* bestselling author of *Becoming Mrs. Lewis*

"Sonja Yoerg's *The Family Ship* is a fearless, timeless story of a family in crisis. Join the Vergennes family on the shores of the Chesapeake and you'll be rewarded with an emotionally charged page-turner of a story, but also with a cast of beautifully rendered characters who each will find a different way into your heart. Rising tides of grief, hope, and loyalty will sweep you away!"

—Kelly Harms, *Washington Post* bestselling author of *The Overdue Life of Amy Byler*

"Building on the metaphor of a landlocked ship on which the children of a large and close-knit family have long engaged in a complex game of make-believe, *The Family Ship* explores the dynamics of love and betrayal, tragedy and healing. Yoerg has crafted a refreshingly unusual and beautifully written story about the ways grief can both break us apart and bring us together."

—Kerry Anne King, bestselling author of *Whisper Me This* and *Everything You Are*

"In *The Family Ship*, Sonja Yoerg has lovingly rendered an imaginative family saga of strength, tragedy, and triumph. The Vergennes family of nine children and their parents is deftly woven and expertly crafted to explore an array of palpable emotions and realistic personalities for a sweeping cast of characters—a credit to Yoerg's remarkable skill and talent as a writer. Like all good family stories, *The Family Ship* begins and ends with love."

—Amy Sue Nathan, bestselling author of *The Last Bathing Beauty*

PRAISE FOR *STORIES WE NEVER TOLD*

"*Stories We Never Told* is a beautifully told story of love and obsession, a gradual unearthing of long-held secrets that can unravel even the happiest of marriages. Yoerg has a real talent for creating compelling and complex characters who wrestle with real-life situations, leaving the reader wondering who to root for until the very end. Yoerg should be on every reader's radar."

—Kimberly Belle, *New York Times* bestselling author of *Stranger in the Lake*

"It's a rare psychological thriller that shows both the dark depths our obsessions can lead to and the unlikely breakthroughs that can let the light in. Sonja Yoerg's *Stories We Never Told* does just that, deftly introducing a brilliant cast of characters for whom detachment and intimacy can be equally terrifying. A taut, clever, and satisfying read."

—Jessica Strawser, bestselling author of *A Million Reasons Why*

"Sonja Yoerg expands her literary repertoire into suspense with *Stories We Never Told*, a tale of obsession, love, secrets, marriage, and the lies we tell ourselves. The prose is lyrical and immersive, and the story builds delicious tension. But the characters are where Yoerg truly shines: they're all so keenly developed, so realistic, and so surprising with their own crackling takes on relationships, academia, and each other that the story itself starts to feel almost immaterial. Until, of course, it shocks the living hell out of you."

—Kate Moretti, *New York Times* bestselling author of
Girls of Brackenhill

"Obsession, jealousy, and secrets smolder into a deadly fire in Yoerg's latest, as a woman's marriage and career implode at the same time her ex's life seems to be on the rise. Astutely observed and beautifully written with echoes of Highsmith's Ripley, this one's got a deliciously diabolical villain to die for."

—Emily Carpenter, bestselling author of
Reviving the Hawthorn Sisters

"Truth and trust relentlessly collide in this beautifully written and riveting page-turner. Talented storyteller Sonja Yoerg will ensnare you from page one—and her determined and endearing main character, twisted by love and betrayed by expectations, will keep you turning pages as fast as you can. Loved this!"

—Hank Phillippi Ryan, nationally bestselling author of
The First to Lie

"*Stories We Never Told* is Sonja Yoerg at her best—gripping characters, sizzling suspense, brilliantly written. I raced through the pages. Bravo!"
—Kaira Rouda, international bestselling author of *The Favorite Daughter*

"*Stories We Never Told* is a superb, slow-burn suspense that brilliantly ratchets up the tension and character development notch by notch, layer by layer, culminating in a chilling, emotional ending. Sonja Yoerg is a master at creating characters you fall into, and her writing is stunning. A must read!"
—Samantha M. Bailey, international bestselling author of *Woman on the Edge*

PRAISE FOR *TRUE PLACES*

"Engrossing and provocative."
—Cynthia Swanson, *New York Times* bestselling author of *The Glass Forest* and *The Bookseller*

"A knockout novel: beautiful, unique, suspenseful, and full of wonder."
—Julie Cantrell, *New York Times* and *USA Today* bestselling author of *Perennials*

"A stunning novel with luminous prose and a story that speaks straight to the heart."
—Camille Pagán, bestselling author of *Life and Other Near-Death Experiences*

"A smart, tension-filled family drama—Yoerg at her best."
—Julie Lawson Timmer, author of *Five Days Left*, *Untethered*, and
Mrs. Saint and the Defectives

"Gripping, emotional, and deeply authentic, *True Places* will have you flipping pages long into the night."
—Kristy Woodson Harvey, national bestselling author of
The Secret to Southern Charm

"Tender and triumphant . . . readers will be swept along in the gorgeous narrative and fall in love with the artfully drawn characters plucked from real life."
—Nicole Baart, author of *Little Broken Things* and
You Were Always Mine

"Readers will enjoy every moment of getting lost in the pages of *True Places*, with its richly drawn, realistic characters and loving attention to the details of the natural world. A beautiful book, all around."
—Susan Gloss, *USA Today* bestselling author of *Vintage* and
The Curiosities

PRAISE FOR *ALL THE BEST PEOPLE*

"Not just the best people, but real people: authentic, quirky, and troubled. I cared for them all."
—Chris Bohjalian, *New York Times* bestselling author of
The Flight Attendant

"Deftly and with the delicate brush of a master, Yoerg draws us into this brilliant, multigenerational saga of love, madness, mysticism, and the markings they leave on a family."

—Christopher Scotton, author of *The Secret Wisdom of the Earth*

"A stirring tale of mothers and daughters, their secrets and their strength . . . a mesmerizing read."

—Lynda Cohen Loigman, author of *The Wartime Sisters*

"A powerful and haunting novel about betrayal and shame, acceptance, and unconditional love. Book clubs will devour it."

—Barbara Claypole White, bestselling author of *The Perfect Son*

PRAISE FOR *THE MIDDLE OF SOMEWHERE*

"Yoerg knows how to keep the pages turning in this fast-paced, action-packed, heart-tugging novel."

—Heather Gudenkauf, *New York Times* bestselling author of *Before She Was Found*

"The perfect blend of self-discovery and suspense."

—Kate Moretti, *New York Times* bestselling author of *In Her Bones*

"Yoerg skillfully explores how the weight of remorse makes the search for personal redemption a test of not just the will, but the heart . . . stunningly descriptive prose."

—Susan Meissner, *USA Today* bestselling author of *The Last Year of the War*

PRAISE FOR *HOUSE BROKEN*

"A stunning debut that will have readers wanting more! Yoerg is on par with Jennifer Weiner and Sarah Pekkanen."

—*Library Journal* (starred review)

"With beautiful prose and an unflinching eye, Sonja Yoerg has created a riveting tale exploring the power of family secrets. *House Broken* is a novel that will burn itself into your memory. The book is, by turns, brilliant, heartbreaking, shocking, and hopeful."

—Ellen Marie Wiseman, author of *The Life She Was Given*

"*House Broken* is a powerful tale of the ways in which families hurt and heal. Gorgeously written with characters that shine."

—Eileen Goudge, *New York Times* bestselling author of *Garden of Lies*

"A compelling tale of a family gone awry and the ultimate cost of maintaining shameful secrets. *House Broken* is everything I love in women's fiction . . . beautiful writing, strong characters, a dash of mystery, and the hope for redemption."

—Lori Nelson Spielman, international bestselling author of
The Life List

THE
FAMILY
SHIP

ALSO BY SONJA YOERG

House Broken
The Middle of Somewhere
All the Best People
True Places
Stories We Never Told

THE
FAMILY
SHIP

A NOVEL

SONJA
YOERG

LAKE UNION
PUBLISHING

391 2997

Text copyright © 2021 by Sonja Yoerg
All rights reserved.

Published by Lake Union Publishing, Seattle

www.apub.com

Amazon, the Amazon logo, and Lake Union Publishing are trademarks of Amazon.com, Inc., or its affiliates.

ISBN-13: 9781542004695
ISBN-10: 1542004691

Cover design by Emily Mahon

Printed in the United States of America

THE
FAMILY
SHIP

PROLOGUE

Jude

1962

Jude's earliest memory was of the day his sister was born, as if becoming a big brother made his brain decide it needed to start keeping track for the long run. As if a promise made at four was meant to be honored forever.

Grandma Jean had been staying with him, the first two nights he'd ever been away from his parents. All Grandma Jean wanted to do was feed him, and all he wanted to do was kneel on the couch where he could see the driveway and know when his parents came home. With the baby.

Jude remembered the nubby feel of the couch under his hands and having to pee but not wanting to go because he might miss spotting the car. He remembered the tight swirl in his chest, excitement and worry tangled together. He remembered that on the second morning, Grandma Jean made him break his vigil and took him to his room to change out of his pajamas, and that was when his parents came home.

Grandma Jean hadn't finished her ridiculous task, and Jude ran downstairs in only his underpants.

His mother bent down and opened her arms. He threw himself into them.

"Easy, son," his father said.

Jude breathed in his mother's smell, and the tangle in his chest loosened.

His mother cupped his face in her hands. "How's my best boy?"

Jude remembered about the baby and looked around the back of his mother for it.

She turned him around by the shoulders. "Go say hello to your sister."

His father had moved to the couch holding something wrapped in a blanket. The something was his sister. Jude had expected bigger. He climbed up next to his father, who unwrapped the blanket. The baby's arms sprang up like a jack-in-the-box. Her face was pink, and so was everything else: her hat, the blanket, her fists. Before Jude could even wonder what he was supposed to do with her, his father put his hand on Jude's chest, then on the baby's.

"This is Verity."

Jude tried it out. "Beridy."

"Verity," his father repeated. "She's your sister, which means you're her big brother. You can see how small she is, how she needs us to take care of her, keep her safe. Not just your mother and me, but you, too."

Him? What could he do, carry his sword around all the time?

Before he could ask, his father said, "She'll grow up faster than you can imagine, but you'll always be her big brother. *Always* means forever, you understand that?"

Jude nodded. Forever was like tomorrow but way out in space.

His father wasn't finished. He lifted Jude's chin with two fingers, and Jude tore his eyes from the baby and looked at his father. "You have to keep her safe, Jude."

"Okay, I will." Jude leaned over and kissed his sister's forehead, feeling thick and heavy, like he had a fever. She was so small and pink and didn't come with any armor or claws or weapons. He worried he wasn't big enough or brave enough to keep her safe, but anyone could see she needed him.

A tiger could eat her in two bites.

PART I

1980

USS *Nepenthe* Roster

Name	Age	Rate
Verity	18	Lieutenant Commander, Captain
Eden	14	Supply Master
Spider	13	Quartermaster
Harper	11	Ship's Doctor
Roy	8	Gunner
Wallace	8	Gunner's Mate
Cyrus	6	Ship's Cook
Nellie	4	Ship's Cook's Mate

CHAPTER ONE

CYRUS

Ship's Log: USS *Nepenthe*
Date: Saturday, April 26, 1980
Time: 1138h
Weather: 59°F, Fair
Winds: 0–5 kn SW
CO: Lt. Commander V. Vergennes

Cyrus checked the eleven pieces of bread in front of him, making sure each had two slices of bologna, and started putting on the top bread slices. A green grape rolled down the aisle between the sandwiches. He popped it into his mouth.

"Hey!" Nellie said. "Mine!"

He smiled. She was only four—well, almost five. Her real name was Penelope, but that was longer than she was, so they called her Nellie. "Just get another one from the bag." He waited to make sure she didn't lose count. Number salad was easy, but only if you were six like him.

Eight red plastic bowls. In each one went six grapes, five raisins, four banana slices, three cheese cubes, and two of something else. Today something else was strawberries, Nellie's favorite, so Cyrus watched her like a spy out of the corner of his eye to make sure she didn't sneak one.

It was his galley, and he was in charge. If he didn't have enough to make everything even steven, he was accountable.

Eight bowls, eight crew on board today. Mommy never had ship lunch. She had peace and quiet. The three biggest got two sandwiches each, so eleven sandwiches and eight number salads. You had to be six and "Be Accountable" and "Be Responsible" to run the galley. The sign outside the wheelhouse told you that every time you walked by—if you were old enough to read it like he was. Right now, though, the plastic banana knife was bugging him. Plastic was for babies. Verity said that if he wanted a real knife, he had to earn it, and what the captain said went.

Cyrus finished the sandwiches, stacked them in a cardboard box, and checked Nellie's work. "Good job, mate."

She grinned and shrugged. "Anyway." Her white sailor hat slipped sideways, and some of her hair sprang out. It was curly like Mommy's and Harper's and Verity's.

Something wriggled inside Nellie's white shirt. It took Cyrus about two seconds to realize what it was. *On the ship. In my galley.*

He came around to her side of the table so he could scream in her ear in private. "What is Vermin doing here?"

She backed up, and her dark-brown eyes went watery. Cyrus was sorry he'd scared her because she was only little. *But for Pete's sake!*

Nellie pulled her shirt out of her pants, and the guinea pig plopped onto the table. "She's helping." Vermin snuffled her way across the table, vacuuming up all the crumbs and dabs of mayo. Nellie clapped her hands. "All clean!"

If the captain or Daddy saw Vermin on board, Cyrus and Nellie would be pulling swab duty until kingdom come. Cyrus lunged for Vermin, but she squeak-oinked and zoomed off with a supersonic waddle.

The horn blasted. Nellie jumped. Another two blasts, both long ones.

"Uh-oh." Cyrus was already untying his apron. "Man overboard."

CHAPTER TWO

VERITY

Verity stationed herself at the stern of the ship on the port side of the engine housing. She clasped her hands behind her back and monitored the actions of the crew. Spider, the quartermaster, cranked the winch to raise the red-and-yellow Oscar flag, the signal for man overboard. Verity's gaze didn't linger on him; he was thirteen and knew what to do. Eden was fourteen and also knew what to do, but that didn't stop her from lounging on top of a supply locker with her feet on the engine housing. Her Dixie cup cap was pushed back on her head, her face tilted up to catch the sun. Verity didn't have time to discipline her now, but she would, or she'd try. She was the captain, and discipline was part of her job whether she liked it or not. She did not.

When the alarm sounded, Harper, the ship's doctor, was catching up on paperwork at the desk inside the wheelhouse. Now she jumped to her feet. She shoved the papers into a folder and flipped up the seat to retrieve the emergency medical kit. Cyrus and Nellie popped up from belowdecks, squeezed past Harper, and scurried to the muster point in front of Verity. Roy and Wallace, eight-year-old twins, came careening around from the bow and dropped the three feet to the deck, nearly colliding with Nellie. Harper, a head taller than the twins, emerged from the wheelhouse and joined the group at the back. As Verity handed out life jackets from the locker at her feet, she realized she'd been Harper's age—eleven—when she first became captain. Harper had been close to Nellie's age then. Would Harper ever take command? She had a better personality for it than Verity did, not at all shy about telling people what to do. *Harper can have the job right now*, Verity thought, *and I can have my own life*. The rush of guilt was immediate, and she pushed the thought aside.

Roy retrieved the life preserver from the wall to the right of the wheelhouse door. He hoisted it in the air triumphantly and twisted around to peer over the side of the ship, scanning frantically. "Who's overboard? Where are they?"

"No questions at muster, Gunner Roy." Verity pointed off the port bow. "A seaman fell in over there. Roy, you throw him the doughnut, but don't clonk him on the head with it."

Eden glanced over her shoulder. "There's no one there."

"Shut up, Eden," Spider said and motioned to Roy. "Hurry up and put on your life jacket before the poor guy drowns. Wallace, be ready to help haul him up."

Verity nodded her approval to Spider, who went back to installing the new weather gauges on the wall near the captain's chair. Wallace unhooked a folded rope ladder from the outside of the wheelhouse. Roy climbed up to the foredeck, dragging the doughnut behind him. He had to be careful because the flat space between the wheelhouse and the bulwark was narrow there, and he refused to hold on to the chrome railings that ran along the top of the wheelhouse and the edge of the bow. When he reached the port bow, he thrust out his arm. "There he is!" Earlier, Verity had placed a Ronald McDonald doll on the lawn as a stand-in for a drowning sailor.

Harper, Wallace, Cyrus, and Nellie gathered along the bulwark, a line of white Dixie cup caps and white uniforms graduated in height. The seriousness of their expressions reminded Verity of when she had been deadly earnest about the ship, too. Her whole childhood had centered on it, and now she had one foot out the door.

Roy tossed the life preserver—a perfect throw, landing a yard in front of Ronald McDonald.

Wallace shouted, "Grab it, Ronald!"

"He's mine, you know." Cyrus shook his head. "So I can tell you he's a goner. Can't swim a lick."

Nellie clamped her hands over his eyes. "Don't watch."

Across the yard, the screen door at the back of the house opened, and a girl emerged. She wore sunshine-yellow bell-bottoms with a bib front over a white shirt. Her loopy, blonde curls were held back by a matching yellow headband. As she scanned the yard, her curls bounced. She looked familiar, but Verity didn't know the younger high school kids, especially not the ones who could have been straight off the cover of *Seventeen*. Whoever it was must've just finished a piano lesson with their mom.

The girl came toward the ship, squinting, peering around, trying to figure out what was going on. Good luck with that.

"Eden? Is Eden there somewhere?"

"Oh God." Eden roused herself from her sun worship, and her feet hit the deck.

Verity frowned at her. "No cursing, sailor."

Eden peeked over the bulwark, spotted the girl, and ducked under the canopy that extended over the deck from the top of the wheelhouse. She crouched below the window to the right of the door. "No way, Jose. No, no, and no."

Harper craned her neck to see who was there, then pointed toward the wheelhouse. "She's right here! Eden! Eden, a friend's here." Harper swung her arm toward the gangway—a wide plank that went from the starboard stern to the ground. "Use that to come aboard, but maybe check with Verity first." She spun and cupped her hands around her mouth to shout, even though Verity was six feet away. "Verity! I mean, Captain! Permission for someone to come aboard!"

"Yes, Harper—"

Harper leaned over the side to speak with the girl. "Did you have a piano lesson with our mom? Was it your first one? How did it go? Our mom's a great teacher. You're really lucky, you know. Eden! We're in the middle of a man-overboard situation here, so pardon us. Ship's business and all that. Plus drowning, possibly. Never a dull moment. Eden! Your friend is here!"

Eden was halfway down the gangway. Verity knew she ought to command her to return, but the look on her sister's face stopped her. Eden was mortified.

Eden racewalked away from the ship. "Hi, Kelsey. I didn't know you'd be here."

Kelsey followed her, but hung back a little, curious. "Yeah, I had a lesson with your mom. But cool your jets a sec. What's the deal with this boat?"

Ship, Verity corrected automatically. *It's a ship*. A destroyer escort, to be precise.

Eden paused, slid her hands into the back pockets of her jeans. She shrugged one shoulder and dropped her eyelids like she was bored out of her skull. This look was new; Eden probably practiced it in the bathroom mirror. "Nothing. Just a dumb game." She circled her arm for Kelsey to follow and started off toward the house again. "You want a Popsicle?"

The rest of the crew had been monitoring the interruption, looking from Verity to Eden and back again. It was Verity's job to take control and erase the disorder of the last few minutes, but instead she watched Eden and Kelsey cross the lawn, chatting and laughing, just two normal teenagers hanging out, no plans, no drills, no line of command. Verity wasn't exactly jealous of Eden, although she did resent her sister grabbing for freedoms that Verity hadn't dared to, at least until recently.

Verity needed the ship because, unlike Eden, she'd never been good at making friends, and it'd only gotten worse lately. Kids called her names, behind her back and to her face: brainiac and Britannica and, the worst one, Cris. Hannah, who was also shy and the closest thing Verity had to a friend, had reluctantly told her what Cris meant. "Short for Crisco. You know, fat in the can." Remembering that, Verity felt the heat of shame.

Wallace and Cyrus began jostling each other, and Nellie flopped down on the deck, knees to her chest, singing to herself. They were getting punchy, probably from hunger. Verity needed to wrap up this drill so they could break for lunch.

She headed toward the bow, where Roy was standing, and scooped up Nellie on the way. "Good job with the throw, Roy. Now let's pull the life preserver back in." She turned to the boys nearby. "Wallace and Cyrus—"

"Look over here, Kelsey!" Roy cried out.

Verity whipped around. Roy was windmilling his arms and staggering, showing off for Kelsey. The bow was too high off the ground for antics like that. "Gunner Roy! Return to your station."

Roy grinned, his eyes on Kelsey, who turned to face him, hands on her hips, eyebrows raised as if daring this little kid to make her attention worth the effort. Eden scowled, impatient to escape further embarrassment.

"Man overboard!" Roy shouted and launched himself off the ship. His legs wheeled, and for a moment he seemed suspended in midair.

Verity winced, unable to look away. Roy hit the ground with a thud.

Silence.

Harper screamed. Roy was flat on his back, legs akimbo.

Verity stood Nellie on her feet and rushed to the gangway. "Everyone stay where you are!"

Spider came out from where he was working behind the wheelhouse. "What happened?"

"Roy jumped." Verity was on the ground, running around the bow, heart pounding. The bow was—what?—higher than the top of their father's head.

Roy was curled on his side, his back to her. He'd moved, so that was a relief. Verity dropped to her knees. "Roy!" She didn't dare touch him.

Spider appeared at her side, breathing hard.

Roy turned partway over. His face was scrunched up with pain, and he was holding his right shoulder. Somehow he was also grinning. "How rad was that?"

Relieved as she was, Verity had to resist the urge to punch him. Everything was a game to an eight-year-old. They didn't have to consider how serious things can get, how jumping off a ship might end up worse than an injured shoulder.

As she lifted him to his feet, she felt the burden of her little brother as a weight in her legs, as if the ship were actually sinking, and she was carrying him to safety.

CHAPTER THREE

MAEVE

Maeve sat at the kitchen table sorting through the mail and eating left-over fried chicken. She ought to be grateful for a moment of solitude, but she never breathed easy without the children nearby. She had come from a sprawling family, eight children plus both sets of grandparents and her aunt Rita all under one roof; being alone meant being lonely. Still, Saturday was the only full day during the school year the children could spend on the ship, and for the most part, they adored it.

To the younger ones, it was an elaborate playhouse, and because the older ones had grown up on its decks, the routines were a comfort, except to Eden, whose interest in the ship had waned after Jude left home. Of all the children, Eden felt Jude's absence most. Maeve could relate; five years on, her heart still ached for him to be part of their lives again. Eden also had a vibrant circle of friends drawing her away from home—and the ship. Maeve's husband, Arthur, insisted Eden spend Saturdays with the family, and Maeve agreed. One day a week away from her friends wouldn't hurt her. If only Eden could exchange a close friend or two for a helping of Verity's sense of duty. Maeve didn't truly wish it, though; the joy of motherhood lay in each child's uniqueness.

The baby kicked inside her. Maeve rubbed her belly as her love for the baby rolled through her. The last one. Nothing gave her more joy than the weight of new life in her arms. All that promise captive in a tiny body, ready to be unfurled like a sail. More children wasn't harder; it was simply more. More love to go around. More life.

And more laundry.

She transferred the circulars to the trash pile and came across a large, thick envelope addressed to Verity from Halliwell College in Roanoke. She weighed it in her hand. No one in her family had gone to anything fancier than a community college, but she knew what a packet this size meant. Why on earth would Halliwell be sending her daughter anything at all? They'd agreed that Verity would only apply to Chesapeake Community College, less than a half-hour drive north and the only option they could afford. Even CCC would be a stretch. As Arthur put it, if Verity couldn't go to classes during the day and sleep in her own bed at night, the school might as well be on the moon.

He had framed the decision in financial terms—it was always easy to hang decisions on lack of money, and the good Lord knew they didn't have extra—but even if money were no concern, Arthur would strive to keep his oldest daughter close. Verity was the linchpin, the commander of the ship in the game of make-believe father and daughter had elaborated together. Maeve often thought her husband ignored how much he had strained to wedge Verity into the leading role she'd held for so long. Yes, Verity was competent, and you would never win a logical argument with her, but mothers were inclined to see their children in terms of their vulnerabilities more than their strengths. Verity was a shy girl, barely eighteen, who was self-conscious about her weight and uncertain about relationships outside the family, making CCC the best next step for her. She could have some independence, meet new people, and still rely on the family when she needed to. Arthur would see how she flourished—as surely she would—and relax his grip. He would see that Verity leaving home to start her own life had nothing to do with how Jude had torn away, leaving a ragged hole. They would never lose Verity like that.

All of which made an application to Halliwell more perplexing. Was it possible her daughter didn't want to stick close to home, that she had other bigger dreams she hadn't shared? The idea was troubling. Maeve vowed to get to the bottom of the mystery as soon as she could.

The window over the sink was open, and shouts from one of the boys snagged Maeve's attention, followed by a scream so penetrating and theatrical the source could only be Harper. Maeve abandoned the envelope from Halliwell on the pile of mail and pushed her plate aside, knowing before she got to her feet that Roy would be at the center of whatever had happened. During his eight short years, he'd already had four broken bones (wrist, tibia, a rib, and a finger), countless sprains, and thirty-plus stitches across three gaping wounds. Last year he had stood too close to a boy at the driving range at the country club where Arthur worked and had been laid out cold by a backswing. Maeve never blamed the boy, though. He could be oblivious, impulsive, or even reckless, but he never meant for anything bad to happen.

Eden and Kelsey were coming in as Maeve reached the back door. Eden headed to the freezer and started digging.

"You getting ice for Roy?"

"Popsicles. But I can." Eden showed the box to her friend. "Orange or grape?"

Just outside, Verity and Spider shepherded Roy in front of them. Maeve held open the screen door, and they piled in.

"I think it's his arm or maybe his shoulder." Verity pulled out a chair with her foot, and she and Spider helped him onto it.

Maeve took the boy's cheeks in her hands and kissed his damp forehead. "No need to be so brave."

"I'm not being brave." His lip quivered, and he rubbed his eyes with one hand.

"Lift your other arm, please."

He looked balefully at his right arm, limp across his lap. "Sorry."

"Verity, did the children have their lunch?"

"Not yet. But it's all ready."

"Eden, please get four sandwiches from the ship and wrap them up quick. Who knows how long we'll be. And you and Verity see that the others eat."

Eden sighed hugely and opened her mouth to protest, but Maeve steadied her with a look. Eden was focused on Kelsey and on herself—behavior you could expect from a teenager—but her brother was hurt, and family came first.

Maeve grabbed her bag and car keys from the hall table and followed four of her children out the front door. Verity and Spider loaded Roy and Wallace into the station wagon. Wherever one twin went, so went the other; no one ever questioned it. Maeve got in the car and adjusted the seat and the rearview mirror. She was barely five-four, and Arthur, who'd last driven the car, was over six feet.

"I'm here, Mom!" Harper ran toward them carrying a bulging folder and a bag with the lunches. She headed straight for the passenger side and installed herself.

Maeve didn't object. As the ship's doctor, Harper kept the family's medical records, reminding her parents when vaccines and dental checkups were due, and updating the files on the ship. Maeve had steered Harper into this role after noticing her daughter collecting subscription forms from magazines and filling them out for fun. Harper had Roy's records, so it made sense for her to come to the clinic. Maeve only hoped the staff were prepared for all the questions Harper would pepper them with.

Verity shut the rear door and leaned on the open window frame. "Don't worry, Roy. We won't launch any attacks while you're getting fixed up."

"Those bad guys better not come too close." With his good arm, Roy mocked aiming an artillery gun, firing.

Wallace, an expert in explosions of all kinds, provided the soundtrack.

"And Verity," Maeve said as she put the car in reverse, "when we get back, you and I are going to discuss the fat envelope you got today from Halliwell."

Her daughter's eyes widened for one long moment before she dropped her gaze. "I can explain."

"I'm sure you can." Verity looked up, wary. Well, of course she was wary. Whatever she had done and however she had managed to do it, she'd done it in secrecy. Maeve offered her daughter a sympathetic smile—and her heart did go out to Verity—but that was all she had time for. "Back soon." Maeve reversed the car, swung it around, and drove off. With any luck, she'd be back in time to talk to Verity before Arthur came home from work and they'd figure out what to do. Maeve regretted not stashing the envelope somewhere; the conversation called for diplomacy, which meant she needed to be there to mediate.

A quarter mile up the road, Maeve spotted a blue sedan coming toward them, crossing the one-lane bridge that marked the border of their property. Maeve pulled into the low grass on the verge.

"Kelsey's mom, I bet, coming to pick her up," Harper said.

"Genius," Wallace deadpanned.

"Nerf brain."

"Doofus goofus."

"Barf bunny." Harper glanced over the seat. "Don't laugh, Wally."

"I'm not."

Maeve heard the laughter bubbling up in his voice. She ought to have stopped the insult ping-pong, but these two loved it too much.

Wallace rallied. "Snot-gobbling potato head."

"Cheese weasel."

Wallace giggled, softly at first, then broke down completely.

"I win." Harper turned to her mother. "Is Kelsey coming every Saturday? Most kids don't like having activities on Saturdays, but maybe her family is different. Do you know them, Mom? Kelsey's friends with Eden, at least it seems that way, so maybe that makes it more fun for her, you know, not just piano torture. Not that it's torture for real, only that it can seem that way—"

Once Harper got started, there was no point in answering her questions. She either answered them herself or moved on to something else. Harper had begun talking in earnest before her first birthday and had taken only short breaks for eating and sleeping since.

Maeve waved at Kelsey's mother as she went past, then drove over the bridge. When Arthur had first shown her the property late in 1971, she hadn't been keen on the idea of living on a quasi island. But Arthur explained what the Realtor had told him, that most of the time the bridge spanned marsh, so at low tide you could walk right across on the land. By the time Arthur had finished giving her the tour, Maeve agreed the advantages of the property outweighed the watery moat. The white clapboard two-story house had four bedrooms, two bathrooms, and a large, sunny kitchen, a huge improvement over the duplex in Marionville they had been shoehorned into at the time. In addition to the house, there was a detached garage with an unfinished room above, which they could use for storage. Maeve had looked out the kitchen window and imagined their children ranging over the enormous yard and splashing in the river during the sweltering summers. Four acres could hold all the children they wanted and then some. Arthur promised he would clear the island of barbed wire, fishing gear, and whatever else had been discarded by the previous owner, Cary Shackleford, an oysterman who had first lost his trade, then, just as slowly, his life. Arthur had made good on his promise, as he always did, and over the last eight years, Maeve had gotten used to the ever-changing marsh that separated them from the rest of the world. Now whenever she crossed the bridge on her way to somewhere, she felt a pang, like she was saying goodbye to someone dear, and when she crossed it again on her way home, her heart lifted a little.

The thirty-six-foot custom-built dead rise came with the property. Cary Shackleford could've sold it long ago but had no use for money, and his children's disinterest in the boat equaled their father's love for it. He had left it to chance whether the new owners would recognize its simple beauty and put it on the water where it belonged. Over the long years of Shackleford's poor health and the additional years during which the property remained unsold, the boat had fallen into disrepair. Arthur had originally intended to spruce it up and sell it, but that wasn't what happened. Now Maeve, Arthur, and the children could not imagine their life without the boat that had become a ship, and it was somehow right that it wasn't out on the river. Certainly it seemed safer for the children while it sat on solid ground, kept upright by steel props. The point was moot, in any case. The only dock on the island was nothing more than an interrupted sequence of rotted boards, and they could never afford a berth at a marina.

Maeve turned onto the main road and glanced in the rearview mirror. "You okay there, Roy?"

"Yes, ma'am."

"What was going through that head of yours when you decided to jump off the ship?"

"Nothing."

"Same as always," Wallace said, and laughter filled the car.

CHAPTER FOUR

HARPER

Near six, just before dinner, Harper heard the rumble of her father's truck and jumped up from the porch steps. The truck took forever to crawl to a stop. Harper itched to run over and tell him everything, but he liked to get out of his truck and make it at least halfway up the walk before hearing what he called the *Vergennes Daily*. Harper didn't get that; she wanted to hear everything right away, preferably before anyone else. But here she was, waiting with Roy's medical folder at the ready, jigging from foot to foot, her mind already three paragraphs deep into the lead story.

Her dad was fussing with something on the seat beside him, organizing his whatnot. He worked at the Greenridge Country Club, in charge of facilities, a fancy word for everything that might break, or need painting or adjusting. The club had a golf course—duh!—and also a pool and tennis courts and a marina, so there was plenty to fix. Her dad had help, at least four people, which he said was equal to about two and a half real workers on a good day. Gray Reynolds owned the place and was her father's boss. They'd served together in the Korean War, which was the sort of thing that made you friends forever.

The other thing about Mr. Reynolds? Whenever the club got new stuff, which was all the time, he let their dad take home the old stuff. It wasn't charity, because her dad wouldn't stand for that. More like recycling. Why throw away a couch just because they changed the color of the walls and it didn't match anymore, or a ping-pong table just because it had some scratches and a busted leg? Last summer her dad had come home with a pile of kid-size life jackets, perfectly fine except being faded from the sun and maybe a broken strap. Now when they did dangerous drills, like man overboard, they could be super safe. Except if you were a klutzy showoff like Roy, who needed padding over his whole stinky body.

Her father got out of his truck like a hermit crab leaving its shell.

"Hi, Daddy!"

He pushed his cap off his forehead and smiled really big. "How's my girl?"

When he got to the porch, he put down his stuff and opened his arms. Harper threw herself into them, and her father hoisted her right off the ground. She breathed in his smell of cut grass and machine oil and himself. He set her back on the step.

"I'm perfectly fine, Daddy, thank you for asking, but man oh man I wish I could say the same about Roy."

He frowned. "Again?" He gently steered her toward the door. "Just a quick recap, Harper. I'm sure your mother will fill me in."

"She's resting upstairs."

He paused at the door. "Oh?"

She shrugged. "Just tired from the baby, I guess." Harper spotted her chance. "So right before lunch Verity calls a man-overboard drill, and everyone did everything just right except for Eden, but that's not exactly a news flash. And I'm not tattling, I'm just summarizing. Kelsey, who is in Eden's class and who seems super cool and nice, had a lesson with Mom, and when she finished she came out looking for Eden—"

"What's this got to do with Roy?"

Harper took a big breath. "Almost there, I promise. So Kelsey shouts for Eden, and Eden leaves the ship without asking Verity, and they head in for Popsicles even though it was almost lunch—" Her dad's eyes wandered. He wasn't as patient as her mom, so Harper put the pedal to the metal. "—and Roy is on the bow with the doughnut getting ready to rescue Ronald McDonald, and he starts showing off and shouts, 'Man overboard!' and then, can you believe it, he overboards himself right up into the air like there really was water down there and not regular ground, and he goes *smack* and doesn't move for a long time, well, maybe just a couple seconds, but then he does—"

"The injury, Harper?"

She opened the folder even though she had it memorized. "Fractured right collarbone immobilized with a sling. No medication administered. Expected recovery time is four weeks, but he's got an appointment on May fifteenth at four in the afternoon because my records show Roy is a fast healer."

Her father half smiled. "He needs to be, doesn't he?"

"Yes, sir."

"Thank you kindly for the information. The rest I can see for myself as soon as I get inside." He opened the door and made room for her to go in.

They went through the living room into the kitchen, which was kid soup on a high boil. Verity was at the stove—a scary sight.

"Daddy! Daddy!" zinged around the room. Their dad ruffled the hair of the ones he could reach, and he scooped Nellie off the floor along with her Raggedy Ann doll that had exactly one strand of yarn for hair.

The only one not moving was Roy. He was slouched at the table, looking like someone had peed in his oatmeal. In fact, Harper was dead certain Roy would rather eat pee oatmeal than have a sling on his arm. To be fair, bones were living things, and breaking them hurt like the dickens, not that she knew personally because she wasn't a daredevil idiot.

Their dad gave Roy a long look, but Roy was keeping his eyeballs to himself. Daddy sat down with Nellie stuck to him like a burr. "What's cooking there, Verity?"

"Spaghetti. Mom made the sauce this morning, so that's lucky for everyone."

He nodded. "Listen up." He didn't say it loud, but he didn't have to. Daddy wasn't a yeller because he expected you to do what he asked using his normal voice. "I want to go check on your mother, but Verity can't cook with all of you swarming in here. Spider and Cyrus, you set the table. Harper, you get the drinks. If you're not helping in here, you're outside or you're reading. Let's work together."

"Anyway, I can read," Nellie said. "I can even read outside."

Their dad kissed her cheek and scanned the room. "Where's Eden?"

Verity answered without turning around. "At her friend Kelsey's."

"Saturdays we eat together. She knows that. Did she ask your mother?"

"Mom was taking Roy to the doctor."

Their dad set Nellie on the floor and stood up. "Well, Roy, be glad you've got so many brothers and sisters. Chances are no matter what foolish thing you get up to, one of them is going to outdo you."

Harper covered her mouth to stop herself laughing. She happened to see Verity's face change from her concentrating-on-not-burning-the-spaghetti face to her freaking-out-but-please-don't-notice face, and Harper's urge to laugh went poof. Maybe Verity would end up today's headliner in the *Vergennes Daily* after all.

Harper didn't wait to be asked twice and started taking glasses out of the cabinet. Her dad went back through the living room and left down the hall to where his and Mama's bedroom was. If Harper could finagle a minute alone with Verity, she'd flat out ask her what was up. Verity might tell her, and she might not. That was the problem with being eleven and the middle kid: she was too mature for Go Fish and fart jokes, but the older kids treated her like she was practically one of the twins when the honest-to-God verifiable truth was she was closer to Spider's age by one whole year. Sometimes her whole life felt like Monkey in the Middle, and she never ever won.

Maybe that was why, when she wasn't doing her duty as the ship's doctor, the person she most wanted to be with was her mom. Some people might have thought that having so many kids would make it hard for any one of them to feel special, but that wasn't how it worked. Their mom made all of them feel special, like if they were her only kid, she would be 100 percent perfectly happy. A mom like that didn't play favorites, but that didn't stop Harper from being sure that her mom felt she was more special than any of the others.

Harper lugged a gallon of milk to the counter and filled the glasses—halfway for Cyrus and Nellie in case they spilled.

"Ready!" Verity carried the giant pot to the table. "Nellie, please go get Daddy—and Mommy, too, if she wants to eat."

"Anyway," Nellie said, "I can do it. Just watch." She walked off but looked over her shoulder every two steps.

"I'm watching. Skedaddle."

Harper sat down, suddenly pooped out from a busy day on the job. The others swarmed around, and she compared their faces. Maybe she was special to her mom because they looked alike. Everyone said so. They were both on the small side, but not runts, and had the same wavy chestnut hair, same hazel eyes that went toward green when they were really happy. Spider looked exactly like their dad, all legs and arms and straight, dark hair, and the rest of them were a mix, each a spoonful of a two-flavor soft-serve swirl, with freckles sprinkled on Wallace's face. From the photo on the piano, Harper knew Jude had freckles, too, at least when he was little. She could barely remember what he looked like since she had been only six when he left, and didn't have a clue what he looked like now. If he walked through the door this minute, she might not know him. It was too weird. She ought to feel bad about it—he was still her brother—but the only thing she felt was, well, weird.

The bowls of spaghetti went down the table. When Verity got to Roy's, she said, "Want me to cut it up for you?"

Roy sent her a squint-eyed glare that would've melted ice. "I can do it. I can do everything just fine!"

Their dad came in, and his face said he'd heard Roy loud and clear. "No cause to speak to your sister in that tone."

Roy stared at his fork. Any of the rest of the kids would have said sorry. Not Roy.

Their dad lowered himself into the seat at the head of the table. "Your mother's taking a nap, so keep it down." Once everyone was served, Daddy said grace and everyone dug in. "Verity, dinner smells wonderful. What would you think of promoting Wallace to gunner?"

Roy's fork clattered against his bowl. "No way, Jose!"

Daddy ignored him, waited for Verity, who chewed on her lip. She hated giving orders that made anyone unhappy. Daddy was always pushing her to get over it, but Harper had come to the conclusion that it was like trying to teach a duck to bark. Not that Verity was a duck, but she was definitely Verity.

"Maybe we can try it out."

"'Maybe' isn't much of an order."

Verity twisted the spaghetti around and around her fork until it was dizzy. "I'll go over assignments at muster tomorrow afternoon."

Their dad raised one eyebrow. He'd made Verity the captain, so in theory he couldn't boss her around. When the ship game had started, their dad was on board a lot, building things and teaching them stuff, but then he let Verity take over more and more. He was still their dad, of course, so things got complicated. In the house, he and their mom were in charge. On the ship, it was Verity. In between it got confusing, which was why Harper always had a squirrelly feeling in her stomach when there was ship talk in the house, and house talk on the ship.

No one could be two people, not without tripping over yourself and falling flat on your face, which might or might not be better than jumping off a ship. Just ask Roy. Or Harper, who was a little girl according to some people, and nearly an adult according to herself.

CHAPTER FIVE

Spider

Ship's Log: USS *Nepenthe*
Date: Sunday, April 27, 1980
Time: 1543h
Weather: 57°F, Fair
Winds: 5–10 kn SW
CO: Lt. Commander V. Vergennes (not aboard)

Inside the wheelhouse Spider was polishing parts of a compass with Brasso and figuring out how it went back together. He hunched over the desk, pulled up his knees, and slammed them on the underside of the table.

"Ouch!" He rubbed his knees, then went back to polishing the compass he'd taken apart.

He'd grown four inches in a year and kept forgetting how long his legs were. Too big for the ship, really, but fact was, he liked tinkering with things, same as his father. Working together on the engine this spring had been sick. They'd even run a hose to it and fired it up during a battle just for the noise. The little kids got all amped. Heck, he got amped, too, forgetting it was a boat on the lawn and the only real enemies around were the mosquitoes. That was the thing about the ship; if you grew up totally wrapped up in that reality, it was hard to let go, even when you knew better. That was why Spider didn't understand Eden, who was now scrubbing the hull under orders from Verity, punishment for having vamoosed with Kelsey. Spider understood Jude even less. His brother had given up being captain and gone on to prove what a selfish and irresponsible jerk he really was, and Spider, for one, was glad he was gone. If only their father would give Spider more credit for how accountable and responsible he had become.

Spider went back to figuring out the compass. His father would be showing up soon—he always spent time on the ship on Sunday afternoons—and Spider wanted to prove he was making progress. The compass had come with the boat, and even though the boat wasn't going anywhere, his father liked everything shipshape. What was the use in having something around if it didn't work? Problem was, he'd pulled apart the gimbal, the gadget that kept the compass level when the ship tilted. His father had given him a hint last night at dinner, saying the compass wasn't magnetic; it was a gyrocompass—a quirky choice for an oysterman. "Seems our Mr. Shackleford had the mind of an engineer," his dad said. Spider immediately went searching for his gyroscope, a birthday present from two years ago. By some miracle, he found it in a box in the dining room. (They called it the dining room even though they only ever ate in the kitchen. The piano was there, and all their toys and games and books.) Now Spider picked up the gyroscope, spun it around in his hand, wondering if it might have been smarter to take it apart first. Too late now.

According to Spider's dad, Chesapeake oystermen could navigate with their eyes closed, but when the bay got socked in with fog, anyone could get turned around, so the boats all had compasses. Spider had a hard time imagining they didn't need a compass all the time. The bay was a maze. They lived on a tributary of the Severn, a little squiggly worm on the map between the York and the Rappahannock. The Severn emptied into Mobjack Bay, which spilled into the Chesapeake. If someone plopped Spider in a boat at the mouth of the Chesapeake, he'd never find his way home without a map, a compass, and a lot of luck—and that was saying something, considering that as quartermaster, he was the ship's navigator.

Spider picked up the two gimbal rings. Maybe one compensated for pitch and the other for roll. He slipped the small one inside the bigger one and lined them up, grinning to himself. He was a geek—so what? Better than most of his classmates, who spent all their time listening to trippy music and getting wasted. Better a geek than a loser like Jude.

Outside on the deck Roy and Wally, Cyrus, and Nellie were playing slapjack, hooting and hollering after every palm smack. They were in uniform, but Verity wouldn't run drills or assign duties until later, if at all. Sundays started at eight sharp with chores, two hours of torture followed by more torture, church. At least they got a big dinner afterward, usually with biscuits and gravy, his favorite.

Heavy footsteps on the gangway. A slap as one of the kids claimed a pile of cards.

"Hi, Dad!" Roy had recently started calling him "Dad" instead of "Daddy," which was way younger than the rest of them, including Spider, had made the shift. "I just won this whole pile!"

"Best one-armed card shark on the ship, I reckon."

Without turning around, Spider knew their dad was patting Roy on the shoulder, ruffling his hair. Roy had broken the number one rule on the ship (no monkey business) and had been forgiven in two seconds. Sure, he was only eight and deserved some slack, but Spider had never broken rules like that even at that age. He cared too much about what his parents thought of him, especially his dad. If his dad thought Roy was so special, then what was wrong with Spider?

His dad sidled into the wheelhouse, stooping. With all the gear they'd added, it was tight for him in the entry. The floor dropped four inches halfway in, so he moved between the wheel and the table so he could stand up straight.

"How's it coming, son?"

"I took it apart."

His father nodded and squinted at the pieces littering the table. "You figure out how it works?"

"Starting to. Thought I'd clean it up first. You ever pulled apart one of these?" Spider wasn't sure which answer he wanted. If his dad knew how to do it, Spider would feel foolish for doing it wrong, but if neither of them could figure it out, then taking it apart had been dumb.

"Can't say that I have." He squeezed into the seat across from Spider. "Tell me what you've got."

Spider took a deep breath and pointed to a small wheel. "This wheel spins free inside a cage made up of these two rings I cleaned, exactly like my gyroscope."

"Those are gimbal rings, but the whole suspension device has a nickname." His father lifted his eyebrows. "A spider."

Spider grinned. "Cool." He'd never crawled as a baby, scooting around on his hands and feet instead. Verity had called him Spider, and it stuck, even after kids at school started teasing him. Stupid jokes didn't bug him. Spider pointed to a device with electrical leads sticking out from it. "I'm guessing that's the motor that drives the wheel."

"You guessed right. And you didn't take it apart, which was smart." Spider beamed. His father picked up the rings, put one inside the other just like Spider had. "It may seem like a small thing, son, coming to grips with how something works. But it's not just fiddling."

34

Spider was polishing the compass case, but his attention was like a laser on his father's words, the weight of them, handed across this table like stones.

His dad shifted in his seat, rubbed one hand along his chin. "We were coming back from Japan, heading to Midway, then maybe San Diego, home. They didn't give us those details, but we were headed in the right direction. Two days from a decent port and this storm blows in from the west. Never seen anything like it. Made us all think the name 'Pacific' was some kind of inside joke."

His smile was crooked. Disastrous things could seem funny when you'd made it to the other side. Spider leaned toward his dad, not wanting to miss a single word. He hardly ever talked about the war, wasn't much of a storyteller in general.

His father went on. "The day before this other fellow, Wes Schultz, and me had been fixing the winches for the racks of lifeboats. Since we'd taken fire in Wonsan Harbor, they'd always been a bit catawampus, but nothing you'd give priority to." He sat back, spread his hands. "You can see where this is going; I'm not much of a storyteller. Suffice it to say, when the swells hit thirty feet, that ship was pitching something fierce. We were all belowdecks and secured, but we could tell from the screeching and shuddering that what wasn't nailed down tight was gone. And those winches? They held, which was a good thing, because next to us a sister destroyer didn't fare so well. We ended up needing every single one of those boats, son."

Spider swallowed. "Were all the men saved?"

"Nearly." He shook his head slowly. "Nearly."

They sat a moment in silence. Spider felt proud his dad had shared the story with him, only with him.

His father cleared his throat and gestured to the array of parts. "Never leave things broken." He pushed himself to standing. "And never underestimate water."

That was the lesson. Spider wouldn't forget. "I won't. Thanks, Dad."

"Don't forget your homework." He registered the slump in Spider's shoulders and smiled at him. "Consider it something broken that needs fixing."

After his father left, Spider fiddled with the gimbal awhile longer, soaking in the contented feeling his father had left behind. For the first time in a long while, he believed his father thought he was special and could live up to his real name: Arthur Jr.

CHAPTER SIX

VERITY

Verity was in the laundry room, sorting through the hamper she shared with Eden and Harper, figuring she could start a load, then finish her homework, leaving her a whole evening free to read or watch TV.

Her mother called to her from the living room. "Verity, could you help me with something?"

"One sec." She started the load, her heartbeat picking up. Her mom had given her the envelope from Halliwell yesterday. Verity knew she had to talk to both her parents about it, but she'd asked her mom if she could talk just to her first.

She must've sounded desperate—she sure felt it—because her mom agreed. "I don't see the harm. Read it over, then we'll talk." Verity had read everything in the packet over a million times, then stashed it in the pantry, where nosy Harper wouldn't find it.

Verity found her mom in the nursery, off the hall to her parents' bedroom. Her mom sat in the rocker, her hands on her swollen belly, her face pale. She'd not been well since yesterday and looked beat.

"I don't need you to do anything, love," her mom said. "I just wanted to get away from little ears."

"I figured." Verity pulled over a small stool and sat with her hands folded in her lap so she wouldn't chew on her thumb. "Mom, I'm sorry I didn't tell you and Dad about applying to Halliwell."

"I have to say I was surprised by it, and a little hurt." Her mom paused. She hardly ever admitted being wounded by her children. "Was it your idea?"

Verity looked at her hands. "Mrs. Castle suggested it. You know, the new guidance counselor. And I thought there was no point in upsetting anyone when I probably wasn't going to get in anyway."

"But you did." Her mom's voice had softened. Verity looked up and nodded. Her mother gave her a small smile. "I'd be lying if I didn't admit to being proud of you, despite how you handled it."

Relief loosened the knot in Verity's stomach. "There's more, Mom. They offered me the Grantham scholarship. It's full tuition, plus work-study."

"Goodness, Verity." She scooted forward and opened her arms. Verity fought back tears as her mother hugged her and kissed her cheek.

Verity returned to the stool and wiped her eyes. She'd said everything now, and her mother wasn't as upset as she'd imagined.

Her mom turned to the window, thoughtful. "I don't know what to say, honestly. It's a shock." She swept back a strand of hair and looked at Verity. "You have to promise to talk to your father the first chance you get, and then the three of us can go over it once I'm feeling better. I know you're avoiding telling him, but it's not right to hide this from him."

"I know. I promise." The knot in her stomach returned. Was there any way she could convince him? She'd give it her best shot and hope her mom would do the rest.

~

At eight o'clock that evening, the kitchen was finally empty, and Verity sneaked into the pantry for one more look at the Halliwell brochure. The photo on the front was mesmerizing: three students, one girl and two boys, sprawled on an impossibly green lawn, books opened casually around them. One of the boys was writing in a notebook, and the other was laughing. The girl smiled as she flipped back a perfectly smooth curtain of blonde hair. Verity wondered what the joke was. She wanted to be in on it, even if she was just the fourth person, out of the frame, pretending not to hear.

For all Verity knew, all private colleges were like this. Mrs. Castle had recommended Halliwell because it was in the top twenty liberal arts colleges in the country and the only one in Virginia. She'd loaned Verity the catalog from the shelf in her office, and Verity had pored over it during her free period. She didn't know what she wanted to study—she got As in everything—and the course offerings at Halliwell made her dizzy. How would she ever decide? Astronomy sounded so cool, but so did marine biology. She put the brochure back into the envelope and stashed it on the shelf.

A scream from upstairs. Eden.

Footsteps hammered above her head, down the hallway, and back again. Verity raced to the stairs and nearly collided with Harper, whose eyes were so wide Verity's heart started pounding.

Behind Harper, Nellie scrambled down the stairs in her footie pajamas, her mouth full of toothpaste. "I don't like screaming at bedtime."

Harper turned around and clamped her hands over Nellie's ears. "It's Mama. There's blood."

Verity's hands went cold. "Where is she?"

"In our room."

Nellie squirmed out from under Harper's grip and glowered at her. "Anyway, don't do that. It's not polite."

"Sorry, Nells."

"I'll get Daddy," Verity said. "You stay with the little ones. Keep them out of there."

"Out of where?" Nellie said. "I want to go to that place."

The children's clinic in Three Rivers was for stitches and sprains; that was where they had fixed Roy's collarbone yesterday. The new hospital in Gloucester was the next step up and where their dad said he was taking their mom. Verity didn't know if her mom had bleeding during her other pregnancies, but she guessed not. If something dramatic like that had happened, there'd be a story around it, like how Eden had arrived three weeks early and had almost been born on a bus. The thought of something happening to the baby was awful. And to her mother even worse.

Verity hadn't gotten a good look at her mom because their dad whisked her out the door and into the car so fast. He'd always been like that when it came to their mom, ready to drop everything to take care of her. Sometimes Verity wondered if his attention was too much on their mom and not enough on the rest of them, but then, their mother's attention was on them like a search beam all the time, no matter what, so maybe that was how it balanced out. Their mom could be there for them because their dad was the rock behind her. Whatever the reason, her dad wouldn't dream of letting anyone else take their mom to the hospital to have a baby or because she was sick—not even an ambulance—and the rest of the family just had to deal with it.

Now it was almost eight thirty. Eden came into the boys' room, where Verity was trying to stop a pillow fight between Roy and Wallace before Cyrus woke up. She motioned to Verity, who followed her out into the hall.

"I can't get the blood up." She looked like she might cry. Eden was tough most of the time, but when she was scared, she seemed more like eleven than fourteen.

"Just get one of the old towels from the laundry and cover it for now. Can you do that?"

"Okay."

Harper was sitting on the top step staring at the front door and made room for Eden to go by. Harper was awfully quiet. No doubt she was worrying about their mom—they all were—but there was something about Harper and Mom, like they shared a single soul that happened to be divided up into a talkative kid and an adoring mother.

Verity was about to go reassure Harper when Cyrus started wailing. He was a heavy sleeper, but when he did wake up, all heck broke loose. He'd had a nightmare, Verity figured. As she crossed the hall, eager to get to him before he woke up the world, Roy burst out of the room and careened off the opposite wall—with his good shoulder, thankfully. Wallace tumbled out after him.

Chaos was around the corner. All Verity wanted was to go to bed and hide under the covers until everything was normal again, with her mom well and her parents in charge. But everyone was relying on her, so she made a snap decision. "Listen up, everyone. Put on your whites if you can find them fast. We're going to the ship."

~

Ship's Log: USS *Nepenthe*
Date: Sunday, April 27, 1980
Time: 2044h
Weather: 55°F, Clear
Winds: 0–5 kn SW
CO: Lt. Commander V. Vergennes

Twilight had already given way to darkness, so Verity mustered her brothers and sisters in the kitchen. Spider had ventured out with a flashlight to turn on some lights, just enough for safety.

Verity scooped Nellie into her arms and stepped outside. Two white lights shone, a floodlight onto the gangway and a smaller one over the covered area in the aft section. Spider also had turned on the red light on top of the wheelhouse that served to warn other vessels. Verity motioned to the others. "Fall in line, sailors."

Eden took Cyrus by the hand, and the others followed. The air was cool with a faint breeze stirring the new leaves on the sycamores along the riverbank. As they crossed the lawn, everyone was subdued to the point of reverence, as if they were going not onto the ship but into a church, although they were never this quiet in church. The ship, Verity realized, was their true church because they went there to show respect for order, for diligence, for their higher, more disciplined selves. Sure, it was made up, but what difference did that make?

Nellie wriggled out of Verity's arms, pushed a mop of curls from her eyes. "Anyway, can we play Go Fish?"

"In a minute, sure." It was a school night and late for games, but it was more important for her brothers and sisters to be settled. To be honest, being on board settled her, too. "Wallace, you take first watch. Roy, you're next. Harper, you're after Roy. Eden, record the assignments in the log." To Verity's surprise, Eden headed into the wheelhouse.

Spider sat on the engine housing, placed his feet on the rails and his hands behind his head. "We can navigate by the stars tonight."

"Where are we going?" Cyrus asked, yawning. He had put his uniform shirt on over his train pajamas.

"Secret mission."

Wallace climbed along the starboard side of the wheelhouse toward the bow to assume his watch. "I'll be able to see Mommy and Daddy coming home from here."

The drive was visible from most parts of the ship, but Verity didn't say anything. "Harper, you're in charge of entertainment."

"Yes, sir." Harper winnowed her way through the sprawled legs and entered the wheelhouse. She screamed.

"What is it?" Verity hurried to the wheelhouse, fearing further catastrophe.

"Here, let me!" Eden pushed Harper aside, scrambling for something in the locker. "I've got it!" She held something in her hands, but the shadows made it hard to see. Whatever it was, it was moving.

Verity moved closer. Light fell on white, brown, and russet fur. "Vermin! What are you doing in here?"

Nellie pushed by Verity and stretched out her arms to Eden. "Here, Vermin. I missed you."

Verity didn't have the heart to take the guinea pig away and put it inside the house, in its cage, as she clearly should have. "Keep track of her, Nellie, okay?"

Harper and Eden emerged from the wheelhouse. Harper carried two decks of cards. Eden held up several packets of M&M's, a couple of which had been chewed open. "Permission to distribute candy rations, Captain."

"Where did those come from?" Verity asked.

"As supply master, it is my job to ensure the ship and her crew are provisioned for every possible emergency." Her expression was dead serious.

Verity felt a surge of love for her sister and smiled. "Permission granted."

~

Verity had put Nellie and Cyrus to bed during Roy's watch, and by the time Harper relieved Roy at ten, he was so tired he could barely stand. He roused Wallace from where he was wrapped up in a blanket against a locker.

Eden rubbed her arms. "I'm freezing. I'll walk you guys back." She used the canopy support to swing herself up to the gunwale and onto the gangway. Verity winced as the canopy bent under her weight. Eden knew she was too big for that maneuver, skinny as she was, but if a rule could be bent or snapped in half, Eden would jump at the chance. Verity wished she were more like Eden, more carefree, more of a rebel, because then she might have become used to facing the consequences of breaking rules—like the consequences waiting for her when she told her father about applying to college in secret.

Verity and Harper stood along the starboard side and watched them leave. The twins marched with their arms around each other's shoulders toward the back door and its yellow light.

Harper turned to her. "Why haven't they called?"

"Because it's too late, and they don't want to wake us," Verity said.

"Or because they don't have any good news."

"Remember Daddy always says that bad news travels faster." She said it as much to reassure herself as her sister.

Harper nodded. "If they come back tonight, they're going to make us go to school tomorrow, so I guess I better go to bed, too."

Verity was glad she didn't have to suggest it. She didn't like telling the older kids what to do. "Good idea. I won't be far behind you."

"Promise you'll wake me up when they get home."

"I promise."

Verity put away the cards, collected the empty M&M's packets, and returned the blankets to the berth in the bow. She was tempted to lie down there; she still fit in the triangular cushioned space—barely—and the years of memories it held comforted her. The spring she had turned ten, she'd spent her first of dozens of overnights in that berth. Jude was on a Boy Scout overnight, and she was jealous, so her father had suggested she sleep on the boat. Snug in the berth, she'd peered out the two small glass hatches at the stars shimmering in the velvet sky until she drifted off to sleep. As she dreamed, the dead rise was still only a boat, but a boat on the verge of becoming a ship. She woke at dawn to birdsong and the croaking of frogs in the marsh. Her father appeared minutes afterward, as if signaled, bearing orange juice and a blueberry muffin so she didn't have to break the magic of her bravery.

While she ate her muffin, her father showed her the wheelhouse and explained what all the gauges and levers and instruments did. She asked him if it was like the ship he'd served on in the war, and that was how the transition from boat to ship started. An oyster boat was mildly interesting, but a destroyer escort was something else.

As the sun climbed above the horizon and eventually above the treetops, Verity and her father sifted through the contents of the lockers: mostly old traps and rotting ropes and rusted tackle. Her father knelt by the pile of gear and made a sweeping gesture with his arm, taking in the whole boat. "I was planning on selling it, you know."

"Is it worth a lot of money?"

"The bay's stuffed with old boats, so probably not. At least not in the condition it's in now."

"Are you going to fix it up?" She knew he was good at fixing everything, so of course he could fix a boat.

"I don't like broken things, that's for certain."

They hadn't talked more about the boat that day, but three days later, he came home with a bag from the army-navy store in Three Rivers. In it were four white shirts with blue ties and four caps like the ones in *McHale's Navy*. "For you, Jude, Eden, and Arthur Jr. Considering your mother has her hands full with Harper and the twins, I thought I could provide a little entertainment for the rest of you. We can always sell the boat later."

"We're going to play on the boat?" Verity couldn't believe her ears.

"Not a boat. A ship." He corralled everyone, handed out the shirts and caps, and led them to the dead rise. "There's a lot you'll need to learn about being sailors, but first things first: the ship's name." He pointed to faded and chipped lettering along the back. Verity hadn't noticed it before. *N-e-p-e-n-t-h-e.*

Jude was hanging back. At fourteen, he was wary of getting roped into kids' games, which made Verity sad because before he became a teenager, they'd played together all the time. Maybe the boat would bring them closer again.

Jude sounded out the name. "Neh-peen-thee?"

"Who knows?" their father said. "Might find it in the dictionary or the encyclopedia."

"Not me," Jude said. He wasn't keen on books during the school year; forget about the summer.

"I'll do it," Verity said. She loved the encyclopedia more than she'd ever admit.

Later that day, she reported back to her father, who was on the couch with Harper in his arms. She was sound asleep, her mouth a perfect pink circle. The encyclopedia was heavy, and Verity balanced it on the arm of the couch. "Daddy, it's pronounced Nuh-pen-thee. It's Greek, and it means a magical potion that takes away sadness."

"Is that right?" her father said.

She nodded. "Helen of Troy—she lived in Greece a long time ago—gave it to some soldiers to help them forget their troubles. Here's what it says." She opened the book to where she'd stuck her finger. "*A drink of this, once mixed with wine, would guarantee no man would let a tear fall on his cheek for one whole day, not even if his mother and his father died.*"

Her father whistled through his teeth. "Strong stuff. What else did you learn?"

"Helen's father was Zeus. He was a powerful god, and when she was born, he put a constellation in the sky just for her."

"Which one would that be?"

"Cygnus. The swan."

After all the little kids were asleep, her father led her and Jude outside again. The night was bright and clear.

"I don't know a thing about Greece, but I do know my stars." Away from the house lights, he squatted beside them and traced the constellation with his finger: the wings, the tail, the long neck. "It's one of the biggest. The middle part is the Northern Cross."

She could see it easily and wondered what other creatures and objects the night sky held. She knew about the Big Dipper, but that was it.

Jude said, "We learned about it in Scouts. The Cross runs like that now, on an angle, but in the winter it stands up straight."

"That's right," their dad said, putting his hand on Jude's shoulder. "Stands on the horizon like it was planted there."

It made Verity dizzy to think of the earth spinning like that under the stars, and she glanced over at the ship. "Nepenthe is a good name, don't you think?"

"Good or bad, that's her name," their dad said. "The USS *Nepenthe*."

Now Verity stood alone on the deck while Cygnus and all the other constellations wheeled slowly overhead. She thought of Jude and wondered if he ever looked at the sky, remembering that night, remembering when their father had been proud of him. She hoped so. She missed him from time to time, mostly when something stirred a memory of being kids together. Now she wasn't even sure she would know him anymore, which upset her. How could someone be your big brother, your first friend, then become a complete stranger? Or was Jude more like a ghost, here and not here?

Headlights skittered through the trees along the road. Wheels crunched on the gravel, then stopped. The lights went off, and she heard a car door open, just one. Her father had come home alone. Verity bit her lip and told herself it wasn't necessarily bad news. Her father would come out to the ship after checking on everyone else, so she could stay put. She'd been taking care of everyone the whole time, and for this one moment, she didn't want to have to do the right thing, just the easier thing. She lay down on the portside lockers and scanned the sky, hoping for a shooting star and knowing ahead of time what her wish would be.

Not ten minutes later her father called to her from the lawn. "Hey, Verity." His voice told her that her mother was all right, and the tightness in her chest eased. When he reached the gangway, he said, "Permission to come aboard."

She got up. "Permission granted. How's Mom?"

"Seems to be fine." He paced to the stern, casting his gaze around the night shapes. "They're keeping her until tomorrow, but she seems fine."

"I was scared."

"I know you were." He wrapped her in a hug. He wasn't super affectionate with her or the other older kids, but boy did it feel good now. "Thank you for looking after everyone." He let her go.

"Sure. We came out here, just to get their minds off it. They might be tired tomorrow."

Her dad's voice was gentle. "That's fine, Verity. Tired is fine."

She was tired. Keeping all the kids safe and easing their worry was hard work. Her earlier nostalgia for her big brother fizzled, and instead she resented that he hadn't been here to help her. Was that how Eden and Spider would feel about her if she went away to college? Her mind had been so preoccupied with worry for her mother that she'd forgotten her promise until now. Her father was right here, and she had to tell him about the fat envelope, about her deception. She sat down with the weight of it.

"I have something to tell you, Daddy."

He stepped closer, rubbed his chin. "Sounds serious."

"It is. Mom made me promise to tell you as soon as I could, so that's now."

"Okay." He sat on the engine housing, not quite across from her. "Let's hear it."

She took the ripping-off-the-Band-Aid approach. "I applied to Halliwell College. It's near Roanoke."

His eyebrows went up practically to his hairline, but he didn't say anything.

"I heard from them yesterday. I got in. And they offered me a scholarship that covers tuition and work-study for the rest." When she said it out loud, just like that, it seemed almost normal. But it still didn't seem real.

Her father stared at her, level and composed. "I don't know why you'd do that without telling us. We talked about it, and you were going to CCC. Did you think you could just make a decision that big without bringing us in?"

She hung her head. "I'm sorry. I didn't think it would work. I was just hoping. Mrs. Castle said I had a good chance."

"Mrs. Castle isn't part of this family." His tone was stern. "You shouldn't have surprised us with this, Verity. It's not right. What's wrong with CCC, at least for a year or two, especially with another baby on the way? Family comes first. You leaving would break your mother's heart."

"We didn't get much of a chance to talk, but Mom didn't say no." She felt her throat go tight, like she was being strangled. "Dad, it's not that far . . ."

"Roanoke is a good four-hour drive. If you have to work for your keep, you wouldn't be coming home hardly at all." Verity opened her mouth, but her dad put up his hand. "All I can say for now is maybe we'll talk about it another time." He stood. "We've all had a long day."

He was right. Her mother was in the hospital. Now wasn't the time. "Okay, Dad."

"Your mother's coming home tomorrow, thank goodness, but not first thing, so we'll need to pull together for the morning." He started down the gangway. "Set your alarm for six thirty."

"I will."

Verity glanced at the sky, one last chance today for a shooting star, but the stars stayed right where they were, blinking from a distant heaven.

CHAPTER SEVEN

CYRUS

.

"Cyrus? Wake up."

Before he even turned over, he knew it was Nellie, and he knew she was crying. He could hear the tears in her words even though she was whispering because Roy and Wallace were sleeping and the last thing anyone in the whole world wanted to do was wake up those two.

He sat up. There was a little light from under the door and a little more from the window because the backyard was out there and the light over the back door must have been on. He put a finger on Nellie's lips, and she backed up so he could get out of bed, and he took her hand because she was only four and tippy-toed her across the room and out the door.

The night-light in the hallway was on so people didn't crash on the way to the bathroom, but no one was moving around or talking, so it had to be late and everyone was sleeping, or else everyone was playing Quakers' Meeting but probably not.

Cyrus stopped to wipe Nellie's cheeks. It didn't feel good to have wet cheeks.

Nellie's room was downstairs and all the way over by Mommy and Daddy's room, but that was where she needed to be, so Cyrus led her along like a dog on a leash. He almost laughed about that and then remembered Daddy had to rush Mommy away to the hospital, and all of a sudden he felt sick and not like laughing, not even a little.

In Nellie's room the pink-shell night-light made the darkness also pink.

"Story," Nellie said as she climbed into her bed. Cyrus climbed in, too. The bed smelled like her all the way through, and also like tears, probably from the pillow.

"Okay." He got comfy, but then he saw the crib against the wall, and his worry for Mommy exploded like a gigantic firework into worry for Mommy and the baby.

Nellie poked him in the arm. "Start."

When she was tired or upset, she got bossy.

Cyrus rolled over so he faced Nellie and not the crib. "Once upon a very long time ago, there was a girl who was not quite five, meaning she was four, and she wanted to go on a magical trip." Cyrus held his breath because if Nellie started asking why this early in the story, he was doomed, but she didn't. "And she lived all by herself on an island in the ocean with butterflies and palm trees and rocks made of butterscotch and rivers made of water."

"Anyway, water's not exciting."

"It is if you're thirsty. And butterscotch makes you thirsty."

"Oh! Is it me?"

"Maybe."

"Is her name Nellie?"

"Penelope."

"That's my name."

"I know. So she plays in the sand and eats butterscotch—"

"—and drinks water—"

"—and drinks water and dreams about her impossible magical trip."

"Where?"

Cyrus had to think hard here because Nellie never wanted to go to the same place twice. She might only be four, but she never forgot. Sometimes the place was magical but also dangerous, like a deep cavern in the sea with treasure but also several-headed algae monsters that spit slime. Tonight was not a good night for danger. He needed someplace nice.

"Into the clouds," he said. Nellie was quiet, which meant she was thinking about it. Cyrus kept going. "But she's only dreaming about it. She can't get there, not even if she wishes so hard she gets a headache."

"I don't want a headache."

"Luckily, while she's building a sandcastle and dreaming, a white boat comes sailing by with a bright white sail, and there's a boy wearing a white shirt and white pants, and he waves to her."

"He's friendly."

"He is. And when she waves back, her arm lifts her in the air, and she waves some more, and she goes higher and higher, and the boat and the boy are below her now, but not for long because the boy and the boat are floating up, too."

"Oh wow."

"The boat is even with her now, and Penelope waves herself over and touches her toes to the deck, which isn't hard like a real ship, but soft like a pillow. 'How do you do,' says the boy."

"'How do you do,' says Penelope."

Cyrus didn't appreciate it when Nellie started telling the story like it was hers, but he let it go. As long as she wasn't crying, it was okay for tonight. Because if she cried, he'd cry, too, and he absolutely didn't want to. For crying he'd wait until Mommy was home so she could tell him it was okay.

"'I am Sir Cyrus,' says the boy. 'We can sail into the clouds, if you wish. All you have to do is think of white.'"

"That's hard."

"Think of things that are white."

"The boat."

"The moon."

"The sail." Her voice was getting slurry.

"The boy's clothes."

"Marshmallows."

"Clouds," Cyrus said, yawning. "Marshmallow clouds, sailboat clouds, moon clouds. Vanilla ice cream clouds." Nellie's eyes closed, and her mouth hung open in a little O. "Toilet paper clouds. Golf ball clouds. Sheep clouds . . ."

CHAPTER EIGHT

MAEVE

Maeve hadn't slept much. The hospital room was too bright and noisy. Funny thing for a woman with so many children to complain about, but it was the wrong kind of noise—mechanical and intrusive.

A nurse came in and picked up the chart from the end of the bed. "How are you doing this morning, Mrs. Vergennes?"

"Just fine. Ready to go home." Maeve was relieved beyond measure that her sheets had not been stained with blood since she arrived.

"We'll just see what the doctor says. He'll be by in a little bit." The nurse took her pulse and her blood pressure, wrote in the chart, and took her breakfast order. "Be back in a jiffy!"

Maeve was more tired than she'd ever been when pregnant, but other than that she felt fine. All she wanted was to go home, pull each of her children into a hug. Her arms ached for it, and she knew how they would fret about her and the baby, each in their own way. That was one of the things she loved most about her children, their individuality, how they came into the world already themselves, with their own light. Her only job was to help them shine.

She worried about Arthur, too, more than she did about the children, excepting Verity, perhaps, and only recently. Despite Arthur's competence and loyalty, he had a vulnerable center. She'd seen it plainly the day they'd met.

The Roseville Fair had always taken place the last weekend of June because the organizers, the Granger brothers, knew their tiny town couldn't draw anyone away from Fourth of July celebrations in other, somewhat larger towns. Roseville was as far south as you could get in Virginia without falling into North Carolina, just big enough for a hardware store, a feed store, a diner, an inn with a special-occasion restaurant, and two hair salons. Maeve's family owned the diner, and she and her seven siblings worked there as soon as they were tall enough to reach up and set a table. Business was such that once the kids were older, most of them were not required for service, and they found work or trouble in other parts of town, or as far as their bicycles or broken-down vehicles would take them.

Maeve first performed at the Roseville Fair when she was twelve. The song she practiced at home until her voice was hoarse was "Comin' Thro' the Rye," backed up by her two eldest brothers on fiddle and banjo. When the song ended, the crowd got up from their folding chairs, whistling and clapping for so long Maeve felt her cheeks burn. They wouldn't let her get off the stage, booing every time she inched in that direction. She was their hometown girl, sweet in her pigtails and pinafore.

"Sing another one!" several people shouted.

She didn't know what to sing. Her brother Bo whispered in her ear: "'Danny Boy.' Just you." Her favorite song, but one she sang only to herself. He gave her a big smile and nudged her toward the microphone.

It was in the right place, but Maeve pretended to adjust it. When she couldn't stall any longer, she closed her eyes and pretended she was alone in her room. She took a deep breath, and the first note came to her from that special place she could not describe. She sang.

"Oh, Danny boy, the pipes, the pipes are calling
From glen to glen, and down the mountainside.
The summer's gone, and all the roses falling,
It's you, it's you must go and I must bide."

The crowd was so quiet she thought they might've packed up and left. But no, when she finished the song and finally dared to look, half of them were wiping their eyes.

The Granger brothers asked her back every year after that, and she grew up, her hair shorter and styled, her skirts fuller. The crowd grew a bit each year, strangers eventually outnumbering the locals, but Maeve's voice stayed sweet and true.

In 1955, a carload of young men stood at the back of the crowd, listening to the bluegrass band from down the road and drinking root beer. Maeve noticed they were still there when it was her turn to take the stage; she was seventeen, and the well-dressed, upright young strangers were bound to catch her eye. She and her brothers opened with Kitty Wells's "It Wasn't God Who Made Honky Tonk Angels." As she finished the first round of the chorus, the tallest of the young men left the others, making his way closer. By the time Maeve was singing the last line, he was close enough for her to see the slight smile on his face and the glint in his eye.

The song ended, and the crowd, most of whom had been coming for years, called out, "'Danny Boy'!"

Maeve waited for the cheering to die down, and for her heart to slow. She closed her eyes and sang. That song meant something different to her every time she sang it, so the singing was as much to find out what it meant today as it was a performance. Maybe that was what made it special, for her and everyone who heard it. Haunting and full of love, and oh so quiet and strong.

"And I shall hear, though soft you tread above me,
And all my grave will warmer, sweeter be,

For you will bend and tell me that you love me,
And I shall sleep in peace until you come to me."

She closed the last note soft as a whisper. As if waking from a dream, Maeve opened her eyes. There was the young man, holding himself as quiet as a fishing heron afraid of scaring something off, or breaking a spell, except he wasn't looking down into the water. He was looking at her, and letting the tears run down his face.

He found her between the stage and the hot-dog stand and held out a bottle of root beer. "Figured you'd be thirsty after that."

He wasn't handsome exactly, but his eyes did shine, and that little smile of his was something else. Maeve accepted the bottle and noticed his hands, long fingered, strong, scrubbed.

"Kind of you, Mr.—"

"Vergennes. Arthur Vergennes."

"I'm Maeve Bradley." She extended her hand and he shook it. "You have people here, Mr. Vergennes? The Roseville Fair doesn't draw from very far." His accent already told her he hailed from somewhere well north, but it was something to say.

"I don't know why not. That voice of yours is like a bell."

Maeve blushed but didn't look away. Something about him made her less conscious of herself than she normally was. She knew she wasn't a beauty, just an average-looking girl with a trim figure and a heart filled with music. She believed in the words in the songs, believed in the most tender and thunderous feelings.

"Are you just passing through, Mr. Vergennes?"

"Arthur." He gestured to his friends in line at the hot-dog stand. "We've come down from Norwalk on the way to Charleston."

"Well, Arthur, I'm sorry to bear bad news, but you and your friends are off course."

He laughed. "By design. We're stationed in Norfolk and thought we'd get away from the water for a spell."

A navy man. Later she would learn he'd served in Korea, and although he had barely touched that foreign land, the experience had left its scars regardless. She also learned that Arthur worried a great deal and blamed himself unnecessarily when life went sideways. At that moment, though, all she cared about was that he was standing in front of her and looking at her like she was the only girl at the fair, and maybe in the world. In the end, it was all that ended up mattering. Inside her huge family, she often felt like a bee in a hive: necessary, valuable, but hardly unique. When she was with Arthur, there was only her.

Arthur's laugh faded, and he turned solemn. "When the music starts again, Maeve, I'd be honored if you'd dance with me."

She smiled at him, not blushing this time. "Only if you buy me a hot dog first. I'm starving!"

The night was clear and moonless. Stars filled the sky, and the drifting tunes of the bluegrass band filled the air. Arthur's buddies were eager to leave for Charleston, but he bought them beer after beer and, abstaining himself, promised to drive through the night while they slept.

He held Maeve close as they danced and stayed glued to her side when they rested between numbers. She felt the town watching them, wondering what spell this stranger had cast on their special girl. Maeve let them wonder, not caring what they might be speculating. She might be a small-town girl, but she knew to trust the rightness of certain things. Fate had dropped Arthur into Roseville that day, and when fate cast its net, there was no use in struggling. It was better just to dance.

~

And there he now stood in the doorway of her hospital room, a bunch of daisies in his hand. He smiled like a kid at Christmas getting his first bike, and tired as she was, her heart did a little skip.

"Let's get you home," he said.

They chatted on the way about nothing at all: Roy's shoulder, a golf event at the club, the likelihood that the washing machine wouldn't last the year.

Maeve asked, "Did Nellie make it through the night all right?" She had never been a sound sleeper, and any disruption in the family routine only made her sleep more fragile.

"Cyrus was in bed with her when I got home. I left him where he was."

Maeve smiled. That boy was an angel. She pictured her two youngest curled up in bed together, their little round faces, their innocence and goodness, and felt a pang of anxiety for them. They would be hurt in this life, there wasn't any avoiding it—look what had happened to Verity. Maeve couldn't help but wish that, just for once, these two children—all her children, really—would be cushioned from pain. It wasn't realistic, but that didn't stop her from wishing it.

"You've gone quiet," Arthur said.

She reached across the seat and patted his leg. "Just missing home." She couldn't share what she'd been thinking. Arthur was too practical a man for such impractical sentiments, and that was fine with her. She didn't need him to feel the same things she did, only to love her. That he did with a force that seemed to grow stronger with time made her wonder if, after twenty-five years, Arthur's love for her was completely unbounded. He gave and gave and gave to her and wanted nothing in return other than her presence in his life.

He had given her all the children she desired, even this last one when she'd already turned forty-two. He had hesitated only because he worried about her. She reassured him that giving birth and raising children were her special gifts, like loving her was his.

They crossed over the bridge. The house came into view. It was early afternoon, so the children were in school, but Maeve nevertheless felt their presence. They were tethered to this place, to her and Arthur, to the boat that sat beyond the house waiting for its crew.

Arthur pulled in, levered the gearshift to park. "You going to lie down, Maeve?"

"I'm tired of lying down. And there's a lot to do, I suspect."

"Nothing pressing. I've got to go back to work, but I'll stop at Anderson's on the way if you make me a list."

"I'll see when we get inside."

He hadn't opened the door, and Maeve sat with her hands on her belly, waiting.

He twisted on the seat to face her. "I love you, Maeve."

"I know you do, Arthur."

"I don't know if you do. I don't know how to tell you how much." His eyes swam with tears. "I need words I don't have."

She laid her hand on his cheek. "It's all right. I really do know."

He smiled, but he wasn't completely reassured. He never was. She could tell him she loved him a million times, and it would not calm him, not at his center. In any case it wasn't her love for him that worried him, but that she might not understand how much he loved her. He might be right. How could anyone measure the depth and extent of their most tender feelings against someone else's?

She touched the end of his nose with a finger. "Let's go in."

CHAPTER NINE

HARPER

The girls' room had three twin beds sticking out from one wall and three desks on the opposite one, but only Verity's was a real desk. Eden's was a vanity Daddy had found at the Goodwill. The varnish was peeling off, and Eden picked at it the whole time she sat there, like it was an animal with a scabby hide. Harper's desk was actually a table, long and thin, meant to go behind a couch or somewhere. Daddy had painted it yellow, her favorite color, so it wasn't completely awful.

Verity's bed and desk were farthest from the door, Eden's were in the middle, and Harper's were closest to the door. Their room was the biggest bedroom in the house, but that didn't mean that if you were sitting on Verity's bed like Verity and Eden were that a person in Harper's bed, in this case, Harper, couldn't hear what you were saying even if you were whispering. Harper had sensitive ears—that was what their mom said. Harper didn't like spying on people, but how else was she supposed to know what was going on? Was it her fault that Eden and Verity forgot that she was there once she stopped talking? The three of them had shared a room for more than a year, since Harper got too old to bunk with Roy and Wally. In other words, when her parents finally realized she was an actual girl. Moving in with Verity and Eden was like joining a new club, one without random hitting and explosions. Verity hadn't minded, but Eden sure did. Like the distance between ten and not even thirteen was something Evel Knievel couldn't jump on a motorcycle.

Ever since Roy dove overboard a little over two weeks ago, Harper had been 100 percent sure Verity had a secret. A ginormous secret. Her sister was lucky she was good at school because if she was forced to survive as an actress, she'd starve to death. Their mom kept looking at Verity out of the corner of her eye, like Verity might do something unexpected, which she had never ever done even once as far as Harper knew. And Harper made it her business to know.

Harper lay perfectly still with her back toward her sisters. Earlier, outside the bathroom, Harper had overheard Verity telling Eden she had to talk to her after Harper fell asleep. Harper stole some iced tea from the fridge after dinner to help stay awake. She'd been waiting so long and struggled to keep her eyeballs open, and finally Verity was spilling.

"Why do you need me to be the captain on Saturday?" Eden said for the third time.

"I already told you."

"And I don't believe you. No way the yearbook staff are going to Richmond." She had also said this three times. "How about if I check with Maybelle Archer? Her sister, Ruth, is my friend, remember?"

Harper was getting annoyed with Verity, too, and now Eden had called her bluff. Out with it!

"You can't tell," Verity said.

Harper could just see Eden rolling her eyes. "Like I would."

Verity was quiet a minute, then gave in. "I applied to Halliwell College, and I got in. Mom and Dad haven't decided, but I think Dad's going to say I can't go even though I got a scholarship that would pay for practically everything."

Harper had never heard of Halliwell College, but if Verity hadn't been sure she'd get in, then it must be the hardest school in the US of A because Verity was a brainiac, a word you should never say out loud to her. Harper ought to know. She'd said it once, meaning it as a compliment, and Verity sat on her, and Harper's lungs nearly collapsed. Verity was almost always calm and nice, but everybody had a brittle place that snapped just like that. What if Halliwell College was really far, like Alaska? She'd hardly ever see Verity. Harper bit on her lip so she wouldn't cry.

Eden was shocked. "You applied in secret?"

"Uh-huh."

Eden let out a low whistle. "Sounds like my MO, except the actual going-to-college part."

"You don't want to go?"

"I'm definitely not keen on the studying, but if it gets me away from Commander Asshole, sure."

Verity's voice was so low, even Harper's owl ears strained to hear. "You shouldn't call him that."

"Come on, Verity. He's a control freak and also a regular freak." Eden shifted around on the bed. "Like you love playing captain. Get real, Verity."

Verity was quiet, and Harper knew she was frowning. "I don't mind most of the time. It was my game, remember? I started it."

"So what? I don't get you. It's not like you signed a contract."

The silence was long and awkward, and Harper wondered who would be captain if Verity went to Alaska. Spider? The crew would spend the whole day taking things apart. Bor-ing.

Finally Verity said, "I need you to help me, Eden. I want to see Halliwell. Mrs. Castle said she'd take me on Saturday."

Verity was running away, Harper thought, just like Jude. Well, she was running away and coming back, because college probably started in the fall like all school did, but then she was running away again. Holy Toledo. Just the idea of Verity leaving made Harper feel like a run-over toad.

"It's creepy you would go with a guidance counselor," Eden said.

"What else am I supposed to do? She expected Mom and Dad to take me, but of course that's ixnayed. I said Dad works on Saturday and Mom's too pregnant to sit that long in a car, which is all true, by the way."

"Yeah, your lies are golden." Eden sighed. "Okay, I'll do it for twenty bucks."

"I don't have twenty dollars!" Verity was shout-whispering.

"Ten, then. Knowing you, you still have your birthday money." Eden was right. Verity was a tightwad—and Eden had holes in her pockets. She asked, "But what's the point in going to see it if the commander won't let you go?"

"I have to. I can't just give up like that, plus Mom is on my side. She knows I'm going but warned me not to get my hopes up." She paused, and Harper knew she was chewing on her thumb. "I'll probably hate it."

"Oh yeah. A college like that has got to be terrible. To make the brochures, they use fake buildings and fake kids, and force them to look rich and smile big. In reality it's just one never-ending bummer." Verity was trying not to laugh, so Eden kept going. "The ship is more luxurious. I'll bet the dorm rooms are smaller than the bow berth and every day you get three meals but it's always the same: bologna sandwiches and number salad."

Verity laughed for real now. "I like number salad!"

Harper couldn't keep quiet one second longer. She threw off the covers and swung her feet to the floor. "Gosh, I sure hope Daddy doesn't find out. You'll be in so much deep doo-doo, Verity. You, too, Eden." Her sisters stared at her with their mouths open. "Five smackeroos, and I'll keep this on the q.t."

Eden snort-laughed. "I'm not giving you anything."

Harper crossed her arms and gave Verity the hairy eyeball. She deserved it for being a traitor and jumping ship.

"I don't have another five, Harper."

"That's okay. I don't need it right now. You can write me an IOU and pay me when you get your allowance." Harper squirmed a little; she didn't get her kicks squeezing cash from her sisters. To be honest, she was doing it for their sakes. Because if they paid to keep her quiet, they wouldn't worry about her telling.

"Don't blab," Eden said.

"I don't blab."

Eden exchanged a look with Verity. "You have diarrhea of the mouth, Harper."

It felt like Eden had just given her a rope burn in her chest. She knew she talked all the time—she wasn't stupid—and kids at school said that exact thing to her. It was gross and mean. Harper glared at Eden but didn't say a word. She got back under the covers, pulling them up to her chin. "If you don't mind, I'm going to sleep now. That is, if you're finished plotting crimes for the night."

"Good night, Harper," Verity said.

"Sweet dreams, you grifter," Eden said.

Grifter? What in the world was a grifter? Harper was unbelievably drowsy but hoped she could remember to look it up in the morning. For now, she'd give Eden the benefit of the doubt. "Good night, you guys."

~

The next morning everyone was getting ready for school. There were too many of them for one trip, and the bus stop was too far to walk, nearly two miles, so their mom made two trips unless she didn't need the car, and then Verity drove the older kids. Daddy wanted a car at home all the time now in case Mommy had to drive herself to have the baby. He didn't trust the ambulance to come right away because of how far out they lived and said their mom would know with plenty of time. "Why don't you have it while you're in town at the store?" he joked. "You'd be most of the way there."

That day Verity and Harper stayed behind with Nellie and Cyrus while Mommy dropped off the others. Her general rule was that two big kids could look after two little ones, what Spider called man-to-man defense. Verity could handle two on her own, maybe three, because she'd had lots of practice.

Harper left her backpack by the door and went into the kitchen, where Nellie was frowning at her empty cereal bowl.

She lifted it up and showed it to Verity, who was wiping the table. "Anyway, can I have more?"

"Only if you're quick." Verity poured Rice Krispies and milk into the bowl, put the milk in the fridge, and signaled to Harper to follow her into the pantry. Even though it was hardly bigger than a coat closet, they used the pantry for private conversations. Cyrus had named it the Room of Secrets. When you had this many siblings, you had to have secrets.

Verity left the door ajar so she could keep an eye on Nellie.

"What's shakin'?" Harper asked.

"About last night." Verity was super serious. Uh-oh. "Please don't be that person."

"What person?"

"A person who takes money to keep quiet about something."

"Oh, you mean don't be Eden."

Verity's brow wrinkled. "Well, not exactly, but also a little bit yes."

Harper was confused. "Why should I keep quiet for free when Eden gets ten dollars?"

"Because Eden is also doing a job for me. She's being captain. But Eden's not a good role model in this case."

Harper was looking up at her sister, trying to figure out the real message. "You do mean don't be like Eden."

Verity sighed. "Be Harper. Be the curious, fun, talkative kid." She reached out, tucked a loose piece of hair behind Harper's ear. "Don't grow up too fast, at least not so fast that you don't know who you want to be before you get there."

Harper didn't know why, but her chest went tight, and she felt really small all of a sudden. Verity was looking at her, not waiting exactly, but wondering if she had said the right thing maybe, and it hit Harper harder than it had last night that Verity was planning to leave, to go somewhere else on her own, without her, and the thought was heavy, making her knees bend a little.

"You okay?" Verity was worried now.

"Sure. Sure, I'm okay. Thanks." But while these words were coming out of her mouth, Harper was thinking about being eleven and in the middle, and how demanding five dollars from her sister was all about trying to be older than eleven instead of exactly eleven. Verity gave good advice and was the nicest sister, and that was why Harper would miss her. "I'm sorry about the money. You don't have to give it to me."

Verity smiled a little. "It doesn't matter. I just don't want you to grow up the wrong way. Not that I have a clue what the right way is." She pulled Harper into a hug. Verity wasn't a big hugger, but she ought to have been because her hugs were primo. She squished you flat, and you didn't care.

Nellie shouted from the kitchen, "Mommy's here! Mommy's here!"

Verity let go of Harper, and they shuffled out of the Room of Secrets. Only today Harper had learned that it was only for secrets from the outside. On the inside it was for the truth, even if the truth hurt.

CHAPTER TEN

MAEVE

When Verity told Maeve that Eden was taking over as captain so Verity could visit Halliwell, Maeve guessed money had exchanged hands. Eden would never give up her Saturday to direct activities on the ship, even if the alternative was simply sitting on her bottom and ignoring Verity's orders. Maeve didn't approve of her children paying each other to keep secrets or do favors, but she decided to make an exception.

For the last three weeks, she had been working on getting Arthur to let go of his anger and hurt over Verity's deception and concentrate instead on how they might afford for Verity to go to Halliwell—both practically and emotionally. It had been slow going, as she'd known it would be. Arthur could be stubborn, especially when he felt he'd been wronged, and Maeve had trouble making the argument for a fancy college over CCC, especially for the first year or two. Arthur wouldn't approve of Verity getting her hopes up by visiting the school and imposing on the guidance counselor to do it. He'd also see it as pressure on their decision-making; in this he wasn't wrong. If Verity fell in love with Halliwell, it would make it that much harder to say no. But Maeve wasn't going to stop her daughter from seeing the place that had made her such a generous offer, so she reluctantly agreed to back up the yearbook-trip cover story. Having a big family meant balancing everyone's needs, desires, and peculiarities, and sometimes that balance could be achieved only with a little stealthy maneuvering.

Maeve perched on the edge of the couch with the laundry basket at her feet, folding and sorting clothing into piles. All the windows were open—it was a fine day in a May that had had nothing but fine days—and the sounds of her children playing on the ship drifted in to her. From the raucous cheers and whoops, Eden had obviously decided to allow Roy and Wallace to use the old ball machine from the club that Arthur and Spider had converted into an artillery gun. It fired one tennis ball at a time, and the lock on the swivel meant it only fired away from the ship. Nevertheless, it launched balls fifty feet, and the children burned off a lot of energy setting up targets and collecting the balls scattered everywhere.

Maeve bent over to collect a handful of socks, and a wave of dizziness came over her. When she straightened, the dizziness subsided, but her temples throbbed. Maybe a tuna sandwich and an apple for lunch hadn't been enough. At seven months along, she usually was eating more, but she had had an appetite. Probably it was her age. As soon as she'd finished with the laundry, she would eat something.

"Mommy!" Nellie raced in from the kitchen and threw herself into Maeve's lap—what there was of it.

"Careful, little bug." She pulled her daughter into the crook of her arm and kept an eye out for her sharp little knees.

"Is the baby coming today? Because I'm bored."

"Not today. You don't want to play on the ship?"

She shook her head. "Anyway, I'm hungry and tired."

"Sounds serious." Maeve leaned back and glanced at the wall clock in the kitchen. Two fifteen. Her watch strap had broken, and she hadn't had a moment to get it fixed. "How about a snack and a story?" Laundry was hardly ever an emergency, and nothing could spoil an afternoon faster than a cranky four-year-old.

Nellie brightened. "The birthday book." Her birthday was tomorrow, and *Happy Birthday to You!* by Dr. Seuss had been getting a workout for the past two weeks.

"The birthday book it is. Why don't you find it and meet me back here?" Nellie toddled off, talking to herself. Maeve used both hands to push herself to standing, and the pain in her back came right along with her. Maybe a hot pad while she read to Nellie.

In the kitchen she put some crackers and grapes in a small bowl for Nellie, and cheese and crackers on a plate for herself. She returned the cheese to the fridge and yawned, overcome by the exhaustion that had been plaguing her all day. She always loved this stage in her pregnancies, feeling full and strong, the welcome periodic surprises of the baby turning over, stretching, kicking. By eight months she would be anticipating the birth, and the welcoming of new life, but at seven months, the joy was still in the pregnancy. Not this time.

The back door opened and Cyrus flew in. Had all her children forgotten how to walk?

His face was red and sweaty, and he held his fists tight by his sides. "They made me the target! They shot the gun at me when I was picking up balls! They aren't supposed to do that!"

"They?"

"Roy and Wally!" It came out "Rolly." Maeve reached out for him, but he was too angry. Revenge suited him better at the moment. "You got to punish them, Mommy!"

Maeve sighed. She ought to send him to the ship to work it out with Eden, but her back hurt, and Nellie was waiting. "I will talk to them. I promise."

"No talking! Lock them up somewhere. Nice kids like me don't stand a chance."

His face started to crumple, and she pulled him to her. "I'm about to read to Nellie." She stroked his bangs off his damp forehead and kissed it. "You want to listen in?"

He nodded but didn't look up at her, and she figured he was thinking he was too big for afternoon story time and should return to the ship, his duties, and the dangerous world of his twin brothers. When her children were poised at a crossroads like this, Maeve kept quiet. One of the most important lessons of growing up, one every person learned again and again, was that growth was never a straight line. One day you were a brave six-year-old who could handle whatever your siblings threw at you—often literally—and the next day you yearned for the shade of your mother's care. Maeve would never have insisted Cyrus be six every day, whatever that meant. Heck, there were days when she herself was as adrift and confused as she had been at sixteen. If Eden had burst through the back door this minute, hurt and feeling small, Maeve would have read *Happy Birthday to You!* to her, too.

She slipped off Cyrus's shoes and led him by the hand to the living room couch, where Nellie had wedged herself between piles of clothing. Maeve cleared a space for the three of them and rested her feet on the coffee table. Nellie handed her the book, and Maeve began to read it by heart. As her two youngest nestled closer, Maeve thought, not for the first time, that the ship was a mixed blessing. When Arthur had first hatched the idea, Maeve had agreed it sounded fun. Who wouldn't? She'd never expected that eight years later, life on the ship would have come to mean so much to their family. They couldn't afford, either in time or money, sports and activities for so many children, not living where they did. In a way, the USS *Nepenthe* defined them. The ship was more than an elaborate playhouse; it was a place where their children could play and learn and work together, right in their backyard.

Jude had never taken to it. She told herself it was because he'd been too old to accept it, but in her heart she understood that he wasn't cut out for it. He didn't like machines and rules, didn't like being corralled and defined. Music was his language. When Arthur had taught him to play chess, Jude had insisted the black and white pawns gang up and take down whichever queen was vulnerable. Now he was gone, and she missed his creative take on things. She missed his music. She missed him.

The ship made parenting easier, she couldn't deny it, but Maeve worried from time to time that the rigid roles and hierarchy didn't allow her children to backslide. It wasn't just Jude. Rules provided their own comfort—every parent understood that—but there was more to growing up than knowing your job and doing it right. There were hard days, days you couldn't cope or were mysteriously sad. There were times when you felt smaller than you were, or simply too different, and what you needed was not a chain of command but someone who'd accept you as you were right then. Arthur failed to grasp this; his solution was to always stand taller. She and Arthur would never see eye to eye on this.

Maeve sighed and read the next page, on which the Birthday Bird declared that no one was "you-er than you," and made it a cause for celebration. Well, at least the Birthday Bird agreed with her.

Nellie burrowed deeper into the space under Maeve's arm. Cyrus draped one leg over Maeve's, his knee coming to rest against the bottom of her swollen belly. His sock was twisted and bunched, exposing his ankle. Maeve's chest tightened, as it often did at casual glimpses of her children's bodies, so small, so new, so perfectly made.

She smiled to herself and read on.

～

"Mom?" A hand on her shoulder. "Mom?" Eden hovered over her.

"What is it?" Maeve blinked into the half light of the living room. "Did I fall asleep?"

"Yeah, and you're really pale. Should I call Dad?"

Maeve pushed herself upright. "I'm fine. Just give me a minute." Her head was fuzzy, and the ache in her back hadn't eased. "Are Nellie and Cyrus on the ship?"

"In Nellie's room. When I came in, you were all passed out. I thought you'd wake up when I carried them off." She peered at Maeve again. "You sure I shouldn't call Dad?"

Maeve waved her hand. "I'm fine." She got up to demonstrate it was true. "I'll just get something to drink." She picked her way among the furniture and laundry piles, and Eden followed. Maeve pulled a ginger ale from the fridge. "Want anything?" Eden shook her head. "Everything okay on the ship?"

Eden rolled her eyes. "Everyone's alive."

Maeve smiled and sipped the ginger ale. The sweet taste woke her up some, but she felt weak as a kitten. Probably from napping so heavily.

Eden stole a look at the clock. Maeve followed her gaze and couldn't believe it was nearly four. "Dad'll be home soon, right? Because I'm about to mutiny myself out there." She hesitated, looked at her mother, and chewed her lip. "Or maybe Spider can entertain them. As usual, he's been doing his own thing all day."

Maeve nodded. "Ask Spider to take over, Eden. Nicely. And thank you for looking after everyone today."

"Sure, Mom. As long as you're okay."

"I'm fine. I'm just fine." If she said it often enough, it would be true.

Eden left, easing the screen door shut behind her. Maeve checked the fridge to make sure she had defrosted hamburger for dinner. If she threw together macaroni and cheese and a salad, Arthur would cook the burgers on the grill. He was always willing, if she asked, even after he'd worked a full day. It was a small thing, but especially helpful since he could monitor the kids in the yard at the same time. Such a trustworthy husband and father. Maeve put the box of elbow macaroni on the counter where she couldn't miss it, knowing chaos might intervene at any moment. She was about to check on Cyrus and Nellie when they came running from the living room into the kitchen.

Nellie screamed, "I'm first! I'm first!" as she chased Cyrus past the table. Cyrus one-armed the screen door, and they both disappeared outside, Nellie's shouts receding. She must've had a good nap.

Maeve rubbed the small of her back, then filled a pot with water for the macaroni and set it on the stove. While she waited for it to boil, she scraped back a chair and slid into it. She drank her ginger ale and resolved not to tell Arthur about her headache and fatigue unless she felt the same tomorrow. Or Monday, because tomorrow was Sunday, which meant chores and church. Arthur would insist on her seeing someone, so it would be the hospital again. Yes, Monday would be soon enough.

~

By five thirty, Maeve had managed to finish putting away the laundry, and had assembled the macaroni and cheese. It wasn't much, but it had required all her effort. The kids had abandoned ship a short while ago, and Eden absconded to her room, closing the door emphatically. At least she hadn't taken off to a friend's house without permission. Roy and Wallace had come in covered head to toe in mud, the result of a tennis ball search gone awry, and although she'd had Spider drag them back outside and hose off the worst of it, they needed a bath. Cyrus and Nellie, too. The four youngest were occupied with Bugles and Hawaiian Punch for now, but it wouldn't last.

Harper placed her glass in the sink. "Can I help with anything, Mom?"

"You're an angel, Harper. A salad would be great."

"I'm an angel, too," Nellie said. "But I don't like salad except number salad."

"You like cucumbers." Harper opened the fridge and peered into the crisper drawer. "And carrots."

"I hate carrots," Wallace said.

Roy nodded. "We hate carrots and cucumbers."

Maeve raised her hand. "Enough. Put whatever you want in the salad, Harper."

"Even frogs?" Cyrus asked.

"Yes. Chef's rules." Maeve stepped out to the living room, where Spider was lounging on the couch with a comic book. "Could you get the kids in the bath? Two at a time?" It wasn't a task he'd done before, as it usually fell to her, Verity, or, in a pinch, Arthur, but she didn't see why he couldn't manage it.

He didn't look up. "The hose wasn't good enough?"

"Not really. They need soap—and clean clothes. It would be such a help to me."

He dropped the comic on the couch. "I got it, Mom. No problemo."

Spider stood, and Maeve swore he'd grown an inch since breakfast. She placed a hand on her belly. *Don't even dream of growing up that fast.*

Spider loped over to the kitchen table. "Who wants to be a suds monster first?" A chorus of groans.

Cyrus's nose crinkled. "I'll be first with Nellie because we don't want to use their stinky, dirty water." He was obviously holding a grudge from earlier, which wasn't like him.

"Let me help," Maeve said as she lifted Nellie from her chair. Nellie wound her arms around her mother's neck, her palms sticky against Maeve's bare shoulders from Hawaiian Punch. The room went blurry at the edges, and Maeve steadied herself against the back of a chair.

Cyrus bumped against her leg, and her knee gave way. Her head was a balloon, and her limbs floated away from her body. Nellie grasped her as she tilted forward and her strength leaked away.

Nellie's head. *No.*

Maeve twisted, tucked her shoulder under her daughter's head as her legs collapsed and the world went dark.

CHAPTER ELEVEN

HARPER

Oh my Lord.

"Eden!"

Mommy was standing there holding Nellie one second and lying on the floor the next.

"Eden!" Harper didn't know why she was screaming for Eden except she was the oldest except for Mommy, and since Mommy was the problem, there was no use screaming her name. "Eden!"

"Stop screaming, Harper!" Spider screamed.

He bent over their mom, but he wasn't doing anything other than staring at her hard. He was scared, and that made Harper even more scared. She scooted around the table and picked up Nellie, who had slipped out of their mom's arms as she fell and hit the floor on her butt and fallen backward and hit her head. She wasn't crying yet because she hadn't figured out what had happened. Harper didn't see any blood on her sister's head or clothes.

"Nellie, it's okay." Harper's thoughts ran around in her head like they were on fire. She held her sister close, then thought she really ought to check her, and leaned her away a little. "Did you bump your head? Show me."

Nellie was dazed, like she'd just woken up, but then she caught up to what had happened and put her pudgy hand on the side of her head above her ear. Tears started running down her cheeks. Harper dried them and kissed her. "It's okay. It's okay."

Spider looked up at them. "Is she really okay?"

"I don't know! I think so. Can't you wake up Mom?" Harper's heart was beating loud in her ears, mixing in with Nellie's crying.

Eden waltzed in. The annoyed look on her face said she had been expecting to have to break up a stupid fight. She saw their mom on the floor and stopped short.

"What happened?" Eden knelt beside Spider and their mom. Harper had been avoiding looking at her mom because the whole thing was terrifying, but she did now. Mommy was so white Harper couldn't even describe it, like the whitest thing ever, and Harper felt sick. Eden put her hand on their mom's cheek and tapped her a little. Harper could tell Eden didn't know what to do, either.

"Someone call Dad," Eden said.

Spider got up, started for the phone, and stopped in his tracks. "He's gotta be on the way already. Maybe we should call an ambulance."

"Okay," Eden said, nodding. "Okay."

Nellie was crying, and Harper wanted to put her down because she was heavy and Harper didn't feel so good herself, but she was frozen in place. She lowered Nellie to the ground—even though it seemed mean, it wasn't as mean as getting dropped for the second time in five minutes. Harper sat and held Nellie's hand, and Nellie stood there, howling. Cyrus came over and hugged Nellie, but then he started crying, too. It felt like their whole world was coming to an end.

Mommy's eyes opened.

"Wallace!" Eden was fierce. "Get Mom a glass of water."

For the first time in his life, he didn't argue.

Mommy tried to sit up, and Eden helped her. Eden twisted to glance at Harper and gave her a little nod, and Harper let out a big breath. Their mom looked around like her kids were a crowd of strangers who had shown up in her kitchen out of nowhere. "Gracious, what am I doing down here?"

"You dropped me," Nellie said, hiccuping. "I hurt my head."

"It's okay, Mom," Eden said. "You fainted, maybe."

Wallace handed Mommy the glass of water. It was too full and some spilled. "Sorry."

"It's okay." Mommy's voice was thin and a little croaky.

Harper was learning that when things were the worst, people say *okay* all the time.

Spider walked back into the kitchen, his shoulders dropping with relief when he saw Mommy was awake. "Do you want me to call an ambulance, Mom?"

"I don't think so." She drank some water, wiped her mouth with the back of her hand. Nellie crawled over to her and sat beside her legs.

"Do you want to get up?" Eden asked, sounding hopeful but also like maybe it wasn't such a hot idea.

Mommy closed her eyes for a second, opened them again. "Not yet."

Harper was feeling steadier and had ideas again. "I think someone who can't get off the floor is someone who needs an ambulance."

"I don't know, Harper. I'll feel better in a minute." Their mom didn't sound sure, not even halfway to sure.

"Dad'll be here soon, Mom," Spider said.

Harper got up. Someone needed to take action. "You don't know that. Anything could happen. Maybe he stayed late at work. Maybe he got a flat tire or picked up a hitchhiker and has to take them somewhere. And even if he is going to be here soon, whenever that is, Daddy's not an ambulance and he's not a doctor."

"Daddy's a daddy," Nellie said.

"I'm calling an ambulance." Harper headed for the phone.

Roy jumped up. "I'm helping."

He still had his arm in a sling and felt left out all the time. For instance he couldn't be the one to get water for Mommy. So of course he had to help dial 9-1-1 because everyone knew one finger couldn't possibly dial three numbers. Brothers were the most annoying invention.

She picked up the receiver, and her finger shook as she tried to poke it in the nine hole. *Calm down.* Cyrus could do it, maybe even Nellie. The problem wasn't the dialing, it was what she was supposed to say after someone answered. Roy was breathing down her neck, or actually down her elbow since he was shorter. "Give me some space, Roy."

"You might mess it up."

"I'll mess you up if you don't back off." His face was all twisted with worry, and she felt bad. "Okay, okay. You watch while I do it." He nodded, real solemn.

The front door opened, and Daddy walked in like it was the most normal day.

Harper had never been more relieved to see someone in her life. She dropped the phone on the cradle and rushed over to him. "Daddy, I know you don't like news right away but this is different."

Roy was beside her. She'd forgotten about him. "She's right. Mommy's on the floor."

Their dad frowned down at them. "Where is she?"

"In the kitchen," Harper said. He was halfway there already, and she skedaddled after him. "I was calling an ambulance. Should I still do that?"

Without turning, he raised his arm. In two steps he reached Mommy. He touched Spider's shoulder, and Spider moved away. Daddy dropped his keys and his lunch box on the table and squatted beside her. "What's going on, love? Did you fall?"

Harper scooted around to the other side of the table so she could see.

Mommy brushed her hair from her forehead. "I fainted, I think. I've been dragging all day."

Daddy picked up her arm, put two fingers on her wrist. He frowned again. "Your pulse is weak, and I don't like how pale you are." He looked around at all the kids. "Where's Verity?"

"She had a trip today," Eden said. "I filled in on the ship."

He didn't like this one bit, but if he knew the truth, he'd like it less. "When's she back?"

Eden shrugged.

The secret Harper had been hiding was right there in her mouth, and she clamped her lips together to hold it in. Secrets were slimy and could slip out without you meaning them to.

Their dad told Spider to help him lift their mom into a chair, which they did but not easily. Next came the instructions.

"Eden, get your mother a glass of orange juice and something to eat—a banana would be good. Need to get her blood sugar up. Harper, you take Cyrus and Nellie to your room, get them settled down." He looked at the twins. "You two go straight into the bath. Spider will set you up, but then you do the rest yourselves, and don't leave a mess." Eden was pouring the juice, but everyone else was staring at Mommy. Their dad sighed, realizing how worried they all were. "I'll take care of your mother. Just do as I ask."

The boys left. Nellie was on the floor, hanging on to their mom's leg and sniffling.

"C'mon, Nellie." Harper waved her over. "Daddy says so. You, too, Cyrus."

Cyrus got up, circled around the table, and took Harper's hand. He tugged on her arm, and she bent over so he could whisper in her ear. "Are we having dinner ever? I'm super hungry."

Mommy had owl ears exactly the same as Harper. "Arthur, the children will need to eat."

"They can wait, Maeve." Eden handed him the juice and put a banana on the table. "Drink this down," Daddy said to Mommy. He peeled the banana with his big hands and broke off a piece and waited for their mom to finish the juice.

In two seconds he was going to tell Harper to hurry up and go, but she wanted to see if the juice and the banana worked. She didn't want to be upstairs worrying about it. She'd rather be right here worrying about it. But Daddy's head started to swivel around, so she scooted Cyrus and Nellie in front of her and herded them out of the kitchen. Nellie was holding her hand to her head, and Harper realized they hadn't told their father about Nellie getting clonked. As the only medically trained person available, Harper would just have to look after Nellie herself until Daddy could. She took Nellie's hand, and Cyrus's, too, and led them upstairs, having decided she'd get them in their pj's, then come back down for some ice.

In the girls' room, Harper pulled Nellie's shirt over her head, then did Cyrus's. They looked so little like that, with their naked bellies showing. She liked being responsible for them, taking care of them, keeping them safe. It made her feel useful, and at least twelve, maybe thirteen.

Cyrus was frowning. "Is Mommy going to be okay?"

"Sure she is. Daddy's taking care of her."

He nodded, satisfied. But it got Harper thinking that if Verity hadn't been away, she'd be taking care of Nellie, making sure her head was okay. If Verity was going to be in Alaska or wherever for college in a few months, did that mean Harper had to act even older than she felt already? She hadn't liked being confused and scared about calling an ambulance, but she would've done it if she had to. It was just hard to do things before you were ready.

Like remembering that Nellie's clothes were downstairs. Harper picked up a T-shirt of hers off the floor. "You like this one, don't you, Nels? Because of the rainbow?"

Nellie nodded and Harper slipped it on. "Let's go tell Daddy about your head."

CHAPTER TWELVE

VERITY

Mrs. Castle was an extremely nice person and a terrible driver. Verity hadn't slept well last night and expected to be nervous about visiting Halliwell. What she hadn't expected was that she would fear for her life during the whole trip. Mrs. Castle didn't seem to understand which half of the road was hers and liked the piece in the middle best. She looked around all the time, talked with her hands (both at once!), and got confused when other drivers beeped at her or gave her the finger.

"I don't like to make generalizations about people, but I have to say the drivers out here in Richmond are awfully rude." Mrs. Castle shook her head. "Used to a different style of driving, is my best guess."

"Do you drive much around home?" It was the most polite question Verity could think of.

"Not a great deal. My husband does most of the driving, insists on it, in fact. I drive myself to school, of course, and that's about it!" Mrs. Castle threw her hands in the air for emphasis, and the car veered into the breakdown lane.

Verity closed her eyes and thought back to the college tour. The student guide had talked a blue streak about the buildings and the courses and the extracurriculars, but at first all Verity saw was how different the other kids were from the ones at her school—compared to her, especially. They were cool and sophisticated, as if they'd been born in a dorm room, had always studied in a grand library with a rotunda, had kicked their first ball across a perfectly manicured lawn, as if living at a college with matching brick buildings with snow-white columns were the most normal thing in the world. Verity had been to Chesapeake Community College a few times for events or school trips, and it was nothing like Halliwell. It was more like her high school: worn and gritty.

Mrs. Castle must've read her thoughts. "Now that you've seen Halliwell, Verity, you should have all the information you need to decide."

"I just need to talk to my parents." Which made her anxious, and a little angry, if she could admit it, because if it were up to her, she'd send in the acceptance form today. Sure, she'd felt out of place at Halliwell, as she'd known she would, but that disappeared pretty quickly, and Verity saw the college for what it was: learning served on a silver platter. All the libraries and labs and lecture halls, all the activities and performances and clubs. Meals whenever you wanted them, cooked by someone else. She'd been overwhelmed, but that didn't stop her wanting to jump into the middle of it. She hadn't felt like that for years, not since that creep Wes had stolen something from her, something she hadn't even known she had and couldn't describe. Her power, maybe. When she'd walked across the campus today, in and out of the buildings, she'd felt it come back to her, like a wave coming over her and carrying her out to sea. She was still worried about knowing how to swim, about keeping up, but she was certain she was ready to give it a shot.

Mrs. Castle turned to her with a serious face. Her arms twisted with her, and the car lurched to the right. "Whoopsie-daisy." She corrected the steering and cleared her throat. "I don't mean to pry, dear, but I have the sense perhaps your parents aren't as thrilled about Halliwell as you and I are."

Unsure of what to say, Verity stared out the window at whatever town they were driving through east of Richmond; she hadn't been paying attention. One house after another, most with kids, judging by the swing sets and bicycles in the yards. What did all these families think of their kids leaving home? They all had to leave sometime, start their own lives. How did the kids and their parents decide when was the right time? Maybe there was no such thing as the right time. Look what had happened with Jude. Gone at seventeen. No one had thought it was the right time, but it had happened anyway. Maybe you just had to leave.

"I was prying, I guess," Mrs. Castle said. "I'm sorry."

"Oh no. It's okay." Verity picked through her thoughts to find the right words. "We have a big family, and my parents want us to be together. We do everything together: chores, church, dinner every night." She almost mentioned the ship, but it was too complicated— and a little embarrassing. "Being together is kind of like our constitution. It's who we are."

"That's lovely. It really is. And so important in making you the wonderful young lady you are." Mrs. Castle paused and for once kept her eyes on the road. "But everyone grows up. I'm sure your parents know that."

"Sure they do. We're going to talk about it."

Mrs. Castle said, "I see."

But she didn't. Verity hadn't considered leaving home for college until Mrs. Castle planted the idea. Going clear across the state, not to mention out of state, was rare for kids from her school. The only ones who did had parents with desk jobs who'd done the same. Neither of Verity's parents had gone to college at all, so CCC seemed like plenty to them, and to her. Mrs. Castle had widened Verity's horizons and left her with swirling feelings of fear, pride, doubt, and hope.

They crossed the bridges over the York at West Point, and the sickly smell from the pulp mill clung to the back of Verity's throat. A few miles later, they passed the sign announcing Gloucester County and its founding date, 1651, and Verity breathed out a sigh. Fields of newly planted corn lined by loblolly pine. Little brick houses with white trim and Buicks under metal carports. Double-wides with peeling paint and abandoned cars rusting in the long grass. Bait-and-tackle shops with ice machines by the door, and small Baptist churches with the signs out front with a proverb or saying in black lettering: "If Jesus was a hitch-hiker, would you give Him a lift?" Verity couldn't say she liked any of this, but it was familiar. When you were a shy, overweight girl from a backwater, familiar was comforting. She was too afraid to know exactly what she wanted and smart enough to know she ought to want something more. Now that she'd been to Halliwell, she had a better idea of what "more" looked like.

The day was fading into evening as Mrs. Castle turned onto River Road. The clouds that had hung in the sky all day had spun to the west and settled low in long, thin strips that caught the lengthening rays. Every shade of orange and pink and yellow ran in layers along the horizon, the sun itself a ball of magenta fire.

"You really are away from town here." Mrs. Castle's driving was steadier. Maybe she had been calmed by the familiar surroundings, too.

"It's only twenty minutes into White Marsh."

"Seems like more."

Verity nodded; she'd heard other people say the same thing. When she visited people who lived in town, she found it weird to be able to see into the neighbor's yard, or into their kitchen. It was all what you were used to, she supposed. No surprise then that Halliwell had made her uncomfortable. Given time, she would get used to it, the way she assumed Jude had gotten used to living in an apartment in Richmond, something she could not imagine.

They turned left onto the unnamed road that led to the Vergennes house. The trees thinned out, exposing stands of reed grass and the broad expanse of river beyond. As they crossed the bridge, a great blue heron lifted from the water, dangling its feet behind like an afterthought.

"This is a tricky little bridge." Mrs. Castle peered over the side, and Verity was ready to grab the wheel if the car started heading that way, too. "Does it ever flood?"

"Not often. A few times in all the years we've been here."

"What did you do when that happened?"

"I only remember one time for certain. We just stayed put until it went down."

She laughed lightly. "I suppose you didn't have too much choice!" She stopped the car alongside Verity's father's truck and put it in park. "I hope today gave you a lot to think about."

"It sure did. Thank you so much for taking me, Mrs. Castle."

She patted Verity's arm. "Delighted. You let me know after you speak with your parents. The deadline's a week from Tuesday."

"I will."

Verity waved to her guidance counselor as she drove off but didn't go straight inside. The evening air was cool, and a light breeze carried the silty smell of the water to her. She stood on the porch looking out toward the ship and the trees lining the river, asking herself whether she was truly ready to take on this battle. She was eighteen, so the decision could be hers alone. She didn't like that idea. She loved her parents and wanted them to stand behind her choices. It was hard to know what was right just by thinking about it. What she needed was two selves, one to go to CCC and live at home for at least two years, ease into college life that way, and the other to jump into the deep end of Halliwell College. She was willing to be half as happy on either path rather than risk doing the completely wrong thing, especially if it meant alienating her parents—maybe her whole family.

Verity stepped off the porch, walked past the driveway to see the eastern horizon hidden by the house. Last night the moon hadn't been quite full, but now it rose round and bright between a gap in the trees. Seeing the moonrise from this spot reminded her of when Uncle Henry, her dad's only sibling, had visited not quite two years ago. He owned a Ford dealership in Frederick, Maryland, and visited maybe twice a year, staying at a hotel in Gloucester because he "didn't want to add to the burden." He'd been divorced twice and didn't have kids, so Verity always figured he didn't visit more often because the Vergennes mob was too much for him. But the last time he was here, he had taken her aside, close to where she now stood, and tried to explain her father to her. Something Uncle Henry had said had gotten under her father's skin, and Uncle Henry was leaving early.

"You're sixteen now, so I want to clear up a few things." He spoke formally, like he'd rehearsed what to say. That wasn't like him; he talked freely and often. That was her father's biggest gripe about his brother, that he talked too much and said too little.

"Okay," Verity said, feeling like she was betraying her father with that one word.

"Your father's a good man and I love him. You know that, right?"

She nodded, although she'd honestly never thought about it. Family loved each other, so it was logical. On the other hand, her father and Uncle Henry seemed more like two dogs who'd given up trying to bite each other.

"All right then. Because I know for a fact that he can get wound up about things, so wound up he doesn't know what to do with himself." He looked straight at her as he talked, his eyes exactly like her father's but also not the same at all. "You know what I'm saying, Verity?"

"I think so." She did and she didn't. Her father definitely got "wound up about things," but that was just him, and it confused her to have Uncle Henry point it out, like her father had a limp that she'd failed to notice.

"Like the way he was complaining about the fellow he works with, that Italian fellow."

"Mr. Amici."

"That's the one."

Her father didn't like Mr. Amici, the dining manager at the club, because he had it in for her father, always interfering and making him look bad.

Uncle Henry was rubbing his chin, just the way her father did. "I've met Mr. Amici on more than one occasion, and we have some mutual friends. He's not a difficult person, Verity, not from what I know. But your father thinks Mr. Amici is out to get him simply because the man's trying to do his job, and sometimes there's a conflict with the job your father does. It's not personal, that's my point. But to your father, it is."

Verity frowned and scratched at her elbows. "Why are you telling me this, Uncle Henry?"

"Because your father is complicated. Hell, we all are! But he's a little more complicated than most. Your mother keeps him as steady as I've ever seen him, but zebras don't get polka dots, if you catch my meaning." He winked at her and smiled. "I'm telling you because you're getting older and might see some things for yourself and wonder about it. But your father's always been touchy, always. The war didn't help, but it never does." Uncle Henry laid his hand on her shoulder, gave it a squeeze. "Don't worry about it, Verity, but remember what I said. If your father gets wound up and thinks the world is against him, remember what I said. None of it has a thing to do with you." He gave her shoulder another squeeze, then turned her around gently and pointed at the sky. "Will you look at that moon, Verity? Aren't we on the most amazing planet to have one as pretty as that?"

At the time, Uncle Henry's confidences about her father hadn't meant a great deal. She knew her father, knew people could get under his skin and stay there, irritating him from the inside. Now, staring at the silvery moon on her own, she thought about it again. Jude had really gotten under their father's skin, and their father had gotten under his. Uncle Henry claimed none of it had anything to do with her, but in this case anyway, he was wrong. It had *everything* to do with her, not that Jude or her father seemed to notice, caught as they were in their Mexican standoff. That fact had gotten under *her* skin and stayed there, making her sore and angry and afraid to be herself. Mrs. Castle opening the door to Halliwell might have changed all that.

Verity checked her watch. Seven thirty—later than she expected. Her guilty conscience insisted she offer to get up early and jump-start chores before church. Maybe she'd make muffins in the morning. She stepped onto the porch, and the front door opened.

Her father stood silhouetted in the doorway. "I thought I heard a car but then couldn't figure out why you didn't come in."

"Hi, Daddy." She couldn't read his face in the poor light. A lump formed in her throat at the possibility he knew where she'd really been. "Sorry I'm late."

He stepped back to let her through. "Really could use you, Verity. Your mother's not well at all."

Her head buzzed in panic. "What's wrong?"

"She's dog tired. It's too much for her when she's this pregnant." Her dad looked beat.

Verity felt a surge of guilt. To hide it, she busied herself unloading her bag and jacket. Hadn't Eden kept the kids on the ship most of the day? Maybe she had been wrong to trust her sister. And now her mother was ill. "Where's Mom? Can I see her?"

He walked off toward the kitchen. "She's lying down in our room. I'm cleaning up from dinner. Eden's getting Nellie's presents organized."

Nellie's birthday tomorrow. Verity had forgotten all about it. Who was supposed to make a cake? Was it her? "I'll finish the kitchen, Daddy. Let me just say hi to Mom."

Spider was on the living room floor with Roy and Wallace surrounded by erector-set pieces. Spider consulted the instructions spread out in front of him. "That long piece there, Wally."

Wally selected an eight-inch piece of metal. "This one?"

"Compare it to the picture." Spider pointed at the instructions and waited while Wally looked back and forth between the piece and the drawing.

Spider was the most patient of all of them. He wasn't sweet like Cyrus, but he took everything in stride. Or seemed to. Verity was coming to realize that people weren't always who they seemed to be all the way through. Her own recent behavior surprised her, so who knew what Spider was like inside.

"Hey, Verity," Spider said.

Roy beamed up at her. "Eden was the best captain! We shot a gazillion rounds and had to find them in the mud and everything!"

"We got in trouble." Wallace didn't look up from the pieces he was lining up. "Cyrus ratted on us. He's a baby."

Spider shrugged. "There was some friendly fire."

Great, Verity thought. "Cyrus is smaller than you two, that's true. But he's a member of the crew and ought to be treated with respect."

Wallace rolled his eyes. Verity turned away, frustrated. Couldn't she be gone for a single day without all this? Maybe if she sneaked away more often, they'd learn to cope without her. As soon as she thought it, though, she felt bad. She was their big sister, their captain.

She crossed to the hall leading to their parents' room, thinking about what part of Halliwell she'd tell her mother about first. It was all so exciting, how could she choose? The door was ajar, and she knocked lightly.

"It's me, Verity."

"Oh, you're home. Come on in, love." Her voice was thin.

The roller shades had been lowered almost to the sills, and the only light came from a small lamp on her father's side of the bed. Her mother was wearing what she'd had on when Verity left this morning, a pale-blue sleeveless cotton maternity shift. The natural waves in her hair had gone limp, and her skin was so pale, Verity worried it might be serious.

Her mother patted the bed. "Come sit."

"Just for a minute. I need to help Dad." Verity perched on the mattress.

Her mother reached over and took her hands. "I feel so useless lying here. How was the tour?"

"It was great. I'll tell you more when you're better." As much as Verity was bursting at the seams to tell her mom about Halliwell, this obviously wasn't the time. "And don't worry about chores, there's plenty of us to do everything."

Her mom nodded, leaned back against the pillows. "I don't remember being this tired with any of you."

"Did you call the doctor?"

"He's on vacation until—what's today? The seventeenth?" Verity nodded. "Until the end of next week, I think."

"But someone must be covering for him."

"Sure. Your father said he'd call tomorrow if I'm not better." She sat up straighter, as if something had occurred to her. "Will you check on Nellie for me? I dropped her when I fainted, and I'm worried about her head."

"You fainted? And dropped Nellie?" Verity's voice rose with alarm. Why hadn't her dad told her that?

"I'm fine, but please check on her, Verity."

"Going right now."

Next door the nursery smelled of sawdust and guinea pig. The shade was down on the only window, but Verity could see enough to open the window and let fresh air in. Vermin rustled in her cage, and Nellie sighed in her sleep. Verity touched the back of her hand to her sister's forehead, which was warm, not hot, and dry. Verity bent down so her nose was an inch from Nellie's neck and breathed in her sweet smell.

She returned to tell her mother Nellie was fine and found her still, with her eyes closed.

"Sleep well, Mom," Verity whispered. She watched her mother for a moment, switched off the bedside lamp, and left to help with the children, dragging the weight of guilt and resentment and worry for her mother behind her.

CHAPTER THIRTEEN

Spider

Ship's Log: USS *Nepenthe*
Date: Sunday, May 18, 1980
Time: 1640h
Weather: 73°F, Cloudy/thunderheads
Winds: 10–15 kn SE
CO: Lt. Commander V. Vergennes

The whole crew was in uniform and lined up on deck in two rows facing Verity. Their dad was there, too, at the back behind Spider, wearing his navy cap in honor of Nellie's birthday. Their mom was the only one missing, and even though she hardly ever came aboard, it felt weird because of Nellie's birthday. Everyone hid their worry for Nellie's sake. Their mom had been at the table for lunch (hot dogs and potato salad, Nellie's favorite) and cake (vanilla with pink icing, made by Eden and Harper, with a lot of whisper-hissing), but it might have been better if she had stayed in her room, because she looked like a ghost. So not like their mom. She tried to make a joke about it, saying she was just old and pregnant, but no one laughed. Cyrus told her he didn't mind her being old and pregnant, which was when Verity shooed them all outside before someone started crying. Their mom was never sick, never more than a cold, and it made Spider feel like he was sick, too.

Verity saluted and everyone saluted back. "Welcome to the USS *Nepenthe* special celebration of the birthday of Penelope Vergennes. Step forward, Private Penelope."

Nellie obeyed. She twitched with excitement and looked over her left shoulder, then her right, grinning so wide her face almost split.

Verity nodded at Spider. "Quartermaster Arthur, please present the honorary signal flag."

It had been Spider's idea to give Nellie her own flag. He hadn't been sure if it should be an *N* or a *P*, but decided on *P* because *N* was a blue-and-white checkerboard that meant "negative." Luckily the *P* was just a blue field with a white square in the middle. He'd found a plain blue flag in with other flags, and his mother had given him an old pillowcase to cut the white square out of, so all he'd had to do was sew it on. Not that it was easy. When each kid turned ten, their mom showed them how to sew on a button and fix a tear in a shirt. If he'd known sewing could actually be handy, he'd have paid more attention.

Spider pulled the rolled cloth from his pocket and handed it to Nellie. "Congratulations, Private. The flag is the letter *P*, and it means 'all aboard; the ship is ready to sail,' which seems perfect for today."

Nellie unrolled it and held it by the corners. "Oooooo."

"With your permission, Penelope, I'll fly it now."

"Yes, please."

Everyone watched as Spider ran it up the pole they used for special signals. The flag snapped in the breeze. Spider checked to make sure his dad had seen he'd done it correctly, but he was staring at the house. His mind was on their mom, which made Spider feel like a turd for focusing on his stupid flag.

"Anyway," Nellie said, "I'm five, and my flag is the prettiest."

"Attention." Verity waited for all eyes on her. "The other honor I'm proud to announce today is a promotion."

"Who could it be, I wonder?" Eden asked, knowing the answer.

"I wonder," Spider said.

Roy put his hands on his hips. "I'm not wondering. I'm impatient."

Verity reached into her shirt pocket and lifted a ribbon bar for them to see. Technically Nellie should have gotten an insignia for her sleeve, but it was too much sewing. Plus the bars were more fun. "This promotion is well deserved. As we sailed across both smooth and turbulent seas, this sailor never failed to help provide us with tasty and filling meals. Her number salad is, I think we can all agree, first rate."

"I think it's me," Nellie whispered to Cyrus. He nodded and put his arm across her shoulders.

Verity continued. "As a member of our crew, we value this sailor's cheerful outlook and team spirit, so it is with great pleasure I announce the promotion of Penelope Vergennes to Private First Class." She stepped forward, bent down, and pinned the bar on Nellie's shirt.

"It was me!"

Spider shouted, "Hip, hip, hooray!" and the whole crew joined in for two more cheers.

Their dad clamped Spider on the shoulder. "I'm going back inside. I don't want to spoil Nellie's day, but resting doesn't seem to be helping your mother feel any better."

"What's wrong, do you think?"

"I don't know. I left a message with the doctor on call before I came out. I'll try again if I don't hear back soon." He stepped over the bulwark and was down the gangway in two strides.

Spider watched his father cross the lawn, a determined set to his shoulders, but also hunched from tiredness, Spider guessed. His dad wouldn't call a doctor unless he thought it might be serious, and that was doing a number on Spider's nerves.

Wallace was tugging on Spider's sleeve. "Where are we sailing?"

"What?"

Wallace pointed at Nellie's signal flag. "All aboard and ready to sail, but everyone is fighting about where. You're the navigator!" He was whining, something he almost never did. Spider put a hand on his shoulder and looked up to see Harper and Roy facing off.

"Timbuktu!" Roy said.

Harper leaned in until she was an inch from his nose. "That's stupid. You can't get to Timbuktu on a boat!"

Roy shoved her, and Harper shoved him back. Spider was about to break it up when Nellie pulled Harper down by the arm and clamped her hand over Harper's mouth. "Anyway, it's my birthday. No yelling."

They were all keyed up, unsettled because of their mom. Spider squatted down so he and Wallace were eye to eye. "Hey, I'm like you, buddy. I take my orders from the captain." He pointed to the wheelhouse. "Looks like she's ready."

Verity emerged from the wheelhouse. "Attention. All hands on deck and at your stations. We are setting sail to Katroo." The twins moaned and Verity ignored them. "We can anticipate hostile forces on the way to the home of the Birthday Bird."

Roy, Wallace, and Cyrus climbed onto the bow and began reeling in the lines. Harper and Eden did the same at the stern.

"Coordinates for Katroo coming up, captain." Spider gestured to Nellie. "Want to help me with the maps?" He led her into the wheelhouse and grabbed a pair of rolled maps from behind the captain's chair.

"Verity!" Their father ran halfway across the lawn and stopped. "Verity! Spider!"

Spider dropped the maps, ducked out of the wheelhouse, his heart beating a mile a minute. It had to be their mom.

Verity was already on the gangway. Eden jumped to her feet. "What's going on?"

Spider didn't answer. He flew down the gangway, vaguely aware of the other kids calling out, scrambling after him, Harper screaming, Eden shouting at them, corralling them.

Their dad had disappeared into the house. Spider caught up to Verity at the back door, and they scrambled inside.

Their dad was in the kitchen, pacing. "I need help getting your mother in the car. I'm taking her to the hospital." He headed for their bedroom.

Spider glanced at Verity, who looked terrified. He took off after their father with his sister behind him.

In the bedroom, their dad had a knee on the bed, trying to lift their mother. Her eyes were half-closed, and she was limp.

Spider rubbed his sweaty hands on his pants. "What's wrong with her?"

"I don't know. The doctor says to get her to the hospital, and he'll meet us there." He gestured to Spider. "Come around this side and help me get her up."

Together they moved her to the entry. She was taking some of her own weight but not much. Sweat trickled down Spider's back from the effort, and he felt like he was moving through syrup.

Verity edged past them, her eyes wide. "I'll get the door."

Spider and his father maneuvered her outside, down the steps, and to the station wagon. Verity ran ahead, opened the passenger-side door.

Their mother cried out in pain and bent over. Spider held on tight to her arm, blinking back tears.

Verity ran back to them. Her lips trembled. "Are you having the baby, Mom?"

Their dad shook his head. "It's too early, so I hope to God she isn't."

At the car, Spider stepped to the side so their father could get their mother into the seat. She seemed to be in her own world, her eyes still mostly closed, almost like she was praying.

Verity wiped her eyes roughly with the heel of her hand. "Can you drive, Dad? I mean, maybe an ambulance is better?"

Their dad shut the door and stared at her with a heavy face. "I'm fine. The ambulance takes too long. You think I'd take a risk with your mother?"

"No, Dad. Never." She backed away and came over to Spider. He put his arm around her shoulder.

Their dad got behind the wheel, started the car with one foot on the gravel. The other kids had cut across the lawn from the ship and were slumped in front of the car. Their dad glanced at their mom. She was moving a little. She opened her eyes. Spider wanted to say something to her but didn't know what. It was all happening too fast.

"It's all right, Maeve." Their dad stroked the back of their mom's head. "Everything's going to be all right." He turned to the kids, his eyes not quite focused. "I'll call you when I've got news. All of you be good now."

Spider nodded and scuffed at the dirt, a huge painful lump in his throat. Roy lifted his good hand and waved, his face crumpling, and Wallace did the same.

Harper was fighting tears. "We love you, Mommy and Daddy."

Nellie ran to the passenger door and yanked on the handle with both hands. "Mommy!"

Verity stepped in, lifted her away, and held her close. "Mommy has to leave, but she'll be back later."

Their father shut the door, put the car in reverse, and drove away, wheels crunching on the gravel.

Spider went to stand with his brothers and sisters. Wallace reached up and held his hand, and out of nowhere tears pooled in Spider's eyes. Harper was crying softly, and Eden put her arms around her. Nellie had her head buried against Verity's neck. Verity met his gaze. She was worried—who wouldn't be?—but she was also serious. He got the message. They were in charge. Verity, Eden, and him. They needed to keep it together, keep everyone safe. The younger kids didn't realize it, there was no way for them to know, but this was especially true for today, Nellie's birthday.

CHAPTER FOURTEEN

Maeve

Her body was weightless, drifting, nearly transparent. Her will was inside her body, but never before had she been aware of these two things being separate, except perhaps when she woke from a dream, when her mind swam on in the dream state, as if it were real, as if it mattered, and her body was plainly in the bed, head on the pillow, covers drawn up, the weight of the material world present in the most mundane and usual way.

Maeve heard Arthur speaking and caught words, phrases. She was in the car—she had been put in the passenger seat. They were going to the hospital; her mind had latched on to that. She had to hold on to her will until they got there, at least until then, until they could reattach her body to her will. But how?

She willed her mouth to speak, but her lips would not part. Her tongue was not hers to govern and lay heavy behind her teeth.

She willed her eyes to open. A flutter of light.

Dark.

What is happening? What is wrong with me? floated by, no more than a dust mote in the sunshine, and was lost. She had many questions, the largest of which was, *Why?* It proved too large for her to hold up. Questions were burdens, and she let them drop to the ground.

She willed herself to breathe in. The breath fell out.

She willed herself to breathe in. The breath fell out.

She willed herself to breathe in. The breath fell out.

The simplest of all rhythms wouldn't sustain itself.

Her hand was on her belly, on her baby. The baby was part of the drifting body she could not harness, but it was most definitely also an object of her will. She reached out to hold the child within that power. She didn't know how to manage it, and yet she tried. Trying was everything. It was all she had. For herself. For the baby.

Alive.

Breathe.

Sing.

Yes! Her will alighted on and captured a wisp of breath.

"Oh, Danny boy
The pipes
The pipes
And I shall hear
Warmer, sweeter be"

CHAPTER FIFTEEN

JUDE

Jude was sitting on the floor in his apartment living room, working out the chord sequence for a new cover the band was adding to their set list. The song leaned toward the folk side of folk-rock—not Jude's taste—but Marvin was the lead singer and the boss. Jude was grateful to be playing backup and figured he could tweak the arrangement, give it a cooler vibe.

The phone rang in the kitchen. He didn't feel like answering it— it was never for him—but his two roommates were out. He put his Martin to the side and stepped over all the crap to get to it.

"Hello?"

"Jude, it's me. Eden."

She always said her name, as though he'd forget his sister's voice. She was allowed to call him on his birthday, and the big holidays, and she'd risk it if she needed to unload, like when she got into trouble. One time their father caught her drinking leftover cocktails at a country club event she'd been roped into helping with, and another time a teacher caught her making out in the boys' bathroom. Jude had last talked to her just a few weeks ago. He remembered the date because she was complaining about not being allowed to go out with her friends for her birthday. "Dad's got trust issues," she'd said, and he'd had to laugh. Anyway, another call so soon got his feelers up.

"Hey, Eden. What's up?"

"It's Mom. Dad just took her to the hospital, the one in Gloucester."

"Is it the baby?" Strange to call it "the baby" when it was really Jude's new brother or sister. He was so remote from his family, he'd lost touch with who they were to him. Who they had been.

Eden's voice was throaty, like she'd been crying. "No, it's not the baby. I mean, maybe? I'm scared, Jude. Mom was white, totally white, and she fainted while she was holding Nellie. Nellie's fine, but I've got a bad feeling."

Jude sat up straighter. "What kind of a bad feeling?" There were lots of reasons Eden was the only one who called him aside from his mom. She was an outsider in the family, a rebel, and so was he, although he hadn't thought of himself that way until after he'd left. He was seven and a half years older than Eden, but they'd always had a connection, understood each other without trying. Jude had finally figured out why: she was intuitive, and so was he. Verity and Spider, and their dad—especially their dad—were hard-core logical. Their dad made intuition and other things you couldn't easily explain seem unimportant, dumb even. Which category the younger kids fit into, Jude wasn't sure. Harper had been only six when he'd left home five years ago, and the younger four were strangers to him. Over those years, he'd talked to his mom about once a month, and had seen her several times, but never his father. He wanted Jude to crawl home with his tail between his legs, which wasn't happening. Verity and Spider also never came along with their mom, which hurt Jude but didn't surprise him. They were holding on to their anger or trying not to piss off their dad. How would he know?

Eden's tone was low and serious. "Jude, it's the worst kind of bad feeling. Mom's been tired for a while, napping all the time, which you know isn't her thing. Something's really wrong."

If it'd been going on for a while, why hadn't his mom let him know? Most of the time he could put his family out of his mind, but every once in a while, like right now, it hit how much he cared about them and wished he weren't on the outside. "Gotta believe in your gut, Eden. You think I should go there?" It was crazy to ask a fourteen-year-old what to do, but she was inside the family, and he wasn't.

"That's why I called."

"Dad will be there." Dad, who had kicked him out of the house. Dad, who made it hard for him to see his family. Dad, who'd written him off.

"I know. I still think you should. For Mom."

Jude pictured Eden in the hall at home, standing next to the couch, twirling the phone cord in her fingers. In his mind, though, she was nine, a little girl with knobby knees, huge eyes, and long, stringy hair. He had seen her two years ago, had driven out to Gloucester for the chance, but his memory insisted she was still nine. "You're brave to call me, Edie."

"Possibly stupid."

He laughed a little. "Possibly." He checked his watch—it was almost five—and thought about how long it would take to get to the hospital. An hour, maybe more with traffic. "I'll go see Mom. Maybe Dad will step out to grab a coffee, and I can sneak in." It'd be harder than that, but Eden needed to hope. Truth was, if he wanted to see his mom, and he did, then whatever happened with his dad happened.

"Give her a hug from me when you see her, okay? I never got to do that." She was crying now, and his throat closed up. It hit him how sick his mom must be. He wanted to reassure Eden, but the words would be empty; he wasn't about to bullshit her. If only she were there, he could give her a hug. The thought of it made his chest ache.

"I will, Eden. If I can call from the hospital and let you know what's going on, I will. Otherwise, I'll call when I get back."

"Thanks, Jude. Bye."

"Bye, Edie."

He hung up and looked around the apartment, at the shabby furniture, the crap piled everywhere, how it wasn't like a home, really, just
a pad where three guys crashed. The place had all the warmth of a bus
station. If his mom saw it, she'd be so low, thinking that how he lived
showed how he felt about himself. She wasn't wrong. He was trying to
get his act together. He had two part-time jobs, which didn't add up to
one decent salary. His uncle had gotten him a job with another Ford
dealership, washing cars mostly, but also occasionally talking to custom-
ers about cars. Jude also ran the board and lights at the Night Train, a
decent bar by the station that hosted music on the weekends. It was his
way into the music scene. Uncle Henry had given him a 1963 Nova,
which looked like hell but got him where he needed to go. Jude made
rent and kept out of serious trouble, which in Richmond was saying
something. When he told his mother about his life, the one he'd created
without her, without his father, she accepted it. No judgment, just love.

Jude shook off the thoughts. He went to his room, grabbed a jacket,
and snagged his wallet and car keys from the upside-down milk crate
next to the mattress on the floor.

He'd never been to the hospital in Gloucester; it had been built
maybe three or four years ago. Gloucester wasn't much of a town, so a
brand-new hospital shouldn't be tough to find, assuming his old beater
didn't break down.

~

Jude suspected something was wrong when he had to drive through
the visitor lot twice before he found an empty spot. He locked the
car, pocketed the keys. The area outside the emergency entrance was
crowded with people hugging each other, crying. Little kids dressed
in pajamas hung on to the arms of their parents, who all look dazed

or broken. Three men huddled together, smoking, shaking their heads. Almost all the people were black and seemed to know each other.

He wove through the crowd, found the door, pulled it open. The scene inside was unreal, and his heart started to race as he took it in. It was a small hospital, but the emergency lobby was crammed with sixty or seventy people. Crash carts had been abandoned against the walls. The floor was smeared and spattered with blood, lots of it. To Jude's right, a teenage girl sitting in a chair was holding a blood-soaked bandage to her head. The woman beside her, her mother probably, rubbed her back, looking around as if hoping someone would help but not expecting they would. Both the girl and her mother were wearing yellow T-shirts, same as many others in the lobby and, now that he noticed, outside, too. The only word Jude could make out on the girl's back was *Choir*. What the hell had happened?

The reception desk was in front of him, he guessed, but he couldn't see it for all the people. Double doors to the right opened, and a man in bloodstained scrubs pushed an empty wheelchair in, headed for someone Jude couldn't see but whose cries he could hear above the rest of the noise, a cry of deep pain, a horrifying sound. The whole place was a nightmare.

He squatted down to talk to the girl and her mother. "Can you tell me what's going on?"

The mother shook her head, her eyes bloodshot and sore looking. "An accident. A truly terrible accident." She gathered herself, rubbed her daughter's back again. "The Rappahannock youth choir were on their way back from Baltimore. The bus went off the road, down an embankment. Forty children—" She wiped her eyes with the handkerchief crushed in her fist, then stared at her daughter, in disbelief. The girl was in shock, maybe, but in one piece.

Jude said, "That's awful. I'm sorry."

She nodded, looked heavenward, then at Jude. "You have people here?"

"My mother. And my father. I need to find them." He straightened. "I'm really sorry about the accident."

Another woman approached them, reaching for the mother, sobbing. Jude backed away.

The crowded room was hot and stuffy, and the distress was contagious. Sweat ran down Jude's back as he scanned the room again, circled the perimeter, then made his way toward the desk, becoming more nervous about running into his father with every step. He hoped his mother had already been admitted, that someone was taking care of her. Not finding either of them in the middle of all this had to be a good sign.

He spotted a tall white man to the left of the reception counter and froze. It had been five years, but he hadn't forgotten his father. He looked the same, exactly the same. How was that? Jude was about to call out to him, but his mouth had gone dry. Jude slipped through the crowd until he was behind his father, who was arguing with a nurse in scrubs holding a clipboard. He swallowed a couple of times to ease the lump in his throat.

His father was keyed up. "You can't tell me how long it will be? Why in God's name not?"

"As I've said already, we're out of her blood type. We're waiting on some from Richmond, but I don't have an ETA." She frowned and shook her head. "I'm so sorry." She gestured to the mayhem surrounding them. "We're doing our absolute best."

"But that's my wife! She needs the blood!"

"I don't want to call an orderly, sir. We're busy enough. Please step aside."

Jude's mind raced to digest the information. Why did she need blood? His hands were sweaty, and he wiped them on his jeans. "Dad."

He reached to touch his father's shoulder but pulled back as his father spun around.

His father's eyes widened. He blinked at Jude as if he weren't real.

"Dad." Standing eye to eye with his father made his heart pound. He was seventeen again, and his father was furious with him, yelling at him to get out of the house. He'd been so scared then, Jude realized, scared of how his father hated him, how he wanted him gone. So he'd left. Now Jude broke away from his father's shocked stare and rubbed his eyes, tried to refocus, remember why he'd come. "Eden called me. Please tell me what's going on."

"I don't—" He hid his face in his hands. Jude couldn't guess what emotion he was trying to hide or control, but it had to mean his mom was really in trouble, and that terrified him. After a moment, his father left the counter for a less congested space, and Jude followed. In those few seconds, his father had gotten himself together, his expression now a block of steel. "I don't know why you're here. This doesn't have anything to do with you."

It hit him like a slap in the face. A jolt of anger rocketed through his body. *Fuck you!* was on his lips. He closed his eyes, held it back. This was not about his father.

"Just tell me. Please." Jude was pleading and he didn't care.

His father looked at him long and hard. Jude held his gaze, and he could tell his father was surprised Jude hadn't reacted before, and he mellowed a little. "They don't know. At first they thought there was a problem with the placenta, that it came away from the womb, that she's been losing blood that way for Lord knows how long."

"But they don't think that now?" The noise and heat in the room ratcheted up. He felt light-headed.

His father shook his head. "They did an ultrasound but didn't see anything. But the main thing is she and the baby need blood. Her heart stopped once already." He pursed his lips, struggling to continue.

"Oh, Dad."

"They gave her one pint." He lifted his index finger in the air and shook it, trembling. "One measly pint."

"Why? I mean, sure, there's the accident, but—"

"When people come in seriously hurt, they don't have time to blood type them. They give them O negative as long as they have it." His forehead creased, and lines of pain formed around his eyes, his mouth. "They gave her one pint. But she's O negative, too, which means that's what she has to have. She has to." He gestured to the catastrophe surrounding them. Tears ran down his face. "And now it's all gone to these poor broken children. I can't blame anyone, I really can't, except myself for not bringing her here sooner."

Jude's head cleared. He reached out to his father, squeezed his arm. "Dad, it's okay." In that moment, he felt a surge of longing for his family. It happened sometimes when he spoke to his mom or to Eden, but it was a bigger deal to feel that way in front of his dad. The guy was such a mess right now, it was hard not to pity him, to wish that he could help him in some way. Jude fought back the tears flooding his eyes.

"What's okay? How is any of this okay?" He wriggled free of Jude's grasp, the cords in his neck straining, his eyes searching. He was so damn desperate and raging—at the hospital, at Jude, at the world—Jude almost couldn't bear to watch.

Jude took a deep breath. "Because a while back I gave blood as often as I could. For gas money."

His father stared at him with a mix of fury and frustration.

Jude pulled out his wallet, found his donor card, and handed it over. "Dad, I'm O negative, too."

~

All the beds were full—the gurneys, too—so the nurse had him lie on a couch in the staff lounge and stuck a needle in his arm almost before he was prone. On the way there he'd scanned for his mother in every room they had passed, but gave up when all he'd seen were busted-up kids.

Jude twisted his head on the cushion to watch the bag fill, willing his heart to pump his blood faster. His father had wanted to come with him. Jude was good with that, but the nurse had refused and walked away before he could object. He guessed word of his dad's freak-out had spread.

Now that the nurse had stopped dashing around, Jude could read her name tag. He knew from the car business that using someone's name made them more likely to be on your side. He also knew that everything was negotiable, in theory. "Brenda, how many pints can I give her right away?"

"Two, but don't be in a rush. It'll take at least four hours to get the first one in her." She monitored the line, the bag, him. "When this one is full, I'll bring it to her, get her started, then check with the lab. If they can spin down the next one, it'll go faster. But they're backlogged."

"I don't care if I pass out. Just take whatever she needs." His throat went tight.

Brenda nodded but didn't say anything. The strain was obvious in the set of her jaw. On a night like this, she was making no promises. She wasn't even going to bother to hope.

But Jude was. He wasn't just hoping his blood would save his mother, he was also hoping it might bring him back home. Until he had seen his father, Jude hadn't owned up to the size of the loss he'd been carrying. When he was seventeen, he'd told himself that he'd eventually leave home anyway. He practically had been kicked out, but it wasn't such a huge deal. In actual fact it was an enormous deal. Just because you'd grown up didn't mean you didn't need your family. Even if you hardly saw them, you still needed them.

"All full." The nurse unclipped the bag from the stand and handed him a Mountain Dew from the staff fridge. "Drink this down, rest up, and I'll be back." Her footsteps on the linoleum were absorbed into the commotion in the hallway and treatment rooms.

Jude sat up slowly and snapped open the soda. He took a long drink. On the wall opposite him was a calendar with the days marked off. Today was the eighteenth. How could he not have noticed that?

Nellie's birthday.

PART II

1975

CHAPTER SIXTEEN

JUDE

"Give me a hand, Jude." His dad was navigating the hallway, his arm around Maeve. She had one hand under her enormous belly and the other braced against the wall with every step. Jude maneuvered past his siblings to help. His father pushed open the screen door, and they shimmied through.

"It's all right," his mom said. "I can walk now."

But his father didn't let go, so neither did Jude. At the car, his father slid the passenger seat all the way back. It didn't look like his mom could possibly fit in there, but she did. Her forehead was sweaty, and her cheeks were bright pink even though it was maybe seventy degrees. The other kids crowded around. Verity was rocking Cyrus on her cocked hip; he was a little over a year old and crying for his mom.

Buck up, Buster. Time to stand in line because another one's on the way.

Their dad hustled around to the driver's side, pointed at Jude, then at Verity. "You two are in charge. If you don't hear from us, there's no news. Make sandwiches for dinner if you can't find anything else. And don't wait up. Babies come when they are good and ready."

"Arthur," their mom said, "this one's ready and then some."

Jude caught hold of the twins and braced them against his legs while their dad backed up and drove off. Why was it that his siblings had to be born on a weekend night? The twins had come on Christmas Eve, a Friday, not that he would have been allowed to go out that night anyway. And Cyrus's birth had meant missing prom because Verity, twelve at the time, wasn't old enough to handle the five younger ones on her own. Jude loved Cyrus, just like he loved his other brothers and sisters, but what was wrong with being born on a Tuesday? Jude went to school all week and worked at the club every weekend for his dad, mowing and weeding. No wonder he looked forward to weekend nights like they were the second coming of Christ. He was seventeen with senior year looming in the fall, and full-time work at the club the whole summer, so freewheeling weekend nights were scarce. Losing this one pissed him off, not that he'd let it show.

Roy was yanking on his arm. "Jude! Jude! Take us on the ship!"

The twins weren't allowed on the ship except if someone was watching them every second. Jude wasn't going to be that someone, not tonight. "How about we make a fort instead?"

Verity started back toward the house with Cyrus. "Maybe include Harper. This one's ready for his nap. I'll check on Eden and Spider once he's down."

Verity was super mature for her age. Being the oldest girl in a huge family did that to a person, he guessed. He tried not to be a chauvinist pig and did his fair share so everything didn't fall to her. Verity might not be the most exciting person—Eden and Harper had more spark— but she was a good teammate.

"Good plan, Ver. Divide and conquer."

Jude wore out the twins and Harper, and by seven thirty all three were asleep. Spider was building a model airplane in his room; Verity had told him to turn off the lights by nine, but Jude wasn't going to play the heavy if he stayed up later. Spider would put himself to bed when he was too tired to hold the pieces steady. Verity was playing with

Cyrus in the living room. He'd get cranky, go to sleep, and then wake up again way too early. By then, with any luck, his parents would be back. Remembering how much newborns cried, Jude recalculated and decided the longer the new baby stayed at the hospital the better. If they weren't home by noon tomorrow, Jude would drive into town and get pizza for everyone—a treat. His dad had left some emergency money. If being stuck at home with seven younger kids for twenty-four hours didn't count as an emergency, he didn't know what did.

Jude was lounging on the front porch drinking a root beer, his feet on the railing, watching the color drain out of the sky. It was his favorite time of day, the end of one thing and the beginning of another, but wrapped up together. A yin-and-yang thing. He'd always been more of a yang kinda guy, wanting to stay up late, sleep in, drawn to discovering a light in the darkness and not the other way around. Explained why he had never gotten along that well with his dad, who was all about sunrise and packing the day with useful activity. At night, the agenda was no agenda.

In the distance a car clattered over the bridge hidden by a stand of trees. It wasn't his parents; they would've called to say the baby had been born before heading home. Way too soon, in any case. A black Mustang appeared—his best friend Boone's car. Boone had called earlier to make plans for the night, and Jude had delivered the babysitting news. *Guess he isn't taking no for an answer. Cool.*

Boone parked and got out along with two guys Jude knew vaguely: Wes and his sidekick Beetle, who was maybe five-three. Wes was a Rayburn, and that was never good news, but Jude didn't know the guy and didn't want to judge him like that. Boone said he wasn't that bad, but Boone had a habit of downplaying things.

"Jude!" Boone trotted up to the house and slapped him on the shoulder. "Thought you could use some cheering up right about now."

"Got that right." He nodded to the other two, wondering what Boone had said to them. One crack about the Waltons, and Jude would be done.

Boone craned his neck, eyeing the backyard. "Free and clear?"

Ten minutes later, they were settled into chairs around the firepit. There wasn't a lot of wood to burn, but it was good to have something to look at.

Beetle poked the kindling tepee with a stick, knocking it over and snuffing out the beginnings of the fire Jude had made. "Oops."

Jude didn't say a thing, just set it up again, lit it. Back in his chair, he watched Wes carry a cooler from the car. Jude assumed it wasn't lemonade.

Wes offered him a Schlitz, and he took it. "Thanks." His father would've gone ape if he'd caught him drinking with friends. His father hardly drank at all, maybe a beer or two a few times a year. Jude had mentioned once that Boone's dad offered him a beer at home once in a while, hoping it might be something Jude and his father could do, too. Jude had imagined lifting his beer can to his dad's, smiling at each other. But no way. His father had gotten pissed at the suggestion, saying Boone's dad was setting a bad example by breaking the law. Jude didn't make a crusade out of drinking like some guys, but getting a little loose could be fun. After that discussion with his dad, though, he'd been careful. Tonight seemed like the perfect night for indulging, like payment for babysitting.

Beetle asked Jude and Boone if they'd seen the trailer for *Jaws* yet.

Boone shook his head. "Would've if we'd gone to *Death Race 2000* tonight." He shrugged, leaned back in his chair. Jude felt bad for screwing up his best friend's plans and scuffed the grass with his foot.

"I've seen the trailer twice," Beetle said, scratching his neck in a way that made him look exactly like a bug.

Jude swallowed back a laugh and Beetle acted it out, doing the Massachusetts accents, snapping his arms to make the mouth of the shark. They all gave him grief, but he was hilarious. Another round of beers got passed around. Boone gave Jude a knowing smile, like "See, they're not so bad," and Jude had to give it to him.

Wes gestured with his beer toward the boat, the bow dimly lit up by the firelight, the rest in deep shadow. "That your dead rise?"

Be weird not to own the boat in your yard. "Yeah."

"Take it out much?"

"Hasn't been in the water since we moved here three years ago and probably for a lot longer before that."

He squinted into the dark. "Can't see for sure, but the hull looks clean—new paint, maybe? You fixing it up?"

Boats were a popular topic here because everyone had at least one, mostly for fishing. Jude hadn't known anything about boats when they first moved here, but he'd learned a few things since. Innocent questions about this particular boat could lead to an awkward place, though, and Jude didn't know what to say. Wes was being friendly, and the beer had loosened all of them up, so Jude spilled.

"At first my father was going to fix it, maybe sell it, but he started letting us play on it. Not me, so much—I was too old—but my brothers and sisters." This wasn't exactly true. Making the boat a ship had been Verity and their father's idea, but Jude had been the captain for several months. Then he'd gotten a guitar for his fifteenth birthday—his mom had overruled his father on it—and playing ship was suddenly for babies. Verity had kept bugging him to stay as captain because she didn't want to be in charge, but his music and his friends had become more important than any game. His dad wasn't happy about it, but his mom convinced him it would be good for Verity to take the helm. She was right, as usual, and Jude got his freedom. Sort of.

Beetle said, "No way my dad would ever let us play on his boat."

Boone jumped in. "The Vergennes crew aren't playing. They're the damn navy." Wes and Beetle laughed, thinking he was joking, and Jude was relieved to leave it at that, but then Boone went on. "No joke, man. They've got uniforms and ranks and missions. The whole enchilada."

Beetle said, "You're shitting us, right?"

Now Jude had to explain. He never should have started. "My dad was in the navy, and with so many kids, he figured it was a way to keep all of us busy, out of the house, working together. He's big on responsibility and discipline."

"My dad's big on discipline, too," Wes said. "But he doesn't need a boat or uniforms. His fists do the job." He crushed his beer can, stood up. "Who's ready for another?"

~

They'd been there maybe an hour when the light over the back door came on. Verity stepped out and let the screen door slap closed. She stood there and rubbed one foot up and down her other leg, like a cricket. Her legs sticking out of her shorts were long and skinny, something that had happened all of a sudden.

She was squinting into the dark, trying to make out who was there. "Jude?"

"It's cool, Verity. It's just Boone and a couple buddies of his."

One leg went down, the other one cricketed up. "Okay." She didn't sound like she meant it. Verity was wary of trouble, but she also didn't like to challenge anyone, including him. "Cyrus is asleep."

Her way of reminding him of their babysitting duty. Like he didn't know. He could feel Wes and Beetle on the verge of snickering, making some remark he'd have to respond to. So he had a baby brother, what was the big deal? "That's cool. I'll be in later. Something comes up, this is where I'll be."

She lifted her hand, awkward. The light was over her shoulder, so he couldn't see her face, but he knew her hesitant smile. "Okay, then. Have fun." She darted inside and left the light on.

Wes tipped his beer into his mouth, draining about half of it. He swiped his hand across his lips and nodded toward the back door. "Who was that?"

"Verity. My oldest sister."

"How many you got again?"

"Four brothers and three sisters. Plus one more on the way."

Beetle let out a low whistle. "You're not Mormons or anything, are you?"

Boone punched his arm. "Ever hear of a beer-drinking Mormon, you half wit?"

Beetle rubbed his arm but let the subject drop, to Jude's relief. His family was weird—its size, the ship, living so far from town—and he didn't appreciate having his nose rubbed in it. He felt bad to be ashamed about his own family, but the fact was he'd rather be normal. Wasn't that the point of normal?

Beetle leaned forward, pulled a baggie out of his back pocket, shook it in front of them. "Care to partake?"

"You bet," Boone said.

What a surprise. Boone was always up for whatever. The only way he managed to stay on the straight and narrow was to hang with Jude, just the two of them. They had their own thing, the music they liked, the fishing, the pickup basketball at the Gloucester city courts. Jude had smoked weed a couple of times. He could take it or leave it.

"I'm good with beer."

"Same," Wes said. "That shit just makes you dumb and hungry."

"So no change then," Beetle said, and got a punch from Wes on his other arm.

Jude laughed, finished off his beer, and loped over to the cooler for another one. He snapped the flip top, took a sip, and caught sight of the first stars shimmering over his head.

Nice night to be born, kid. And you'll have beautiful May birthdays your whole life.

CHAPTER SEVENTEEN

SPIDER

Something woke Spider up. The first thing he noticed was that two fingers on his right hand were glued together. The second thing was that he was still in his T-shirt and shorts, but the light over his desk, where he'd been working on his airplane, was off, so someone had done that. Probably Verity. He remembered about the baby—the new baby, not Cyrus—and listened into the darkness for crying, but there wasn't any. No crying, no baby. Not yet. Across the room, he could just make out Roy and Wallace, two lumps side by side in their mini beds. Twins were special, but Spider was glad there was only one of him. He liked to do stuff on his own and didn't want a shadow.

He wondered what had woken him up because he always slept hard—dead to the world, Mommy called it. Once lightning hit a tree and it fell onto the house, not in the middle, but on the garage side. He slept through that. He slept through the tooth fairy, too. And Santa, every single Christmas.

He swung his feet onto the floor and turned on the light, angling it toward the wall so the twins didn't wake up. He listened again, and this time he heard something. Shuffling. And a higher sound that made the skin on his arms prickle. Spider walked to the door, following the sound, and was out in the hallway when he realized he'd heard it before. A deer had jumped in front of the station wagon. His mom had told him and Eden and Harper not to get out of the car, but she forgot to say, "Cover your ears." The deer had made that sound, hurt and sad and scared all at once.

Spider went past the closed door of the girls' room and listened again. Maybe it was Cyrus crying. But Cyrus slept downstairs in the same room with the things for the new baby, near Mommy and Daddy's room. Cyrus's door was always open, so if he cried, the world heard it. This sound was closer. Like from the bathroom at the end of the hall.

The door was shut.

Now that he was near the stairs, noises from the backyard drifted up to him. Jude's laugh, and another boy's, maybe his friend Boone, but maybe not.

A scraping sound from inside the bathroom, and grunting.

"Who's in there?" He didn't say it loud enough, so he said it again. "Who's in there?"

"Go away." A boy. Or a man.

"What are you doing in our bathroom?"

"Go away, kid."

That deer noise again. His heart beat faster.

"Verity?" Spider twisted the knob. Locked. The knob had a button on the inside that you pushed in to lock it. The littler kids were always locking themselves in, on purpose and on accident, but his parents didn't want to get rid of the lock because otherwise no one could shower or poop in private.

Maybe he should get Jude. But then he had a better idea, a quicker one than going all the way downstairs and outside. He went to the linen closet and found the pin taped to the back of the door. He stuck the pin in the tiny hole by the knob. The button popped.

"I'm coming in!" He pushed open the door.

Verity was up against the far wall between the sink and the tub. Her eyes were so scared Spider's stomach dropped right onto the floor. A man was pushed up against her, his back to Spider, and one hand over Verity's mouth. His pants were falling down.

He turned halfway around. His face was red and sweaty, and his eyes were crazy like in a cartoon. "Get out, you little brat!"

That did it. Spider took two giant steps and kicked him in the back of his legs and clawed at him. He kicked him again and again. The man swung at him. Spider ducked and got smacked on his shoulder. He fell. Verity pulled her shirt down and hugged herself.

"Jude!" Spider screamed. "Jude!"

The man stepped over Spider, pulled up his pants, and stormed out into the hall and down the stairs.

Spider sat on the floor staring at Verity. She was crying and shaking all over. He couldn't decide whether he should chase the man or stay here with her. He was too scared and confused to think straight.

Verity fell onto her knees.

He crawled over to her. "Hey, hey." He picked up her hand. It was sweaty and cold. "It's okay now."

Spider didn't understand what he'd walked in on, other than that big man was hurting his sister, but he did understand that Verity was not even close to okay. He got up, closed the door, and pushed the button in, in case the man decided to come back. It was the only thing he could think of.

"It's okay now," he said again because he couldn't think of anything else.

CHAPTER EIGHTEEN

VERITY

Once Spider saw she was okay, that she wasn't bleeding or dying, she asked him to get Jude. Verity stayed on the bathroom floor, hugging her knees. Her shoulder hurt from her arm being twisted up her back, and she was sore on her hip from hitting it against the towel rail. Other than that she was okay, like Spider had said. She wiped her face with her sleeve and told herself to stop crying. The boy was gone. She didn't want anyone to come into the bathroom except maybe her mom, but even then she'd have to explain everything, and she didn't think she could do that. She chewed on the meaty part of her thumb and tried to remember exactly what had happened.

It had been maybe eleven o'clock, and she was leaving the bathroom. Someone was coming up the stairs. They still hadn't heard from their parents, so it couldn't be them; it had to be Jude. She started to tell him she was going to bed and realized it wasn't him, but a boy about his age, not tall but big, husky. He had to be one of the boys from the backyard, but she hadn't seen them clearly in the dark. His brown hair was long, almost to his shoulders, and his mustache hid his mouth. His eyes were red and swimming a little, and he held on to the railing at the top of the stairs like he needed to.

She waited in the bathroom doorway, not sure what to do.

"Hey," he said, his voice hoarse.

"There's another bathroom downstairs."

He stepped closer. "Verity, isn't that right?"

She nodded. He grinned.

She was wearing her Raquel Welch *Kansas City Bomber* nightshirt. When she first got it, it hung past her knees, but now it felt too short. She pulled at the hem. His eyes went to her chest, and she looked down and saw she'd made her nipples show by stretching her shirt. She let go of the hem and took a couple of shuffling steps back into the bathroom.

"Weren't you just coming from there?" he asked.

"Yeah, but—"

He came right up to her, so she backed up. There was nowhere else to go. She pointed behind him. "You should go downstairs."

He smiled and reached out, slid his hand along her neck under her hair. "Don't be like that."

She pulled away, looking for a way around him, but he filled the whole doorway. Her pulse was a drum in her ears.

"Give me a kiss." He breathed close to her mouth, and she turned her face away. The sour smell of beer made her stomach sick. She tried to slip past him, but he caught her arm, brought it up behind her. Not hard, but when she tried to pull away, she got nowhere.

"Let go of me!"

He pushed her arm up higher, and closed the door with his other hand, locked it, fixed her with his eyes. "You're pretty, you know. I'll bet boys have already kissed you."

One boy had, and she hadn't liked it, and she hadn't not liked it. Verity tucked her chin, set her lips in a hard line.

He ran his hand down the front of her, stopped at her underwear. "I'll bet the boys have already done a lot more than kissing, haven't they, Verity?"

"Help!" It came out strangled. She opened her mouth to really scream this time, and he clamped his hand over her mouth. It tasted like dirt and sweat. Her throat went dry. She tried to scream, but he pressed harder, knocking her head against the wall. He let go of her arm and pushed harder on her face, bracing his elbow against her shoulder while he undid his pants. She hit him with her fist, but he was like a snake, quick at the strike. He grabbed her wrist and twisted it up behind her, way up this time. A bolt of pain shot through her shoulder. He pushed his hips against her, panting. She twisted her legs away, tried to crouch down, anything to get away, but he forced her back up the wall. She twisted away from him again.

"Is that how you want it? From behind?" His breath was hot in her ear. "Well, okay then."

She screamed again and again into his hand. The pain in her shoulder sharpened, and her vision blurred.

"Who's in there?"

Spider.

The boy shouted for him to go away.

But he didn't. He unlocked the door.

~

Alone in the bathroom, Verity was desperately thirsty. She got to her feet, filled the glass by the sink, spilling half of it because her hands were shaking. She drank it down, gasping.

Jude walked in, Spider behind him.

Jude frowned. "Are you okay?" He reached for the doorframe and missed, stumbled, then righted himself. He was drunk.

"Who was that guy?" Verity's voice sounded weak to her own ears, like a small girl's.

Eden appeared in the doorway. She pushed her way past the boys, took Verity by the arms. "What happened? Why are you crying?"

Verity shook her head. She didn't want to frighten her.

Eden looked at Jude, scowled, then turned to Spider. "What happened?"

"Some friend of Jude's—"

"He's not my friend!"

Spider ignored him. Verity sent Spider a look to stop him talking, but he ignored her, too. "I heard noises from my room. He wouldn't let me in. The door was locked, so I opened it with the pin. He was attacking Verity."

Eden stared at Verity, but Verity wouldn't look her in the eyes. It was too much, all of them talking, wanting to know. "I'm fine. Please leave so I can take a shower."

Eden nodded. "Okay, okay. That's a good idea. Do you want me to stay with you?"

Verity shook her head. Eden had just turned nine. She didn't know what "attacking" meant any more than Spider did. And that was good. Verity wished she didn't know, either.

Eden hesitated. "Should we call Mom and Dad? At the hospital?"

Jude's eyes were half-closed. "I don't think . . ."

"You shut up!" Spider shoved Jude, and he stumbled backward into the hall. "You just shut up, you stupid!"

Spider lurched for him, and Jude caught his brother by the shoulders. "Hey, little fella. Hey, hey."

"It's all your fault!" Spider twisted away and stood there shaking with anger.

Eden looked terrified. "I'm calling the hospital. Mom left the number by the phone, so I'm calling."

"I'll help." Spider turned to Verity, maybe hoping she would guide them. She was the one who always knew what to do.

What were her parents going to do? Her mother was having a baby. She couldn't just stop. And her dad needed to be there. He was always there when the babies came, was always there for their mother. "Don't call them. I'm fine."

Eden and Spider weren't convinced. Verity was certain she didn't look fine. She wasn't acting fine. Nothing that had happened was close to fine, but if they kept staring at her for one minute longer, she was going to scream and never stop.

"I'm fine," she said softly. "I'm going to take a shower. You guys get a glass of milk and go back to bed."

"Okay," Spider said. He jabbed his thumb toward Jude, who was slumped against the wall with his eyes half-closed. "What about him?"

Verity didn't say a word. She nudged Eden into the hall, slowly closed the bathroom door, and locked it. She leaned her forehead against the door and listened to Spider's and Eden's footsteps on the stairs. She tried to take in a deep breath, but it was like someone was sitting on her chest. She checked the lock again and ran the water in the shower, holding her trembling fingers under the spray until it got warm. She started to pull off her nightshirt, but she couldn't. She didn't want to see the body that the boy wanted, that he had grabbed and tried to take for his own.

She wished she could toss her body in the trash.

The water was still running. Verity sank down on the bath mat and cried.

CHAPTER NINETEEN

MAEVE

Early on Sunday afternoon, Arthur drove while Maeve held their new baby, swaddled tight for the ride home. Arthur turned off the main road and glanced over at them for the twentieth time.

"Don't fuss, Arthur. She's perfectly fine."

"And you? I'm sorry about all these bumps."

"I don't feel a thing." It was close to the truth. Her body was numb, in that state of shock peculiar to having just given birth. The pain would come soon enough, and then she would heal. Maeve stared at the baby's wide-set eyes and pouting mouth. "She looks like Eden the most, I think. She has her eyes."

Arthur grinned. "You said that about Harper, and she's the spitting image of you."

"True. No matter because she's lovely."

"Our Penelope."

Penelope Wray Vergennes had come into this world two minutes past midnight. Maeve had been certain she would deliver her in the station wagon, but as Arthur had said to the children, babies come when they are good and ready, and Penelope had decided to linger on her way out. Arthur had been a wreck, as he always was. The obstetrician knew he'd keep pestering him, so he allowed him in the delivery room. Maeve didn't mind. When she was in labor, the entire population of Richmond could be present, and she wouldn't give a hoot.

Just shy of the bridge, Maeve asked Arthur to pull over. "The kids are going to give her a nickname no matter what we say, so we might as well decide on one."

"Penny or Nellie, I suppose." Arthur studied the baby as if she might offer an opinion.

"Nellie, I think."

"Definitely Nellie." He leaned across, kissed Maeve's cheek, and touched a finger to the baby's cheek. "You ready for this, Nellie girl?"

The day was bright, and as they approached the house, Maeve was surprised none of the children were outside. Arthur had called at six to relay the news about their new sister, and called again, speaking briefly to Verity, before leaving for home. She had reported they were all fine, he had said, but had begged off quickly to deal with an argument between the twins.

The ship came into view. No one was on the deck, from what Maeve could see. Perhaps they'd just finished lunch and would explode out the back door any moment.

Arthur parked. "I'll come around and hold her while you get out."

"Okay." Maeve searched the house windows for movement. Arthur opened her door. "Isn't it awfully quiet?"

He shrugged. "Long may it last."

Arthur led the way up the walk. The closer they got to the house, the greater her sense of dread. Everything looked as it had yesterday, but something had shifted, which made no sense because Verity had said everything was fine.

Everything was not fine.

Arthur held the door for her, smiling. Maeve scolded herself for giving in to thoughts driven by the roller coaster of postpartum emotion and returned her husband's smile.

"The baby!" Harper jumped up from the couch and ran full tilt toward Maeve.

Arthur intercepted her, gently holding her by the shoulders. "Easy now, girl."

"Hi, Daddy. Please let me go. I need to see my sister right away." She went up on tiptoe. Maeve lowered the bundled baby and watched Harper's face. No one got more excited about a baby than a six-year-old girl.

Harper broke out in the sweetest smile Maeve had ever seen. "Oh, Mommy, she's sooooo cute," she whispered in reverence. "Can I hold her?"

"In a minute, love."

"Incoming," Arthur said as Roy and Wallace barreled in from the kitchen, followed by Cyrus staggering to catch up.

"Let us see!" Roy shouted.

Arthur headed off the twins with one arm and scooped up Cyrus with the other. "Your sister is sleeping, so keep it down, okay?"

Maeve gave the boys a peek at Nellie.

"What does she do?" Wallace asked.

Maeve said, "Mostly she sleeps, like Cyrus did when he first came home."

Roy and Wallace exchanged looks.

"Boring," Wallace announced. They ran off into the kitchen, whooping and running in circles.

Jude appeared in the doorway, his eyes creased the way they were when he was short on sleep. The children had kept him up, no doubt. "Hi, Mom, Dad. Great that you're home." Roy hid behind Jude's legs and Wallace lunged for him. Jude steadied the boys. "Hey, you two, how about we head to the swing set?" They cheered and stormed the back door. Jude followed and called over his shoulder, "Back in a flash."

Maeve frowned and started for the kitchen, thinking it odd that the others hadn't come to greet them. Maybe they were upstairs with music on. She stopped to listen but heard nothing other than Harper talking nonstop at her elbow.

Arthur was behind her. "Maeve, where do you want to rest? Here on the couch?"

"In a minute." With the rush of the smaller children, she'd forgotten about her impression that something was amiss. Now the feeling returned. She entered the kitchen. It was messy, but that was expected and unimportant.

Spider sat alone, elbows propped on the table, his palms flat against his temples, a comic book open before him. He had to have heard them come in.

"Hi, Spider. Everything okay?"

He lifted his head. His hair was rumpled, and he had bags under his eyes. "Just tired." Nellie mewled and Spider straightened, as if he'd forgotten about the baby. He gave Maeve a thin smile and came over. "Did you name her yet?"

"Oh my gosh!" Harper's hands flew to her cheeks. "I can't believe I forgot to ask that. In my head, I call her 'the baby,' but of course she has to have a real name because she won't always be a baby, and that's not a great name anyway. Is there anyone whose name that is? 'Baby'? That would be cute but also weird."

"Penelope," Arthur said.

"Oh, that's so sweet! Penelope. Pen-el-o-pe. How do you spell that? Sounds like so many *e*'s."

Arthur put his hand on her head, and she zipped and latched her mouth closed with two fingers. It was a signal and response they had worked out for when Harper needed to give others a chance to talk. "Where are Eden and Verity?"

"Upstairs."

Arthur pulled out a chair. "Why don't you sit, Maeve? I'm just going to change Cyrus, then check on the girls."

"Thank you, Arthur."

Spider leaned against her side and looked at the baby, who had started to cry in earnest. "She looks like a prune. A cute prune."

Maeve kissed his cheek. "I have a feeling something's wrong. Want to tell me about it?"

He glanced at the back door, frowning. Was he worried Jude would overhear? Why would that be? "Maybe ask Verity, Mommy."

Harper said, "I want to know, too."

Maeve studied Spider for a moment, wondering if he didn't want to talk with Harper there. If Maeve pressed him, he would tell her. There wasn't an ounce of deviousness in him. He was so like Arthur, not only in his looks but in his plain speaking. And in the way he worried so. She brushed his bangs off his forehead. "I'll ask Verity, love." The baby's cries were ratcheting up. "I need to feed this little one. Why don't you two go outside and see if Jude needs help with the twins?" They both seemed reluctant to leave, and Maeve regretted her suggestion. "Or you can stay, get to know your new sister."

Spider cupped his hand under Penelope's head. The gentleness of the gesture sent tears to Maeve's eyes. "I think I'll go work on my airplane."

"You do that. Maybe later you can show me."

He was already leaving, his shoulders drooping under some private burden.

"Oh my gosh! I almost forgot!" Harper scampered after Spider. "I made a card for the baby. It's in my room." Their footsteps were loud on the stairs, louder than seemed possible, given their size. Harper was still talking. "Of course, that was before I knew her name was Penelope. Do you think I should add that, Spider? It says *baby* now. I could add it."

Maeve unhooked her nursing bra, lifted her blouse. "Shhh, shhh." Penelope's cries sputtered as she latched on. She'd already gotten the hang of it, no problem. Maeve sighed and counted the blessing.

~

An hour later, Maeve was dozing on the couch with the baby on her chest when Spider tapped her on the arm.

"Mommy?"

"What is it, love?"

He bent to whisper in her ear. "I'm ready to tell you what I didn't want to tell you before."

"Okay. I'm ready, too." In truth, she wasn't. Verity had been skittish when she and Eden had come downstairs to see the baby. When Maeve asked her about it, she said she was fine. That had clearly troubled Eden, but she hadn't said anything. Eden was their child of secrets, which was both a virtue and a fault. From the moment Maeve had come up the walk, she'd been waiting for her children to open up to her. Whatever the secret was, it involved Jude, because he'd been uncharacteristically helpful with the children—as if he were compensating for something.

Maeve gestured for Spider to sit beside her. "Just tell me what happened. Whatever it is, it's going to be all right."

He sighed, his shoulders rising, then dropping. "I fell asleep I don't know when, and then I woke because I heard a weird sound. Or I woke up and then I heard a weird sound." He pulled back a little to see her reaction. She smiled to encourage him. "So I got up, and the sound was coming from the bathroom, and I knocked and said, 'Who's in there?'"

"What sort of sound was it?"

"Grunting and shuffling and I don't know what else."

His ears had turned red, and Maeve was suddenly very scared. "Go on."

135

"And the man in there tells me to go away."

"The man? What man?" Maeve's heart raced, and she stroked the baby's back to calm herself.

"I didn't know who it was, either, but the door was locked, and I went and got the pin to open it. You know, from the linen closet." He looked at her again, and she could tell he was proud of remembering how to do this.

"Such a smart boy." She wanted to ask about the man, and she would, but her son had to tell her his own way. She kept her tone as steady as she could. "So what happened when you opened the door?"

He paused. "Mommy, the man in there was attacking Verity."

Her mind flew into a panic, but she didn't want to frighten him. He might stop talking. "Attacking how exactly?"

"I don't like this part."

"It's okay, love. It's just words."

He sighed. "He had his hand over her mouth and was pushed up against her. She was fighting him, Mommy."

Maeve closed her eyes, breathed. "What else did you see?"

"He kinda had his pants down."

Maeve let out a cry, and Spider flinched. Why hadn't Verity said anything? Maeve had to go to her now, talk to her. Maybe call the police. She sat up and shifted the baby to cradle her so she could face her son directly. "It's awful you saw that, Spider. And I'm very worried about Verity, so I'm going to see her right away. Tell me one more thing, okay?"

"Okay."

"Who was this man? Do you know him?"

"I don't know him, but Jude does."

"Jude?"

"Sure. Wes is his friend."

Maeve paused, gathering herself, hanging on tight to her emotions. "You did the right thing in telling me, Spider. Now would you please find Verity and ask her to come to my room?"

~

Maeve sat on her bed with her arm around Verity and listened to her daughter recount what had happened, a recounting that was as halting as it was heartbreaking—and frightening. Maeve thanked God that Spider had unlocked the door when he had. Verity told her everything in a calm, matter-of-fact tone, which Maeve supposed was how her daughter was managing to cope with what had happened. Verity finished her story and laid her head on her mother's shoulder.

Arthur entered their room. He seemed confused as to why Verity was in Maeve's arms, but stuck with his original intention. "Maeve, I'm making sandwiches. Can I bring you one? Tuna?"

Maeve nodded. She knew she had to tell Arthur about Verity's attack right away but was torn about whether her daughter should be there when she did. The girl might be embarrassed, even though nothing had been her fault. Maeve was also concerned about Arthur's reaction. His temper flared on occasion, and the surest thing to set it off would be a threat to one of their children, or to her.

Verity figured what was coming, and solved Maeve's dilemma for her. She stood, crossed her arms in front of her chest. "Chores didn't get finished this morning, Mom. I'll see what we can get done now."

"Thank you, Verity." Her daughter was so brave. It pained Maeve that she had to be, and yet she was proud of her strength.

Arthur bent over the bassinet beside the bed. "Will you look at that angel?"

"She's beautiful, Arthur."

He came over to her, took her hand. "Did you get any sleep?"

"A little," she lied. "Arthur, sit down a minute. I need to tell you something." He sat facing her, full of concern. "Something happened last night."

"What sort of something?"

"Boone came over and brought two friends."

"Jude had friends here last night?"

"Yes, and I don't know the details."

"That boy. The nerve." Arthur got up. "I'll get the details right now."

Maeve took his arm. "Arthur. Sit down. Please."

His eyes widened, and he sat.

Maeve held on to his arm and told him about Spider waking up, unlocking the door. Telling it from Spider's perspective made it easier, but not much. She still pictured her daughter fighting against a man bent on harming her.

Arthur ignited. "His pants were down? Good gracious, Maeve! Is she all right? She's just a little girl!"

"He didn't get any farther than groping her and scaring the daylights out of her. Verity was sure of that."

"How sure?"

"She understands what sex is. She was sure."

He was breathing heavily, and his eyes darted around. "Who is it? Who's the boy?"

"Verity didn't know him, but Jude told her afterward it was Wes Rayburn."

"Those good-for-nothing Rayburns!"

Penelope startled and began to cry. Arthur got to his feet and yanked open the door. "Jude! Where in God's name is Jude?"

Maeve held her breath and prayed Arthur would get hold of himself. She heard a faint reply from Verity.

"Verity. My girl." Arthur's voice faltered. He went out into the hall, and Maeve imagined he was hugging their daughter. After a moment, he said, "Please find Jude. Tell him to come here." Arthur came back into the bedroom. Some of the anger had melted out of him. For herself, Maeve was too exhausted for anger at her son or anyone, although she knew it would come later. All she felt was a thick, round ache for the damage to Verity's innocence.

Penelope was crying louder.

Maeve beckoned. "Would you give her to me, Arthur?"

He picked the baby up, gentle and slow, his face crumpling. "Just a little girl. She's just a little girl." He placed her in Maeve's arms, then crossed to the window.

A few minutes passed, and Maeve could only guess what was storming through his mind. She settled the baby on her breast, felt the tug and release of the letdown.

Arthur broke the silence, his voice steady now. "What were those boys doing here, Maeve? Were they drinking?"

"Yes. Verity said Wes smelled of beer. Jude, too."

"Damn him. Damn that boy."

Maeve didn't know if he was talking about the Rayburn boy or their son. Her thoughts were scattered by dread, and her entire body was consumed by the deep ache of exhaustion. She concentrated on Penelope's tiny fist encircling her index finger and on the hope contained there.

There was a rap on the door, and Jude leaned in. "Is now good?"

Arthur turned from the window, waved him in. "This isn't going to be a long conversation."

Jude looked at Maeve, then at his feet, ashamed, as he ought to be.

Arthur said, "Jude, who came over here last night?"

"Boone, and two guys I don't know well, Beetle, um, Timothy Hunt, and Wes Rayburn. I didn't know—"

Arthur put up his hand. "What time?"

"Around eight. I put the twins and Harper to bed, and Verity was taking care of Cyrus, so I figured—"

Arthur ran a hand through his hair. "You figured you'd have a party."

Jude stuck his hands in his pockets. "It wasn't a party."

Arthur scoffed. "Were all of you drinking?"

"It was just a few beers."

"Just a few. I see." Arthur turned away, went to the window again, as if he could see those boys out there, leaning back in their chairs with empties scattered around.

Apologize, Maeve willed her son, but he stood there like a statue. He always got his back up when Arthur confronted him. It was painful to see how they locked horns so quickly. Maeve moved the baby to her shoulder, rubbed her back, thinking about when they had brought Jude home from the hospital, first-time parents, proud and nervous. She had become a mother, become herself, because of Jude. She kept her eyes unfocused on the bedcovers and waited for the pain to ease.

Arthur spoke. "Just a few, but enough so this Wes fellow tries to rape your sister. Your thirteen-year-old sister." His back was still to Jude, and somehow this made everything worse.

"Dad, I had no idea." His voice was catching. "I honestly didn't."

Arthur left the window and stood next to the bed, looking down at her and the baby. "We didn't have any idea, either, did we, Maeve? No idea that our son could be so irresponsible, take such a foolish chance with the safety of our family for the sake of a few beers."

Silence, except for the baby fussing. Maeve blinked back tears. Jude had been irresponsible, no doubt about that, but was it his fault Wes had attacked Verity? Maeve couldn't work it out; her thoughts slid uselessly around in her head. She was so very tired. Her husband could handle this for now.

Arthur swallowed hard and stepped right up to Jude. "You'll finish out this school year, and then you'll work for me this summer as planned. You can keep your room, provisionally. No friends are allowed here, and your curfew is ten o'clock. You will do chores and help take care of your brothers and sisters whenever we ask, no questions. I'm not going to promise you anything beyond the end of the summer, and I don't care that you've got another year left. If you want to stay in this family, son, you have to earn the privilege."

Jude's mouth fell open, and he looked to Maeve for support. Her son had a good heart, she knew he did, so why wouldn't he apologize? Even if he wasn't responsible for what Wes did, he ought to be sorry for drinking with his friends when he was in charge of his siblings. What if one of the children had injured themselves? He was the only one who could drive to the hospital, the only one strong enough to carry the older children. As her mind touched on all the things that might have befallen her family, her anger found a toehold. Jude was no doubt ashamed for what had happened but afraid that acknowledging it would mean shouldering some of the blame—in front of his father. Maybe Jude would reflect on it and realize the magnitude of his selfishness and find some courage. Seventeen-year-olds were still children, but they nevertheless had to be accountable. She felt for him—of course she did—but she wouldn't fix this for him, not now.

Maeve met her son's gaze. He saw that she would not catch him in this free fall and was fearful. This outraged her; he should have been afraid the moment he learned what had happened to his sister.

Arthur pointed a finger at Jude's chest. "The first time you break the rules is the last time, so don't test me." He folded his arms across his chest. "It may not seem like it, but I'm giving you a chance. The rest, Jude, is up to you."

~

Hours later, Maeve settled the baby in the bassinet at her feet in the living room. Penelope was fast asleep, but Maeve wouldn't put her in the nursery, where she might wake Cyrus, certainly not tonight, and probably not for a few weeks. Verity was curled up on the far end of the couch, her feet tucked under her, her head resting on a throw pillow. Her eyes were closed, but Maeve doubted she was sleeping. Maeve reached over and tucked the blanket more snugly over her daughter's back. Her throat closed, and tears flooded her eyes again—too many times today to count.

Poor, dear girl.

Exhaustion pressed down on Maeve. She checked her watch: only seven o'clock. She ought to take a shower. She wanted to be clean, get the hospital smell off her body, but she couldn't summon the energy. This terrible tragedy—Verity's innocence shattered, Jude's betrayal of trust—had gutted her. She admitted she was resentful, too. Today should have been about the joy of welcoming Penelope into their family, a celebration. Maeve could only hope that this day didn't follow the baby into the future, into the birthdays stretched out in front of her.

Above Maeve's head, Arthur's footsteps creaked across the boys' room. Maybe he'd finally gotten Spider to sleep, or at least close enough to leave him on his own. The boy was fretful because he knew what he had seen and what he had told were important, and disturbing to everyone, but he didn't understand all the reasons why. Maeve would find a way to explain it to him soon, but not tonight.

She didn't hear Arthur on the stairs, so he'd probably gone to check on Eden and Harper. He was making the rounds, trying to tuck in the strands that had unraveled. Her heart went out to him for creating calm where he could. She'd be doing the same if she had the strength, and if she didn't know Verity needed her right there, within arm's reach. Part of Maeve wished Arthur would stay upstairs, or at least confine his attention to the twins, Harper, Spider, and Eden. She could manage the babies and Verity. It might be cowardly, but Maeve could not bear the disappointment she knew she would see on Arthur's face, his disappointment in his eldest son.

Jude had gone to his room over the garage as Maeve had asked. Sent to his room like a small boy. It was all she could think of to stop anything worse happening, especially between Jude and Arthur. Her husband had kept his temper, but it didn't need further testing. And neither did her own anger.

She couldn't imagine what the next three weeks would be like, Jude living here like he always had, yet on probation. What would she and Arthur say to the younger children? Every one of them had been on edge today, whether they knew what had transpired or not. Families created their own weather, and today was dark and stormy for everyone. Tomorrow would likely be no different. As for the day after that, well, they would see. Maeve used the clean diaper on her shoulder to wipe her eyes and rub her nose.

Verity pushed to sitting, looked at the sleeping baby, then at Maeve. "Mom, you should go lie down. I'll bring her to you if she wakes up."

"I'm fine."

"You just had a baby."

Her sweet, generous daughter. Maeve opened her arms, and Verity leaned into them. "You are all my babies. Always." She kissed the top of her daughter's head, squeezed her as tight as her tender body allowed, then let her go.

"Where's Dad?"

"Upstairs. He'll be down in a minute."

"Is he going over to the Rayburns'?"

She sounded anxious about it, with good reason. Maeve was worried, too, but not as worried as she was about her own children. The Rayburns could take care of themselves. "I don't know. I don't see what good can come of it, but your father has a right to speak his mind."

Verity pulled at a lock of hair. "I'd rather just forget about it. Why is it up to Dad? It happened to me, and I don't want him talking about it, not to the Rayburns, not to the police, not to anyone." Her voice was thin and high, like a little girl's.

"I know. But it's hard to let something this serious go."

Verity's eyes flooded with tears—the first time Maeve had seen her cry today. "I don't want anyone talking about me like that, about what that boy did."

"I'm so sorry. I wish I could wipe it all away."

Verity was crying so hard now she was choking on the words. "I know what people are going to say about me." She swiped at her eyes hard with the heels of her hands. "Tell Dad not to, okay? Please?"

"I'll talk to him. Of course I will." Maeve pulled her daughter closer, stroking her hair, heartbroken she could not promise her more.

CHAPTER TWENTY

VERITY

The next day Verity was riding the school bus, staring out the window at the river and the trees and the sky. Some of the bus windows were open, and a cool breeze blew through smelling like new grass. No one talked to her or bothered her, like usual. Her best friends lived north of school and took a different bus, so she usually read the whole half hour, or stared out the window. Jude was here, too, because the high school and the junior high were in the same place. Harper, Spider, and Eden were on the elementary school bus.

Jude sat way in the back with the three other juniors who rode the bus. Boone sometimes picked Jude up at the bus stop and gave Verity a ride, too. Not anymore. Their father had lumped Boone in with the other boys who had been there Saturday night, and Verity was supposed to steer clear of all of them. It was too bad, because there was nothing wrong with Boone. As far as she knew. She was less sure about that sort of thing now, meaning boys and men and what they might do.

Last night had been just awful. Her dad hadn't gone to the Rayburns', and he hadn't gone to the police, but he had come down hard on Jude. Maybe if Verity hadn't begged her dad not to tell anyone, he might not have been so mad at Jude. Her father couldn't undo what happened, so he needed to do something, blame someone. Verity was only thirteen, but she knew it didn't matter what her dad or anyone did. She could've gone over to the Rayburns' right now with a gun in her hand and shot that Wes dead, and it wouldn't have changed what happened, not even a little. Adults were dense like that, thinking what happened or didn't happen to Wes or to Jude was the important thing. That those boys needed to learn a lesson and be held accountable and not think they could get away with it.

What was "it" anyway?

Verity watched the trees whiz by and decided that the "it" Wes had gotten away with was making her feel naked. Since the attack, she kept checking to see if her clothes were on right, and even when they were, she was aware of her naked body underneath and worried about it. A boy who was big enough—and certainly a man—could grab her and get under her clothes and hurt her if he wanted to. He could stick his penis inside her. He could just do that. Even if he were stopped or caught, punished by her father or by the law, he could still leave a girl naked. What were the police going to do about that?

The girl sharing her seat was Wendy Swanson, a sophomore. She lived in a big house with a long dock and a new boat. Wendy was popular enough that she didn't need to worry about sitting next to Verity. It was just a seat, and wherever Wendy sat was the right place, the best place. Almost every day she had a new hairstyle. Today it was a side ponytail with a twist at the top. Her hair was a pretty kind of dark blonde. Everything about her was a pretty version of something normal. Usually Wendy gabbed the whole ride with Maxine Fields, but Maxine wasn't here, so Wendy was flipping through *Seventeen*. Verity could see part of every page, and even without looking at it, she knew it was all about being pretty, or hip, or cool, or sexy. Verity and her friends spent a lot of time thinking about how to look right, look cool, without spending money they didn't have. They all wanted flared jeans. They had to fit right, her friend Julie said, meaning tight around your butt. Verity had wanted those jeans as much as her friends did. She had asked for a pair for her birthday but didn't get them.

Wendy noticed Verity peeking at the magazine and turned to her. "You've got such pretty green eyes, you know." She tilted the magazine so Verity could see it. "See how they put on the eyeliner? Taupe would be good for you. You should try some." She gave Verity a bright smile. Her lips were coated in a frosted-peach color. "Boys go crazy over eyes like yours." She nudged Verity with her shoulder, like they were sharing a secret. "I bet you know that already, you lucky girl."

Verity felt her face catch fire, and she turned to the window.

Boys go crazy.

Don't they ever. Crazy enough to do just about anything.

~

Fourth of July and so far the only fireworks were the ones exploding in her house. Verity was hiding in her room with the door closed, but she could hear raised voices—her father's and Eden's—and the quieter hum of her mother's. If Jude was down there, and he had to be because this was about him like everything had been lately, he was keeping pretty quiet.

School had let out exactly three weeks ago, on June thirteenth, a Friday the thirteenth, which at the time felt like the luckiest day ever. Verity planned to stay at home all summer and never worry about running into Wes Rayburn, never wonder if word had gotten out about what had happened, or some twisted version of it. If Wes bragged about it, she never heard. She didn't know whether Jude had said anything to Boone or Beetle. They must have known something happened that night, with all the kids awake and Wes eager to leave all of a sudden, but Verity never talked to Jude about it, and he never brought it up, either, not that he was around much. He went to work, wolfed down his meals, did his chores at lightning speed, then hid in his room. Whether he was hiding from Verity, from their dad, from the whole family, or maybe even from the entire world, Verity couldn't tell. She just wanted to forget about it, and not talking to Jude made that easier. Like it never happened.

Verity kept busy helping her mother with baby Nellie and, when Cyrus and the twins were napping, leading activities on the ship with Eden, Spider, and Harper. She still felt raw, like she had sunburn on the inside of her skin, and she never went into the bathroom without thinking about Wes pushing her up against the wall and grabbing her. She cut her time in there, taking short showers and fixing her hair in her room. She dressed differently now, too, even at home with just her family. She hid her skin, wearing a shirt over her bathing suit to go swimming, and chose pants instead of the short shorts that were the only ones she had—all anyone had. It was already hot, though, so she had dug out a pair of kelly-green gym shorts that hung almost to her knees. Eden rolled her eyes clear into her skull when she saw Verity in them. Verity ignored her. All she wanted was to know when she would feel normal again, so she had it to look forward to. No one had the answer to that question.

The argument went on downstairs. Verity closed her book—she couldn't concentrate anyway—and followed the yelling. If this was about Jude, it was about her, for better or for worse. What was she saying? For worse.

In the living room, Harper was playing with the twins, tossing a nerf ball around, and doling out Goldfish as a reward for just about anything. Outside the rain was coming down in sheets, hammering on the metal roof. Roy and Wallace had to burn off energy somehow, and everyone else who might have entertained them was arguing in the kitchen. As Verity passed by, Harper gave her a pained look.

Verity half smiled and shrugged. It was becoming her signature move. She leaned against the opening to the kitchen. Her mother was at the stove, heating something in a small pan. Cyrus was clinging to her skirt and looking up at her with a worried look. "Almost ready, love," her mother said.

Her father was at the head of the table, leaning on his forearms. Jude sat at the opposite end, slumped back in the chair, his long legs stretched in front of him, his jaw working and one foot jiggling.

Eden was pacing the length of the table. "Daddy, it's a holiday! You can change a rule for a holiday."

"I can, but I don't see why I should."

"Because I need to go to the fireworks, and I can't fly there!"

"Lower your voice, Eden." He pointed a finger at her. "My last warning."

She stopped pacing and let out a muffled groan of frustration.

Verity got it now. Eden wanted to meet her friends at the fireworks in town but needed a ride and someone to supervise her. Jude could have taken her, but Verity guessed their dad didn't trust him to watch out for Eden, not with a big crowd.

"Dad," Jude said. "I said I'd go with her, didn't I?" ·

"You did. But Eden's nine, and I'm not convinced you take your role seriously."

Jude and their dad stared at each other. There had been a lot of stare-downs in the weeks since Nellie was born, like they were both afraid of what words might do. It made Verity mad that Jude and her father had taken what happened to her and made it all about themselves. It left her feeling invisible. She didn't want attention, the opposite, in fact, but also didn't want to be erased.

Eden stomped her foot like a toddler. "My friends will be there and so will their parents."

"Whose parents? And they're going to be watching you and not talking and drinking with their friends?" He shook his head. "I don't think so."

Eden huffed, and Verity was sure their dad was going to send her to her room, but he didn't. None of this was Eden's fault. She was a kid who wanted to see fireworks and hang out with her friends on the Fourth.

Her mother slipped Cyrus into the high chair, locked him in with the tray, and tied a bib around his neck before he knew what was happening. "If it stops raining, we could all go, Arthur."

He was quiet a moment, rubbing his jaw. "I don't know." He never simply said no to their mother. Never.

Verity said, "I can stay with Nellie, Cyrus, the twins even."

"You don't want to go?" Eden screwed up her face, trying to imagine a world in which anyone would rather babysit than go out.

Verity shrugged.

Jude sat up, put his hands on his knees. "Yeah, that's a great idea. We'll all go, one big happy family, with me on a leash. A real short one." He hung his hands from his wrists in a begging posture and started panting.

Cyrus grinned, and the food in his mouth leaked out.

"Jude," their mom said. "Don't make things worse."

"Make things worse? Mom, you have no idea what I've been putting up with from Dad at work."

She raised her eyebrows and poked another spoonful of food into Cyrus's mouth. "I guess I haven't—"

"For the love of God, Maeve, don't listen to him." Their dad spread his hands. "He's just trying to make you and everyone else feel sorry for him."

Jude laughed and shook his head. "Sure, sure. Perfectly normal to ask your son to dig out the sewer lines."

"It sure is when he works for me. You think I never dug out a sewer line?"

Jude's sneer sent a wave of dread through Verity. *Stop*, she wanted to scream at him. *Stop making things worse.*

"For the record, Daddy," Eden said, hands on her hips, "I do feel sorry for Jude. You've ruined his summer."

Their dad smacked his palm on the table. Cyrus startled, knocking the dish out of their mom's hand, sending it crashing to the floor. Eden threw her hands in the air, stormed past Verity, and ran through the living room and up the stairs.

From what Eden knew, Jude was being punished for drinking beer, so their dad's behavior was going to look extreme to her. That was the problem with this whole mess: everyone saw it differently, and everyone cared more about their own perspective than anyone else's, including Verity. Their mom was the exception.

Their dad went to the high chair and bent down next to their mom, who was picking up the pieces of the bowl. "Maeve, don't cut yourself. Let me get that."

Jude's arms were crossed over his chest. His expression was a little victorious and a lot mad. "You know what, Dad, Mom? You guys are so big on consequences, maybe before you went and had so many kids, you should've thought about the consequences of forcing the older ones to raise them for you."

Their dad jumped to his feet, his eyes blazing. "Get out!" He thrust a pointed finger toward the front door. "Get out of my house!"

"Arthur, no!" Their mom reached up and clung to his arm.

Jude slipped by Verity and hustled out of the kitchen.

"Jude!" their mom shouted after him. The front door slammed. Their dad stood there with his wife hanging on to him, broken shards all around her.

Verity held on to the doorjamb. Jude shouldn't have said that. It was plain mean. They'd been doing fine, working together, helping each other like a family should, right until the attack. Now they were coming apart, and it was her fault. If she'd been smarter, none of this would've happened. The moment she'd seen a stranger standing there in the hall, she should've locked herself in the bathroom. Or she could've darted across the hall and locked herself in her bedroom. He wouldn't have been expecting it; it would've been easy. Instead, she stood there, telling him about the other bathroom, being nice when she already knew trouble was coming. Even after he grabbed for her, she could've screamed loud enough for maybe Jude to hear, or for Spider to hear and go get Jude. She had been stupid. So stupid.

Her father looked toward the door. Verity couldn't tell whether he hoped Jude would come back or was relieved that he hadn't. Finally he let out a big breath. Her mom let go of him, and together they picked up the broken dish.

"It'll be all right, Maeve," her dad said as he dumped the shards in the trash. He didn't sound convinced.

In the nursery next to her parents' room, the baby started to cry.

"I'll get her," Verity said, eager to be anywhere else.

As she lifted her sister from her crib, Verity wondered which of her siblings would be marked by the attack and her stupidity in allowing it to happen. Jude, for certain, and Spider and Eden, who, even if they didn't quite understand what happened, would put two and two together in the years to come. Harper might not ever learn the true story, and the younger ones, if they heard about it at all, wouldn't know it firsthand. It would be like a story that happened in a book, not real.

"Wouldn't that be nice, huh, Nellie?" She held the baby close, cradling her head in her hand, and kissed the top of her head. "Wouldn't that be nice?"

Babies are wonderful, Verity thought, *because of everything they don't know. They don't know how to pretend, how to hide themselves. They don't know how to walk across a floor of broken china acting like everything is fine.*

CHAPTER TWENTY-ONE

MAEVE

After Jude stormed out, Verity left to quiet the baby. Maeve went to the stove, spooned Cyrus's food into a new dish, and placed it on the table out of his reach, her hands steady, though her insides were in turmoil. "Arthur, that wasn't like him, what he said about us and the children."

Arthur shook his head and frowned. "I don't know what's happened to that boy."

"Do you think you're being too hard on him?" She meant it as a sincere question and trusted Arthur to take it that way.

"No. I honestly don't." He enclosed her in his arms. "I know it's hard for you. Heck, it's hard for me, too, but he's going out into the world soon, one way or the other, and I want to be sure he knows what responsibility means, what family means." He let go and held her by the shoulders. "That's what we're doing here, Maeve darling, isn't it?"

"Yes. Yes, it is."

He was right. Maeve was always torn when it came to consequences for her children. Parenting was empty without them, but it pained her to be in charge of making her children unhappy, even in the interest of learning and growth. When her heart and her intellect were at odds, her heart had the louder voice.

~

That evening they ate early, without Jude. Everyone was used to Jude acting independently, and they didn't comment on his absence. Dinner was unnaturally quiet, though, the current of recent discord vibrating around them. Maeve understood that one sour note could ruin a song. Her family was a beautiful piece of music that sounded best when each individual instrument was tuned and in rhythm. Jude and Arthur had been discordant for a while, and Maeve could hardly hear Verity at all.

After dinner, Maeve and Verity put the little ones to bed while Arthur rounded up blankets, a cooler, flashlights, and bug spray, and loaded Eden, Harper, and Spider into the station wagon to see the fireworks. Maeve kept peering out the windows, checking to make sure the lights were on over the garage. Jude was cooling off, she assumed. Tomorrow she would talk to him even if Arthur wouldn't. She'd encourage him to acknowledge the harm he'd let befall his sister. If he did that, Arthur would find forgiveness. So far Jude was focused only on Arthur, as if he could prove his innocence by railing against his father's punishments and taking potshots at their decision to have a large family. Anger was an easy emotion, especially for boys. Shame and regret were rooted deeper, and Maeve hoped her son would find his way there, for Verity's sake. For tonight, though, she'd leave him be.

Now at eight thirty, Maeve sat on the living room couch cradling Nellie with Verity curled up beside her with a book. The windows were open, letting in the sound of the wind stirring the tops of the trees and making the trunks of the sycamores creak. The rainstorm had moved away hours ago but had left the wind behind.

The wind paused. Tires crunched on the gravel, and headlights swept across the ceiling and disappeared.

Verity closed her book. "Too early for it to be over, isn't it?"

"Would've just started. Please have a look, see who it is."

Verity went to the window. "Looks like Boone's car."

Maeve wrapped a blanket around Nellie, rose, and slipped on her sandals. "That's not good."

Together they went out onto the porch. The overhead light was on, and the security light on the corner of the porch roof lit up the walk and part of the drive.

Boone was leaning against his car. "Hello, Mrs. Vergennes, Verity. Happy Fourth."

"You, too, Boone. Is Jude expecting you?"

"Yes, ma'am."

Why would Jude call Boone? Her chest tightened with worry. "I didn't know about it." The light over the garage stairway came on. Jude appeared wearing a backpack and carrying a large duffel bag in one hand and his guitar in the other. Her heart lodged in her throat.

She crossed the lawn to meet him, Verity behind her. "Jude, where are you going?"

He paused but didn't put down his belongings. "I was going to come in and tell you. I just can't deal with Dad the way he is."

"Jude, now—"

He stiffened. "He said 'get out,' remember? I'm getting out."

"He didn't mean it like that. He was just angry."

"I'm sick of him being angry and taking everything out on me."

"But where are you going?" She'd never imagined he would leave, that it would even occur to him. He lived here; he was her son.

He gestured toward Boone and the car, his jaw set. "To Boone's for now."

She reached out, wishing to touch his face, but his look was so closed off, her hand dropped to his arm instead. "Oh, Jude."

He took a step to the side, closer to Verity. He seemed so brittle, like he might come apart if something knocked against him. "I never meant for anything to happen to you." The words came out in almost a mumble. Maeve could tell he was overcome with emotion, and it pained her to see him in so much turmoil.

"I know," Verity said, her voice barely a whisper.

Apologize, Maeve thought. *Tell her it was your fault, in part.* Maeve couldn't demand it of him, or even suggest it. It had to come from him to be real, and he was too full of anger and spite and shame and Lord knew what else to manage it. Maybe it was better if he went. Maybe it was the only way he could find a way back.

Resigned, Maeve said, "Please let me know where you are. Will you do that?"

"Sure, Mom." He adjusted his grip on the duffel.

"What do you want me to tell your father?"

He looked at the ground, then out over the top of her head. "Tell him I quit."

She let out a long breath. The baby squirmed in her arms, mewling. There was so much she could say, so many directions in which to take this moment, but her son was leaving, and right now she couldn't stop him, as much as it pained her to realize it. She had to let him go. Anything else was just weight to hang on him, and she saw he was weighed down enough, hard as he was trying to hide it.

Maeve reached for him with her free arm. He set the bag down, hugged her tight. When he let go, Maeve turned to Verity, for her chance at a hug goodbye from Jude, but she was halfway back to the house, her feet quiet on the dark grass.

~

It had never occurred to Maeve on that night, nor during the dozens, then hundreds, of days and nights that followed, that Jude would not return home. Surely he would tire of sharing a room with Boone, of not belonging properly to his friend's family. He would miss his brothers and sisters, and her, if not his father. He would long, as everyone does, for the familiar. He would chafe at being broke. He would initially embrace, then come to resent, his freedom.

She turned out to be wrong about all those things. She didn't mind being wrong, but she did mind what it said about her and her son: she'd lost hold of him. She, who had carried him inside her those long months, who brought him into the world and fed and cared for him for seventeen years. Her first child, the emissary for all the others. She'd lost him and wasn't sure how to get him back, how hard she ought to try, for his own sake as well as hers. She loved him as much as she ever had, but there was more to raising a child than love.

Over those many days and nights Jude was gone, Maeve consoled herself that children always left home eventually. The rupture was inevitable, but did it always feel like this, that it happened because things had gone wrong, not because it was the natural order? What did it mean—about Jude, about their family, about her—that Jude left in the night, without warning, and didn't come back?

A week after he left, Maeve called him at Boone's house and suggested he get in touch with his uncle Henry about the possibility of summer work, to keep him occupied and give him purpose. He followed her advice and moved to Frederick. A summer job was what she had in mind, nothing more. He'd come home for his senior year, to graduate. She and Arthur told the children that Jude was away for the summer, like other seventeen-year-olds who worked at summer camps and the like, and the younger ones accepted it. Verity knew there was more to it, of course, but didn't talk about Jude or ask to get in touch with him. When Maeve brought it up with her, she grew quiet or changed the subject. Eden missed Jude the most. At first she insisted on talking to him whenever Maeve called him, once every few weeks because of the price of long-distance calls. When school began, Eden turned her attention to her friends, pulling away from all of them as much as Arthur would tolerate.

Arthur, like Maeve, expected Jude to tire of his self-made life, to miss his family, and return to the house on the island where he belonged, with humility and bearing an apology. In mid-August, however, enrollment forms for the new school up north arrived at the house, a gut-punch to them both.

"He's made up his mind, then," Arthur said.

"He's young. His mind will change a dozen times." Her husband shot her a skeptical look. She was convincing herself, she realized, because now that her son had chosen to go to school in Frederick, it was clear he'd dug in. Arthur had, too. "Won't you call him, talk to him about coming home?" It had to come from Arthur.

"The boy crossed a line once when he failed to keep his sister safe, then he did it again when he failed to own up to it and deal with the consequences."

"But if you reach out, maybe he will own up."

"Henry's got a phone, Maeve. Jude can start building a bridge today if he chooses to." He rubbed his chin, shook his head. "He decided to leave home. What am I supposed to do? Run after him?"

"Would that be so terrible?" She heard the pleading in her voice but, as a mother, could not afford pride.

"For him, yes. I can't learn this lesson for him." Arthur saw her distress and pulled her into an embrace. "I'm sorry, Maeve. I miss him, too, despite everything."

She believed him. Time was what the situation needed, not confrontation. Still, their son, their eldest, had left and would not return for his senior year. Maeve always held a wellspring of hope and patience, but with Jude gone she struggled, albeit silently. Her belief in their family, once inviolate, had been tainted, but she would never give up on her son, not even if she never found a way to bring him back home.

~

On a Tuesday in mid-October, Maeve left the twins with Linda Lewinski, a woman in White Marsh who ran an unofficial day care, strictly cash. Maeve could afford childcare only rarely, and with gas prices so high, the four-hour round trip to Frederick was a luxury. She and Jude spoke every few weeks and not for very long, and she filled in Arthur and the other children on his news. She'd chosen today to visit because Jude didn't have classes on Tuesday afternoons. Nellie was four months old and would sleep most of the journey, and Cyrus would be easy as long as he was with Nellie.

Jude was waiting on the doorstep when Maeve pulled up to the curb. He met her on the sidewalk, accepted a hug, but pulled away first, bending to wave at Cyrus and Nellie through the car window.

"I thought we could go to the park," he said. "It's just a few blocks."

She smiled at him, at his plan, wondering why he didn't suggest they go inside. Maybe later. Maybe he didn't want her to intrude. The idea was both alarming and hurtful. "That's fine, Jude. The stroller's in the back."

Maeve carried Nellie in a sling, and Jude took charge of Cyrus's stroller. They caught up on small things at first: Jude's new school, his classes, the other children. When Maeve volunteered a tidbit about Verity, Jude nodded but didn't follow up. At the park, Maeve nursed Nellie and watched Jude push Cyrus in a bucket swing. Jude seemed leaner, older, even though it had been only a few months. She ached for him to come home and felt the pinch of failure knowing he wouldn't, not yet. The fact that he appeared to be completely fine was both a relief and a slap in the face.

Nellie fell asleep, milk drunk. Cyrus tired of the swing and raised his arms. "Jude. Out." Only he said "Chude," and Maeve and Jude shared a smile.

Maeve said, "Let's walk, okay?" It was easier to talk about difficult things when you were beside someone instead of facing them.

With Cyrus in the stroller and Nellie in Maeve's arms, they headed through the park. It was larger than it appeared from the children's area. The maples and oaks and birches were a riot of color.

Maeve said, "Jude, your father will be reasonable if you meet him halfway. I hope you know that."

"I don't know that at all. He isn't happy unless he can blame someone. I'm the fall guy."

"He does want you to take responsibility, but that's not the same as blaming."

He stopped short. "Isn't it? What happened was not my fault. Sure, I shouldn't have been drinking, but there's no way I could've known that Wes was such a sleazeball."

Maeve said, "But if you hadn't been drinking, you might've questioned what was going on, been more alert." She had wondered about this more times than she could count. Why would that boy have bothered to go inside? Wouldn't he just have peed in the bushes?

Jude blinked hard in frustration. "Not you, too, Mom. Wes went inside to take a leak. Whether I was drinking or not, I wouldn't have thought anything about it because it's totally normal."

"But his demeanor might have tipped you off. Can't you imagine that?" She was desperate to get him to own up to his part in what happened and show some contrition. The fact that it was like pulling teeth told her he was fighting against something, shame and regret, the inability to relive that night and act differently. She searched his face for some sign of these feelings but wasn't sure she saw anything but the same wall he'd put up months ago.

"I can imagine a lot of things. I can imagine a father who would actually confront the guy whose fault it was, but I notice Dad didn't even go to the Rayburns or the police. Instead he put it all on me."

"That's because Verity didn't want him to. She was worried about her reputation, things getting twisted."

His eyes flashed in anger. "Right. I get that. But what about my reputation? What about my being basically kicked out of the family?" He nodded ruefully. "Like I said, I'm the fall guy."

"We didn't kick you out, but I'm sorry that's how it seems."

"I remember Dad saying, 'Get out of my house.' Seems crystal clear to me."

"He didn't mean for you to leave."

"Oh yeah? I guess that's why he's been asking me to come back every single day, huh?"

Maeve was trapped. She'd urged Arthur to reach out to Jude countless times, but he continued to assert that Jude needed to show contrition first. Maeve realized how similar her eldest son and her husband were in this regard—stubborn with a tendency toward self-righteousness—and resented acting as a go-between. She wanted to knock their heads together. For both Arthur and Jude, Verity's attack was less about Verity than it was about them and their broken relationship. Jude couldn't apologize to Verity because, to him, it was no longer about her. It was about his father. Maeve didn't know how to change that. She wouldn't script an apology for Jude.

They continued in silence past a narrow sand-filled court, where a handful of elderly men congregated around an array of balls. Maeve idly wondered how the game was played. A man and a woman in their fifties approached along the paved walkway, and as they neared, Maeve was struck by their resemblance to each other: the same aquiline nose, high forehead, thick, wavy hair. Their stride was similar, too. Siblings. The sight reminded Maeve of what else she'd come to say.

"Jude, do you know about what happened to your father's sister, Annie?" She knew the answer, but it seemed the right way to start.

"Only that she died young, in an accident." He turned to her. "A car accident, maybe?"

Maeve nodded. "She was fifteen. Your father was seventeen, same as you. They were close. Henry was older, already out of the house, but Annie and your father were really close." Nellie fussed, and Maeve repositioned her and rubbed her back. "Annie was at a school dance with her friends. Your father was supposed to pick her up, but he was working on a bicycle he was fixing up for her, a birthday gift, and lost track of time. Annie accepted a ride with the brother of one of her friends. They went off the road, straight through a guardrail. The brother was injured badly, but he recovered. The sister had scrapes and bruises, as I remember. Annie was thrown from the car."

Jude stopped. "Mom, why are you telling me this?"

"The boy had been drinking, Jude. Annie must not have known, or she wouldn't have gotten in the car with him."

Her son frowned with annoyance. "There's a moral to this story, I bet. A lesson for yours truly."

"There's no moral. Just tragedy, one your father carries with him to this day. He believes that if he'd done what he was supposed to do, if he'd taken care of his sister, she'd still be alive."

Jude was quiet a long moment. "Dad thinks it was his fault? That's ridiculous." He turned to her, his face softer. "Don't you think so?"

"It's not that simple. Your father loved his sister and wished he'd paid attention, because in the blink of an eye, he lost her forever. He wasn't the one drinking, and he wasn't behind that wheel, but regret is complicated. I can't tell you how much I wish your father would let go of that regret about Annie, for his own sake, and for the sake of everyone around him. But we carry what we carry, and if you love someone, you carry it, too."

He swallowed hard, then began walking again. She fell in beside him, wishing she could catch up to his thoughts as easily as his stride. After a few moments, Jude spoke. "Seems as though because of what happened to his sister, Dad needs someone to blame no matter what. Sometimes it's him, and this time it's me. Is that it?"

Maeve shook her head. "Your father's not wrong, Jude, and he's also not completely right. Just like you."

~

On the drive home, Maeve sang to Nellie and Cyrus until they grew drowsy and fell asleep. She revisited her conversation with Jude, wondering if she got through to him at all. He seemed so settled in his new life, and in his thinking. Jude seemed fine. He was going to school and pursuing his music, and his uncle had no complaints whatsoever. Maeve was reassured by this but also perplexed. Was she simply blind to the harm his leaving had caused both to himself and to the others? Was she lumping it in with the usual changes kids experienced?

That was the difficulty. All children had problems, phases they went through, hurdles to overcome or run straight into. But since Jude had left home, she found herself tracing every problem or change back to the attack on Verity and the fallout from it.

The connection was clearest with Eden, who was vocal about missing her brother and was angry at her father for being too hard on Jude. She had turned to her friends, and would spend all her time with them, Maeve was sure, given half a chance. Was this normal for an outgoing nine-year-old girl? She played on the ship only when she had nothing else to do or if Arthur insisted, which Maeve interpreted as a show of allegiance with Jude. Or was it? Maybe she just didn't like the ship game.

Then there was Spider. He'd always been introverted, but recently had reduced his pool of friends to exactly one, and often chose not to see him. Had he turned inward because he missed his brother? Spider also seemed keener to please his father, more eager to show him his projects, his schoolwork. Was he filling in the space Jude had left in his father's affections? How was it possible to know?

And Harper. The girl had always been talkative, but lately it had become nonstop, as if she were afraid of what might be said, or simply felt, in the void. Eden, Harper's natural playmate, couldn't tolerate the chatter, so Harper had started shadowing Maeve, appearing at her side at the sink or following her through the children's rooms while she was tidying. Maeve didn't mind, but she expected Harper to become more independent, not less. That was the trouble. Growth, with or without a tragedy, was never a straight line.

And Verity. Well, at least there Maeve understood what was going on. Her daughter hadn't seen her friends more than a handful of times all summer, and now that school had started again, she was even more of a homebody. Verity had also gained weight, about fifteen pounds, Maeve guessed. She was going through puberty, but it didn't take a psychologist to see it was related to the assault. Maeve had tried to talk to her about it on several occasions, but Verity shut her off, saying she was fine. Maeve also spoke with the school counselor, who had then called Verity into the office for a chat, after which Verity refused to talk to her mother for two weeks. Maeve's only option was to let Verity work through it on her own, which felt less like letting go and more like giving up.

The closer Maeve got to home, the harder her resolve became to never give up on her children. She loved them absolutely and, more, wanted to learn how to be a better mother. She didn't want to be blind to their problems or sweep troubles under the rug. She didn't want them to leave home bruised and misunderstood. When Jude had left home, Maeve had had faith that, given time, she could right all the wrongs and love their family back to healing. Now she worried that in time the younger children would forget about Jude altogether. She worried she would lose faith, and become a different kind of mother, one with doubts and regrets, and one with children who harbored dark mysteries.

As she turned down their drive, Maeve knew that what had happened to Verity, what had happened to them all, had already changed her. Her spirit would never again be as light, nor her heart quite as full.

CHAPTER TWENTY-TWO

JUDE

Jude stood on the sidewalk outside Uncle Henry's house with his hands in his pockets, watching his mother drive off. He missed her already and was sorry the visit hadn't gone better. She came all that way to see him and try to make peace between him and his dad. He did feel sorry for his old man, losing his sister like that, but it didn't change the fact that Jude was on his own here with Uncle Henry because his father had made it impossible for him to stay. His father had come down on him like a ton of bricks, making him feel like he was the one who hurt Verity, like he was a bad person. One slipup, and all the good things he'd ever done for his family didn't count for squat.

When the car was out of sight, he let himself in and went to the room in the back, what used to be the den but was now his. It wasn't much, just a twin bed, an old dresser, and a desk his uncle had helped him make out of two sawhorses and a cheap pine door. It worked fine. His uncle didn't have many rules, but Jude didn't itch to get in trouble, so he didn't need many. The worst thing was he had to be careful about not bugging Uncle Henry with his music. Once he had saved some dough, the first thing he'd spring for was a set of headphones.

He picked up his guitar and played for more than an hour, erasing his mother's visit by concentrating on learning a bear of a new riff until his fingers accepted the rhythm, made it their own. He got that round feeling in his chest, and in his belly, and his mind cleared. Zen, though he'd never admit that to anyone.

Hungry now, Jude put away the guitar and headed to the kitchen. The fridge had nothing he could just grab; he'd eaten a leftover baked potato and some pickles for lunch. He checked the stove clock, saw it was after five. Maybe he ought to make something for dinner, not just sponge. He tried to help when he could. Okay, not always, but he wasn't a complete mooch. Maybe his guilty conscience was something his mother left behind.

Fair enough.

He scrounged in the fridge and the cabinets. Uncle Henry liked to cook, so there was more than condiments. Correction: his uncle didn't like going out much, thought fast food was gross, and didn't have a wife, so cooking was what was left. Jude found some tuna, cheese, and bread: tuna melts. Everyone liked those, right? He dug out a head of iceberg, a cucumber, and a bottle of Thousand Island dressing for a perfectly balanced meal. Jude tuned the radio on the kitchen counter to WASH. Creedence came on, and Jude started chopping, one foot tapping the beat.

~

A while later, Uncle Henry wiped his mouth with a paper napkin and pushed back from the table. "Not bad, not bad at all." He gave Jude the side-eye. "You buttering me up for a reason or just getting ready to be a bachelor?"

Jude smiled. "No reason. It was easy." He took another bite of his tuna melt, way behind Uncle Henry, who ate like someone was gonna steal it away. "My mom came to see me today."

"I wondered when she might. Everything all right?"

"Well, she's not happy about me taking off—not that I am—but you know." Jude had told his uncle everything that had happened, and he suspected his mother, and maybe his father, too, had called his uncle at some point to explain. Who knew what his uncle really thought of the situation?

"I do."

"She told me today about what happened with your sister." Jude said it casually, not knowing what sort of territory he'd just wandered into.

He nodded. "Makes sense that would come up, given the circumstances." So he had noticed the parallels, too. "But you and your father are different people. That's the lesson here."

"I don't get what you mean."

He got up, went to the fridge for a beer. He had one, maybe two a night. "Losing Annie marked all of us. That's a fact. But it marked your father more than anyone."

"Why?"

"Because he takes things hard, and he takes them personal."

Sounded about right. "So did your parents hate him for forgetting to pick her up? What did they do to him?"

He popped the top on the beer, shook his head. "If they blamed him, they kept quiet about it. Annie was dead—they didn't blame anyone other than the drunk who drove off the road, and even then they knew he was just a kid, just a stupid kid who did a stupid thing and ruined his own life in the bargain."

Jude pulled back. "You mean they didn't punish my dad?"

"That's what I'm trying to say. They didn't have to. Your dad took it all on himself."

"What do you mean?"

"Day after the funeral, he goes to the recruiting office in Dover, enlists." Uncle Henry took in Jude's reaction. "Never put the two together, I take it."

"No, I sure didn't." Jude shook his head. "So he punished himself."

"That he did." Uncle Henry set down his beer, picked up their plates. "I'm on dish duty, then I'm watching the game. Reds tied it up last time, so let's see if they can pick up another one."

Jude didn't care much about baseball, or about sports in general. But his uncle's team was in the World Series, and Jude didn't exactly have much else going on. And there would be snacks.

"Cool. I've gotta finish up some history, then I'm in."

Back in his room he left the door open so he could hear Uncle Henry cleaning up. The one thing he hadn't gotten used to since he'd left home was how quiet it was here. Even though he was the new guy at James Monroe High and didn't fit in yet, he'd take the clanging, buzzy, swaggering, dopey noise of high school to this eerie quiet any day. Growing up with so many siblings, silence had been rare.

Jude opened his history book and thought about what he'd said about his father, that he'd punished himself for his sister's death by enlisting. Was that what Jude was doing here in this too-quiet house, exiled from his family, punishing himself? He'd chew on it sometime when he didn't have homework, not that it mattered, because he wasn't going back.

While Jude read about the Treaty of Versailles, he left the door open, and the window, too, even though it was chilly. The neighbors two doors down had three kids, and they usually played out in their yard in the afternoon. If they weren't out, and Uncle Henry wasn't home, Jude turned on the radio in the kitchen and set it to a talk station.

It wasn't that he missed his family, exactly. He was just used to the noise.

~

Over the next few weeks, Jude did get used to the relative quiet of Uncle Henry's. It helped that his new high school was large and rowdy. When he wasn't working at the dealership, he stayed after school, hanging out at the edges of the established groups like a stray dog hoping to find a warm place to sleep. His music was his ticket in. Once a couple of kids learned he played guitar—and well—he was allowed in the door. Jude would be moving on to something else after graduation, someplace cooler than Frederick, and that made it easier not to care about friends. Turned out not caring made him more popular than he'd ever been.

The Sunday before Thanksgiving, Eden called to ask if he was coming home for the holiday. "Only if you truss Dad up instead of the turkey," Jude joked, then felt bad. "I wish I could, to see you anyway."

"It's okay," Eden said, like she'd known the answer. "The day after I'm going to Marcie's." She went on about Marcie until their mom took the phone. She'd overheard the conversation—it was impossible to have a private one in that house—and told him the twins and Cyrus had chicken pox. "No one's sleeping."

"Sorry, Mom." A weird feeling came over him, and he realized he felt guilty about not being there to help, followed by a fresh surge of anger at his father for teeing up this mess. "Uncle Henry says we can go to Eva's in Philly." Eva was one of Uncle Henry's exes who liked big crowds at Thanksgiving. As his uncle put it, it was easy to fit in even if half the people there hate your guts.

"Is there room in the car for me?" his mother asked, laughing, but her voice was heavy with exhaustion. "Enjoy yourselves. Love to you both."

∼

Jude weathered Thanksgiving, but his first Christmas away was the pits. All Christmas Eve, Jude kept expecting the phone to ring, wanted it to, even though he didn't know what he would say. If his mother invited him, would he give in and take the bus down? The last time they talked, it was early December and she hadn't mentioned it. Now it was almost too late. He passed the hours playing guitar, working on an original song, and watching movies with his uncle. Thankfully Uncle Henry didn't go in for sappy holiday flicks. Halfway through *The Legend of Lizzie Borden*, the phone rang. Uncle Henry was in the kitchen getting snacks and answered it, and called to Jude.

He covered the receiver with his palm. "If you want to go down there tomorrow, I can drive you. Or go by yourself. Or stay here. It's all fine with me."

Jude nodded, and it hit him how pitiful he was, a teenager in exile. He took the receiver and turned from his uncle before he could see Jude was feeling sorry for himself. "Hello?"

"It's me, Eden."

"Oh. Hey." Eden. Not his mother. The familiar hot mix of disappointment and anger bloomed inside his rib cage.

"Merry Christmas Eve!" She wasn't a terrible actress for a nine-year-old, but Jude heard the strain behind the cheer. "What're you doing?"

"Watching a movie about a girl who hacks her parents to pieces." What did he just say? God, he was such a jerk.

"Really? I couldn't watch that. Does Uncle Henry let you watch whatever you want?"

"Kind of. It's his house, his TV." He looked out the kitchen window. There was nothing to see except the lights strung along the eaves of the house next door. He imagined the kitchen window at home. The trees lining the river were visible even on the darkest night, and twinkling lights came from the stars whatever the season. Homesick. He was homesick. "What's everybody doing?"

"Oh, you know. Nothing special. Mommy and Daddy are in the dining room doing secret stuff, and I gave Harper a quarter to keep watch."

"They don't know you're calling?"

"Uh-uh."

Jude pictured her in her pajamas on the bottom step, looking over her shoulder. His nose stung and he rubbed it. "Well, I'm happy you called. It's super cool to hear your voice."

"I'll remind Mommy to call you tomorrow, in case she forgets." She was quiet for a moment, like she was figuring out what else she could do to make things right, to bring things back to normal. "Harper still believes in Santa, did you know that?"

"I'll bet you're good at not spoiling it for her."

"Really good." Her voice was full of pride. "After we say goodbye, I'm going to eat Santa's cookie."

Jude laughed. "You'd better go. Merry Christmas, Eden."

"Merry Christmas, Jude. Sleep tight."

"Don't let the bedbugs bite."

The next day, he slept in until nine. Uncle Henry fixed his usual weekend breakfast: fried eggs, hash browns, bacon. The only reason it seemed like Christmas was that his uncle whistled to the songs on the holiday radio show. They didn't have a tree. "All that stuff is for kids," Uncle Henry had volunteered a couple of weeks ago.

After they ate, they exchanged presents—one each, they'd agreed. His uncle seemed to actually like the electric popcorn popper Jude picked out for him. When Jude opened his, he grinned from ear to ear.

"Headphones! Man, you're the best." Jude had never hugged his uncle, not since he was little, so he stuck out his hand. The handshake made this Christmas their own, instead of a pathetic version of what Jude had been used to, or what his uncle had been used to, whatever that was.

"I'll do the dishes," Jude said, pushing back his chair.

"And I'll see how the bowl games are going."

The wall clock said ten fifteen. Jude went over to the phone and angled the receiver in the cradle, leaving it off the hook. His uncle wasn't expecting any calls that Jude knew about, and anyone else could call back later. Jude had other plans. He would clean up, watch a little football with Uncle Henry, put the phone back on the hook, then walk into town and catch a movie. He didn't know what was playing and didn't care. It was just a day. Tomorrow he would go to work at the dealership, and his friends would be free again, and everything would go back to normal. He even had a New Year's party to go to at the house of a girl he liked quite a bit. Before he knew it, his last semester of school would be starting.

The one thing he wasn't going to do this Christmas was hang around waiting for his mother to call. He didn't want to hear her voice, full of regret, or blame. He didn't want to wonder if she'd tried to get his father on the phone. Most of all he didn't want to hear his brothers and sisters in the background full of Christmas joy. He wasn't feeling mean or spiteful; it wasn't that. He simply didn't want to hear it. He'd had his Christmas with Uncle Henry, and his own life now, and that was that.

PART III

1980

CHAPTER TWENTY-THREE

JUDE

He'd been watching the clock on the wall of the staff room for a solid hour, the second hand twitching from one hash mark to the next, the minute hand moving through sludge. The nurse, Brenda, had taken the first pint and now was making him wait for an hour—until eight fifteen—before she'd take the next. The good news was she confirmed the second pint would be spun down so it wouldn't take as long to transfuse into his mother. In the meantime, Jude had flipped through every magazine stashed under the table by the fridge, but his attention jumped around so much he couldn't read more than a phrase or two. His father was out there in the lobby or maybe in the room with his mother. He didn't know, and right now he didn't care. He just wanted to give that next pint.

Brenda rushed through the door. "You eat that sandwich I gave you?"

"Yup. And the orange juice. How's my mother?"

"Stand for me, please." She looked him over, took his wrist, felt his pulse. "How do you feel? Light-headed? Dizzy?"

"I'm fine."

She narrowed her eyes at him, judging. "Okay, let's start and see how it goes."

Jude lay down, and seconds later his blood flowed into the bag. "You didn't say how my mother was."

She kept her focus on the bag and the line. "What do you say we just get this to the lab?"

~

After the second pint he did feel weak. He drank more orange juice and dozed, finally falling asleep.

His father leaned over him. "Jude?"

He rubbed his eyes, propped himself up on one elbow. "How is she?" The creases around his father's eyes and mouth had deepened. Jude's stomach dropped.

His father hung his head. "She lost the baby."

The baby. It took Jude a minute to register that it was his brother or sister. He knew it, of course, but he hadn't felt it until now. The distance it opened up inside him burned wide and hot. "And Mom?"

"The transfusion helped, but then the baby . . . she's just so weak." His father pulled over a chair, lowered himself into it as if he'd never sat down before. "The placenta wasn't the problem. There wasn't any rupture or bleeding."

"Then what's wrong with her?"

"They don't know. They just don't know. She has to stay, though, at least tonight. They've moved her to a room."

"Can I see her?" He almost didn't dare to ask, even though that was why he'd come. He felt like he was on the edge of something—a way forward, or a way back—and was afraid of losing his chance.

His father nodded. "Sure you can. They said maybe in an hour, give her some rest."

Jude's shoulders dropped with relief. "Are you going to stay here tonight?"

"I hadn't thought it through." He got up, paced the room. "School's tomorrow, but maybe the kids shouldn't go. Or maybe it's better if they do." He stopped as if he'd hit a wall. "Oh, my Maeve. My sweet Maeve. She wanted that baby with all her heart."

Jude watched as everything he had resented about his father—his rigidity, his certainty—dissolved into grief. Jude felt sorry for him and didn't know what to do or say. So much time had gone by since they'd had anything to do with each other. Eden had pulled Jude into this—and he wasn't sorry she had—but it was hard to jump into the deep end.

A nurse came in, glanced at them wearily, then grabbed something from the fridge and headed out again. His father stopped pacing, checked his watch, rubbed a hand over his face.

The room was stuffy, and the tangy smell of sweat and blood and antiseptic irritated Jude's throat. "I'm going to get some air." He got up. If his father wanted to tag along, fine, but Jude wasn't issuing any invitations. He paused in the doorway. "I'll check with the desk in an hour, okay?"

His father nodded once but didn't look his way.

This is not about him, Jude reminded himself as he wound his way down the busy corridor. *Not today.*

Jude went outside. The scene wasn't as chaotic as it had been, but there were still people greeting late-arriving relatives, or hanging out in groups, getting some fresh night air like him, or having a smoke. No one stood alone. Everyone had an arm around someone's shoulder, a hand in theirs, a friend or a spouse to mirror their anxiety or grief, a familiar face tilted at a sympathetic angle. A pregnant woman sat next to an elderly man on a bench. His head rested on her shoulder, his eyes closed, his fingers laced between hers. Whatever they had lost, they had each other in this moment. That couldn't erase their grief, but it could contain it.

Jude looked away and headed down the sidewalk between the buildings, following the lighted path. He'd almost forgotten what family meant, what his family had meant to him. Living with Uncle Henry had been easy, but it was temporary—they both knew that—and that put a limit on how close they became. His uncle was helping Jude out, not adopting him. Jude liked his roommates, and the situation had been pretty stress-free, but they were roommates, not best friends. Not family.

Today he'd seen too much, and he didn't know what to think. Starting with Eden's call, he'd heard too much need, seen too much crying. He'd felt sorry for his father, truly sorry, and pissed off with him at the same time. He hadn't even seen his mom, but there he was, trying to save her life, by some fluke. The baby brother or sister he'd barely known about, practically never thought about, was dead, and it made him feel awful in a way he couldn't understand, like when he thought about Nellie and realized she'd had one birthday after another without him. He was so far removed from his family, he didn't even qualify as a ghost.

The sidewalk ended abruptly at the corner of a building, like no one was expected to walk there in the first place. Jude stood out of the reach of the lights, wondering what would've happened if he hadn't been home when Eden called. He would have found out eventually about his mother, and the baby, but as a story, from Eden maybe, or in a recap from his mother months later. It hit him that his mother might not have survived if he hadn't answered Eden's call. His throat closed. Who would've called him with that news?

There was no way around it. Five years down the road, whether he liked it or not, Jude was still part of his family. What part, that was the money question.

He zipped his jacket and stood there a few minutes longer, his feet at the edge of the concrete, his hands in his pockets, staring out at distant lights punctuating the dark, places he knew nothing of and didn't care about. His father wasn't about to make it easy for him—when had he ever done that?—but Jude didn't have another family, and feeling this alone was too hard to take.

CHAPTER TWENTY-FOUR

MAEVE

The nurse helped her sit up and held a water glass fitted with a straw so she could drink. "Do you think you can eat something, Mrs. Vergennes?"

Maeve ought to say yes. She needed to do what the doctors and nurses suggested. She needed food, she needed to regain her strength. But her sadness was a crushing weight. She couldn't even cry. She didn't have the will.

Earlier—how much earlier she really didn't know—she had been feeling better, stronger because of the blood transfusions. Then the back pain had begun, hard and sharp, and minutes later, contractions. She had known what was happening and had been powerless to stop it. A doctor had been in the room when the contractions began, a serious middle-aged man who'd been in and out since she had arrived. He called for more staff. She asked him if the baby would be all right, knowing it would not be, that it was far too young, that her body would make its own decisions. *Expel* was the word that came to mind, a harsh one, and correct.

It was over before her fear could build. Her legs spread apart, her back seized. The contractions doubled her over, blinded her. Liquid gushed out; she felt it, but she could not bring herself to look. More contractions, again and again. That part was familiar, like a sick joke. Someone held her hand, sponged her brow.

Maeve must have passed out, because the next thing she knew, she was lying back against her pillow. A nurse was shifting her hips. Another was pulling away the blood-soaked sheets.

"A boy or a girl?" Maeve had whispered.

One nurse rolled the dirty sheets into a ball, stuffed them into the laundry cart, and wheeled it away. The other unfolded the clean sheets, tucked them in, brisk, efficient. When she was finished, she came to the head of the bed and placed a cool, damp washcloth on Maeve's forehead, held it there. "A boy, Mrs. Vergennes. I'm sorry."

A boy. Daniel. She'd been saving the name.

Now, hours later, the nurse repeated her question. "Do you think you can eat?"

Maeve shook her head. They would bring something either way. The nurse checked the pad between Maeve's legs, covered her up again, neatly. "I'll be back soon."

"Thank you," Maeve said.

She was alone. Truly alone. She looked down at her stomach, where she had rested her hand so often in the last months in reverence for the miracle occurring inside. She and the child were flesh and blood, bonded in ways she could never put to words. This was especially true for this child, her last, her Daniel. Now he was gone, and her belly was sore and hollow.

Maeve had had a miscarriage the summer of 1960, when Jude was two and a half. She'd been four months pregnant. She mourned the loss, and the pain of it lingered longer than she ever thought it would. Arthur had nothing but sympathy and never hurried her grief. It was plain to her that he was worried she wouldn't be able to have more children and would be disappointed in a way he could not fix, although he never said so. "Women lose babies all the time," she told him. He nodded, but she could see his anxiety was unimpressed by this fact. It wasn't until Verity was born, full term, pink and howling, that he released his grip on this particular fear of his. He had many fears, and most had to do with her.

His fears had always been closer at hand than hers. She had never expected to lead a charmed life; that would be foolish. But unlike Arthur, she didn't search for bad omens, and didn't look for reasons to believe her life was coming apart. If blame could not be easily assigned, or if there wasn't any lesson to be learned for anyone, she let it go. She wasn't optimistic, exactly; it was more that she took life as it was given her and cradled it with as much joy and hope as she could find. If fortune looked the other way, there was no pattern in it, nothing to blame. There was only tomorrow.

Until now, maybe. Lying in the hospital room, she searched for a bootstrap to pull herself out of despair. She had so much, she reminded herself. An adoring husband, so many healthy children, a bounty of love all around her. Yet the void in her heart was yawning, large enough for her to fall into and disappear. That was her fear, her only fear, the inexplicable feeling that the loss of this child was not just the peak of her grief, but the point on which the full and fragile plate of her life spun.

She felt the plate wobble.

~

Arthur came in, his face a patchwork of concern—and something else. Before her addled brain could work it out, a young man appeared behind him. Maeve's breath caught. Jude had grown a mustache, and he was taller, leaner.

"Mom." Jude moved to the foot of the bed.

"Jude. I'm just—" She looked to Arthur for an explanation.

"Eden called him."

Eden. The girl didn't know how to let go of anything, not even a little, and right now Maeve loved her for it so much she didn't know what to do with all of it. The tears that had been waiting flowed into her eyes and down her cheeks. Arthur searched for tissues. Maeve wiped her face with the sleeve of her gown.

Jude came toward her so slowly it felt like a dream. "I'm sorry about the baby, Mom."

Maeve nodded, took his hand in hers. One son taken. One son returned.

A nurse arrived, the same one who'd told her the baby was a boy. Maeve couldn't focus on the names. The nurse held a tray with a syringe and several tubes. "I need to take some blood."

"Take some blood?" Arthur moved between the nurse and the bed. "The problem is she doesn't have enough."

"We don't take blood for no reason, Mr. Vergennes. We need to measure her hematocrit, among other things, to see how much the transfusions are helping."

"It's okay, Arthur," Maeve said.

He regarded the nurse with suspicion, then stepped aside. They all watched as the nurse drew a vial of blood from the line inside Maeve's elbow. When the nurse was done, she checked Maeve's vitals. "Better than a few hours ago. Your son's blood is doing the trick."

"My son?" Confused, Maeve turned to Jude.

He lifted his right hand, showing her the gauze taped across the back. "Plenty more if you need it, Mom."

She opened her arms. He bent down, and she hugged her son with all the strength she could find. Under the smell of unfamiliar soap was the smell of her boy. The enormity of her feelings overwhelmed her again. So much regret, so much pain, and, spreading through her weakened limbs, the warmth of love. After a long moment, she released him.

Arthur was at the window staring out at the darkness.

"Arthur," Maeve said, "you'll be needing some help, don't you think? The nurse said it could be days." He twisted around to let her know he'd heard, but he kept silent. That was fine with Maeve. It was a place to start, anyway. She pressed her hand to her son's cheek. "Jude, now that you've saved my life, could you do me another favor?"

~

Sleep evaded her for hours and hours. The ward was noisy with the comings and goings of the loved ones of the children and chaperones lucky enough to have survived the bus accident. The machines around her bed blinked, light spilled in from the corridor, and the woman in the other bed had left the TV on. The sound was off, but images flickered in Maeve's peripheral vision. She wasn't annoyed, just thoroughly bereft. Her arms were too empty. She longed for home, for the faces of her children and the embrace of her husband.

A nurse came, fresh faced and smiling. The start of her shift, Maeve supposed. She turned off the TV for Maeve, replenished her water jug, brought her an extra pillow, and generally made that awful beige room seem less like a punishment.

"Try to sleep," the nurse said. "Sleep is medicine. The best sort."

Maeve nodded. It was exactly what she would've said to one of her children, and that thought soothed her enough to let exhaustion have its way.

She tumbled straight into a dream in which she looked through the glass of a hospital nursery, cribs arrayed before her, endless rows, endless columns of cribs, disappearing into a distant mist. The nursery had no floor, at least not a solid one, but Maeve had the sense that if she were to step inside—where was the door?—it would support her. The cribs, the bedding, the ceiling were pure white.

Maeve stepped closer, her face nearly pressed against the glass, and looked into the nearest crib. It held a tiny infant, swaddled tight and fast asleep.

Maeve gasped but made no sound. It was a boy, she was sure, and the boy was hers, her Daniel. She put her palm to the window, and the glass dissolved. She stood over the crib of her son, her heart thrumming, full. She thought to reach into the crib, to gather him to her, when she again became aware of the other cribs and their silent, sleeping babies.

They were all hers.

CHAPTER
TWENTY-FIVE

VERITY

Verity was watching *Trapper John, M.D.* with Eden, who was annoying the heck out of her, jumping up every two seconds to see if Jude had arrived. Their father had called an hour and a half ago to tell Verity about the miscarriage and to say he was spending the night at the hospital. Oh, and their long-lost brother was coming to help out. She'd been too stunned to say a word. Her father said he'd explain when he got home and asked her not to tell any of the others about the baby. After he hung up Verity stood there with the phone in her hand, her grief about the baby flooded over by anger about Jude. Eden was at her elbow waiting to hear the news.

"Mom's okay, but Dad's staying the night there." She put the receiver back on the cradle. "And Jude is coming here tonight. To help."

Eden squealed and put her hands to her face. "He's coming here?"

Verity nodded. Eden had always sided with Jude, believing the only thing he'd been guilty of at seventeen was a drinking infraction. Eden knew about the attack, but only vaguely. She hadn't seen Wes like Spider had, and if she'd come to understand more about that night over those five years, she still thought Jude was in the clear. But even that didn't matter because whichever side their father was on, Eden would be on the other. Verity envied Eden her naive black-and-white stance.

Eden was wide eyed. "How long is he staying? I mean, is he really coming home—for good?"

"Dad didn't say." Her sister's excitement was unbearable. "I'm going to watch TV."

Verity marched toward the couch, annoyed she had to keep the awful secret about the baby and deal with the fallout from the news about Jude. Over the years, she'd convinced herself she didn't care one way or the other about Jude. He'd been gone so long, and the mess that had led to him leaving was stashed away in a dusty corner of her mind. Not that she'd forgotten, more that she'd chosen not to remember, and not caring about Jude was part of it. For him to suddenly appear—to help them out, no less—made no sense. If he was so interested in helping, then where had he been all this time she'd been acting as captain and taking care of everyone? Her father said he'd explain later. While he was at it, maybe he could explain why she felt so anxious and resentful. Sure, she was tired, but she'd been coping just fine. Everyone was fed and safe and more or less clean.

Eden stood in front of the TV, hands on her hips. "Aren't you going to tell Spider?"

Spider. He'd be pissed about Jude, having seen Wes attack her and figuring out what it meant later. He'd told her so last year on Nellie's birthday, his face turning red with embarrassment, then flashing to anger. "I can't believe he let that happen to you. Dad was right to kick him out. I hate his guts."

Wanting to put him at ease and avoid the topic herself, Verity had told him she was fine, but Spider had shaken his head. No way Verity was going to tell Spider about Jude now. "You can tell him, Eden. I'm going to watch *Alice*."

Eden had frowned and sat down next to her.

Now it was eleven o'clock. An engine growled out front, too loud for the station wagon. Eden sprang up, knocking over the table lamp, and threw open the door. The screen door hit the side of the house.

"For Pete's sake, Eden!" Verity righted the lamp. Nellie started crying, and Verity went to soothe her. *Not even in the house yet and already causing chaos.*

Verity stayed in the nursery with Nellie until she fell asleep, then stayed a little longer, delaying the inevitable. Finally she went into the hall, leaving the door ajar, and followed the voices into the kitchen.

Eden was opening a bag of bread, chatting brightly, bouncing on her toes like a runner impatient to start a race. Her sister's eyes were on Jude, who was scrounging in the fridge, his head and torso hidden behind the open door. It seemed wrong, like he was trespassing in her kitchen, and she had to fight the urge to tell him to get out.

He must've sensed her there, because he straightened and leaned his elbow on top of the door. His hair was long, almost to his shoulders, and he had a mustache. She couldn't remember ever seeing much more than peach fuzz on him and, even though she knew it was in, didn't like this look at all. He seemed so much older, older than twenty-two, as if something had settled in him. As a teenager he was always getting rubbed the wrong way by things, like Eden. Verity never had the luxury.

"Hi, Verity," Jude said.

She watched him take her in—how heavy she was, she saw that register—and probably seeing the familiar, too, the girl of thirteen. That was when Verity noticed something else in him, behind the settled look. He was scared. "Hi, Jude."

Eden said, "We're making sandwiches. Want one?"

Jude hadn't looked away. Verity slowly turned to her sister. "No, thanks. I'm going to bed."

She left before Eden could ask her where Jude should sleep, before Jude volunteered details about her mother she didn't want to hear from him, before she started caring, even a little, about what her long-lost brother might be scared of.

~

Ship's Log: USS *Nepenthe*
Date: Monday, May 19, 1980
Time: 1240h
Weather: 63°F, Partly cloudy
Winds: 5–10 kn W
CO: Lt. Commander V. Vergennes

Verity sat on a locker eating number salad, her second portion. Eden had refused hers, taking advantage of their parents being gone and leaving the ship after finishing her sandwich. She'd headed straight to the freezer for a Fudgsicle, which she was now licking in the middle of the lawn in full view of the rest of the crew. Helpful. Really helpful. You'd think the fact that they were skipping school today would have been enough for Eden. That and having Jude back.

Wallace leaned over the side and frowned at Eden. "Why does she get to leave like that—and have a Fudgsicle?"

Verity got up and peered through the wheelhouse door and into the galley to make sure Cyrus and Nellie hadn't heard. They were chatting away, oblivious.

"Never mind, Gunner Wallace." Verity sat again. "I'll deal with her later." But she wouldn't. She was too worried about her mom, too tired from taking care of everyone, and too pissed off about Jude.

Roy picked a grape out of his salad and tossed it overboard. Discipline was eroding fast. Verity gave him the hairy eyeball, but he only shrugged and said, "Why isn't Jude on board? Shouldn't he be captain?"

Harper and Spider were on the opposite set of lockers. Harper stopped chewing; Spider shook his head and scowled.

Verity had been waiting for this to come up. She put her fruit to the side and crossed her arms. "Because, Gunner Roy, he lacks the experience for the job." Not to mention he'd been AWOL for five years. "When everyone's finished with their chow, how about we set course for Gibraltar, see if we can't stir up a little trouble in the Mediterranean."

Roy and Wallace exchanged excited looks. Roy said, "We'll have the gun at the ready, Captain!"

"Harper? I'm putting you in charge of spotting today."

Harper spoke around the last of her sandwich. "Getting the binoculars now, Captain."

Spider waited until Harper had gone, then bent close to Verity. "Weird that Jude's here, huh?"

"I'm sorry I didn't tell you last night. I couldn't deal with it, with any of it."

He shrugged, but Verity could see the truth. Anytime the subject of Jude had come up, Spider acted like nothing could be less interesting. It was a show, a cover for his anger. That anger felt like loyalty to her, and she loved him more for it.

Spider said, "He hasn't done anything to yank my chain yet. I hope he doesn't think he can crash in my room because it used to be his. When Dad gets here, he'll straighten things out." He picked up his bowl and Verity's, and stood up. "I just want Mom to come home. I don't care about Jude."

Verity was tempted to tell Spider about the baby. He was being honest with her, and she wanted to reciprocate. But she had promised her father. "Yeah, Spider. Same here."

Spider headed into the wheelhouse, ducking his head through the doorway. He spoke to Cyrus and Nellie—something about cleaning up, and their upcoming mission—then sat at the desk and bent over a book.

Cyrus emerged from the wheelhouse carrying a tub with the lunch supplies. Nellie was behind him with the plastic pail they used for garbage. They stepped over the bulwark, brows knit in concentration, and walked with baby steps down the gangway. They left the containers on the lawn and boarded the ship again.

Cyrus saluted Verity. "Crew has been fed, and the galley is tidy, Captain."

"Excellent job, Cook and Cook's Mate." Verity was about to give them their orders when Roy and Wallace came up the gangway with a bag of tennis ball ammunition. Verity hadn't had a chance to talk to the little ones alone since they had woken up to find Jude there—a brother they didn't have direct memories of. She called the twins over. "So Jude was a surprise, huh?"

Roy said, "Yeah, but he's super cool. He's going to show us how to play guitar and stuff."

"He plays in a band," Wallace said, awestruck.

Verity nodded. Why wouldn't they be excited? "What about you, Cyrus?"

He stole a glance at Nellie. "When we got up, he was in the kitchen and no one else was there. I thought maybe he was a bad guy, but he said he was our brother. I asked him where he came from, and he said Richmond and another place that's long and begins with *F*." Cyrus shrugged.

Nellie had been listening carefully. "I've been waiting for the baby, and it could be a baby brother and it could be a baby sister. That's what Mommy said."

Verity was confused. "I don't—"

Cyrus said, "She thought Jude was instead of the baby." He rolled his eyes. Roy and Wallace snickered.

Verity sighed with dismay. Her mom wouldn't be bringing home a new baby for everyone to adore. Instead they got confusion in the form of Jude.

Nellie looked over her shoulder, to make sure Jude wasn't around, and whispered, "Anyway, he's not cute like babies are. I'm very disappointed."

Verity regretted starting this. Why did she have to have these awkward discussions with her siblings? Why hadn't her father told Jude to come later, like today, so he could answer their impossible questions? And more hard questions were coming. Nellie wouldn't understand what a miscarriage was, nor that she'd been robbed of what Verity herself had experienced so many times—the curious joy of holding a new sibling in her arms. And Nellie might never be told about why Jude left, and so she wouldn't get why he'd been away for so long. Same with Cyrus, and the twins.

Verity took a deep breath and thought about what her mother would want her to say. "We all need some time to get used to Jude being here, but no matter what, be kind." She got to her feet and adopted her captain's voice, sweeping her arm to take in the ship. "Man your stations, sailors. We've got a lot of water to cover."

~

Just before three o'clock, Jude approached the ship. Verity didn't know what he'd been doing inside all this time, but it hadn't been taking care of the kids because, except for Eden, all of them had been out here.

As he came up the gangway, Harper left her station at the stern and blocked the end of the plank. "You need permission to board. You can ask me to ask Verity—she's the captain—or I guess you can ask her yourself since she's right here, but however you do it, you need to ask." She looked over her shoulder at Verity with her eyebrows raised, hoping she'd done the right thing.

Verity nodded.

Jude smiled, but he also looked a little annoyed. "Permission to board, Verity?"

"Captain," Harper corrected.

"Sure, whatever. Captain."

Harper stepped aside, shaking her head as if she couldn't believe this undisciplined hooligan was her brother.

Jude said, "Dad called. He and Mom are on their way here."

Here, not home.

Verity's first thought was that the house was a mess. After everyone had gone to bed last night, she'd spent an hour tidying the bathrooms, the living room, and the kitchen, but it had all been undone during the course of the day. As she imagined her mother walking through the front door, though, Verity realized she couldn't wait to see her mother, that underneath all the taking care of kids and cooking and captaining, she'd been worrying about her, worrying about her going to the hospital and now also worrying about how sad she'd be that the baby was dead. *Dead.* The ugliness of the word froze her.

Jude went on. "I've already cleaned up the kitchen."

"Okay, great." What was next? Should the kids be inside when their parents came home, or should they stay on the ship? Jude was the only other person here who knew what had happened to the baby; suddenly he seemed like a life raft. "What should we do? The kids are going to be excited, and Mom's going to want to be alone—"

"Why's Mom going to want to be alone?" Harper was at Verity's elbow. She was such a buttinsky. "Mom never wants to be alone. What's going on? Dad called last night, I know he did. What did he say?"

Verity looked straight into Jude's eyes for the first time since he'd shown up. Jude looked straight back at her, and instead of seeing the guy who lived in Richmond, the one who had let her down, the one who had broken her family, she saw her brother. He felt something, too, because his expression went soft.

Verity turned to her sister. "Harper, ask Spider to help you get all the gear stowed, please. Jude, can you take Cyrus and Nellie inside, make sure they have a snack and their faces and hands are clean? I'll follow in with the twins, okay?"

"Sounds like a plan." Jude leaned out over the starboard side and called to Cyrus and Nellie, who were coiling a rope on the bow. "Time to go in, guys." They glanced at each other, unsure of his authority.

"Sailors Cyrus and Nellie are granted leave," Verity said. "Jude will escort you."

They scrambled down to the deck and saluted Verity. She saluted back, keeping her expression neutral even though those two always made her smile inside. Whether or not Jude was here to stay, she was the captain of this ship, and she had a feeling her brothers and sisters were going to need the ship and her hand at the wheel more than ever.

CHAPTER
TWENTY-SIX

CYRUS

Mommy was home! Daddy came in the door first and stopped Roy and Wallace from ramming her, so Cyrus slipped by and got the first hug. She smelled funny, like Band-Aids and something worse, and she wasn't as big in the tummy anymore. He wanted to ask if the baby had come out, but they'd had a meeting before Daddy and Mommy came home, and Verity said no questions. No questions at all. Zero. Just hugs and nice words and listening.

Cyrus was good at all those things.

"Cyrus, my love." Mommy kissed his ear but was probably aiming for his cheek and missed. It didn't matter.

Nellie was right behind him like always, and Mommy scooped her in for a double hug. Mommy was crying, but there's such a thing as happy tears so maybe that was it.

Everyone else got their turn, and Daddy went and got Mommy a drink and said to "gather in the living room," which was pretty much where everyone was already. Nellie followed Mommy and Daddy onto the couch, and Cyrus didn't want to be a copycat or a baby, so he squeezed between the couch and the table and sat on the floor. Verity, Eden, and Harper lined up like cross-legged ducks on the floor on the other side of the table. Spider sat on one end of the little couch, and when Jude went to sit next to him, Spider pulled Roy up real fast, and Wallace was in there, too, like a rat up a drainpipe, so now there was no room for Jude. Spider acted as if he didn't like Jude very much. Cyrus didn't know Jude. In between the times someone mentioned him, Cyrus forgot about him being his brother, so when he turned up out of nowhere, it was like someone had picked up the house and given it a big shake. Jude had long hair like Jesus but also a mustache.

When the twins and Nellie stopped wiggling, Daddy leaned his elbows on his legs and made a steeple with his hands, and Cyrus knew this was bad. The steeple always meant bad things, probably because of church.

"I'm sorry, children, but your mother and I have bad news." See? "We've lost the baby."

Cyrus practically sprained his neck looking around to see if Daddy meant what he said.

Eden sucked in her breath and covered her mouth. Harper shrieked, but only a little, like she wasn't sure. Spider was frowning really hard. It was serious, for sure, but Cyrus had an idea that might help.

"Did you look under the front seat? Because remember when Wally lost his G.I. Joe, and we couldn't find it anywhere, not even in the whole entire house, that's where it was."

Daddy closed his eyes like he was about to be hit with something, and Cyrus had no clue what was going on. He twisted around to see his mom, but she had her face covered with her hands.

"Cyrus," Verity said, "*losing the baby* is just an expression. What Daddy's saying is that the baby died and went to heaven."

"Wow," Nellie said.

Died? Went to heaven? Cyrus wanted to crawl under the table. His mom patted his back, telling him it was all right, so he just sat there instead, feeling stupid and sorry. "I didn't know."

"We know you didn't, son," Daddy said.

Harper was crying now, and Eden was hugging her. Roy and Wallace were quiet, not even fidgeting for the first time in their whole entire lives. Cyrus had a million questions but remembered Verity said no questions. How could you find out things if you couldn't have questions? He counted the silent questions on his fingers.

One. Why the baby was dead? Did it fall or get cancer or what?

Two. Did it get born first?

Three. What did it look like?

Four. Did it have a funeral already?

Five. If it did, then how come none of them were invited?

He was out of fingers on that hand and about to start on the next when Verity interrupted his question thinking.

"I'm really sorry, Mom," she said. "You, too, Dad."

Dad? Oh, because it was Daddy's baby, too. But not as much as Mommy's. Not when a baby was little and especially not when it was inside her tummy. Daddies had to wait to own a baby.

Jude made a funny sound in his throat, like a fly had gotten stuck in there. "Can I get you something, Mom?"

"Not right now, thank you."

Nellie squirmed to the edge of the couch and stood up. "Anyway, if the baby is in heaven, then I'm not sad. Mommy can just make another one."

That was true, but it was wrong to think about another baby when two seconds ago this baby was their baby. Was it better to be in heaven or to grow up in a family? Cyrus couldn't stop the questions, and it was making him tired. He didn't know what to think about anything, and the way everyone was crying or quiet or frowning was pushing on his chest. Now he wanted to cry.

Nellie wandered into the kitchen. Cyrus got up and followed her but stopped when he got to Verity. She bent down, and he whispered in her ear. "You said no questions, but what if my question is when we can ask questions again? I don't know how to not ask that, and my head is exploding."

Verity smiled and hugged him. Her hair smelled like strawberries. "Maybe tomorrow, okay? Today we should just think about the baby and about Mommy."

"I don't know how to think about the baby without questions."

"Just Mommy, then."

"Okay, just Mommy." Cyrus turned to look at his mother. She seemed smaller, not just her tummy, but her whole person, the way air goes out of a balloon. Cyrus thought about her hard, thought about how she was the best person in the world and hoped that thinking about her would make her the right size again.

CHAPTER
TWENTY-SEVEN

SPIDER

Spider had thought he was hallucinating when he came into the house this morning and found Jude at the kitchen table. It took Spider a couple of beats to recognize him, even after Verity said his name. The mustache must've thrown him off—that and five years. Spider had been in his room over the garage when their dad called, and if Verity had planned to tell him about Jude, she hadn't gone out of her way to do it. Anyway, it had been a surprise and not a good one. Maybe "What the hell are you doing here?" hadn't been the friendliest opener, but it came from the heart.

Now they'd just heard the news about the baby, and Spider could tell from Verity's and Jude's reactions they'd already been clued in. Jude wasn't even back a day, and he was an insider. Everyone was hanging out in the living room, crying or just being sad, and even though Spider was sad, too, he was also annoyed and needed to book it out of there. He got up, headed for the front door.

His dad called out to him. "Hang on there, Spider. I've got something else to say to everyone." The room went quiet. Spider stayed where he was, holding on to the banister. "Jude was a big help to your mother last night. Turns out his blood matches hers, and he gave her the blood she desperately needed."

Jude's head was lowered, his hands clasped in front of him like he was praying. Mom was smiling at him. She was so white, and she was sinking into the couch like she was going to disappear between the cushions, but her smile was beautiful. It hit Spider that bringing Jude home had been her idea.

His father was still talking. "Jude's going to stay with us for a while until your mother's all better again. I know he's been gone a long time, but we need to pull together." He cleared his throat and looked at their mom, checking to see how he was doing. Spider couldn't believe his parents didn't know what a mistake this was. They'd all been doing just fine without Jude. Mom getting sick didn't change that. Jude could give blood if that was what she needed. He didn't have to live here; he could leave it in the mailbox for all Spider cared.

"Spider?" His father raised his eyebrows. "Jude will be sharing your room. That makes sense, doesn't it?"

His face got hot. Everyone was waiting for him to say something, to say the right thing. Even Jude was acting cool, stretching his legs in front of him like it was no biggie.

"Aw, Dad!" Roy said. "We want him to sleep with us, don't we, Wally?"

Jude reached over, ruffled Roy's hair. The kid beamed.

Their dad smiled at Roy. Of course. "That's generous of you, Roy, but it's better to keep the older boys together. Right, Spider?"

"If you say so, Dad." He was the patient one, the easygoing nerd who kept busy with his models and machines and did as he was told. But no matter what he did, no eyes shined for him. He felt petty for thinking it. In a family this big, how could everyone be a favorite? But look: Nellie was the youngest, an automatic ticket. Cyrus was the sweetest, and no one could help loving him. Roy was their father's favorite for reasons Spider couldn't explain, and Wallace didn't care about favorites and was happy being Roy's less-annoying other half. Harper was their mom's favorite, along with Eden, who got into trouble all the time, sucking in a ton of attention and therefore proving she really was a favorite, too. Otherwise they would have sent her to reform school. Verity wasn't a favorite, exactly, but she was like a second mom, plus the whole ship idea had started with her. Whatever the ranking was, Spider was last. He hardly ever thought about it, but Jude being here made it hard not to, especially when he was being asked—no, told—to give up his private space.

His father had been eyeing him. "Okay, then. It's settled."

Perfecto. Spider nodded and left the house. His father probably imagined he was going to his room to move things around, make space for his brother. Maybe his father thought Spider would take the initiative and get the air mattress from the garage, blow it up for Jude, show him how to pull together as a family. His father was all about taking initiative and pulling together—and following orders. Most of the time, Spider didn't have a problem with any of that, but Jude had been a selfish jerk, had left them all for five solid years. He hadn't even said goodbye to Spider. He had eased out of their lives the way a cottonmouth slid through the eel grass.

Spider stepped off the porch and headed toward the ship. The weak spring sun had ducked behind the high clouds, and though it wasn't even dinnertime, the temperature had dropped. He rubbed his arms, thought about grabbing a sweatshirt from his room, but he wasn't going to be very long. As he crossed the lawn between the house and ship, he checked the back door to see if the kids were spilling out of the house already. He wasn't doing anything secret; he just didn't want to be disturbed.

He made his way to the wheelhouse, and he pulled out a folder from behind the captain's chair. Inside were a bunch of forms; some were copies of real navy forms their dad had found. There were requisition forms that Eden used to request actual supplies from their parents, or made-up ones for missions, like extra rum or ammunition. There were medical forms that Harper filled out when there had been an accident or someone needed medical leave, or when they pretended that a sailor had been injured during a skirmish. There were forms for requesting leave, for reporting dereliction of duty, for reassigning duties or ranks. The one Spider was looking for, though, was at the bottom, because it was hardly ever used: a recommendation from the crew to the captain. Verity had made these to deal with crew complaints, figuring the kids would forget about their gripes before they got around to filling out the form. Spider didn't think their father even knew about them. If he did, he'd say that suggestion boxes were for poorly run businesses, not the navy.

Spider selected a pen from the holder fastened to the wall and sat at the desk. He filled out the date and time. Under recommendation type were several categories: Assignments; Safety; Missions; Personnel; Ship Maintenance; Other. He circled *Other*.

The rest of the page was lined, and the instructions asked for at least twenty-five words. Spider printed as carefully as he could. His handwriting was the worst.

"As quartermaster of the USS *Nepenthe* and second-highest-ranked officer assigned to her, I am writing to warn you about the appearance of a potentially hostile and dangerous person in nearby waters. Jude Vergennes has a known history of treachery and bad judgment, and it is my opinion that he should never be allowed to board, and never ever take part in any duties or missions. We can't afford to leave ourselves at his mercy during these difficult times. Yours sincerely, Arthur Vergennes Jr."

He read it through, folded it in half, and wrote "Captain Vergennes" on the back. He scrounged for a tape dispenser in the office-supply box, taped the letter shut, and propped it up behind the wheel, where Verity would be sure to see it. No one else would dare to open it. The crew was, after all, disciplined.

Spider's stomach growled. He left the ship and headed inside to help keep his younger sibs entertained while someone made dinner. Everyone would be low because of the miscarriage. Underneath Spider's annoyance about Jude was an ache for how his mother was probably feeling. But the Vergennes crew knew how to pull together, and they sure didn't need some guy from Richmond with a beater and a dumb mustache busting down the door, hoping to be the hero.

CHAPTER
TWENTY-EIGHT

VERITY

Verity pulled her humongous calculus book from the shelf in her locker and grabbed her sweater from the hook. It was Friday, and she was a senior, so her last period was free, but she had to wait for the bus anyway. Might as well do homework.

"Hey, Verity." Her friend Hannah was dressed in her blue and gold cheerleading outfit. Why an introvert like her had chosen the most extroverted activity ever invented didn't make sense. Hannah said it was because her trampoline skills made her a shoo-in, but Verity wondered if Hannah had a crush on someone on the football team. She would never act on it, being even less flirty than Verity, but that didn't mean it wasn't true. If Verity had more time for her friends, for even one friend, she'd have known for sure.

"Hey, Han."

"Any chance you're coming to the pep rally?" Hannah was only being nice. Verity wasn't the pep-rally type.

"I can't. My mom's not doing so hot." Verity had told her about her mother losing the baby, but not more than that because, well, saying her mom was tired just invited questions Verity couldn't answer.

Hannah frowned with worry. "I'm sorry. Tell her I hope she feels better." She gave Verity a quick hug. "I gotta fly."

"Good luck!" Verity watched her friend leave. A cramp in her belly reminded her that her period was due any second. Awesome!

She shut her locker and started off for the library. At the end of the corridor, Mrs. Castle came out of the office, spotted Verity, and waited for her.

"Hi, Mrs. Castle." Normally she'd be happy to talk to her, but not today, not with cramps, the mess at home, and what she knew Mrs. Castle was going to ask.

"Hello, Verity. I'm glad I ran into you. I was just collecting work for the weekend, to catch up. I happened to see a note to myself about the Halliwell scholarship deadline."

"This coming Tuesday. I know."

"Have you and your parents come to a decision?" Mrs. Castle disguised it well, but Verity could hear the impatience. Why in the world wouldn't a family jump at this opportunity?

Verity dropped her gaze. "My mom's been sick. She lost the baby."

"Oh dear. I'm sorry." She reached out and rubbed Verity's arm. Mrs. Castle still wanted to know about the scholarship, but didn't know how to ask after that news.

Welcome to my world, Mrs. Castle.

"It's not a good time, so I guess if they really need to have an answer, it has to be no." As soon as the words left her mouth, Verity felt the sour wash of disappointment.

"That's a shame. You've worked so hard."

A flash of resentment zinged through Verity. Why couldn't she just be like all the other seniors and go to games and not have to worry about money and little kids every single second? Why couldn't she just get this one thing? Maybe she would talk to her mother, remind her of the deadline. She pictured it, and guilt shoved her resentment straight out the door. It was selfish to think about herself when her mother was sick and grieving the baby.

Mrs. Castle was looking at her like she could read Verity's mind. "I can talk to the college for you, ask if there's wiggle room. That is, if you don't mind."

"I don't mind. I mean, thank you." Maybe her guidance counselor could buy her some time. Her mother wouldn't be sick forever.

~

That afternoon, Verity, Eden, and Spider got off the bus and waited for Jude to pick them up.

"You'd think he could be on time," Spider said, staring down the empty road. "It's not like he's got a heavy schedule."

Eden stepped in front of him, her feet practically touching his. Her nose came to only his chest, so she had to tip her head back to look him in the eye. "Lay off him."

Spider ignored her.

Verity wasn't crazy about admitting it, but having Jude home did make things easier, especially since their mom was spending almost all her time in bed or sitting on the couch. Jude had taken over ferrying everyone back and forth to the bus—not in his death trap, in the station wagon—and he didn't grumble about chores. Their parents didn't think Jude should have Nellie every day, so she was at Mrs. Lewinski's Tuesday, Wednesday, and Friday until Jude picked her up before the bus stop run. Dad was off on Mondays, so there was only one day, Thursday, Nellie was home all day with Mom and Jude.

Jude had told her he hadn't minded quitting his job at the car dealership, but he was worried about giving up the one at the nightclub. Just the fact that he worked at a nightclub made Dad furious, but Jude pointed out that he had to actually support himself and his dad got a little quieter after that—but not before getting in a dig about Jude being in that position only because he'd failed the family.

Dad was a little testy these days. They all were.

The station wagon pulled up, and Nellie waved to them from the back seat. Eden rode shotgun, and Verity and Spider piled in the back.

"Hey," Jude said.

"How's Mom?" Eden and Verity said at the same time.

"The same. Tired." He drummed his fingers on the steering wheel as he turned onto the road. Spider squirmed beside Verity; the drumming bugged him. "She had me bring her some old photo albums from the dining room, and she looked through those while I was doing the laundry."

Eden peered at Verity over the seat. The idea of their mother sitting alone leafing through a photo album was odd—odd enough to be disturbing. If their mother sat down, she did something productive, like clipping coupons or letting down a hem. On Saturdays, when the kids were on the ship all day, she sometimes treated herself to a few chapters of a novel, but she never idly leafed through anything.

"Anyway, I don't like the photo albums," Nellie said.

"Why not?" Verity asked.

She sighed as if it should have been obvious. "Only one has me in it. The rest are boring."

After Jude parked in front of the house, he loaded them all up with grocery bags. "Nellie and I went shopping. How does chicken and baked potatoes sound?"

"I don't know." Eden started up the walk with a smile on her face, the first one Verity had seen in days. "I kinda love having hot dogs or spaghetti every single day."

Spider took the last bag and caught up with Verity, leaning in to speak quietly. "How many chicken dinners make up for being a jerk?"

Verity sighed. "If I don't have to eat my own cooking, I'm not knocking it." With their mom unwell, having Jude around meant the difference between barely coping and utter disaster. Spider was looking for solidarity, though. "And you don't have to like someone to scarf down their food."

He smiled. "Excellent point."

~

A half hour later, the groceries were put away, and Spider and Eden were in the yard with all the younger kids, playing kickball. Verity checked on her mother—she was asleep—and sneaked upstairs for some Motrin. Her cramps were killing her. She lay down on her bed, waiting for the drugs to kick in, listening to the shrieks and shouts and laughter of her siblings, wishing she were young enough to forget, at least for a while, the way her life had become such a freaking mess. It was like it didn't even belong to her. She imagined having complete control over everything—and failed. Would she even know what she wanted?

The sounds of clanging pots and running water interrupted her pity party. She got up, straightened the bed, and went down into the kitchen. Jude was rinsing potatoes at the sink.

"Can I help?" No one should make dinner for eleven people by themselves, and she was physically incapable of watching someone work while she stood there doing zip.

"Sure. You can do this, and I'll get the chickens in the oven." Jude followed her gaze to the three chickens in two roasting pans lined up on the counter. "They were on sale. Leftovers are good, right?"

"Leftovers are great, but Spider will probably eat one of those himself." She picked up a potato. Since Jude arrived, her conversations with him had been mostly household stuff. She'd watched him, though, the way he was caring to their mom, and how he was trying to get to know their younger sibs. She couldn't imagine what it was like to be him, to have been away for so long, then jump right into the middle. Verity resented all the freedoms he'd had that she couldn't even dream of, and felt uncomfortable with him because he'd never apologized to her about the attack, but that didn't mean she couldn't try to talk to him. "When did you learn to cook?"

"Uncle Henry cooks. I guess he has to because he's in between wives a lot." Jude grinned. "Nothing fancy, but he showed me a few things. Like chicken." He slid the trays into the oven and opened the freezer compartment. "Should we have a vegetable? What's the crowd favorite? Nellie said corn."

Verity laughed. "She'd have it every night. You'll never get them all to agree, so just pick something."

She placed the potatoes on a tray, and Jude put them in with the chickens. Verity began putting away the dishes in the drainer.

Jude leaned against the counter. "So what are your plans for life after high school? College, I'm guessing."

Verity paused with a drawer half-open. "I really don't know."

"Really?"

"Well, I want to go, but it's hard."

"Hard how?"

She studied him, wondering how much to say. She hardly knew him anymore. Before he turned away from the ship and toward music and friends, before there even was a ship, they'd talked like it was nothing. Ancient history, she supposed, but his question seemed sincere, and maybe he could help her figure it out.

Verity closed the drawer. "I can go to CCC, no problem. But the new guidance counselor, Mrs. Castle, she's really nice, and she encouraged me to apply to Halliwell."

"In Roanoke?"

"Yeah. And I got in, with a scholarship that pretty much covers everything."

He broke out into a big smile, and she remembered suddenly how she'd loved him once. It hit her like a burst of sunshine. "That's incredible! What's hard about that?"

Verity played with the dish towel in her hands, bit down on her lip. "Oh, I get it. Dad, right?"

She nodded, and all the emotion she'd been holding back boiled up: resentment for having to put herself last, guilt for applying to Halliwell in secret, worry about her mother having to convince her father, and fury at her father for being so darn stubborn. She tamped it all down, turned to the sink, and filled a glass with water, took a long drink.

"Verity? You know that's bullshit, right?" He came over to her. She was looking out the window, into the yard, where Roy was chasing Harper. Jude touched her shoulder, and she turned to him. He was intense. "You can't spend your entire life being the second mom in this house. It wasn't your decision to have so many kids. You have your own life. Or you should. You can't let Dad ruin things for you."

The room grew still, and Verity sensed him before she saw him, standing just beyond the opening to the living room. Their father stared at them, his jaw working, his right hand squeezing the handle of his lunch cooler again and again.

"Dad," Verity said. It came out like a squeak, and she wished she'd just stayed quiet.

He stepped into the kitchen, set the cooler on a corner of the counter, so gently it didn't make a sound. He was breathing hard enough, though, for Verity to hear. Jude tensed beside her.

Their dad said, "I got in a couple minutes ago, came in quietly in case your mother was asleep on the couch. I heard you two in here, but I went to see your mother first." He took off his jacket, carefully draped it over the back of a seat, treating it like it was something special and not the dusky-green zip-front he'd worn for years. "It's a fine thing for a man to come home at the end of the day to hear he's ruining his children's lives." His tone was level, but his eyes were drilling into Jude.

Verity chewed on her thumb, her heart beating in her ears, wishing she hadn't confided in her brother.

Jude stood taller. "Verity told me about getting accepted to Halliwell and about the scholarship."

"And?"

Verity jumped in. "He was happy for me, is all."

Her father frowned at her, waved his hand. "I know what I heard."

Jude said, "If she won't say it, then I will. It doesn't seem fair to hold Verity back."

Their father stepped forward, smacked a hand on the table. To Verity it felt like a slap in her face. "Who's holding her back? She can go to the community college. I stand by my decision, not that I have to justify it to anyone, especially not to you." He spit out the last word like it was poison.

"CCC's not the same as Halliwell. You know that."

Verity glanced at her brother, hoping to signal him to back down, but he was trained on their dad.

"Here's what I know. I know that because Verity's smart and hard-working, she'll make the best of any school. I know that we need her here to help for a while longer."

Jude shook his head. "How much longer? Until Nellie's ready for CCC herself?"

Their father spun away, his fists clenched tight. When he turned back to them, his glare was steely. "That's not your business. You wouldn't be here to stick your nose in things if it weren't for your mother insisting on it. Just because you hightailed it out of here at seventeen doesn't mean you set a fine example—except as the way to break your mother's heart."

"Dad, Jude," Verity pleaded. "Please stop."

Jude lifted a hand in her direction and took two steps closer to his father, locking eyes with him. He pointed at his father's chest. "What about your heart, Dad, huh? I don't think you cared one bit when I left. Why do you think I stayed away? Why?" He leaned in, searching their father's face, which had gone from angry to uncertain. "I'll tell you why.

Because you didn't care. If you did, you'd have talked to me, reached out. But you didn't bother."

Jude's shoulders dropped, and he went to the stove, checked the heat under the corn. Their father hadn't moved. In the lines on his face, Verity read all the worry and exhaustion and frustration of the last weeks—or maybe the last five years. By avoiding thinking about Jude and what had happened the night of Nellie's birth, Verity had also avoided seeing how it had affected their father. She searched his face and tried to remember what he'd been like before. She couldn't. Maybe he'd been the same. Maybe he'd been just the same.

"You don't understand about family, Jude," their father said, his voice heavy and low. "You never have."

A jumble of voices gathered at the back door. Pellets of rain hit the metal roof.

The children would storm the kitchen if someone didn't head them off at the back door. Verity started in that direction. Jude was faster and slid by her. As he passed, he put his mouth to her ear. "He's full of it and you know it. Get out while you can."

I'm trying, Jude. I'm trying.

CHAPTER
TWENTY-NINE

JUDE

Nellie raised her arms in the air. "Anyway, my waffle is gone."

"Good job." Jude carried her to the sink and helped her rinse her syrup-sticky hands. As he set her down, their father came in and snagged the cooler from the counter. For the week and a half since their mom had lost the baby, he'd been waiting to leave for work until the kids had gone to school. He hovered around their mom, made sure she didn't overdo it.

"You got an apple and two salami sandwiches and four Oreos," Nellie said. "I helped Mommy."

"I saw, Nellie, thanks." He squatted, reached out an arm, and she came in for a quick hug. "Be good today."

"Maybe," she said. "I'm still thinking about it."

Jude ran the water hot for the dishes, squeezed soap onto a sponge.

"Your mother's resting now," their father said.

His voice was lower, rougher, so Jude knew who he was talking to without turning around. "I know," Jude said.

He left without a goodbye.

Fine.

Jude hadn't counted on having a honeymoon period with his father, and his low expectations were set just right. A few days at home were all it took before Jude went toe-to-toe with him over Verity wanting to go to Halliwell. Jude had defended her because she deserved to go, having paid her dues at school and at home. He owned up to feeling guilty about the home part. If he'd been here, her share of the load would've been lighter. It'd also occurred to him that she didn't hang out with friends or show any interest in boys maybe because of what Wes had done to her. Jude had never figured it would weigh her down like that, and if he had been the one to let the wolf in the door, well, it wasn't a good feeling.

Not all his problems with his father had to do with Verity, though. The rest had to do with his father being an insensitive, selfish prick. At least Jude didn't have to wonder anymore whether things would be better between them.

Nellie stood looking up at him expectantly. Today was their first full day together. Last Thursday their dad had stayed until after lunch, so Jude had never had to entertain a five-year-old for six hours by himself. Back before he'd left, taking care of the little ones had always been a group effort.

"Nells, can you get a coloring book or something while I clean up? Won't take long."

She pouted. "Okay, but then we do everything that I want."

He laughed. "Okay."

~

Turned out that Nellie liked the boys' toys, which she never got to play with because they commandeered them. Jude unpacked the erector set on the living-room floor.

Nellie took her time looking over the options and decided to make the steam shovel. "So we can move things."

Her little fingers were good at inserting the bolts and starting the nuts, but when it came to tightening them with the wrench, Jude had to step in. "Let me help."

"I can do it myself."

"How about we do it together?"

She sighed, as if even considering this were beneath her, but when Jude put his hand over hers, she didn't wriggle away. They worked quietly, Jude consulting the diagram and gently nudging Nellie toward the next piece. "Now this one."

"I can do it myself."

"Sure." He tried to remember what his mom would say to Harper, who had been six when Jude left home. "If you're big enough to try, you're big enough to succeed."

"What's *succeed*?"

You're asking me, kid? It seemed his answer mattered, though, so he thought before he spoke.

"*Succeed* is doing things in a way that seems right to you."

She picked up the axle. One wheel was inside the frame, and other one was outside—how did that happen? She showed it to him proudly. "Succeed is easy for me, anyway."

This must be why people loved little kids. They created their own reality, and none of it was a bummer.

～

The steam shovel never came together the right way, and Nellie got bored, so Jude left her with a cut-up apple and went to get his guitar from over the garage. When she was done eating, he showed her two simple chords—G and C—and showed her how to play a single note from each on the piano. She caught on quickly, so he played and sang "Skip to My Lou," calling out the chord changes.

"We're a band!" she said.

"Yup. We're a cool band." He strummed an F chord. "Ready to add another one for 'The Bear Went over the Mountain'?"

She nodded. "Show me."

Halfway through the second verse, Nellie quit. "Boring."

Jude thought for a moment. "Maybe you're ready for a real band song."

She sat up straighter. "Lay it on me."

Jude laughed. Where did she get that? "Okay, this is 'Down on the Corner' by CCR, my favorite band. Listen once, then we'll do it together." He picked up the rhythm, leaving off any embellishments and runs. CCR was better laid down straight anyway. His foot tapped along, and Nellie's legs swung in time on the piano bench. Kid had rhythm. The song was short, and when he finished, he started again, slowing it down and calling out the chords for Nellie to echo on the piano. She missed only one or two.

"Amazing!" Jude said.

Their mother walked in. She'd changed into slacks and a short-sleeved button-up shirt, and had pulled her hair back, which made her face look even paler and thinner, but it was probably less effort than washing it. She was smiling, though, and her eyes were lit up.

"We're a band!" Nellie said.

"I heard," their mom said. "Sounded lovely."

Jude leaned the guitar against the bookshelves. "She's a natural, Mom." Their mother nodded and Jude felt dumb. "Of course you would already know that."

She lowered herself onto the bench next to Nellie, slowly, like she didn't trust her legs. "She's our little metronome, all right." She touched Nellie's cheek with the back of a finger. "But I never would've thought to teach her the way you were doing. I'd say you were a natural, too. Musician and teacher both."

"I didn't do anything special." He honestly didn't think he had, but his mother's words had launched an arrow at his heart. This was what he'd been missing, the line that went from his mother to him, and to Eden, and now to Nellie. Their love for music was the obvious thing binding them together, but there were more connections, threads weaving in and out of all of them. Seeing the pattern of it was seeing his family and seeing his place in it. It made him feel like he was part of something that existed outside his own head, something real, something alive. He realized now that he'd always carried them with him. Jude had no idea how his father fit into all this, if he even did, but for now Jude was starved for that feeling of belonging.

Something of his thoughts must've read on his face, because his mom reached out and put her hand on his knee. She turned to Nellie. "What do you think? Is your brother Jude a good teacher? A special guy?"

"Yes," Nellie said, as she stood up and headed for the door. "I'm ready for lunch, now."

"We'll be there in a minute," his mother said, watching her go. "Jude, you can't know how wonderful it is to see you with Nellie, to have you get to know her. The others, too."

Jude nodded. His mother seeing him trying to be a good brother meant everything to him. "If only it was as easy with Dad. If we had something in common, something like music, some sort of bridge." His mother listened closely. "Did we ever? If we did, I can't remember."

"Not a particular activity, no. You never were one to tag along behind him, never took interest in what he was doing."

"You make it sound like my fault."

"I don't mean to. Some children want to do what adults do, and others couldn't care less." She paused, considering. "Verity started toddling after your father as soon as she could walk. Didn't matter what he was doing. You wouldn't think a tiny girl like that would care about the difference between a regular screwdriver and a Phillips one, but she did."

Jude remembered that about Verity, and thinking it was a dumb thing to do, but also being jealous of how close they'd seemed. "She was trying to please him. That's all it was, right?"

She tilted her head. "Maybe. Or maybe she wanted to learn from him, whatever it was."

"Maybe." Jude wasn't convinced. In any case, Verity wasn't a kid anymore. "You'd think after all her loyalty, being the captain all these years, Dad would do something for her for once."

His mom sighed, nodded. "You mean let her go to Halliwell."

"Yeah, that."

"To be honest, her application to Halliwell blindsided us. It would've been better if she'd been honest about it. And now"—she waved her hand, let it hang there a moment, a placeholder for the child she'd lost, the exhaustion she couldn't shake, then returned it to her lap—"now I just don't know. The college extended the deadline, so I have more time to talk to your father."

"You mean 'work on him.'"

A little mischief played in her eyes. "Maybe I do." She smiled and reached out her arms. "Help me up, please. Princess Penelope doesn't like to be kept waiting."

CHAPTER THIRTY

HARPER

Harper looked over her shoulder to make sure no one was around, then took her mom's purse from the hall table and dug for the piece of paper she knew had to be there. This morning her parents had gone to Richmond, and when they came back, her mom went straight to bed. Harper had to know what was going on.

Bingo! A receipt from Founders Hospital Laboratory Services. Under *Services* was only one thing: bone-marrow sample. Harper felt sick to her stomach because taking something from a bone sounded crazy and also violent, and she had to stop herself from running down the hall and crawling into bed with her mom that very second. Instead she folded the receipt and put it back. It was creepy that hospitals took stuff from your body, then gave you a piece of paper for it like that made it even.

Harper wasn't allowed to update her mom's medical records like she did for her brothers and sisters. Her mom said it was private, which meant there were embarrassing things in there. As if the time Harper accidentally superglued her Barbie to her forehead wasn't? Sheesh.

It had been over three weeks since their mom had fainted and dropped Nellie on her head, then had gone to the hospital and come back without the baby. Harper had been keeping track of everything she could, including pieces of paper that got left out after a doctor's visit and bills that were stacked on the little desk where Mom paid them, and also what Harper happened to hear when she stuck her ear against her parents' bedroom door. School was over on Friday, so soon she'd have more time to figure it out. Her dad had told all of them the doctors didn't know what was wrong with their mom, but they knew something, and Harper wanted to know it, too.

All yesterday she'd been holed up in the dining room chasing words through the dictionary. She was about to pull her hair out. *Transfusion* was easy enough. Her mom had at least two of those. She also got an "antibiotic" for "a febrile condition of unspecified origin." In other words, a fever. Why not just say so? The antibiotic had Harper confused because when she and her brothers and sisters had fevers, all they ever got was a cold washcloth and ice cream.

The word *hematocrit* popped up everywhere, and she'd figured out it meant how many red blood cells you had. Her mom's was low except right after a transfusion. The blood came from Jude, which made Harper think maybe their mom's hematocrit right after a transfusion was really Jude's hematocrit. Jude kept giving his blood, but he wasn't pale or tired, so he had to be making more. Maybe their mom wasn't?

The first time she saw the word *anemia* was on a piece of paper her dad left on his bedside table after the baby died. Written in his neat, square handwriting was *peripartum anemia*. Harper figured he wrote down what the doctor had said so he wouldn't forget. She looked it up, and it was basically blaming it on the baby. But if the baby had gone to heaven, how could it be making her mother lose her red blood cells? Yesterday her mom bumped into the coffee table and got a bruise from her ankle to her knee, which was scary. She wasn't getting better.

∼

Now Harper sat on the stairs, wanting to look up *bone marrow* in the dictionary. Problem was that Verity was showing Cyrus and Nellie how to play scales on the piano, which was in the dining room with the dictionary. It sounded like two demented cats dancing on the keys.

Her dad came down the hall from their bedroom and sat on the couch. Harper watched him, wanting to ask him about the bone marrow, about why her mother was sick, but he looked so sad, sitting there by himself, holding the newspaper in his lap but not reading it.

She plonked herself down on the little couch opposite him. "Hi, Daddy."

"How's my girl?"

"I'm okay. Mom's tired still, huh?"

"Yes, she is." He was looking at her, but it was more like looking straight through her.

"So what did they do at the hospital?"

He sighed hard. "Harper, I know you care about your mother and that you're curious about anything medical, but I just can't be telling you everything."

"Why not?"

"Because you'd have questions, and I don't have the answers." He spread his hands to show her how empty they were. "I promise you that once we know what the heck is going on with your mother, we will tell you—all of you. We're not in the business of keeping secrets." He moved the paper off his lap and patted the cushion next to his leg. "Come sit with me a minute." Harper climbed over the coffee table and curled up next to him. He held her close with his arm. "Sometimes I think that when you ask questions, Harper, what you really want is this." He kissed the top of her head. Her throat was tight and her nose stung.

Maybe, she thought, *that's what you say when the answers you get aren't the ones you want.*

~

The rain started pouring down just when Harper was about to go outside and play with the boys to get away from medical worrying. She headed upstairs instead, and there was Eden, lying tummy down on her bed reading a magazine. Eden always had better things to do than talk to Harper, practically anything really. Point of fact, Eden knew Harper was standing right at the end of her bed, but she might as well have been an ant, one of those teeny-tiny ones you didn't notice unless they crawled somewhere sensitive like along your neck. Harper also worried that Eden's knack for getting into trouble might be contagious. Hadn't Verity warned her about not becoming Eden? But her sister looked almost normal right now, and Harper had questions.

Harper sat on the edge of her bed next to Eden's. "Can I ask you something?"

"Mmm."

Close enough. "What do you know about bone marrow?"

"What?" Her eyes didn't budge from the page.

"Bone marrow."

Eden sighed and did an eye roll that ended somewhere near the night table between their beds. "Harper, what the freak are you talking about?"

"Mom had her bone marrow tested today. I thought you might know something."

Eden frowned. "It's inside your bones, but I don't remember what it does. Ask Verity maybe."

"Verity would tell me very nicely to mind my own beeswax, which is also what Dad said, by the way, not about bone marrow exactly, but about why they went to the hospital today."

She shrugged. "I guess they'll tell us when they know."

"I don't like secrets."

Eden put down the magazine and sat up. "I love them when they're mine, but yeah, I know what you mean." She stared at Harper. "How did you find out about the bone marrow anyway?"

"I might've looked at a piece of paper in Mom's purse."

"Not your first, I'm guessing."

She shook her head. Eden didn't know anything more than Harper, but at least she was listening and not telling Harper to mind her own beeswax. This gave Harper the nerve to open another barrel of monkeys, the monkeys being Jude and Spider. She'd asked Verity a couple of days ago why they didn't like each other, and Verity had said they never had and that was that. Some answer.

"So forget about the bone marrow and tell me something else, okay?"

"Okaaaay." Meaning, *don't bet on it.*

"Why does Spider hate Jude? And why didn't Jude visit us all that time? Daddy always said it was because Jude had done something bad that I was too young to understand and that I shouldn't ask about it anymore, so I didn't, plus I kind of forgot about Jude, from not seeing him and nobody talking about him. But now he's here, living here, so I have all the same questions again. Still."

Eden had her head down and had been playing with the ends of her hair the whole time Harper was talking. Now she tilted her head at Harper like she was trying to figure out what to say, which made Harper's stomach do flips. Eden was the just-spit-it-out type.

"You can tell me, Eden. I'm mature for my age." Why did she have to keep reminding everyone? Geez.

"Look. Something happened a long time ago, the day Nellie was born."

"What sort of something? Who did it happen to?"

"Harper, I don't even know for sure myself. I was nine, and no one talked about it, so that makes it hard to remember." Harper nodded because that did make sense. "And the who is Verity. It happened to Verity. And Spider was there, I'm sure about that, and Jude got blamed."

"Why did Jude get blamed?" Harper was struggling to put the pieces together. "Did he do something bad to Verity?" She stared at Eden, praying she'd say no.

"No, not like that. He'd had a couple beers, that's it. But Dad and, I guess, Spider, too, thought it wouldn't have happened if Jude had been, I don't know, perfect. That's the trouble, Harper, and that's what makes me so angry all the time. We have to follow all the rules every single second and line up like soldiers, or sailors, I guess, and be absolutely perfect."

Was that true? Harper couldn't decide. Roy was definitely a lot less than perfect. Before she could noodle on it anymore, Eden scooted forward so their knees were almost touching.

"I don't know why I'm telling you all this. Maybe because Mom's so sick and I'm scared. If things are bad enough that Dad let Jude come home, then I'm really scared." She stopped and covered her mouth with her hand. "I shouldn't have told you that."

"It's okay. I asked." Harper wiped her sweaty palms on the bedspread. "Plus you don't know squat."

Eden smiled. "I'm worrying about Mom, too. We all are. And I wish they'd tell us something. Waiting and not knowing is the worst."

Harper smiled back, sort of. This conversation had left her brain a jumbled mess.

Eden picked up her magazine, flopped over on her tummy again. "Ask Spider about the bone-marrow thing. He's the resident nerd."

Harper went to find Spider, feeling for the umpteenth time like she wanted to know more but also knew too much already. If she knew what the adults did, would she feel better? She doubted it. But she couldn't pretend to be ignorant like a little kid, so she was stuck in the middle like always.

CHAPTER
THIRTY-ONE

Maeve

Maeve sat at her spot at the kitchen table, on the end closest to the stove. Cyrus was up early, as usual, eating a bowl of Cap'n Crunch and reading yesterday's comics. Every few bites his hair fell into his eyes, and he pushed it away. How long had it been since his hair had been cut? Lord knew. Since she'd fallen ill, time had become unpredictable. It could be stretched out long, a few minutes as full as a day, like this moment here with her little boy, and other times a week could race by undetected, Monday to Sunday gone in a blink. She ought to go to her room, get dressed for another trip to Richmond. The lab at the hospital had promised the results of the bone-marrow test would go to Dr. Weingarten as soon as they were ready, but Maeve hadn't expected they would get a call from the doctor's office the very next day—yesterday—asking them to come in. When she had hung up and told Arthur, he asked why they didn't just tell her over the phone.

"I guess it's not that sort of news, Arthur."

"Now, don't think that way. He just wants to charge us for an office visit." His smile was unconvincing.

The quip touched a sore spot, though. Maeve was afraid to go through the mail for fear of more medical bills. To make things worse, Arthur had lost some days on the job ferrying her to one appointment or another. He said his boss, Gray Reynolds, told him not to worry about it, but as tired as Maeve was, her power to worry seemed only to have strengthened. What if Gray wasn't as forgiving as Arthur made him out to be? She could easily imagine Arthur dismissing his boss's hints that he find someone else to take his wife to the doctor. Surely Gray knew that Verity could drive, even if he might not know Jude was home. It would be like Arthur to be unconcerned about jeopardizing his job in order to be there for her. But where would they be without that job? Other than being in the military, Arthur hadn't had another one, and it wasn't as if there were a lot of opportunities around here.

Cyrus rested his spoon in the bowl and folded the newspaper neatly. "Can you do something with me today?"

"I have to go to Richmond with your father, but I can try. What did you have in mind?"

He tossed his bangs out of his eyes. "I don't know."

"How about I cut your hair?" She smiled. "You look like a Shetland pony."

"Maybe. Or maybe we can play cards."

Normally he'd ask to go looking for frogs or to ride bikes down the road; Roy and Wallace were too wild for him. Maeve wished he felt free to ask for those small activities instead of playing cards because she couldn't manage more. "Come here, my love." She held out her arms.

Cyrus scooted back his chair and climbed into her lap. With no one else around, he didn't mind being her little boy at all.

~

The kitchen filled slowly—Arthur, Nellie, then Verity, all subdued. Maeve excused herself to get ready. When she came back through the living room, she was swept along with Roy, Wallace, and Harper as they tumbled down from upstairs. All were half-asleep but awake enough to elbow each other to be first to the refrigerator. Maeve made it as far as the couch before she needed to sit again from the exertion of dressing.

Spider arrived through the front door followed by Jude a dozen steps behind. Where did they find the energy to bristle for so long? She needed to sit down with them, work through it. Two weeks ago she'd managed to broker a fragile truce between Jude and Arthur. They'd done it for her sake, but she wouldn't quibble. She wanted peace in her family, true peace, but sick as she was, she'd settle for civility.

Spider rubbed his stomach through his shirt, same as he'd done when he was a hungry toddler. "Morning, Mom."

"Good morning, boys. Spider, I know you're starving. Go on."

He shrugged sheepishly and loped into the kitchen.

"Hi, Mom," Jude said. "You're up and ready early."

She couldn't remember if he had been told about this morning's appointment. "More ready than up, I think." She smiled to show she didn't mean for him to worry.

He nodded toward the kitchen. "Can I get you anything?"

"No, I'm fine, thanks." When he waited another moment, his brow knit, it was clear to her he did know about the appointment and was concerned for her. "Really, I'm fine."

Arthur's low, calm voice came to her through the clinking of dishes, the scrape of the chairs along the floor, the subdued chatting of the children. She closed her eyes, listening to the familiar tones, the sweet, full music of it.

~

"Aplastic anemia," Dr. Weingarten said a second time.

Arthur was holding her hand. Maeve looked at him, wondering which of them was going to start with the questions. But the doctor was ahead of them.

"When I ordered the bone-marrow sample, I explained that's where blood cells are made. The cells generally only live about six weeks, so they have to be replaced. People can have anemia for many reasons, like we talked about, and some kinds are more serious than others." He picked up some papers on his desk, moved them to the side, as if they were getting in the way of his making his point. "Mrs. Vergennes, your bone marrow is not making new cells at all. That's what the aplastic part means, that the bone marrow is not working."

Maeve swallowed past the lump in her throat.

Arthur said, "So what's the treatment?"

Dr. Weingarten spread his hands. "We've tried to jump-start things, if you will, with transfusions, because in some cases the bone marrow recovers. It's our belief that your wife"—he nodded to Maeve, careful not to leave her out—"Mrs. Vergennes, will likely not recover."

Arthur cleared his throat. "I don't think you answered my question."

Maeve didn't know where to look. She didn't want to see Arthur's face when the doctor said what she already now knew, and she didn't want to watch the man say it. She turned her gaze to a potted plant in the corner.

"I'm sorry to say that we don't have any promising treatments for the disease."

Arthur made a choking sound, coughed into his hand. "No promising treatments, or no treatments at all?"

The doctor sighed. "We can try one more transfusion from your son, if he's willing."

"Only one?" Arthur said.

Maeve imagined Jude lying on a large bed next to her, his blood flowing out of his body into hers. He became paler, weaker, while she, temporarily, revived. It was a horrific tableau. Her hands, always cold now, were immobile in her lap, frozen solid. If she moved them, they would shatter.

Dr. Weingarten said, "Jude is a good match, but not perfect. We're already seeing signs in your wife's blood work suggesting impacts from histoincompatibility. And, in anticipation of your next question, yes, it's possible that another family member could provide as good a match, but without an identical twin, there will always be problems, serious ones."

Maeve's mouth was parched. She licked her lips. "How long?"

"Maeve," Arthur whispered. "That's not—"

"It's difficult to say," the doctor said. "Another transfusion might buy you some time, but it also might precipitate a cascade of ill effects." He leaned back in his chair, adjusted his tie. He didn't strike Maeve as a timid or cowardly man, so his hesitation struck fear in her. "Perhaps a month, optimistically."

"Optimistically," Arthur repeated.

"Yes," Dr. Weingarten said.

He continued to say other things Maeve did not hear. She did not remember leaving the hospital, or walking to the car, not specifically. She felt Arthur's arm around her, the strength of him. Everything else was blurred. Her vision was narrow and the sunlight harsh. She closed her eyes and allowed her husband to support and guide her, to replace the body that was abandoning her.

On the drive home, somewhere past West Point, Maeve revived a little. The corn in the fields on either side of the road was knee high. She'd be gone before it was ripe.

"That doctor could be wrong." Arthur said, "He gave us two names, says they are top-notch, and I'm going to ask for another opinion. Two opinions."

"All right." If Maeve ever knew all the stages of grief, she could not now bring them to mind. She did, however, remember the first: denial.

~

As soon as they arrived home and greeted the children, Arthur handed Jude the car keys and some money and instructed him to get pizza. "Take Roy and Wallace with you, and any of the others."

He was clearing the way to make phone calls to the other doctors, she supposed. Maeve didn't know what to do with herself. The children swirled.

"Mommy," Wallace said, "I can't find my shoes." He hadn't looked.

"Try the back door." She swayed and reached for the banister.

Verity was at her elbow. "You sit down, Mom. I'll find the shoes." She walked her to the couch, then hurried off.

Nellie appeared in front of her, holding her guinea pig. "Jude says I can't take Vermin."

"She won't be allowed in, and Jude can't leave you in the car."

She thought a moment, then placed a sticky hand on her mother's cheek. "Anyway, me and Vermin decided to stay with you."

Maeve pulled Nellie to her and buried her face in her daughter's shoulder to buffer the moan she could not suppress.

Nellie wrestled free and frowned at her. "It's not nice to growl."

"I would never growl at you. I love you with all my heart." Tears ran down Maeve's face, and she wiped them away before the others could see. This wasn't the time to explain, especially since she couldn't imagine what the words would be. She'd work it out with Arthur.

Maeve gave Nellie a kiss to reassure her and scanned the room for Arthur. He was under the cased opening to the kitchen. The children passed in front of him going one way and the other, issuing a constant stream of chatter. Arthur touched a sleeve or a head or murmured an answer to a direct question, but he wasn't really there. He was in a small private room of his own making, a cell with no doors or windows. He had gone inside to protect his heart, and no matter who came near, he would not break it down. In there he could believe whatever he wanted and put the blame for things wherever he pleased. But it was dark in there, and lonely. Maeve was worried about many things right now, and scared, but Arthur shutting himself away terrified her. Not for herself, not in this moment, but for when she was gone, and all the people in this house would need him more than he could ever begin to imagine.

~

Maeve went to bed early that night, the voices of her older children sifting down to her through the floorboards like falling snow. Her dog-tiredness gave her a certain peace; the lead in her veins slowed the panic she would otherwise have felt. She was too exhausted to worry when she might die, and felt she was already on her way, her limbs so heavy she would sink into the earth were it not for the bed and the house itself. Perhaps the weight was grief. How could she know? It wasn't pity, she was sure of that.

Arthur came in. He put on his pajamas and slid in beside her. She raised one arm, shifted her hips, turned her cheek onto the pillow, and with these familiar adjustments was in his arms, her forehead touching his. He didn't speak, and Maeve could only assume it was because his emotions prevented it, because her husband had always been careful to say everything he could when it concerned the two of them, even if he invariably concluded that his words were a disappointment to the intention of his heart.

Maeve also did not speak but reached out to him with her heart, the only part of her that still felt able.

In the next room, Nellie sighed loudly, rustled in her sheets, and moments later was quiet again. Maeve was grateful she did not have to tend to her. She wanted Arthur to have his sleep, and from the rhythm of his breathing, he was already succumbing.

Her thoughts turned to when she and Arthur first began courting. She'd taken it for granted that the clarity and confidence of his feelings for her meant he was clear and confident about everything, or most things. She was a small-town girl with little experience of men; the ones she knew were uncomplicated, as far as she could tell, so she assumed Arthur was exactly as he appeared. He swept her off her feet and treated her with kindness, respect, and more adoration than she ever dreamed she would find.

It wasn't until after they were married, less than a year after they danced at the Roseville Fair, that she gradually discovered her husband's best characteristics—his devotion, loyalty, and generosity—were not indicative of general personal strength. He was a wonderful husband but not, as she would learn, a robust person.

For sixteen years, from the time Maeve met Arthur until 1972, when they moved to their house on the Chesapeake, Arthur worked at the Naval Air Station in Norfolk. His rank as a navy man had been Machinist's Mate, in charge of maintaining the steam plant that propelled the ship and provided water and electricity. The work itself was never a problem for Arthur; fixing things satisfied him, and he didn't mind getting dirty or putting in overtime. The only part of the job he brought home with him had to do with his fellow workers, particularly his superiors.

"I don't know why," he'd start, shaking his head, "but so-and-so's got it in for me."

At first Maeve just listened. What did she know about work on a ship or about the military? In any case, her mother always said that listening was the most important thing a wife could do. So she listened. First it was Jenkins, another mechanic, who tried to tell Arthur how to do his job. Then it was Yardley, his direct supervisor, always giving Arthur the jobs that were hardest to solve but never with enough time or the right equipment.

"I'm a mechanic, not a magician!" Arthur complained. He didn't go on about it because he saw how it troubled her to think he was unhappy, but he also didn't hide his feelings well. They rode along inside him, pressing against his seams.

He didn't complain about everyone. He had buddies at work, and even bosses he respected, and was content more days than not. But some of the bad days were like storms, and she feared them. After a few years, Maeve began to see what the problem was: Arthur couldn't shake off a conflict, or even a slight. He felt persecuted.

Their fourth child was born in January 1967, and they named him Arthur Jr. They needed more room than their two-bedroom duplex, so Arthur had a solid reason to try to move up to a petty officer rate. He'd been in the service more than long enough, but hadn't been keen on a leadership role, feeling some of his superiors, other petty officers, would make trouble for him. Still, they needed the money.

Maeve tried building him up. "You're a steady worker, and a careful one, Arthur, and people have to respect that. Those men that have a problem with you, well, they're probably just having a rotten day."

"Ah, Maeve," he'd said and given her a kiss. "What would I do without you?"

His CO agreed to recommend the advancement, reluctantly, according to Arthur, and that was when the trouble began. The men who were once his buddies resented his new authority, and his new CO found every excuse to criticize him. The other petty officers would not support him.

"I'd been a grunt too long," Arthur observed, but the knowledge did him no good.

Lying in bed watching him sleep, Maeve recalled the pain of that time, how Arthur's periodic dive into feelings of persecution became an almost daily lament. Only her presence and, to a lesser extent, that of the children could restore him. Maeve never despaired; it wasn't her way, and Arthur's love for her never faltered, his devotion to the family never wavered. How could she fault him?

In the late winter of 1970, Arthur did snap, finally. She never got a clear picture of what happened. Through her navy-wife acquaintances she'd learned he'd lost his temper, thrown things, yelled at his CO. She didn't think he'd hit anyone, because he'd have been court-martialed for that. He was leaving the navy, that was clear, because they wouldn't have him anymore or because he couldn't stay—or both. What did it matter? He was too ashamed, too angry, for her to pursue the details.

There was one stroke of luck, though, and one was all they needed. Gray Reynolds, a lieutenant commander who'd served with Arthur in Korea, returned in the new year from a tour in Vietnam. He'd had enough of the navy, too, for reasons different from Arthur's. He had always respected Arthur, although the gap between their ranks had prevented them from being friends. Later, the difference in their social standing would prevent it still, but it didn't matter. Gray Reynolds bought a golf course on the Chesapeake, an easy drive for all his navy friends in Norfolk. He offered Arthur a job as the head of maintenance and a salary that was more than generous.

Maeve had been pregnant with the twins when Reynolds made the offer. She and Arthur barely discussed the move; it was a blessing, a second chance, a better chance. Arthur showed her the house on the island, with its generous kitchen, its sprawling yard, its dilapidated boat, and she was, after a brief realignment of her perspective, sold on this new life.

That house held everything she loved now. She'd been grateful every day for what they had built there together. And yet, as she lay beside Arthur, with her children tucked into every corner of the house, and the garage, too, she could not dismiss her biggest fear, her only fear, when it came down to it. She and Arthur were strong together, but how would he cope on his own, without her?

Her heart beat too fast, as if racing toward a finish line she had no desire to cross. Maeve willed her heart to steady itself, but she was drowning with fatigue. She turned her thoughts to her children and prayed for them to be strong and generous. It was a lot to ask of them, but what choice did she have?

CHAPTER
THIRTY-TWO

CYRUS

Ship's Log: USS *Nepenthe*
Date: Thursday, June 12, 1980
Time: 1138h
Weather: 59°F, Rain
Winds: 0–5 kn SW
CO: Lt. Commander V. Vergennes

Cyrus counted the sandwiches for the third time and got ten. Last time he got eleven and the time before twelve. Unless there was sandwich magic happening, he was losing his noodle. One last count. He made stacks of two sandwiches to make counting easier. Okay, so it was ten, which was right: Verity, Eden, Spider (that was six), plus Harper, Roy, Wallace, and him.

Now to make number salad. Nellie had a bad cold and was in bed, so he had to do it all by himself. He unloaded the fruit bag. No bananas! Jeepers creepers. He grabbed his slicker and climbed up the stairs and out to the deck. Everyone was huddled in the wheelhouse or under the canopy because it was raining like crazy. He stepped over legs and feet and whatnot.

"No bananas! Be right back!"

He shuffled down the gangway, being careful not to fall on his face, and ran across the yard. Huge puddles were everywhere, but he had on his lucky boots, which were lucky because when it rained he could splash and splash and his feet stayed dry. He was almost at the back door when, out of the corner of his eye, he spied Eden ducking into the shed with someone. A boy someone. The boy someone was pushing a bike, maybe a dirt bike, behind the shed. That looked like hiding. Uh-oh.

Water was running off Cyrus's hood down his face. He went inside, shucked his slicker and lucky boots, and began the banana hunt. Since Mommy had gotten sick, you could never tell where things would end up. He hunted along the counters and in the pantry but no such luck. He was about to hunt in the fridge—bananas don't go in the fridge, everyone knows that, but some doofus might've done it anyway—when Daddy came in.

"What's going on, son?"

"No bananas."

"Guess you'll have to make do."

Cyrus didn't know how to make dew, he thought God did that, but he didn't say anything because he had to get back to the ship and finish lunch before Verity wrote him up for dereliction of duty. He picked his slicker off the floor, put it on.

His father said, "Tell Verity I need Eden to come in from the ship, will you? She was supposed to clean the bathroom upstairs."

"Eden's not on the ship. She's in the shed with a boy." As soon as he said it, he knew he'd made trouble. Why did he never think first?

Daddy didn't say a word, just got his coat from the hook by the door, didn't even bother changing his shoes even though he'd get soaked and unlucky. Cyrus's tummy felt bad for Eden because Daddy seemed to get mad at her quicker than at anyone else, and anyone getting mad these days was bad business because of Mommy being sick.

This mess was the fault of Cyrus's noodle not stopping things coming out of his mouth in time.

He pulled on his lucky boots and his slicker and headed outside into the rain, worried and bananaless. He caught the screen door with his heel in case his mother was napping, ducked his head, and splashed his way toward the boat.

Three giant steps away from the gangplank, he heard screaming, which usually meant Harper but in this case was Eden because it came from the shed, not the boat. He spun around.

"Let go of him, Daddy!"

Eden was yanking their dad by his coat, pulling with both her hands. Her slicker was half-off, and her hair was in straggly, wet clumps like a zombie. Daddy had the boy by the arm and was practically lifting him off the ground like he weighed nothing. It was hard to see with the rain, but Cyrus didn't think he'd ever seen the boy before. His hair hung down in his eyes, and he was really skinny and short.

Daddy acted like Eden wasn't there. He tossed the boy away, and he fell on his behind and shuffled backward like a crab. It was almost funny but not really because the boy looked like he might pee his pants he was so scared.

Daddy towered over him. "She's fourteen, for heaven's sake!"

Eden let go and stood there watching them like it was a wrestling match. Cyrus had seen one on TV just one time at a friend's house, but jeepers creepers he wouldn't forget it ever. Hulk Hogan and two little guys who looked like woolly caterpillars. Cyrus hoped Eden would stay clear of the action.

Their dad was still yelling. "Get off my property! If you ever entertain the notion of coming back, I'll wring your neck!"

The boy found his feet and kept his eyes on Daddy the whole time while he got his bike from the bushes.

Eden was cry shouting. "I'm sorry, Peter! He's a maniac!"

Cyrus covered his ears and shut his eyes and counted to twenty, but his heart was beating really fast, and he lost count at twelve and had to start over. When he got to twelve again, he felt braver and looked.

Their dad was standing there with rain pouring down on his head, looking down the road. The boy wasn't anywhere. The back door slammed, which had to be Eden.

"Cyrus, you okay?" Verity leaned over the gunwale. The rest of his brothers and sisters were peeking out around her. They'd probably watched the whole match.

"Sure," he said. "Lunch is almost ready."

He went up the gangplank, careful as a cat. No bananas was bad, but lots of other things were worse. Way worse.

CHAPTER THIRTY-THREE

JUDE

In the room above the garage, Jude sat on his air mattress with his guitar, playing riffs, nothing solid, just getting his fingers loose, hoping for a long enough session to toughen up his fingertips or maybe even get a little magic happening. When he first had come back home, he thought he'd have tons of time to play, but, man, had he been wrong about that. Not that he was complaining; his mom was in a bad way, and she appreciated him chipping in. That was all that mattered.

It was weird sharing this room with his brother. First off, five years ago Spider had been a little kid, an eight-year-old who'd fall over laughing at fart jokes. Now he was already as tall as Jude, so soon he'd be taller, and his voice was low and throaty—when it didn't squeak. How much Jude had hated that when it was him. That was the thing: he remembered thirteen. He could remember how he felt like a giraffe in a dollhouse, and how his feelings were definitely more intense than anyone else's. Jude *got* Spider, so it sucked that Spider hated him. The kid had swallowed their father's version of the story whole.

The other thing about Spider? He was a neat freak. Jude was afraid he might disturb the perfect order just by breathing or leaving dust mites in the wrong places.

He ran a few progressions up the neck and down again, not worrying about hitting every note clean, just letting his hands find their way. The tightness in his chest loosened up for the first time in too long. He hadn't been home a month, but it felt like three, or like he'd never left, like he'd been battling his father and at odds with Spider the whole time. If he had an escape plan, he could tolerate the bullshit, but without knowing when his mother would recover, the plan was no plan.

The D string was a hair sharp, and he paused to tune it. He was about to start again, but someone came clomping up the outside stairs. Damn.

His father's face appeared in the glass of the door. Jude waved him in and laid the guitar aside, but he didn't get up, hoping the visit would be short so he could keep playing.

His father swung the door open, kept his hand on the knob. He looked like complete hell. "Your mother and I need to talk to you. It's important." There was no anger in his words, none of the edge Jude had gotten used to—and it worried him. "And Verity and Spider, too. They're on the ship. Could you go tell them to come in?"

Jude got up. "Sure. Are the rest of them okay with just Harper?"

"They'll have to be. It won't take long." He turned, stooped and slow, and headed down the stairs.

A few minutes later Jude, Verity, and Spider piled into their parents' bedroom, along with Eden, who already sat cross-legged on the bed at their mother's feet, chewing on a fingernail. The kids looked around at each other for clues and just met more grim and perplexed faces.

"We're in here," their dad explained, "to give us some distance from little ears." He glanced at their mother, who gave a slight nod. "I'm not going to draw this out. The doctors are finally sure they know what's the matter with your mother. It's called aplastic anemia, meaning her bone marrow can't make new blood cells. They thought it might fix itself, but it doesn't look that way."

Their dad rubbed his chin and looked at their mom with a helpless expression that hit Jude low in his stomach.

"It's all right, Arthur." Their mother sat up a little, looked at each of them in turn, her eyes moist. Dread crept up Jude's spine. "There's no treatment for it, much less a cure."

Jude stared at her, then at their father, whose head was bowed.

"Mom," Eden said. "No."

"Yes, darling. I'm so sorry because you know how much I love all of you, how much I want to stay with you, watch you grow." Her jaw was set. She was determined not to cry, and that somehow made it worse, reminding them how strong she was, how she cared more about their feelings than her own. Jude wondered how he had managed without her these last five years. His throat swelled, and he swallowed to ease it.

Their dad said, "The doctors could be wrong. There's always that chance. We talked to two, but there's always that chance."

"How much of a chance?" Jude asked.

He shook his head, which could have meant either he didn't know or he didn't want to say.

"Mom?" Eden said. Their mother didn't say anything, just gave her the most pitiful expression. "No!" Eden jumped from the bed, spun in front of it, arms flailing. "You are not dying! You are not!"

Jude caught her arms, pinned them to her sides, and embraced her with all his might. She struggled, but he held on, not knowing if he was holding on for her or for him.

～

The next couple of days were a freaking mess. Their parents didn't want the older kids to say anything to the younger ones, but it was kinda hard to explain why Eden was crying one minute and shouting at everyone the next, or why Spider wouldn't come out of his room except on direct orders from their dad. When Verity tried to pull captain on Spider, he told her to go to hell. And Verity? She was quiet, way too quiet.

Bad news hit everyone in a different place.

Sunday evening was balmy and dry, green and fresh like spring but earthy like summer. Jude found his parents sitting side by side in lawn chairs near the back door, catching the last of the sunlight. The kids were all on the ship. They'd been hard at it all afternoon, and Jude hadn't heard a single fight break out, despite the frayed tempers. It was as if they really did sail away to a different place.

Jude moved a chair over and sat next to his mother. She gave him a smile. Talking had become an effort. Her skin was pale gray, but the whites of her eyes were brilliantly clear. It didn't look right, and it scared him.

"I'll get started on dinner in a minute." Jude had gotten in the habit of reminding them of how he was helping. He cringed inside whenever he did it—it felt like sucking up—but he couldn't stop himself. He'd been away a long time, missed so much, that even though he and his parents didn't agree on what had happened, or on what should have happened, Jude still felt like he was making up for lost time. With his mother's prognosis, time had become a prized commodity, maybe the only one that mattered.

His parents both nodded, then his father said, "We wanted to ask you something anyway." His tone was soft around the edges like he was in church. That was the way everything felt now, hushed and heavy.

"Shoot."

"The doctor said we might try another transfusion."

"I thought there was no treatment."

"There isn't, but your mother is failing—" He coughed, rubbed his chin, collected himself. "Another transfusion is risky, too, but there's a chance, a small one, mind you, that she could turn it around."

Jude studied his mother's face for signs that this was nothing more than wishful thinking on his father's part. He couldn't suss it out; she was gazing out at the ship, quiet and serene, at least on the outside.

"Whatever you decide is cool with me. When are you thinking?"

"Tomorrow," his dad said.

His mother turned to him, her eyes full of light. "Thank you, son."

~

Jude was in the back seat of the station wagon feeling like a kid again being driven around by his parents. The car was new, or newer, but it hadn't really changed. There was the same trash container on the hump between the footwells in the back, always empty somehow, the same sticker on the driver's side of the windshield for parking at the country club, and, he was sure, the same packet of tissues inside the door pocket next to his mother's leg. He didn't have to look to know there was a tool kit in the back, just in case. This Chevy even smelled the same as the old one, like overheated vinyl and dried-out rubber. Jude's car was about the same age, but smelled totally different.

His father was keeping up a light, mostly one-sided conversation with his mother. She'd been so quiet since she'd gotten the diagnosis. Totally understandable. Jude wanted to talk to her, find a way to make it easier for her, but didn't have the first idea how to start. In the middle of the night, he'd think of what he thought he wanted to say, how much she meant to him, how he always knew she loved him, how she was the best person he'd ever known, but in the daylight there was so much going on with the kids, or she was so weak he couldn't find a way to tell her. Maybe he was just a coward.

Earlier the clouds had been so low it seemed like you could reach up and touch them. Now a couple of hours later, raindrops hit the windshield, just a few at first. Seconds later it started raining like crazy, and his dad flipped on the wipers. The thunk they made with each swipe gave Jude a beat. He laid notes against it in his head, running the fingers of his left hand along an invisible guitar neck. It was like meditation, not that he'd ever tried it, just how he imagined it; a way to step sideways into another world running parallel to this one but much, much simpler. It was the only quasi break he allowed himself from the tragedy surrounding them.

A piercing cry knocked him out of the music. His mother was screaming, an unending high-pitched wail. The car swerved right, hit gravel along the edge, recovered. A flash of panic shot through Jude.

"Maeve!" His father yanked the wheel to the right, on purpose this time. The car bumped off the pavement, onto the soft shoulder.

His mother was clutching her left shoulder. The car came to a halt. His father threw it into park.

"Mom!" Jude leaned over the seat, not sure if he should touch her.

Her scream slid into silence. She slumped, collapsed into the middle space. Her head hit his father's shoulder.

His father twisted to support her. "Maeve! Oh dear god."

Jude scooted across to the passenger-side door, got out, his legs numb. The rain pelted down. In two seconds he was soaked. He opened his mother's door. She was splayed across the seat, head tipped back, mouth partly open. He leaned inside. "Dad, what should we do?"

"I don't know!" His father laid two fingers under her chin. They trembled against her pale skin. "I don't know!"

"Should we get her out?"

"She's not moving." He put his fingers on her neck again. His other hand cupped her cheek. "I can't feel a pulse."

Jude's mouth went dry. "Maybe drive to the hospital?" He looked through the windshield, trying to place where they were. "It's not too far."

His father was wagging his head, his eyes closed.

Jude couldn't feel his legs. Only the rain pricking at his back stopped him from floating away from this whole crazy mess. "Dad?"

A truck pulled up behind them. A woman got out, dark hair pulled back. Maybe forty. She pulled a yellow slicker on as she hurried toward them.

"I saw the swerve back there. Everything okay?"

"It's my mom. She screamed, then she collapsed."

She pushed back her hood, wiped the rain from her face. "I'm a pharmacist, not a doctor, but do you want me to take a look?"

Jude stepped away to give her space. The wipers counted time. The woman was talking to his father in low tones, words Jude couldn't make out over the noise of the traffic on the wet road, over the beating of his heart. Jude held on to the car door, held on tight.

After a minute, the woman straightened, backed out. Her expression made Jude's blood stall in his heart. "I couldn't find a pulse, but we're not far from the hospital, the one in Gloucester." She gestured inside the car. "Maybe you should drive. Can you?"

Jude nodded, but he wasn't sure at all. He just knew he had to.

"I'll follow you," the woman said. "Make sure you get there."

Jude ran to the other side of the car, helped his father into the back seat. His father was sobbing, saying, "Maeve, Maeve," over and over again, shaking his head like he was getting rid of a nightmare. Jude buckled himself into the driver's seat. His mother's head was inches from his leg. Her mouth was open, her jaw slack. He looked away.

Jude blinked hard and took in a ragged breath, tasting the metallic bitterness in his mouth. He signaled a left turn, waited for a gap in the traffic, and drove off as fast as he dared. He checked his mirror. The woman's truck was behind him, and he drew the smallest comfort from it. His hands trembled, and he shivered beneath his soaked shirt. He tightened his grip on the wheel.

In the back seat, his father rocked and keened. The wipers kept time.

At the emergency room entrance, Jude stayed in the car as the orderlies removed his mother from the seat beside him. He didn't watch. He didn't follow her inside, but his father did, as Jude knew he would.

The woman came to the car window. Jude lowered it, water running down both sides of the glass. He wanted to thank her, but he was shaking so hard he couldn't speak.

"You did a good job driving," she said.

He nodded. It was exactly what his mother would've said.

"Do you want me to call someone?" She shifted her hood, and the rain trickled down her shoulder. "Or stay? I can. I was just on my way home."

Home.

The word evoked one thing: his mother. The pain of it rode over him, pressing the air out of his lungs. Jude let go of the steering wheel and dropped his head into his hands.

~

The service was that Saturday. It rained, that was pretty much all Jude would remember, like misery falling from the sky, soaking them all. Their dark clothes and pale faces.

~

Two days in that house, trapped by constant rain, were all he could take. The amount of sadness was crushing; he couldn't breathe. No one was sleeping, and the little kids were fighting or crying all the time. Verity never stopped working, Spider wouldn't look at him, and Harper was way too quiet. Eden escaped to be with her friends. And his father? He was practically catatonic.

Jude was only just figuring out how to fit in, how to make it work, and with his mother gone forever, it now seemed impossible. He hadn't realized how much he relied on her to smooth his path back into the family until she wasn't there anymore. Aunt Sarah, his mother's oldest sister, had come to help out, so he wouldn't be missed, or so he told himself. He'd go for a couple of days, or a week. Hell, he didn't know. He just needed out.

On the Monday after the service, Jude tried to talk to his father about going back to Richmond, but it wasn't clear he was even listening. The next day Jude caught him on the front porch, coming in from the garage.

"Dad, can we talk a sec?"

He stopped only because Jude was in front of the door. He lifted his hands, which were dark with grease. "I'd like to clean up."

"This is quick. I need to know what to do about my place, my room in Richmond. I'm paying rent, but if I'm going to be here longer, it doesn't make sense to keep doing that." He posed it as a practical problem because he couldn't cop to feeling overwhelmed, not to his father.

His father had been looking past him, unfocused. "Do whatever you need to."

The disappointment that swam through him told Jude what his itch to leave was really about. He didn't need his stuff, and he could figure out the rent and all that without driving there. What Jude needed to know was that his father wanted him to stay, be part of the family. Well, he'd gotten his answer. His father didn't want him today any more than he had for the past five years. In frustration, Jude tried to make him understand. "It's not what I need, Dad. It's what I can afford. I want to help here, but—"

"But what? What do you want from me here?" His father looked at him now.

Jude didn't know what to make of his expression. It was like he wasn't in there. Jude pulled back a little.

"You want your job back at the club? You want your room back? You want to sit with us every night at dinnertime?"

"I don't know, Dad. I've got a room I can't afford without a job and need to know where I'm supposed to be. I'm having trouble knowing what's right because I'm upset just like all of us are." Jude let out a long breath, relieved he'd finally come close to saying what he felt.

His father shook his head. "'Course you don't know what's right. You never have." He flicked one hand in front of his son. "Now leave me be."

Jude stepped to the side, reeling from the accusation, and let his father pass. Had everything he'd done since Eden called him that night meant nothing? How could one mistake at seventeen mean more than everything else?

He left that evening, driven by anger and resentment, and missing his mother more than ever. And he took his guitar, the signal to himself that he might not be coming back.

CHAPTER THIRTY-FOUR

VERITY

Verity stuffed a load of laundry into the washing machine, added detergent, hit the "Start" button, and said a short prayer. Twice in the last week the washer had simply refused to start, then, a day or two later, as if recovering from a sour mood, it had decided it would wash a load after all. Verity could barely turn around for the piles of clothing. It all made her so tired. Everything was making her tired.

The washer was silent. She pushed the button again. Nothing.

The doorbell chimed. Verity sighed, stepped between the clothing piles, out through the kitchen, and into the living room. Roy, Wallace, and Cyrus were playing keep-away with Nellie's stuffed hedgehog. She stood in the middle of the room shouting at them, her face red with indignation.

"RoyWallyCyrus, cut it out! Give her back!"

Verity grabbed hold of Cyrus, took the toy from him, and handed it to Nellie. "Nellie, maybe find Harper and let the boys torture each other for a change." Nellie stood her ground.

Verity was torn between wanting to scold Cyrus and to pull him into a hug. It wasn't like him to tease Nellie; he was acting out. They all had been, one way or another.

The doorbell rang again. "Outside," Verity said to the boys, pointing at the back door. Nellie followed her to the entry.

Verity ran a hand over her braid. Had she slept in it and not redone it this morning? She'd been up half the night dealing with the musical beds that had become a nightly ordeal in the week and a half since their mother had died. She didn't even remember which bed she'd woken up in.

An elderly couple stood at a polite distance from the door, both wearing tan trench coats. He carried a huge foil-covered dish. Verity knew them from church, but their name was lost to her.

"Verity, dear," the woman said. "We didn't mean to intrude—"

"We left a message," the man said, smiling to tell her he understood.

"I'm sorry. I haven't checked the messages today." Carmichael, that was the name. "But thank you for coming by, Mr. and Mrs. Carmichael." Behind her, the boys shouted at each other. "Would you like to come in?"

Nellie was at Verity's side, holding her hand. If the girl wasn't distracted by something, she insisted on being in constant contact with Verity. No one else. She even refused her father. "Anyway," Nellie said, "you don't want to come in. It's not nice in there anymore."

The woman smiled at Nellie sweetly, but was also clearly unsettled by the remark. "We just wanted to drop this off, dear. It's a pasta bake from *Good Housekeeping*. Homemade."

Verity took it from Mr. Carmichael. People had been dropping off food regularly over the last ten days. There had to be a schedule, probably organized by someone at church. "Sounds delicious. It's so much help. It really is." The pity in Mrs. Carmichael's face went straight into Verity, like a sudden sickness. She had the urge to go home with these kind people, to wallow in whatever feelings arose in her for as long as she liked. She imagined a soft bed with sheets dotted with pink roses in a room as quiet as the moon.

Mrs. Carmichael extracted a tissue from her handbag, offered it to Verity, who hadn't realized she was crying.

"Thank you, ma'am."

"You poor things." She took a tissue for herself, dabbed at her eyes, and settled her handbag on her arm.

Mr. Carmichael cleared his throat and nodded at the parking area. "Your father's back at work, is he?"

"Yes, sir."

He nodded. "Tell him I'd be happy to lend a hand with whatever needs doing, not that he isn't perfectly capable."

For a split second, Verity considered asking him what he knew about washing machines, but if her father heard about it, and he surely would, his pride would be wounded. Clean clothes weren't worth that. "Thank you. I'll tell him."

Mrs. Carmichael exchanged a glance with her husband. "If you're sure there's nothing else we can do, dear, then we'll be off."

"I'm sure. And thank you again."

Verity watched them go, Nellie hanging on her forearm since Verity needed both hands for the casserole. The service for her mother had been last Saturday, and her father had gone back to work on Monday. He didn't explain his reasoning to Verity or anyone else, just showed up at breakfast in his work clothes and packed himself a lunch from the piles of leftovers. "Funeral food," Eden called it. No one ate much of it.

Grandma Jean, Maeve's mother, and four of their mother's seven siblings had come for the service, but only Aunt Sarah, the eldest sister, stayed past Sunday. Verity hadn't been party to the discussion around that, either, nor when Aunt Faith arrived on Tuesday to take Sarah's place. It could be that Verity had missed hearing about these arrangements, but she thought it more likely that the aunts had worked it out themselves and presented it to Arthur as a done deal. The aunts, grieving themselves, did the best they could. Verity was so lost in her own world of hurt that she didn't pay attention to the adults. Her arms were too full of sad and angry children.

Her father had hardly said a word to anyone since he'd come back from the hospital with Jude and without their mother. He nodded or shook his head when he couldn't avoid answering and wandered around the house and yard tinkering with things like a restless ghost. Then there was the whole business with the burial. For three solid days after his wife died, he stonewalled any questions about funeral arrangements. Verity had been in the living room with Nellie and Cyrus when Jasper Stafford, the director of the town's only funeral home, pulled up to the house. She followed her father to the door when he answered the knock.

Their father didn't invite him in, so Mr. Stafford delivered his message across the threshold. "Hello, Arthur. I've come to see what your wishes are regarding your beloved wife." When her father said nothing, Mr. Stafford went on. "Pastor Feltner says there's a plot at the church, and seeing as your family are regular—"

"I don't want her there," her father said.

"Now, Arthur, as hard as it is, a decision must be made. Time is of the essence."

Verity caught his meaning and thought she might be sick then and there, but she stayed put.

"Bring her here."

Mr. Stafford tilted his head, considering, but only out of politeness. "I don't think you mean that."

"I do." Her father nodded, as if settling the matter with himself. "I'll bury her here."

"I see," Mr. Stafford said carefully. "Now you are within your rights—"

"That's settled then. Plainest box you have. My wife wouldn't have wanted anything more." Her father walked away, leaving the door to swing shut on its own.

A week had passed since that disturbing encounter. Verity watched the Carmichaels drive off and swung her gaze to the right. From where she stood she could see the mounded earth that marked the foot of the grave, but the head of it and the cross her father had fashioned were out of view. She couldn't say her father had been wrong to place their mother within reach, but it wasn't right, either. It wasn't what was done, as far as she knew. They didn't go over to that side of the house very often, but now they knew what they would encounter, and for Verity at least, her feelings were too raw for her mother's body to be that close. Maybe it was different for her father.

Verity carried the dish inside, Nellie in tow, feeling the empty spaces that had cropped up everywhere inside, the void left behind by her mother, the moth holes in the invisible fabric unraveling around her.

~

Late that afternoon Aunt Faith stripped all the beds, not knowing the washer wasn't working. She stood in the kitchen hugging a gigantic bundle of sheets as Verity delivered the news. Of all her mother's siblings, Aunt Faith looked the least like her mother, and Verity was grateful for it.

"Well, shoot. And the sun's out."

"Might as well try it," Verity said.

"I suppose I ought to." Aunt Faith pursed her lips and picked her way over to the washer.

She was a worker, unlike Aunt Sarah, who was a talker. Verity didn't know either of them well. Both still lived in Roseville with their families, as did her mother's eldest brother, Bo, and Grandma Jean. The drive from Roseville to Mobjack was over six hours, and none of it on easy roads, or so her parents had always said, and none of the Bradleys had the time or money to travel on a regular basis. To Verity, Aunt Faith was like an ambassador on a diplomatic mission in an exotic land and uncertain of the natives. Aunt Sarah might've felt the same way but covered it with talk. She grieved more openly, too, and Verity couldn't help but resent that. Her aunt was there to help, not to add to the mess. Verity felt terrible thinking that way, but the other children all relied on her, not on some woman they barely knew. Aunt Faith was better. Verity's father ignored them both, more or less.

From the laundry came the beautiful sound of water rushing into the washer. Aunt Faith stuck her head out. "I charmed it."

Verity smiled. "Might even dry before the sun goes down, breezy as it is." She would take a small victory.

Dinnertime was approaching, and the kids started gathering in the kitchen. Harper came in with Cyrus and Nellie and helped them wash their hands without saying a dozen words. She'd gone terribly quiet since their mother died. It was the most noticeable change in the house, other than the actual absence of their mother, as if their mother had been the movie and Harper the soundtrack.

"Harper," Verity said, "could you get the drinks, please?"

"Sure."

Nellie slipped her still-damp hand into Verity's. "One minute, pumpkin," Verity said, releasing her and sliding the pasta bake into the oven. Verity picked up Nellie and held her close, laying her cheek against her sister's, rubbing her back. Cyrus was watching them like they were eating ice cream that he'd been denied. It broke her heart, but she couldn't be everywhere at once. She put Nellie down, knelt beside Cyrus, and hugged him. He melted into her like he had no bones at all.

Aunt Faith came in with the laundry basket on her hip and took in the scene, biting her lip. "I'll drop these sheets upstairs and get the boys ready."

"Okay," Verity said, and returned to the stove. Food, sleep, and affection. It didn't seem like all that much, but she couldn't keep up. Her mother's voice played in her head. *Do your best. You'll find it's plenty.*

Harper began setting the table. She paused at their mother's place, set it for Aunt Faith, and went around the other side. She counted. "Eleven, right?"

"Nine," Verity said. "Eden's at Melissa's."

"Again?"

"Still." Verity wasn't sure of the exact number, but over the last ten days, Eden had been at her friend's more nights than she'd been home. If their father had noticed, he hadn't said anything. Verity was torn between resenting Eden for abandoning her role as big sister and being envious of her ability to escape the immediate physical reminders of their mother that saturated the house. Eden did what Eden wanted, whatever the price, and Verity was left to shoulder the burden.

Harper said, "I forgot that Jude's not here. I guess that does make nine." She returned the two place settings to the drawer. "Is he coming back? Ever?"

"Beats me." Her sister looked so down about the way the family seemed to be splintering, Verity had to say something, even if she didn't know what to believe. "I'm sure he will. Once these casseroles stop coming, we need him to cook."

Harper gave her a weak smile and wandered into the living room.

Jude. He'd gone back to Richmond two days after the service, saying that while they had an extra set of hands, he'd go back, get some things. He'd fought with their father right before he left; Verity didn't know what about, hadn't asked, and didn't care. They were all dragging themselves around like they were thigh deep in mud. She didn't have one bit of energy to spare, not for arguments, and definitely not for more pain.

The odd thing was that she'd been missing Jude. If she ignored the tension between him and their father, and between him and Spider, he was a steadying hand. Their father thought he was unreliable and selfish, and maybe he had been, but in the month he'd been around, he seemed anything but. Five years had changed him. Living away from home with

Uncle Henry. (What was that like? Verity couldn't imagine it.) Going to a new school, working for his uncle instead of his father, then moving out on his own. Jude hadn't volunteered much about his life, and Verity hadn't asked because she was still angry with him. He was still the brother who'd failed to look out for her, then failed to apologize for what happened because of it. She was waiting for that apology without hoping for it. It'd been so long, it was like waiting for a shooting star.

Verity went back to the stove, Nellie on her hip, Cyrus clinging to her leg, thinking that if anyone should've left, it was her. It was her turn, wasn't it? Before Jude left she ought to have stolen his keys, driven off in his Nova. Didn't matter that she had nowhere to go; the point would be the leaving. It was her turn, but of course now of all times her family needed her. Dreams were one thing, fantasies something else.

~

At six o'clock, Verity placed the pasta bake on the table next to a large salad. Their father had not returned from work, but the kids were all there, except for Eden and Jude, and polished off their milks before Verity could get the food dished out. They were all so thirsty these days. She put the last plate in front of her own place and got another gallon of milk from the refrigerator and refilled the glasses. She sat and said grace.

"Go ahead and eat. Aunt Faith said to start, and Daddy will be home when he's home." His hours had become unpredictable, as if their mother's passing had untethered him.

"This is really good," Spider said around a mouthful. "Who made it?"

"Two old people who cried," Nellie said.

"The Carmichaels from church." Verity passed the salad to Wallace on her right, who acted like it was a hot potato and practically threw it at Cyrus, who picked out three cucumbers.

The front door opened, and everyone shifted in their seats. When their father appeared, he was greeted with a half-hearted chorus of "Hi, Daddy."

He caught Verity's eye and nodded approval at the orderly scene. "Looks like a nice dinner."

"It's really good, Dad," Spider said. He served his father from the dish. Verity's heart squeezed. He always tried so hard.

Their father had taken two bites when Aunt Faith came in, her short blonde hair wet from the shower.

"Hello, Arthur." She circled the table to the opposite end, sat, and helped herself to the food.

Their father stared at her like she was a stranger. Verity took another serving of salad because it was in front of her, and she didn't know what else to do.

Finally, he said, "I thought you'd left."

"Why, Arthur, no, not until—"

"Where's Eden?" their father said, scanning the table. "Where in God's name is Eden?"

Across from Verity, Roy held his fork in the air and stopped chewing. Verity glanced at Harper, then put down her fork and faced her father. "At her friend Melissa's house."

He flattened his palms on the table. "For dinner?"

"I think she's been sleeping over."

Aunt Faith said, "She came home yesterday while you were at work, Arthur, and she asked me if she could stay overnight again." She smiled, looked around the table for some acknowledgment that this was a perfectly reasonable thing to do. Her smile went from natural to pasted on. "I didn't see the harm in it. Sometimes a friend is what a person needs most in times like this."

"That's not your decision to make, Faith." Their father's voice was level, but his left eyelid twitched. It did that when he was tired. It'd been twitching pretty much all the time.

"I didn't see the harm—"

"Of course you didn't! Because she is not your child. It's not your place." He shook his head like it was too heavy all of a sudden.

Verity felt the emotions around the table swell. She couldn't do anything about it; they were buried under the enormity of their collective damage. Their father, who should've been soothing them, easing their way into a life without their mother, was only making things worse. Verity hated him for it.

Aunt Faith said, "I know she's not mine, Arthur. But it was only a sleepover. I wasn't giving her away."

Cyrus had his hands over his ears, but something had gotten through. "Who's giving Eden away?"

"No one," Verity said.

"You'd have to pay someone to take her," Spider said, scowling.

Their father was on his feet. Verity's heart lurched. If Spider hadn't been at the opposite end of a long table, she was certain their dad would have had him by the shirt collar already.

"Sorry, Dad. Bad joke."

Their father sat down but stiffly, like his joints were spring-loaded. He was quiet a moment, gazing at the middle of the table, then spoke softly to Faith. "I think we can handle it from here. I do appreciate you taking time from your family to help us out."

Aunt Faith opened her mouth to speak. The doorbell rang.

"Harper," their father said, "go see who'd be rude enough to come calling during dinner."

Harper went. When their father started eating again, everyone else did, too, but really they were all watching him and straining to hear who might be at the door.

Harper scurried in, breathless. "It's Pastor Feltner. I said we were eating but, oh heck, I left him at the door and—"

"The pastor," Aunt Faith said. "How nice."

From the entry, the voice of Sunday sermons. The pastor was making his way into the house. "I'm sorry to interrupt, but I tried to leave a—"

"For the love of . . ." Their father scraped his chair back and met the pastor in the living room.

The kids on the far side of the table—Spider, Cyrus, Roy, and Wallace—leaned over the table so they could witness whatever was going to happen. Verity put her napkin on the table and sat sideways in her chair. Their father had never been a fan of the pastor, and it was clear from how the man was holding himself that he knew it. His narrow shoulders were pinched forward and his hands were clasped in front, reminding Verity of one of her brothers about to ask an awkward question.

"Good evening, Arthur. As I was saying, I did call more than once and intended to leave a message, but your answering machine is full. Of course you may not realize that, and perhaps there are other messages on there that need your attention, but in any case, I thought I'd drop in to see you. I'm sorry it's dinnertime, but any later and I'd worry about waking the children." He smiled broadly and spread his hands, inviting their father to accept this sensible explanation of why he was standing in their living room.

"I assure you, Pastor Feltner, that despite my beloved wife's passing, I do know how to work the answering machine."

He stepped closer to the pastor, a little too close, from Verity's perspective. She moved to the edge of the chair, not certain how exactly she would spring to action, but her father's behavior since he'd come home had made her jumpy. Pastor Feltner didn't look completely comfortable, either, and took a small step back.

"Of course," the pastor said. "I didn't mean to imply—"

Their father threw his hands in the hair, and the pastor rocked back on his heels. "I cannot believe what is going on here! People we don't even know show up whenever they please to bring things we don't ask for, as if I cannot provide for my family. My sister-in-law here"—he swung around and jabbed a finger at Aunt Faith—"sees fit to allow my daughter to move in with another family without so much as a by-your-leave, and now you come here, in the middle of supper, to inform me of the state of my answering machine! I may have lost my wife, God rest her soul, but I have not lost control of my family or my mind!"

He locked the pastor in a stare, then ran a hand across his chin. Nellie climbed onto Verity's lap, whimpering. Verity's attention was fixed on her father, but she knew the other children were looking at each other, and especially at her, as if she could account for what they'd just witnessed.

The pastor gathered himself and clasped his hands again. "My comment about your answering machine was not the purpose of my visit. I was just trying to be helpful."

Their father cocked his head.

"I came, in fact," the pastor continued, his voice now smooth and low, "to see you, Arthur. To see how you were coping."

The children said not a word. The only sound was the ticking of the kitchen clock. Their father held himself like a statue for what seemed to be minutes. Finally he set his shoulders and gestured to the door.

"If you don't mind, my supper is getting cold."

~

The next day was Friday, but their father didn't go to work. He didn't try to fix the washing machine, either, even though Verity had told him the problem. He had to have seen the piles of laundry; they were hard to miss. After breakfast he disappeared outside, and when Aunt Faith had packed up and said goodbye to everyone else, Verity found him in the garage, sorting through a pile of lumber. He came out to see off Aunt Faith, then went back to whatever he was doing.

Eden came home from Melissa's midmorning and helped Verity clean the kitchen. Since it wasn't raining and Verity was sick of chores, she suggested they get their brothers and sisters in uniform and head to the ship. They hadn't been on board since two Sundays ago, the last full day they had had their mother.

"Why not?" Eden said.

They kept it simple. No big battles, no complicated missions. Harper declared she no longer wanted to be the ship's doctor.

Verity was about to ask her why, but then it dawned on her. Medical records, hospital appointments, and diagnoses were no longer intriguing, just painful reminders. "What do you want to be, then?"

"I dunno." Harper looked up at the clouds racing across the sky. "Is there something with the weather?"

While Spider explained the weather gauges to Harper, Verity sat in the captain's chair with the logbook open in her lap and a pen in her hand so it looked like she was busy. In actual fact, she was making a mental list of everyone who had been there to help care for her family and who had left: her mother, Aunt Sarah, Aunt Faith, Eden, Pastor Feltner, Jude, and her father, on and off. Once upon a time, Verity had her own plan to leave, to go to Halliwell, and see what she could make of herself. Her mother had been her ally, and now that she was gone, Verity knew there was no point in bringing it up with her father. She was trapped. If her family had needed her before, they needed her ten times more now.

She closed the logbook and stared out at the yard and the house. The ship, she realized, was a perfect metaphor for what her life had become. She was stranded with her siblings, drifting out to sea, the home they longed for forever out of reach.

CHAPTER THIRTY-FIVE

SPIDER

Spider sat on the deck, his back against a locker, playing Go Fish with Nellie and Cyrus. It was keeping them happy, or at least distracted. He found that if he concentrated on the cards, tried hard to figure out what the other hands were, what card was likely to be next in the pile, he could forget for a few minutes at a time that their mother was gone forever and that, in general, life sucked.

"Got any threes, Cyrus, my man?"

"Go fish."

"Harsh." Spider picked up a card. A three. Woo-hoo.

"Spider!" his dad shouted from somewhere in the backyard. "Give me a hand, will you?"

Spider peered over the gunwale. His dad stood near the shed, holding the handles of a wheelbarrow. He hadn't gone to work—no explanation—but he'd been working hard at something because his T-shirt was all sweaty. It was hot for the end of June—maybe eighty-five—but not sticky like it would be in a month or so.

"Coming!" Spider put down his cards. "Sorry, squirts."

"It's okay," Cyrus said.

"Anyway, I won," Nellie said, adjusting Vermin on her lap.

"Did not."

"Did, too."

Spider got up. "Why don't you start a new game?" He stuck his head in the wheelhouse. Verity and Harper were deep in discussion. "Dad wants me."

Verity nodded. She glanced through the window at the bow, where Roy and Wallace were untangling ropes. "What are they up to? Practicing knots, maybe?"

"That's optimistic."

Verity smiled. Spider couldn't remember the last time he'd seen that. She said, "I'll keep an eye on them."

His father was already on the move, heading past the cars. Spider caught up with him. The wheelbarrow was full of dusty gray stuff, concrete maybe, and two shovels that rattled against the metal rim. His father didn't stop. "Get a couple five-gallon buckets from the shed, fill them with water, and meet me at the bridge."

"Yes, sir." It was a long way to lug all that water, but if his father asked him to do it, he wasn't going to whine.

"Oh, and grab a level, too."

After he brought the water, they carried four fence posts from the garage to the bridge. Spider didn't ask what they were doing, figuring his father would tell him when he felt like it. That was probably the one thing that his father appreciated about him: he was patient.

With the sun blazing overhead, they dug a hole on either side of the road, close to where it sloped down from the bridge. Spider poured water into the wheelbarrow, and his dad mixed up the concrete. Within an hour, the fence posts were standing in the wet mix, and Spider had come to the unsettling conclusion that something was going up between them. Whatever it was, it'd keep people out, cars anyway, and people, too, at least when the water was high, as it was now from all the rain.

Spider gave his father a sidelong stare, hoping for some explanation, but he was gathering the tools and laying them in the wheelbarrow.

"Better rinse this out before it sets up." He headed back toward the house.

Spider followed a few paces, then looked back at the posts. If whatever his dad was building was to keep people out, he wondered, wouldn't it keep them in, too?

~

Later that day his father left in his truck—couldn't mistake the rumble of the diesel engine—and came back a couple of hours later. He didn't come inside, just beeped the horn. Spider had been watching TV with Eden while Harper and Verity bathed the little kids. Spider and Eden were supposed to be getting dinner ready, but Eden had convinced him there was nothing to do other than reheat a bunch of stuff.

When his father hit the horn, Spider knew it was for him. He got up, stretched his arms over his head. "Don't forget dinner, Eden. Less trouble is better."

"I won't." The defeated way she said it made him think she'd actually take care of it.

Sticking out of the back of the truck was a rusty farm gate. Spider climbed into the cab. On the seat between them was a length of chain and a padlock.

"It's security," his dad said. "If Jude's not around, I don't want Verity worrying. Heck, if Jude *is* around, I don't want Verity worrying. I don't want anyone worrying, period."

Spider nodded and stared straight ahead. Worrying no matter what; that sounded about right. But about what? Old people bringing casseroles? A pastor checking in? It didn't make sense, but it was pointless to argue. He just wondered who would get the combination to the lock.

~

The next morning, when Spider came down the stairs from his room over the garage, his father's truck was gone. Good. Whether he'd gone to work or was doing something else to turn their house into Fort Knox, at least he was out of the way. His father's silence since their mother had died creeped Spider out. You could read anything into it you wanted, any sort of feeling, any sort of attitude. It bothered Spider that his father could just wall himself off like that while the rest of them had to keep things as normal as possible for each other, especially for the little kids. Spider wasn't sure where that line was drawn; was Harper one of the little ones? Either way, the older kids were left holding the bag, especially now that Aunt Faith had been sent packing. Who was looking out for them? Sure wasn't Jude, who'd taken off five days ago, supposedly to get a few things from his apartment. How long did that take? Spider had just gotten used to Jude being there, actually helping, making a difference, and now that his brother had abandoned ship—again—it was worse than if he'd just stayed away. Their mother had died, for freaking sake, and all Jude could think about was himself.

As Spider crossed the lawn to the house, he made a promise to talk to Verity and Eden, see how they were doing. You couldn't always tell from how someone acted; he was the first to understand that. He'd woken up in the middle of the night and felt the wide-open space where his mother had been. He'd cried for who knew how long, worrying about whether she'd been in pain when she died, worrying that he hadn't been as good to her as he could've been, worrying that he'd forget all the details about her—the way her hugs felt, the way she smelled, her smile—and he thought he'd never be happy again. He wouldn't know where to look for the kind of happiness his mother made all around her just by being herself.

Did any of that show on his face this morning? He doubted it.

He opened the front door and knew right away something was wrong. All his brothers and sisters were in the living room, huddled around the wall below the stairs, talking at the same time.

Wallace saw him first. "The phone's gone!" He was excited, like it was a mystery they had to solve.

Roy threw his arms out to the side, blocking Nellie and Cyrus. "Nobody touch anything. There might be fingerprints."

Spider looked at the wall. The bracket was still attached. The paint was lighter where the phone had been.

Verity pointed at the small table below. "The answering machine is gone, too."

"It had to be Dad," Eden said. "Who else?"

"A robber!" Roy shouted. "We better check what else is missing." He motioned to Wallace. "Come on!"

They charged off up the stairs. Nellie looked like she might follow them but hung on to Verity's hand instead. Cyrus stared at Spider, like he knew the truth. It occurred to him that he was the oldest boy or man or whatever. Harper was waiting for him to weigh in, too.

"If Dad took it, it was only to fix it. Remember Pastor Feltner said the machine was full? Maybe it wasn't full. Maybe it was broken." Harper squinted at him, like she wasn't buying it, but she didn't say anything. She was old enough to realize their dad wasn't exactly stable, even before he made off with the phone. Spider's worry about his dad cranked up, but he had to keep it cool for the kids. "I'm starving. Who wants pancakes?"

Harper helped him make the batter while Eden read to Cyrus and Nellie. Spider heated the griddle and stole glances at Verity, sitting in the living room by herself staring at where the phone had been. He hadn't told her or any of the others about the gate. If someone had asked him what he had been doing, he would've said, but his father didn't bring it up over dinner, so Spider figured it was better not to volunteer the information. Now with the phone and answering machine gone, his thinking had changed.

"First batch is ready." He handed Harper the plate and started in on the next batch. When those were done, he put three on a plate for himself and ate at the stove so he could tend to the third batch. Pancakes for eight was a freaking marathon, but it was pretty much the only thing he could cook, so he didn't mind.

When everyone was stuffed, Spider took Verity aside. "I need to talk to you and Eden in private."

"Got it." Verity headed into the dining room and came back with coloring books and crayons. She handed them out to Roy, Wally, Cyrus, and Nellie, and announced there would be special dispensation for a Disney movie tonight if they could manage to play nicely for a half hour. Harper had gone upstairs, so the older kids didn't have to worry about her.

Verity led the way into the Room of Secrets and motioned Eden inside. Spider closed the door behind them and leaned against it as a precaution because there wasn't a lock.

"What's going on?" Eden said. "Do you know something about the phone?"

He shook his head. "That was a surprise. This is about yesterday, when Dad needed my help."

Verity said, "I thought it was some random cleanup or repair thing. He's been on a mission."

"Nope. First I helped him put in fence posts on either side of the road, right before the bridge." Verity and Eden exchanged confused looks. "Then later he showed up with a big rusty gate, said we'd attach it to the posts once the concrete dries and close it up with a chain and a padlock."

"What the hell?" Eden said.

Verity frowned. "Did he say why?"

"Something about keeping you—keeping us safe. But why all of a sudden? Why now?"

"That makes no sense," Verity said.

"None."

Eden threw her head back and her arms down to her sides in frustration, knocking over two cans of beans on a shelf. "I can't believe him!"

"Shhhh!" Verity warned.

Eden dropped her voice to a hoarse whisper. "He's totally losing it. He railed on Aunt Faith, who actually was really helping, then was so rude to the pastor. I hate going to church, but I would never be that rude to that guy, just in case." She took a deep breath, let it out. "Plus he was being nice. And now Dad's locking out the world? What the hell?" Her face was red, and the muscles in her jaw were throbbing. In the silence that followed her tirade, though, it all melted. Her shoulders dropped, and tears fell down her cheeks. "What the hell?" she whispered.

Verity put a hand on Eden's shoulder, like a lion tamer with a prod. When Eden didn't flinch, Verity pulled her into a hug. Spider felt awkward, too big for that space, towering over his sisters, who, despite all their differences, despite all the places they rubbed each other the wrong way, could get past it and hold each other. Spider remembered the way Eden and Jude had fallen against each other in their parents' room, the day they learned their mother was going to die soon. It seemed easy for them, this reaching out, this breaking through. He didn't know how.

When he thought of his brothers and sisters, the older ones, it was usually in terms of where they stood in relation to him, to his parents, like they were pieces in some game whose rules were written in a language he didn't speak. He didn't feel like a pawn or an outsider or whatever it was often because he didn't dwell on that kind of thing. But when he did, he worried about who was up and who was down.

Everything was different now. The system was collapsing. Instead of a steady, driving force, their father was becoming unpredictable. Who knew what was next, what they would all become because of it?

There in the Room of Secrets, his sisters must have felt it, too, the sense of spinning out of control. Verity's arm was looped around Eden's shoulder, and he put his hand on it, then he bent down and kissed the top of Eden's head.

"Ick," Eden said.

Spider knew she didn't mean it.

CHAPTER
THIRTY-SIX

JUDE

Since coming back to Richmond, Jude had stewed about his father pretty much nonstop. The only time it was off his mind was during the few nights he worked the board at the Night Train. The owner had been sympathetic about Jude's mom and his time away, but there wasn't anything he could do about getting him more nights. Jude had too much free time and not enough money. He played his guitar and slept at random times and scrounged food from his roommates. The haphazard meals and weird hours made him miss his family's routines. Odd things popped into his mind—the feel of Cyrus's hand in his, the way Harper pulled on her hair while she ate, the sweet sound of Eden singing Nellie to sleep—but it wasn't enough to outweigh how much it hurt to be nothing to his father. He'd called the house a couple of times, planning to hang up if his father answered, but no one picked up. Out on the ship was his guess.

About two weeks in, on the Fourth of July, he'd spent the morning fooling around on his guitar and gotten bored with it—a sure sign that something had to happen. He decided to call Uncle Henry. He hadn't talked to him since the service, and then only for a few minutes. Jude had no idea what they had talked about.

Uncle Henry picked up right away. "Hello?"

"It's Jude. You making lunch? I can call later."

"Just a sandwich. I'm going to a barbecue later."

"People from the dealership?"

"Nah, a new lady friend is having a crowd. Sounded like the sort of low-pressure situation I might be able to manage in exchange for a plate of ribs." Jude laughed. "Where are you, anyway?"

Jude recounted his conversation with his father, and the dilemma surrounding keeping his apartment.

"If money's the problem, I could help you out, but it seems like you ought to decide where you need to be."

His uncle was opening jars. Jude could see them lined up: mayo, Colman's, sweet pickle. It was stupid, but it gave Jude a pang of loneliness. "I know."

"Here's my two. You've lost your mother, and that's a hard knock, but you gotta think of your father, too. Maeve wasn't just his wife for twenty-four years. She was the center of his universe. His best friend—hell, maybe his only friend. Not making any excuses, not a one, but no man is at his best after losing a person like that."

Jude sighed. "You're right."

"Don't do anything because of me. Make up your own mind."

"Okay. I will." Jude flashed on the thought that his life would have been so much smoother if Uncle Henry had been his father—someone he could talk to, who listened. Jude felt guilty for thinking it, but that didn't stop it from being true.

Uncle Henry had been walking around, but now the line was silent. "That Nova of yours still going?"

"Just about."

"Your dad used to like to work on cars. You could ask him for a hand sorting it out. Might take his mind off things, give you both something to do."

Why hadn't he thought of that? Too busy being angry to come up with ways to make things better. "Thanks, Uncle Henry. I'll do that." Jude felt a sense of certainty and relief that'd been scarce a good long while. "Enjoy your ribs."

"I'll do that. And call anytime."

As soon as Jude hung up, he knew he was going home. He had to make his own decisions, not wait for his father to decide for him. He was an adult! Sure, his father hadn't begged him to stay; he also hadn't told him to go. Jude's brothers and sisters needed him—at least it had started to feel that way—so he'd go back. It was what his mother would've wanted; he was certain of that. Once he settled on it, it felt right to him, too.

It took him exactly two days to find a guy to rent his room from the message board at the club. The room was cheap and in a pretty safe neighborhood, and that combo was an easy sell. The next day, he got some boxes from the liquor store down the street and started packing. He didn't have a lot of crap, so it took only a couple of hours. Everything Jude owned fit in his car, which was either pathetic or minimalistic— take your pick. He'd tried calling home to let them know he was coming, but no one answered, and the voice mail didn't kick in. No one was deleting messages, he guessed.

He lugged his two duffel bags, guitar, and backpack out to his car, loaded everything in the back, then went inside again to leave a note for his roommates with the phone number of the house in Mobjack. He hadn't done that last time, not that they'd had reason to call, but this time he didn't plan on coming back.

He scrounged for a piece of paper and ended up tearing off the flap of a cereal box from the trash. *Stay weird, you guys,* he wrote. *Something*

cool comes up at the club, call me, and I'll meet you. (703) 555-2312.
Considering the state of his car, it was more hope than promise.

~

The day was muggy, and Jude drove with the windows down. His favorite station was doing a Creedence tribute, and that, combined with the warm air flowing through the car and the familiar road running under his wheels, gave him a hopeful feeling, like maybe things had to get this bad before they could get better. He missed his mother, thought about her all the time, but the sense of loss wasn't fresh. He'd had five years of practice.

He turned off the main road, slowing down on the loose gravel. The clouds were thick and low, and the bay was a solid slice of steel. The air stalled inside the car, and sweat trickled down his back. The water looked inviting, and he thought about taking a carload of his brothers and sisters to Gloucester Point for a swim.

The road curved and the bridge came into view. He slowed down to a crawl, not wanting to catch his front bumper on the rise. Something was on the far side of the bridge. A gate? What was that doing there? It was on their property, so there was only one person who could be responsible.

He nosed the car onto the bridge. From there he spotted the padlock. Great. There wasn't any place to park between the bridge and the gate, so he backed off the bridge until he got to a wider part of the road. He parked and went to see what the hell was going on.

There was a yard of dry ground on the outside of the fencing, so getting on the far side of the gate was easy. At high tide, or after a heavy rain, it would be harder. A person could just climb over, but it wasn't as though they got much foot traffic. Jude yanked on the padlock, which didn't budge, and walked to the house, the hopeful feeling from before gone, just like that.

He let himself in. Roy and Wallace jumped up from the couch where they were watching TV and tackled him. "Jude! Jude! Jude!"

Cyrus and Nellie hung back a little, wary or tired, he couldn't tell. Nellie was sucking her thumb, something he'd never seen before. All four of them looked wild, hair uncombed, clothes stained, knees filthy. Things had gone south without him, which made him a dirtbag.

"Where are the big kids?" Jude asked.

Roy and Wallace shrugged. Cyrus pointed toward the back of the house.

"We can watch TV whenever we want," Nellie said. "Unless Daddy is home." She pointed to the open curtain. "We take turns on lookout but not until later."

That didn't sound good. "I'm going to say hi to everyone, okay?"

Roy stood in front of him, his enthusiasm dissolving into worry. "Are you really staying or leaving again?"

"Staying for now," Jude said, and realized immediately how wishy-washy that would sound to a little kid. "I want to stay."

Roy didn't acknowledge the save and went back to the couch. All four of them were bunched up together, not fighting for space, like baby monkeys in a cage. Jude walked away before their sorry state hit him harder.

Verity and Harper were hanging up laundry on the line and didn't see him right away. Jude glanced around for Spider and Eden, but they were either on the ship or out. He called to his sisters.

"Jude!" Harper dropped a shirt into the basket and came over to him. He opened his arms, and she accepted a quick hug, then went back to what she'd been doing. Jude's throat got tight when he saw how much she looked like their mother. It wasn't exactly a secret, but maybe because Harper looked older now, not a little kid anymore, the resemblance was thrown into focus.

Verity gave him a wary smile over the sheet she was hanging up. "You're back."

"Yeah. Sorry about that. I tried to call."

Verity and Harper exchanged a look.

"Something happen to the phone?"

"And the answering machine," Harper said. "Daddy took them. At least we think he did, because why would anyone else do that?"

"Why would he do it?" Again, his sisters looked at each other. He saw now how strained they both were despite the smiles. "And what's up with the gate? When did that happen?"

Verity sighed and picked up a few clothespins from the bucket at her feet. "It just happened. Like the phone. We don't know any more than you do."

"Do you have a key at least?"

She straightened her shoulders. "We're not locked in, if that's what you mean."

"I don't mean anything." The thought had occurred to him, but he wasn't about to admit it. "My car is on the other side of the bridge, though."

Eden burst through the back door, slamming it against the side of the house. She stood with her feet apart and her hands on her hips, and Jude knew he was in for it.

"Decided to grace us with your presence, huh?"

Harper said, "She's in a bad mood because she's grounded for the rest of the summer."

"Think you're so smart, Harper? From what I can see, we're all pretty much grounded."

Jude looked from one sister to another for an explanation.

Verity said, "I can't find the keys to the station wagon." She didn't say *Mom's car*. "I asked Dad, and he said he didn't know, either, then another time he said he'd get whatever we needed."

Eden snorted. "Which is why we're drinking powdered milk and eating canned beans practically every day."

Jude asked, "What happened to the casserole brigade?"

"Daddy," Eden said. "Daddy's what happened."

When neither Verity nor Harper rushed to their father's defense, Jude knew he'd made the right decision coming home. Why was their father pulling this crazy shit? Had he lost his freaking mind?

"I can go get food. I can do that now." He pulled his wallet out of the back pocket of his jeans. "I've got sixteen dollars."

~

By the time Jude heard their father's truck rumble down the drive, dinner was long over. The kids had eaten mounds of Hamburger Helper, corn, and carrots, and at least two glasses of milk each. The feast made them sleepy, and Jude had a hard time lifting the deadweight of Wallace out of the bath. Cyrus fell asleep on a makeshift mattress in the boys' room, and Nellie went straight into Verity's bed—where she ended up every night anyway, according to Verity.

Spider hadn't exactly rolled out the welcome mat. He'd grunted hello to Jude, ignored him the rest of the evening, then grabbed a pillow and sleeping bag and gone outside, to the ship, Jude figured. Hey, if the guy wanted to get eaten by mosquitoes, that was up to him. After Jude had helped get the groceries in, he'd unloaded his car, and although he hadn't unpacked, he was as settled as he was going to be.

He gave his father a good hour to eat, shower, and chill before he left the room over the garage and headed to the house. He didn't know what he was going to say other than this was where he felt he ought to be, that he planned to stay to help because this was his family. His father knew he was there because of his car, and the fact that he hadn't come up to his room and chewed him out already was a good sign.

Jude let himself in and, not seeing his father in the living room or kitchen, went down the carpeted hallway to his parents' bedroom. His dad's bedroom. Before he got to the half-closed door, he heard his father talking.

"Now, Maeve, I know that's what you said, but it's not that simple." A pause. "Yes, of course I know that. I'm doing my best. The children just don't understand." Another pause. "I'm doing my best. It's just impossible without you. I don't want to do it without you. And I'm angry."

The conversation sounded almost normal, as if his mother were a little too far away to be heard or was whispering in response so Jude heard only his father's side. It sent a chill up his spine—talking to a dead person?—but also he felt a pang of something else. Jealousy. If only he could hear his mother's voice.

Inside the bedroom the lights were dim, just a bedside lamp, he guessed. Jude didn't want to interrupt whatever was going on, but he had come to talk to his father, after all. He paused in the doorway and leaned in, about to announce himself, but what he saw stopped him.

His father was perched on his mother's side of the bed, facing the headboard. The bedding had been pulled back, and the pillow lay flat. On the bed next to his father was one of his mother's nightgowns and the pale-blue bathrobe she'd had for years, both arranged as if she were lying with them on. Her slippers were next to the bed.

Jude stood frozen, trying to make sense of what he was seeing. It was so messed up.

His father held one cuff of the robe in his hand. "I can't let go of it, Maeve. I just can't. If he'd driven faster, if we'd gotten you to the hospital quicker, they could've saved you. They could've." His father bent his head and began sobbing, huge heaving sobs that flooded the space between him and his son.

Jude turned away, his mind spinning. He rushed down the hallway, his feet carrying him out of the house, out onto the lawn, where he couldn't hear his father anymore. What had he been saying? That it was Jude's fault his mother had died? That was as crazy as talking to empty clothes. It'd been clear to Jude, and the doctors had confirmed it in front of his father, that her heart attack had been—what were the words?—"massive and immediately fatal." But, sure, blame him.

He ought to leave, grab his bags, go. He looked out toward the bridge, remembered the gate.

He'd have to get the key from Verity or, worse, from his father. He could not handle either the disappointment or the indifference. He turned his face to the night sky, sprinkled with stars, and wished with his whole heart that his mother would talk to him, even if it meant he was as crazy as his father. He'd take that because right now he needed her to tell him what to do. But she wasn't in the sky, or beyond the stars, in heaven, whatever that was. She wasn't anywhere he could find her, and that knowledge filled him with a sadness deeper than he'd ever felt. Jude had thought getting older meant the sharp edges of your feelings got coated with something that made them easier to live with, to swallow. Most of the adults he knew weren't thrown around by their feelings the way he was, or had recently been, as a teenager.

All that was wrong, he guessed. Feelings didn't get easier at all. When you got older, you got knocked down by bigger things. Just look at his father.

Jude climbed the steps outside the garage, his feet as heavy as his heart. It'd been a long, crushing day. If his father was looking around for someone to blame for his mother's death, Jude was a convenient target. He was used to being that punching bag. Given their history, it'd be weird if his father didn't blame him for something.

Jude let himself into the room, flicked on the light, and lay down on the bed, hands behind his head. He decided he would pretend he'd never overheard what his father said. Jude had come back for his brothers and sisters, not for his father. As long as the old man didn't lay his crazy shit on him in broad daylight, Jude would stay right here where he belonged.

CHAPTER
THIRTY-SEVEN

HARPER

Ship's Log: USS *Nepenthe*
Date: Sunday, July 20, 1980
Time: 1225h
Weather: 92°F, Cloudy
Winds: 0–5 kn SSE
CO: Lt. Commander V. Vergennes

Muggy and buggy. That'd pretty much been the story for the last couple of weeks. Now that Harper was ship meteorologist, she knew she ought to refer to it as "high relative humidity" and "ideal breeding climate for biting pests." *Muggy and buggy* was easier.

Roy waved a hand in front of his face to scatter the mosquitoes. "Where's the Skin So Soft?"

"On the desk in the wheelhouse." Technically, the lotion was part of the medical supplies and no longer her problem, but there was no point in being a wiener.

Harper leaned back against the locker and balanced the weather notebook on her raised leg. She'd found the notebook in the dining room, crammed in a box with a bunch of random paper and coloring books and whatnot. Normally she'd have had to ask permission to just make off with something like that—it had a hard cover, and the paper was super smooth—but nothing was normal anymore, and if Daddy wasn't right there, permission was something you just gave yourself. She entered the temperature, humidity, and barometric pressure in a table and tried to take readings three times a day. When Spider first showed her how to read the gauges, he'd said she could check it against the newspaper, but since they didn't get the newspaper anymore because Daddy didn't pay the bill, either the gauges were right or they weren't. Every week she made a graph of the daily averages using a ruler to connect the dots and different colors for the different measures. It was something to do.

Two weeks ago she'd asked her dad to take her to the library to get a book about weather. It'd been after dinner, pretty much the only time to nail him down. He got up super early and left for work and didn't take time off like he used to, sometimes not even on Sunday, not that it mattered since they didn't go to church anymore. Funny how you could miss something that dorky.

"Next time I go into town, sure."

"When's that going to be?"

He rubbed his face, like he was trying to wake up. "I don't know, Harper." He got up, put his glass on the counter. "Won't the encyclo-pedia do?"

She didn't answer. As he left the room, he clapped a hand on her shoulder, the way he did with the boys. It was worse than not being touched at all.

Harper hadn't wanted to go into the dining room where the ency-clopedia was because the piano was in there. But her father hadn't given her much choice, so she went before she changed her mind.

She found the switch on the wall, and even though she turned her head to the left, where the bookcases were, she still saw the piano, and the floor went soft and she had to hold on to the doorknob tight. Her mom was all over the house, and inside her brothers and sisters, but the piano was purely hers, like another leg. Harper swallowed hard and went over to the encyclopedias with the piano behind her. It was easier like that.

That night she read about the weather and wanted to take notes, and that was when she found the notebook. She came back again and again, and it was never as hard as the first time and even came to feel a little like she was hanging out with her mom in there.

Back on the ship, Roy stood in front of her holding the lotion bottle upside down. "It's empty."

"Tell Eden. She's in charge of supplies."

He didn't move. Wallace was off to the side and watched him like he might detonate. Roy had been so un-Roy lately.

"She's not here, is she!" He tossed the bottle overboard, threw his arms in the air. "None of you older kids are any good! You don't know how to be an adult! You don't know how to be a mom!" Tears were running down his cheeks. "I hate you! I hate all of you!" He leaped over the gunwale and practically threw himself down the gangplank, wheeling his arms to keep his balance as he hit the ground.

Verity was coming out of the wheelhouse when the yelling started. Harper expected her to run after Roy, expected her to do something, but she just stood there. Wallace followed Roy off the ship, no salute, no permission, and ran after him all the way to the back door. They disappeared inside.

Harper stared at Verity. Cyrus and Nellie had come up from below, and Spider came up to the ship from the shed. They all watched as Verity froze solid on the deck. Her hands were shaking, then her shoulders shook, too, hard, like she was being electrocuted.

"Verity," Harper whispered, though she didn't know why. "It's okay. It's just Roy. He didn't mean it."

Her whole body was shaking now, like it was the middle of winter, except she was sweating, too. Harper wanted to do something to help, but her mind was like a broken gauge. She repeated herself. "He didn't mean it, Verity."

Spider shouted from the lawn, "Everything okay up there?"

Verity looked right at Harper. Her eyes were bloodshot, and she swayed like a pine in the wind. "It's too hard, Harper. This is all too hard. I can't do it."

Harper didn't know what to say. None of this was fair. She looked at Nellie and Cyrus in their white caps, their faces painted with worry, and thought about how mad Roy was and how Wallace worried twice, once for himself and again for Roy. Harper thought about how Jude was okay to have around but not the answer, either. He was their brother and he was trying to help, doing the cooking and whatnot, but no one could fix what was wrong. Ever.

They all needed to forget about their sadness and worry for a while, even if things would be exactly the same after.

Harper stood and gave Verity her sharpest salute. "Captain, I propose a long mission." She was winging it but felt she was on the right track. "At least overnight, sir. Maybe longer."

Verity blinked once, digging herself out of her funk, then nodded slowly.

Verity and Eden and Spider—and Jude—couldn't make up for their mom being gone or for their dad being a ghost and acting crazy. None of them could fix everything that was wrong, but while they were on the USS *Nepenthe*, they could pull together and honor her. They could try. Ship's business.

"Harper," Verity said, checking the ship clock, "see if you can catch the weather on Channel 7. Let's hope it's a good night for a sail."

Harper hesitated. As of two weeks ago, they were absolutely forbidden from watching TV unless their dad gave permission. He'd threatened to get rid of it when Verity had let the little kids watch cartoons on Saturday morning and hadn't run it by him. He was at work now, but you never knew.

"That's an order," Verity said.

～

While Harper waited for the weather to come on, she jumped up and checked the driveway every few minutes for her dad. Roy and Wallace were sitting on the floor with their noses practically touching the TV screen. It was just the news, plus some ads, but they'd been starved of TV, so even Mr. Clean grinning like an idiot would do.

Wallace pointed at the screen. "Weather guy's on!"

Duh, dinobrain, Harper thought but didn't say. She and Wallace didn't do the insult game anymore. Maybe they only ever had because it made their mom smile.

The weather guy looked like Tweedledee and had a really low voice. "The low-pressure system that's responsible for the high humidity we've been experiencing throughout the viewing area will likely break by tomorrow night. Expect thunderstorms, heavy at times, continuing through Tuesday, tapering off Wednesday morning as a high moves in." The guy gave a sideways smile to the camera. "It's always something, right?"

Roy twisted around. "Weather's okay tonight, then, right, Harper?" She'd told the twins about the plan for a long mission.

"Right." She tried to hear what the weather guy was saying now. He pointed at a map of the Atlantic; she recognized it right away from the snatches of other weather reports she'd seen.

"—tropical depression forming in the south Atlantic. We'll keep an eye on that in the coming days. In the meantime, back to you, Judy."

～

Between the noon weather report and dinnertime, the idea for an overnight on the ship had turned into a major production. Harper wasn't exactly sure how it happened. It might've started with Eden, who had wandered out to the boat looking for lunch. She ended up suggesting to Cyrus and Nellie that they make treats for the overnight.

"Brownies, if we have the ingredients," she said as she chewed her bologna sandwich.

"We don't know how," Cyrus said, frowning.

Nellie pulled her thumb out of her mouth. "Anyway, we're not allowed to use the oven and burn down the house."

"Jude will show you guys, and I'll supervise," Eden said.

"Hey, look." Spider leaned on the starboard side of the wheelhouse and pointed to the row of signal flags.

Harper studied them. "Oh! One for each of our first letters. In order."

Spider tied off the line, jumped down to the deck, and they all stood there and admired them. This was theirs: the mission, the flags, the duties, the ship.

"How about some lights?" Verity said. "Like Christmas."

Spider smiled. "Roy, Wally. You're my deputy electrical crew. Let's make her shine."

Harper watched them leave the ship, the twins running and jostling each other playfully for the first time since—well, the worst day ever. It made her feel hopeful, like even if things would never be the same, maybe they wouldn't always be terrible.

~

Humidity in the air made for colorful sunsets; that was one of the many things Harper had learned about weather. That evening, the Vergennes kids sat on the ship's lockers, or on the bow, eating frozen pizza off paper towels and watching the fireball of a sun sink behind the trees, turning the sky more shades of orange, red, and pink than there were in the Crayola 120-crayon set. They passed around a gallon of milk, drinking out of the carton because who wanted more dishes to wash? Their manners had slid a little—okay, maybe a lot—and they'd stopped wearing their white uniforms every time they were on board. Verity didn't enforce it because it was too hard to keep up with the regular laundry. They'd become the Bad News Bears of the navy. So what.

Around six, Jude came out of the house carrying another tray of pizza and the radio from the kitchen. "Thought you sailors could use some tunes." He handed the pizza to Spider. "I've had mine, so do your worst."

"Thanks, man." That was warm and fuzzy for those two.

Verity took the radio. "You wanna come up?"

That was a first. Why not? He was their brother. Even Spider didn't even freak out at the suggestion.

Jude looked at all of them wedged into every corner of the ship and smiled. "Thanks for the offer, Captain. How about I pull up a chair?"

Eden tuned the radio to a pop station, but with the volume low so no one would get crazy. Spider lay on his back on the engine housing, one hand behind his head, the other one shoving his tenth slice of pizza in his mouth. "The lights are rad. We should keep them up."

Harper looked around. They'd kind of gone overboard, pun intended. There must've been eight strings of lights, white ones and colored ones, ones that blinked and ones that didn't, strung up along the gunwales, the rails, and the canopy, and twisted in the signal-flag line. She and Eden had made paper stars, the way they'd learned to do snowflakes, folding the paper and making little cuts everywhere, and taped them on all the windows. Harper couldn't remember the last time she'd done anything with Eden other than argue or cry.

Harper reached for another slice of pizza and saw it was the last one. She nudged Eden, who sat cross-legged beside her. "You wanna split this?"

"Sure. I'm so hungry tonight."

They all were. It was like they'd left a part of their heartache behind when they set sail that night.

The sky went inky. The air didn't exactly cool, but Harper's shirt stopped sticking to her back. Cyrus unwrapped the tray of brownies and passed it around. Verity handed one down to Jude. "Little Jeannie" came on the radio. Eden, an Elton John superfan, knew all the lyrics to all his songs, even the weird ones, and she sang along, softly. She had the best voice of any of them, except their mom, of course. Nellie laid her head in Verity's lap and played with the frayed ends of her shorts. Two seconds later she was fast asleep. Harper was about to doze off herself.

Spider bolted upright and pointed at the drive. "The truck."

She'd forgotten about their father. Completely forgotten about him.

Verity was facing the other way, and eased Nellie off her lap so she could kneel on the locker and see the drive. Roy and Wallace had been lying on the bow stargazing, pointing out constellations to each other but mostly making them up, but now they were quiet and went up on their elbows.

The truck came to a stop. They heard the truck door close and the crunch of his feet on the gravel. Then the footsteps stopped. Jude had left a light on in the house, so when their father changed course and headed toward the ship, having no doubt seen it lit up like a Christmas tree, they could just make him out in the darkness.

"What in the Lord's name is going on out here?" He did not sound happy.

Verity got up and went to the gunwale. Harper, Eden, and Spider did, too. Jude got up out of his chair.

"We're staying here tonight," Verity said.

He waved his arm. "Who said you could put up all those lights? Who gave you permission?"

Spider said, "I put them up."

Roy said, "We helped!"

Their father took a step closer, his hands on his hips.

"On my orders," Verity said.

"Is that so?"

"Yes."

Not "Yes, sir," Harper thought. She stole a look at Verity. She was serious as serious could be.

Jude said, "It's a harmless party. They deserve it."

Their father glared at him, then turned to Verity. "It's foolish non-sense. Waste of electricity! You think we've got the money to burn it like that?" He was right below them now. Jude moved closer, his back nearly against the hull. Their father hadn't shaved in ages, and his beard made him different—not in a good way. He looked mean. "Get off the damn boat and come inside and go to bed. All of you!"

Nellie had woken up and was hanging on Verity's arm. Cyrus had wedged himself between Eden and Harper. No one said a word.

Their father trained his glare at Roy and Wallace on the bow. "Jude, go grab those two!"

Jude put his hands on his hips, shook his head.

Their father scowled at him, then turned back to the rest of them. "Didn't you hear me? I said get off the boat and go to bed!"

"No," Verity said, almost too quiet for their father to hear. Almost.

"What—"

"No!"

"I don't know who you think—"

"No!" Verity gripped the rail like she was hanging on to it for dear life. "We are not coming inside!"

"No!" shouted Nellie.

Their father glared at them all, his jaw working. Harper worried for a moment that he would board the ship and punish them, one by one. Would Jude stop him? Their dad wasn't a hitter, maybe swatted their bums once or twice when they were little to bring home an important lesson. But they were older now; what exactly could he do, especially if they stuck together?

Something like that must've been going through his mind, because when none of the kids said anything, just held their positions on the ship, under their captain's orders, he let it go. Their father stalked off back the way he'd come, disappearing into the darkness.

Good riddance, Harper thought, and felt only a little guilty for it.

CHAPTER THIRTY-EIGHT

Cyrus

Ship's Log: USS *Nepenthe*
Date: Sunday, July 20, 1980
Time: 2125h
Weather: 78°F, Clear
Winds: 0–5 kn SSE
CO: Lt. Commander V. Vergennes

Cyrus finished his watch at 2000h, which was eight at night if you weren't on the ship, but he wasn't sleepy, not even a little. He was lying in the bow berth next to Spider, who was also not sleepy. The whole ship felt awake, not just the crew—the whole ship. Cyrus remembered back when he was little how he'd had an elephant named Elephant, and when he got sick with a bad fever, Elephant woke up for real. Not "came alive," but woke up because Elephant had always been alive to him, always real, just not awake until then. That was how the ship felt now, like a gigantic boulder that all of a sudden was taking long, deep breaths.

"You okay, my man?" Spider asked.

The bow berth was the same as the galley; you just added boards in between the counters and put cushions on top. Spider had started sleeping there even when it wasn't an overnight because he didn't want to share a room with Jude.

"Uh-huh."

"Excited about the Bermuda Triangle?"

"Sure, but do ships really disappear there?" It'd been worrying him since Verity announced the next mission. She and Eden and Spider had put their heads together and decided.

"That's what they say. Our mission is to find out, get close enough without being in danger."

This also had been worrying him. "If the ships disappear, then how do you know exactly where the Triangle is?"

Spider smiled in the dark. It was funny how smiles showed up like that. "I'm the navigator, so leave that to me."

"Okay."

Cyrus listened to someone shuffling across the bow overhead and tried to remember who was on watch. Wallace had relieved him, so maybe Roy. Cyrus thought about the twins on the bow when their father had ordered them all to get off the ship, how their father had expected them all to do what he said and was surprised they didn't, but most disappointed in Roy and Wallace, like he could chop them off from the rest. Cyrus didn't feel as bad about disobeying his father as he thought he would. He didn't want to go inside with his father, didn't want to go anywhere with him anymore. He wanted to say something to Spider about it but didn't know what. They had all decided the same thing.

"I'm going to sleep now," Cyrus said, turning on his side to face his brother.

Spider reached out his arm, and Cyrus took hold of it, tucked it against his chest, and folded his knees up so Spider's hand was on his thigh. The arm smelled like Skin So Soft and pizza and summer air. "Sweet dreams, my man."

Cyrus closed his eyes. Somewhere out near the river, an owl hooted once, twice, three times. Another owl, farther away, answered. Were there owls in the Bermuda Triangle? Seemed like there ought to be. Also, palm trees and white monkeys and pirates standing over their treasure on beaches made of black sand. As sleep crept into the berth and crawled over him, Cyrus imagined many mysterious and beautiful things waiting for them far out in the Atlantic Ocean, and he was glad, so very glad, he had disobeyed his father. He was, after all, a sailor, an accountable and responsible one. He couldn't have his mother anymore, but he wasn't giving up his ship.

With that settled in his mind, with his brother's arm against his chest, and the ship's lights twinkling below the stars, Cyrus drifted into sleep.

CHAPTER
THIRTY-NINE

VERITY

Ship's Log: USS *Nepenthe*
Date: Monday, July 21, 1980
Time: 1005h
Weather: 91°F, Overcast
Winds: 10–15 kn S
CO: Lt. Commander V. Vergennes

Verity had seen their father leave in his truck a half hour ago, but the crew had been too engrossed in launching artillery at the Bermudan sea monsters to notice. They hadn't left the ship since the confrontation with their father, and if he was on their minds, no one let on. Eden was playing what she called "motivational massacre music" over the radio at full volume, and the rock beat energized everyone. Harper and Nellie broke out into an impromptu dance routine to "Rockin' in the U.S.A." and Verity laughed harder than she had in an awfully long time. It felt like a betrayal of the grief she ought to be feeling, and also extremely good, like a cold shower on a hot day.

"Hey, sailors!" Jude yelled out from the back door. "Chow's ready whenever you are."

Verity smiled and waved at him. He'd been pitching in like crazy since he came back, not retreating to the garage all the time, and more important, he'd stuck by them last night. If she could count on him to stay stuck, she'd feel less like everything was on her. She didn't dare ask him, though. What if he had plans to leave? She couldn't handle it. "I'll send them in two at a time, okay? So they can use the bathroom and get cleaned up."

He gave her the thumbs-up. Verity called to Cyrus and Nellie, "Ship's Cook and Ship's Cook's Mate are granted temporary leave." They were bleary from interrupted sleep, and their hair and clothes were a mess, but their limbs were looser, their faces more relaxed as they toddled down the gangway. After a resupply and some housekeeping, Verity planned to extend their mission for at least another day.

Jude scooped up Nellie and took Cyrus by the hand. It'd been only a few days since Nellie would let anyone other than Verity hold her. Such a small step but huge for Nellie and Verity—and Jude.

"Where you guys been?" Jude asked.

"In the Bermuda Triangle," Cyrus announced proudly.

"Cool. I'll bet it made you hungry." Before he turned to go back inside, he caught Verity's eye. He was pretty far away, but if she had to guess, he wanted to be forgiven for leaving her vulnerable and then abandoning all of them, and for leaving again. It was hard for him, she got that, but really all he had to do was ask.

~

Twenty minutes later, Verity put Eden in charge and took the twins in to eat. They burst into the kitchen, jabbering to Jude about blasting sea monsters and rescuing lost ships. Cyrus and Nellie were finishing their eggs and toast, swaying over their plates with exhaustion. The doorbell rang and Verity startled. Since their father had installed the gate, not a single person had come to the front door. People might've gotten as far as the gate and turned around, but there was no way to know, especially with the phone gone.

"You want me to get it?" Jude asked, frowning.

"No, I got it. Wallace, Roy, go upstairs and get cleaned up. I promise you can go back to the ship if you do a good job, okay?" She was already at the door, shooing them up the stairs. "Jude'll get you breakfast. Be good now."

Verity smoothed her hands over her hair and discovered a tangled braid she'd forgotten was there. Her white trousers were stained, as was her shirt, but there was nothing she could do about that. What did it matter, anyway? She opened the door a few inches. It was her father's boss, the owner of the country club. She pulled the door wide. "Mr. Reynolds. Hello."

When she unlatched the screen door, she spotted the policeman next to Mr. Reynolds. Her heart stopped. Everyone knew Sheriff Mooney, and everyone knew that the police didn't come to your house unless there was trouble—or very bad news. Her knees started to melt, and she gripped the doorframe.

"It's all right, miss," the sheriff said. "Your father is fine. We just wanted to talk." He was a big man, his undershirt showing in the gaps between the straining buttons of his uniform, half moons of sweat under his arms. He offered her a weak smile.

Her feet wouldn't move. Mr. Reynolds stood there, a golf cap in his hands. He wasn't very tall, but he was squared off and solid looking, like a barricade, and his crew cut made his head look square, too. He had on a striped polo and tan slacks with a sharp crease down the front. She'd never gotten the impression that he was friendly, but he was without question a good man. She'd always felt that, even before she learned how generous he was to her family. It was his eyes, she thought now. Everything about him was squared off, but his eyes were soft and blue. She relaxed a little.

"Morning, Verity," he said. "Sorry to intrude this way, and we didn't mean to frighten you. Mind if we come in?"

She glanced at the driveway, confused for a moment about why only her mother's car was there—the keys still missing—but then she remembered the gate. They'd walked in from the bridge.

"Sure. I mean, no, I don't mind." She should do better. What would her mother say? "I could make coffee."

"We won't trouble you for coffee, but thank you."

They followed her inside. Jude came in from the kitchen to see what was going on and stopped short when he saw the sheriff.

Verity said, "Mr. Reynolds, Sheriff, you remember my brother Jude."

"Of course, of course," Mr. Reynolds said.

"Jude," the sheriff said.

The men shook hands.

"Dad's fine," Verity said to Jude.

He nodded, but his expression matched the concern she felt. He tilted his head toward the kitchen. "How about I send those two out to the ship?"

"Good thought." Verity listened for the boys upstairs and heard no more than running water and chatter. She pushed clothing and toys into a pile to make room for them to sit. Jude came back and joined her on the love seat, and Sheriff Mooney and Mr. Reynolds took the couch.

"What's this all about?" Jude said.

Verity felt a twinge of annoyance that he would take the lead in the conversation, but let it go.

The sheriff was perched on the edge of the couch, his elbows on his knees. He'd taken off his hat and held it by the brim. "Your father's been leaving regular every morning, I take it."

"Sure," Verity said. "He's been at work. Really long hours."

Mr. Reynolds picked something invisible off his trouser leg. "In point of fact, he hasn't worked a day since, well, since your mother passed."

Verity and Jude exchanged stunned looks. "What do you mean?" she asked.

Mr. Reynolds spread his hands. "I told him to take all the time he needed, and I meant it."

"He hasn't been at work?" Verity couldn't get her mind around it. She pictured him leaving early in the truck, coming in late, sometimes after dinner, day in and day out.

Jude said, "He hasn't been here. I mean, I was gone awhile, but since I've been back, he's only here at night."

Sheriff Mooney said, "We got complaints from the hospital in Gloucester, and the one up in Richmond. And also Dr. Weingarten."

"Complaints about what?" Jude asked, his voice tight.

"At first your father was asking a lot of questions about how they took care of your mother, about their decisions, what they said, what they did. They knew he was grieving and tried to be mindful of that, but he kept coming back, day after day, a little angrier every time." Sheriff Mooney stopped, sat back, resettled himself. "They asked him to stop coming, but he didn't listen. Two days ago he threatened the doctor and his receptionist and got the police up there involved. They served a restraining order on your father yesterday and notified our department. The hospitals have informed their security not to let him in. It's a bit of a situation."

Verity's throat was so dry she didn't think she could ask a single one of the questions flying through her head. Mr. Reynolds and Sheriff Mooney were looking at Jude and her with sympathy, and also seemed sorry to bring bad news into their house, a house they had to know was held together with baling twine.

"So where is he now?" Jude asked.

Mr. Reynolds shrugged. "I haven't a clue, son."

"What I need to know from both of you," Sheriff Mooney said, "is whether everything is okay here, from your point of view."

Okay? Verity thought. *How could everything be okay?*

"I've kept the paychecks coming," Mr. Reynolds said. "I didn't want any of you to do without."

Verity found her voice, shaky as it was. "We appreciate that, sir." She'd had to ask their father for cash last week since they'd gone through what was in their mother's cashbox after the casseroles stopped coming. She'd found five twenties on the kitchen table the next morning, but it wouldn't last forever. Mr. Reynolds had used the past tense, which meant he couldn't keep paying someone who didn't turn up for work. What would they do then?

A clatter of footsteps as Roy and Wallace ran down the stairs, shouting, "We're ready for breakfast!" They rounded the corner and stopped short when they saw Verity's and Jude's faces—and the sheriff and Mr. Reynolds.

"Whoa," Roy said. "Who's under arrest?"

"No one." Verity pointed toward the kitchen. "Have some juice and I'll be there in a minute." The twins stood there staring at the sheriff.

"C'mon, hotshots." Jude got up and herded the boys out of the room, their feet dragging on the floor.

Verity watched them go. This disturbing information about her father began to sink in. If he was acting crazy like this, what would happen when he came home? It was all too much. She put a hand down on the seat to steady herself. "What do we do when he comes home?"

Sheriff Mooney tilted his head. "Same as always, I reckon. As long as he stays away from the doctor and those hospitals, there's nothing to be done."

"If he doesn't come by the club tomorrow, I'll stop by tomorrow evening," Mr. Reynolds said. "See if I can get him to come back to work. Aside from the fact that we need him, a routine will do him good."

They made it sound so simple, Verity thought. Like a conversation would set everything right. For nearly a month her father had been letting them all think that even though he wasn't doing much for them at home, wasn't caring for them or holding them or even doing the damn dishes, at least he was going to work. However strange and distant he'd been at home had been balanced by the normalcy of holding down a job. It meant he couldn't be that bad off, and therefore neither could they, right?

Wrong. Verity was scared, for herself, for her brothers and sisters, for their family. The word brought tears to her eyes.

"Hey now," Mr. Reynolds said softly. "It'll be all right. If anything comes up, you've got my number, don't you? You can just call me."

"Thank you, Mr. Reynolds." She stopped herself from glancing over her shoulder at the place on the wall where the phone had been. She wanted to go along with their optimistic view of things, the idea that Mr. Reynolds would talk to her father tomorrow and straighten things out. Mr. Reynolds and Sheriff Mooney had seen the gate; they didn't need to know about the phone.

The men got to their feet and made their way to the door. Verity followed them out to the porch.

"You're doing a helluva job, Verity, you and Jude," Mr. Reynolds said. "If you don't mind me saying so, your mother would be proud."

Her eyes misted. She pushed her hair back from her forehead and cleared her throat. "Thank you both for coming by. I appreciate it."

They said their goodbyes. Verity watched them go down the walk single file, then fall into step beside each other across the lot and down the drive. She felt the urge to run after them, call them back, sit them down again, tell them everything, tell them about the washing machine, and the hundred dollars that wouldn't last, about the kids sleeping in piles because they were sad and frightened, about how she didn't trust Jude would stay and she worried about Eden, about how Harper had stopped talking, about how she'd wanted to go to Halliwell College, about how she could've gone but was afraid, and now she'd missed her chance, about how, most of all, she missed her mother, missed her all the time, even when she slept, and couldn't see how that feeling would ever go away. She hardly had a minute to herself now, but being busy didn't help much. She walked around bleeding.

Mr. Reynolds and the sheriff disappeared around the corner behind the stand of pines. Verity stayed a few minutes longer, then went in. Roy and Wallace had finished eating, so she sent them out with instructions to have Spider and Harper come in.

Jude was washing dishes and shut off the water. "We should talk about Dad."

"What for?" Verity said, her anger rising, not at Jude necessarily, but at the situation she was left to cope with, and mostly at the fact that their father was on the loose, doing more harm than good. They were barely keeping it together, and he was out there threatening people and missing work. "Mr. Reynolds is coming tomorrow. Let him deal with it. I've got a ship to run."

She grabbed a piece of toast and started for the door.

Jude intercepted her, put a hand on her shoulder. "Let me make you some eggs, okay?"

His touch deflated her anger a little, exposing raw pain. "Okay." She rocked on her heels, closed her eyes to avoid his gaze. One drop more of emotion and she would disintegrate.

"This is all so messed up." He sighed and let go of her. "Go clean up, and your eggs will be ready when you're done."

She went upstairs, limp and bruised, thinking what a relief it was to be told what to do.

CHAPTER FORTY

SPIDER

Ship's Log: USS *Nepenthe*
Date: Tuesday, July 22, 1980
Time: 1815h
Weather: 86°F, Overcast
Winds: 0–5 kn SSW
CO: Lt. Commander V. Vergennes

Spider's stomach growled. He checked the ship's clock: 1815h. Earlier Verity had said they'd eat inside, but no one had called him in, and he'd lost track of time. He'd been working on the horn mounted on the starboard side of the big window, a project his dad had promised to help him with way back when they actually did stuff together, and he was ready to test it out.

The crew were getting a lot of mileage out of the Bermuda Triangle idea. Who could resist monsters, pirates, and lost ships all wrapped up in a mystery? Plus Verity wasn't being as strict as she used to be. Everyone still followed her orders, but she also let them do their own thing. For Spider that meant messing around with the maps, batteries, and, best of all, the engine. He had to make sure their dad wasn't around because he'd have a conniption. Spider tagged along with Jude on a grocery run so he could fill the fuel canisters with his own money, just for fooling around, making noise with the engine. Jude hadn't given him the third degree over it, so that was something. His brother had been generally not a douche since he'd come back, and Spider was thinking he'd go back to sleeping in his room. It was his, after all, and the mosquitoes were a bitch.

He craned his neck to see if anyone was on board. Harper was outside the wheelhouse checking the weather gauges. Everyone else had gone in, he guessed. He pushed the button next to the wheel and kept his eye on Harper. The horn went off, louder than his wildest dreams.

Harper jumped a foot in the air, clamped her hands over her ears, and let out a bloodcurdling scream louder than the horn. Spider doubled over laughing.

She spun toward him. "You snot-faced, scum-brained, evil little cockroach! You scared the bejesus out of me!"

He tried to wipe the smile off his face, but he couldn't. "Sorry."

"Like hell." She picked up the notebook she'd dropped. "I've got to catch the weather report."

"I'm coming."

Harper was over the gunwale and navigating the gangway. "Tell it to someone who gives a rat's ass."

She never used to swear, Spider thought. Never. Their parents wouldn't tolerate it, and neither would Verity. He did feel bad about getting Harper's goose and would make it up to her later, once she simmered down.

The other kids were eating already: grilled cheese and tomato soup and leftover pizza. Spider wolfed down two sandwiches and a bowl of soup at the table, then grabbed a slice of pizza and joined Harper and Jude in front of the TV.

"Look," Harper said, pointing to the screen. "That tropical depression is a hurricane now. Earl."

"Sounds like someone's creepy uncle," Jude said.

"Hey," Spider said, "it's in the Bermuda Triangle." He smiled at Harper, but her eyes were glued to the screen.

The graphic switched, now a curved cone showing where the storm might go.

The weatherman swept his hand along the wide part of the cone. "Early projections predict possible landfall on Friday or Saturday, most likely on the Carolina coast, although a lot can change between now and then, both in terms of the storm's location and its strength. We advise viewers all along the eastern coast to stay informed as we monitor the progress of Hurricane Earl."

"That includes Virginia, doesn't it?" Harper looked from Jude to Spider, her eyes wide.

Jude shrugged. "It includes most of the coast from DC south, so yeah."

"Well, isn't that kind of a problem?" Harper said.

"I doubt it," Spider said. "I mean, don't they always stay south?"

"Shows what you know." Harper's tone made it clear she hadn't forgiven him yet for the horn. "The Chesapeake-Potomac hurricane of 1933 was one of the worst ones ever. Note the word *Chesapeake*. Forty-seven people died."

"Okay, so once." Jude stretched his legs out in front of him. "Sports are on."

They must've had the sound turned up, because all of a sudden, their father was standing in front of the TV. *Crap*, Spider thought.

"Hey." Jude jumped up to turn down the sound.

His father beat him to it, switching the set off. "Now that I can hear myself think, hello." The room was too quiet, like everyone was holding their breath.

"Hi, Daddy," Harper said.

"Hi, Dad." Spider stood up with his plate, eager to get out of there. "How was work?"

His father's face went dark. "Did you talk to Mr. Reynolds yesterday?"

"Mr. Reynolds? No. Why?" Spider glanced around to see if maybe someone else knew what the heck was going on. Verity was in the kitchen doorway strangling a dish towel. Eden stood behind her looking as confused as he felt. Jude was conducting a detailed examination of his fingernails. "I don't know anything, Dad."

"You sure?" His eyes darted back and forth. He was super keyed up. If it wasn't his father, Spider would've thought he was on something.

"Dad," Jude said, real calm, "don't put this on us."

Their father squared his shoulders, jutted his chin. "You don't think I know what's going on? You don't think I know you were talking to my boss and Sheriff Mooney yesterday?" All his focus was on Jude, who kept his eyes down.

What was Dad talking about? The sheriff had been here? No one ever told him anything.

Verity stepped into the room. "The sheriff and Mr. Reynolds only talked to Jude and me. It wasn't like we had any choice. They just showed up."

"And somehow you forgot to tell me?"

"You weren't here until late, and we were—"

"On the boat. Yes, I know. On the boat."

He said it like it was a dirty thing. Not a ship with a captain and a crew. A boat.

"Yes," Verity said.

Spider could see she was chewing on something, deciding whether to spill it. He didn't know why the sheriff had come, but it usually wasn't to give someone an award. Spider sat back down, tried to disappear into the couch.

Jude was nodding, like he'd just made up his mind. "Okay, so maybe we should've told you about those guys showing up, but maybe you should've told us that you haven't been going to work for a month."

"That's none of your business! None!" Their father wasn't a yeller, but he sure was yelling now. He wasn't just mad, he was freaking tense, the tendons in his neck sticking out, his jaw working, his arm muscles rigid, his face bright red, like he might explode, or catch fire. Cyrus, Nellie, and the twins clustered around Verity, all those eyes as big as saucers. Eden, too. Their father spun in a slow half circle, taking them all in, then turned back to Jude. Spider felt a surge of protectiveness for his brother. That was how bad it was.

"Dad," Jude said, real soft. "Let us get the kids on the ship, then we can, I don't know, talk. You, me, Verity." He glanced over at Eden, then at Spider. "Whoever." He said it like those hostage negotiators on a cop show, like their dad had a bomb. Maybe he was the bomb. Spider tried to swallow but couldn't.

Their dad stood there for what seemed like a full minute, eyes trained on Jude. "None of you understand. Even if I explained it to you, you wouldn't understand. It's like you're all against me."

"We're not against you, Dad," Verity said.

Their father dismissed her with a wave of his hand. "The doctors, the nurses, all of them. They didn't do what they should've when your mother was there the first time and lost the baby. They didn't give her the blood!"

Verity tried again. "Dad, let's talk in a minute. Let me just—"

"They put her last. They put my Maeve last." He shook his head slowly, then jerked up his chin, pointed at Jude. "And you. When she had her attack, you drove. I couldn't. I just couldn't." His finger was shaking. "You drove, but you didn't go fast enough. You didn't get her there in time. What were you thinking, Jude?" His voice broke. "Didn't she matter enough to you?"

The color left Jude's face. Spider looked at Verity, trying to see if she knew anything about this. Could it possibly be true? He couldn't remember who had told him what, but it sounded like their mother had died in the car, right away. If Verity knew different, she wasn't saying anything.

Jude sprang to his feet. His eyes were bloodshot, and his mouth was pulled tight. He came around the coffee table, stood a punch away from their father. "Fuck you."

That stunned their father—all of them. In that split second Jude got out of there, yanking open the door and slamming it behind him so hard the windows rattled. Spider felt it in his bones.

Verity didn't wait to see what happened next. "Everyone, back to the ship." Eden nudged the twins and Cyrus toward the back door. Nellie had wrapped both arms around Verity's leg and didn't move. Verity pointed at Spider and Harper. "That's an order." Harper scooted toward Spider, and he knew it was so she didn't have to cross in front of their dad to get to the kitchen. For Harper to be that scared of him—they'd always been tight—well, it shook Spider.

Their father watched everyone head outside like they were walking right off the face of the earth. Spider followed Harper but hung back a little. Their father was so messed up, it wasn't right to ignore it. If he hadn't been going to work all this time, if he had all these crazy ideas about what happened to their mother, if the sheriff had come to see him—it was too much to pretend it wasn't happening. He looked his father in the eye, thinking he'd say something helpful, but there was nothing in his father's expression that invited it. Nothing at all. Spider had spent so much energy clawing his way into his father's good graces, had tried so hard to be the son he'd be proud of, and now Spider was practically offering himself on a platter as the last kid who wasn't going to walk out on him, and guess what? His father didn't give a damn.

Spider marched outside with his brothers and sisters. Verity waited by the door for him, and together they crossed the lawn to the ship.

CHAPTER FORTY-ONE

HARPER

Ship's Log: USS *Nepenthe*
Date: Friday, July 25, 1980
Time: 1235h
Weather: 90°F, Partly cloudy
Winds: 15–20 kn SSW
CO: Lt. Commander V. Vergennes

Harper was sneak-watching the noon news, hoping to catch the weather. She'd been playing cat-and-mouse with her father for three days now, ever since he yelled at them and practically accused Jude of not caring about their mom and maybe not doing enough to stop her from dying. Verity told all of them it wasn't true, but still. Right now her father was on the garage side of the house clearing the drains. It'd rained two days straight, and the gutters were overflowing, and there was a lake on that side of the house. Harper hoped he didn't come in because she needed weather information, and she needed it badly.

Their dad had put the radio back in the kitchen, but whenever Harper went to listen to the forecast, the radio wasn't in its spot on the windowsill. None of the kids knew where it was—she'd asked—so her father had taken it. She listened for it, even sneaking down the hallway to his bedroom, but never heard anything more than him talking to himself, not exactly normal, just not the radio.

Since he'd been caught not going to work, he was around a lot, popping up in one room or another like he'd come through a wall. He'd take off in his truck without warning, off to who knew where. Verity kept everyone on the ship most of the time, afraid he'd start yelling again. When it rained hard they'd all be squished into the wheelhouse and the galley and get cranky and sweaty. Jude played spy and told them when it was safe to come inside, and they'd make a break for it.

Somehow Harper and her brothers and sisters had gotten on one side of things and their dad on the other. She didn't know how they'd get back together, or if they ever would, and it made her sadder than she'd ever been. She didn't think there could be anything worse than losing her mother, but there was: this. At night she worried something might happen to Verity, or to Eden, or to Spider, or even to Jude since he was one of them now, and it was hard to sleep.

Getting rid of her hurricane worry would help. It could've fizzled out by now, nothing more than a tropical storm. That would be some good news.

The newswoman said, "Over to you, Frank. What's the latest on Hurricane Earl?"

Still a hurricane. Crap.

A colorful map appeared, and Frank swept his hand from right to left. Harper was trying to figure out where Chesapeake Bay was exactly.

"Yesterday morning, Earl hit the Turks and Caicos Islands as a Category 2. That slowed it down a little, but now it's heading north—or northwest, rather—picking up speed and gaining strength. Top winds are now recorded at over one hundred and thirty miles per hour, making it a Category 3."

"Gosh," Harper said.

Frank the weatherman pointed at the screen with its familiar cone. "As this projection indicates, we don't know exactly where Earl will go. Our best guess is it will make landfall in the next twenty-four hours, most likely between Wilmington and the Outer Banks, although—"

The screen went blank. Harper picked up the remote and clicked the "On" button. Nothing. She got up and punched the button on the TV. More nothing. She checked the plug, and it was plugged in same as always. Weird. She went into the kitchen just as Eden and Wallace were coming in from outside.

Eden went straight to the fridge. "Is there any more bologna?" She opened the door, stuck her head in. "Huh. Light's not on."

Oh, Harper thought. She flicked the switch for the overhead light. Zip. "Looks like the power's out."

"There's no storm," Wallace said, going from room to room trying all the lights.

"Freaky," Eden said. "Maybe we should ask Dad."

Harper wagged her thumb toward the side of the house. "He's out there."

"Forget it." Eden grabbed the bologna, handed it to Wallace. "Lemonade sounds good. It's so damn hot." She cradled a giant bottle in one arm, stopped in the pantry for paper cups, and left, Wallace trailing behind her.

Harper tried the lights one more time, then got out of there before her father came back and found a way to blame it on her.

~

"Maybe no one paid the bill," Verity said, chewing her sandwich.

Eden took a swig of lemonade from the bottle. "By *no one*, you mean Dad."

"Well, yeah. Mom always paid the bills."

"It's not like it's hard. Unless there's no money."

That stopped them talking. Was their father working again? Who was going to stick their head in the lion's mouth and ask?

"Are we going to be homeless?" Cyrus asked.

"We've got the ship," Eden said. "And it's not like we had air-conditioning or anything."

Cyrus stood up, looked at the house like there was a birthday party in there he hadn't been invited to. He didn't say anything, though. He was full of silences. They all were.

Harper went back to eating her sandwich, more like nibbling it. She leaned out from under the canopy so she could study the sky. The wind was up, blowing the tops of the pines flat, stirring up the river. Clouds were shooting across the sky like they were late for something, and she wondered again about the hurricane.

Spider was watching her. "You catch the forecast?"

"Power went off just when they were getting to the good part. But Earl's still a hurricane, and it'll make landfall in the next twenty-four hours."

"Anyway, that's the same as one day," Nellie said.

"You're right," Harper said. "They say it like that to be scientific." That reminded her of the gauges. She hadn't checked them since first thing this morning.

"Where?" Spider asked.

"Where, what?"

"Where's the hurricane hitting?"

"They said the Outer Banks. Is that South Carolina? But honestly they didn't sound so sure." Harper retrieved her notebook from the wheelhouse and recorded the temperature (93 degrees) and the humidity (84 percent). The barometer read 29.5, the lowest she'd ever seen. There was a storm coming, no doubt about that. The only thing she couldn't tell from that one reading was how big.

She put away the notebook and started telling Verity about the pressure, which meant explaining the entire nature of weather to her.

Verity was listening but seemed like she couldn't believe that little gauge had anything to do with a hurricane. Harper got to the point. "If it keeps dropping fast, it means a really big storm."

"Keep an eye on it," Verity said, making Harper feel proud of doing her job.

~

They spent the afternoon hunting down a pirate ship off the coast of one of the tinier Bermuda Islands. When Spider announced he finally had it in his sights, Wallace started feeding cannonballs—tennis balls, duh—to Roy. He'd launched a few, and everyone made explosion noises when they landed. Normally only the younger boys did that, but ever since the special party, the crew did most things together, even silly things like explosion noises. It was fun if you didn't think about how stupid it was.

Roy swiveled the gun to port, then pointed toward the drive. "Dad's talking to Jude." They'd all taken to reporting their father's position. No one wanted to run into him unprepared.

Verity stuck her head out the window so she could hear, but it was impossible with the wind. Their dad took out his wallet, handed Jude some bills.

"For the electric bill, maybe?" Verity said. "You can pay it at the bank. I went once with Mom."

Everyone had stopped eating to watch their father and Jude, to see if there'd be more yelling, or worse. Nothing bad happened, though. Their dad went around the side of the house again, and Jude came over to the boat.

"I'm going into town, see if we can get the juice back on. Anything from the store, Verity?"

She thought for a sec. "Ice, in case it doesn't come on soon. All that milk and meat will spoil."

"Ice cream," Roy said.

"Yeah, chocolate ice cream," Wallace added.

Jude smiled. "Not when we don't have power, you clowns."

Spider said, "Maybe some candles—and batteries for flashlights. Do we even have flashlights?"

Eden let out an exasperated sigh. "I hate this! It's like frontier days or something! How long do we have to put up with this crap?" Her eyes got huge—an idea had just exploded in her head. "Hey, can I come with you?"

The twins shouted, "Me, too! Me, too!" Nellie joined in, and so did Cyrus, not to be left out. Harper kind of wanted to go, too, but didn't want to seem like a baby. Eden begging to go was different; one foot was always out the door.

Verity had a look on her face like if Jude wanted to stuff all of them in his car and drive off into the sunset, he was more than welcome. Harper tried not to be hurt by it, but being a burden stank.

Verity said, "Eden, I'm not going to stop you." Eden nodded. Verity knelt down so she was face to face with Nellie. "Do you really want to go with Jude?"

She screwed up her face, thinking. "Nope."

"Then I don't, either," Cyrus said.

"Jude, you okay with these two?" Verity pointed at Roy and Wallace, who had such sweet smiles you could practically see the halos.

"You guys aren't going to give me any grief, are you?"

They shook their heads. Verity gave them a once-over, raked their hair sort of flat with her fingers while they did their best not to squirm. She rubbed a dab of mustard from the corner of Wallace's mouth and gave them each a kiss on the top of their heads, which made Harper's stomach twist because it was exactly like their mom.

"Good enough," Verity said. "Don't beg for treats at the store."

Eden grabbed the small woven bag she'd started keeping with her. Harper knew it had a mini hairbrush in it, and lip gloss, and, she guessed, money. She imagined what it would be like to constantly be prepared for the moment when you'd need to look good, and maybe have the chance to buy something just because you wanted it. Harper felt like she was stuck at the mustard-on-your-face stage. Maybe she could find a bag like that but not too similar. What would be the point, though? She was marooned on this island, just like on *Gilligan's Island* except no coconuts and no rich people.

She watched Eden cross the lawn, sidestepping the puddles near the drive, with her short shorts and her long, long legs.

Verity was watching, too. "How much you want to bet she ends up at Melissa's house?"

"Why didn't you stop her?"

Verity turned to her. She was tired, Harper could see that, but there was more. Under her captain's mask, she was sad. "Roy was right. I'm trying to be an adult, but I'm not very good at it. If I knew how to give up, I just would, I really would. But I don't." She pushed her hair off her forehead. They were both sweating like crazy, just standing there. "If Eden ends up at her friend's, it's not the end of the world, not even close." She stared off into the distance, her face to the wind. "Sounds nice, actually, don't you think? A house with a mom? Someone who knows what they're doing? I'd settle for one actual adult who knew how to keep Nellie from sucking her thumb and Roy from losing his cool. Someone to keep the washer going and the electricity on and the fridge full."

Harper didn't know what to say. Those thoughts popped up all the time, but she pushed them out of her mind as fast as they came in. She didn't have answers. Verity wasn't looking for answers anyway. She was talking to herself.

Nellie tugged on Verity's arm. "Are we still in Bermuda?"

Verity didn't answer.

CHAPTER
FORTY-TWO

JUDE

Roy and Wallace raced each other to the bridge, stoked to ride in Jude's car. They probably thought it had air-conditioning. Jude had hoped his father would offer the truck—the twins could've ridden in the jump seats—but no such luck. The boys were play-fighting each other on the bridge, waiting for Jude and Eden to catch up. The tide was out, but water was standing under it.

Everyone piled in and rolled down the windows. Hotter than hell in there. Eden didn't complain, which made Jude certain she was going to ask him a favor. He remembered fourteen. Being stuck at home with no phone and no power—no TV!—was the pits.

"Everyone pray," Jude said as he turned the key in the ignition. It caught the third time.

He switched on the radio. The last verse of "Sailing" was playing. Christopher Cross made Jude want to slit his wrists, so he lowered the volume before anyone could object.

As he swung out onto River Road, Eden inspected herself in the visor mirror and put on some lip stuff.

Here we go.

"I was wondering," she said, casual as can be, "if you could drop me at Melissa's. It's on the way." Jude didn't say anything, figuring she'd worked out at least two scenarios. "Or I could help with the shopping, and you could drop me on the way back."

"Unless you sent smoke signals, they don't know you're coming."

"Do you know smoke signals?" Wallace asked Eden.

"Dummy," Roy said, punching his arm. "She doesn't smoke."

Eden waited through this with great patience. "They won't mind. But I can also call from the pay phone at the store."

"You've got it all figured out," Jude said.

She turned to him, desperation all over her face. "Please?"

"What'll Dad say?"

"He'll say you're grounded for infinity years," Roy said.

"Jude, that's my problem. It's just a girlfriend's house. You can talk to her mom and everything. I have to get away, just for one night."

If their father had been acting like he ought to, Jude wouldn't seriously consider it. But as far as he was concerned, all bets were off. Why shouldn't Eden see her friend? "Sure. Call from the store."

As they got closer to town, the traffic was heavier than usual. Not heavy for a real city but definitely for Gloucester. A dozen cars were backed up at the light just inside the city limits.

"Is there some sort of holiday we missed?" Eden asked.

"We miss all the good stuff," Roy whined.

Jude shrugged. "Maybe a festival, or some kind of event, like a concert or a car show."

Roy and Wallace both jumped forward, leaning into the front seat. "Can we go?"

"We don't even know what it is."

Eden laughed. "They don't care. They're like me, just trying to have a good time. Right, guys?"

Twenty minutes later they made it to the center of town and parked behind the BB&T Bank. Jude jogged around to the front. A note taped to the inside of the glass door read: "*Closed early due to storm. Stay safe!*" The traffic made sense now. Back in the car, Jude told Eden and the boys about the note, and what it likely meant, keeping his voice calm even though worry was inching along his spine.

Eden groaned. "And no power for who knows how long. I'm definitely staying at Melissa's—maybe for the rest of the summer!"

Jude pulled out and turned north toward the Pic 'n Pack. The parking lot was jammed, and they crept along in the line of cars trawling for a spot to park. He concentrated on avoiding the people pushing carts and the cars backing out. It was a mess. The wind blew hats off, sent receipts floating through the air. A man stopped a cart next to them filled with bottled water and canned goods. Emergency rations.

"The hurricane must've turned north," Jude said. It was so unlikely, though. One hurricane here. One.

Eden twisted to face him. "So that means what?"

"Nothing definite." He gestured to the people scurrying everywhere. "People do tend to panic."

"Especially when there's actually something to panic about."

A truck reversed out of a spot on their left, braking only inches from Jude's front bumper. "Hey!" Jude shouted, but the truck was already pulling away. Jude swung into the spot, turned off the car. "Let's get what we need and maybe ask someone what the news is, okay?" He pointed at Wallace, then at Roy. "No monkey business. You can see what a zoo it is here already. Got that?"

They nodded, and he hoped the message sank in. The whole situation concerned him, and he wished he'd decided to run this errand on his own instead of trying to score brownie points with his siblings. Too late now.

Jude, Eden, and the twins stopped in front of the ice locker outside the store. A handwritten sign had been taped to the door. A corner had come loose and was flapping in the wind.

"*Gone,*" Eden read. "*And there won't be more.*"

"Ever?" Roy asked.

It was a good question. Jude headed inside before he had to answer it. He wanted to ask what the emergency was, find out the details, but what could it be other than the storm? Everyone had their heads down, rushing, and the folks coming into the store behind them were pushing ahead. All the carts were being used, so they grabbed baskets and wormed their way through the crowded aisles, scrounging for what was left—baked beans, a bag of apples, three boxes of Saltines, and a box of Mounds bars. No one really liked them, but fuel was fuel. If everything in the fridge went bad, they'd need something. All the batteries were gone, but they found two scented candles. Jude silently cursed his father for not paying the electric bill and for making off with the radio. Without the news, they'd been blindsided by a serious storm. Only Harper had saved them from being totally in the dark. Jude scanned what was in their baskets. With what they had at home, it would be enough. He could go hungry, and his father could get fucking takeout.

They got in line to pay. The crazy scene in the store had stunned the twins and Eden into silence. Jude gently nudged the woman in front of them. "Excuse me. The power is out at our house, so we haven't had an update on the storm."

The woman frowned. "Your power's out already. Lord help us."

"No, it's just . . . Anyway, what's going on?"

"They thought it was gonna hit the Carolinas. You heard that, right?" She didn't wait for a response. No one could possibly be out of touch for that long. "It did, but then it went back out and started going north. It's a Category 2, or maybe a 3, I can't keep track."

"And it's aimed here?" Eden asked, her voice high and tight.

"Here, there, they never know exactly, do they? Virginia Beach, maybe? But with the full moon and the tide, the timing's bad." The line moved, and she quickly unloaded her cart, focused on her own business. She glanced at Jude, Eden, the boys. "Winds'll be strong, no doubt about it, but it's the flooding you gotta worry about." Her cart was empty, and she shoved it forward and spoke over her shoulder. "Early morning. That's when it's gonna peak. So they say." She shrugged as if weather people were just as unreliable as everyone else.

Back at the car, they stowed the bags in the trunk. It had taken them an hour and a half to shop, and they still didn't have ice. The rain started falling, big fat drops. Jude stacked the baskets, left them with the carts, his mind racing to think what else he could do. Maybe stop at the bait shop for ice?

"I'm going to call Melissa," Eden said. "Who knows if that lady had a clue. Maybe it's all hype."

Jude nodded. "Don't take too long." She was already walking away. Roy and Wallace were elbowing each other for no reason. "In the car, guys."

"Are we going to the festival?" Wallace asked.

"Just get in." They needed to get home, pack some things, move everyone out before the bridge flooded. Good thing his car was on this side of it.

~

Eden slumped in her seat, her feet on the dash, curled up in misery. No one had answered the phone at Melissa's house. Eden had wanted to drive there, but it was another twenty minutes. Jude didn't think they had that luxury and wanted them to stick together in any case. The rain was hard and steady, the wind blowing it sideways. If he hadn't known about Hurricane Earl, he'd have thought it was just a bad storm instead of a warm-up to a possible disaster. The twins had been asking questions since they'd overheard the woman at the store, and Jude had answered as best he could. To be honest, he didn't know much about hurricanes. It wasn't as though they lived in Florida.

Heading south on Highway 17, they passed a hundred cars or more heading the other way, coming up from Newport News or wherever. It was unnerving swimming downstream like that.

Jude turned east onto the 219, and the engine hiccuped, nothing it hadn't done before, but it sent a chill up his arms. He drove as steadily as he could, wipers lashing back and forth, never actually clearing the windshield. He should've changed them months ago, but it hadn't seemed important then. A few hundred yards later, the engine hiccuped again, then sputtered, making the wheel tremble in his hands.

"C'mon," he said under his breath. "C'mon."

"What?" Eden said, not really interested.

"Nothing." There was no point in worrying her. The boys had gone quiet in the back seat, either tired or anxious about the storm or bored—who could tell?

Jude wondered if he ought to stop, check the plugs, the wires, whatever, but didn't have much confidence that he wouldn't make things worse. As they came over a low rise, the power went out of the car. He pressed the gas pedal down, all the way to the floor. The engine sputtered a few times, then went silent.

No, not now. Not now.

The car glided down the incline, coasted on the flat. Jude nudged it onto the shoulder just as it came to a halt. He smacked his hand on the steering wheel.

Eden sat upright. "What happened?"

"I don't know." Jude set the hand brake, turned on the ignition, holding his breath. It sounded like it would catch, and it did for a second, but then the engine gave up. "It's dead."

"Can you fix it?" Roy said, thinking of his father, no doubt. He could fix anything.

"I don't really know cars." He looked around. They were on the flat, that was a plus, but their house was several miles away. He pushed down the feeling of helplessness growing inside him.

Think. Make a plan. These guys are relying on you.

There was a house not too far ahead, one he remembered from driving by a million times. "I'm going to take a quick look under the hood, then go get help at a house up the road."

"I'll be here where it's dry," Eden said.

Jude spent twenty minutes jiggling spark plugs, checking for loose wires, scanning for leaks, but nothing jumped out at him. He must've tried to start the car a dozen times, getting wetter each time he went out. Not a single car went by. They were stuck.

It was almost seven, and Roy and Wallace had already eaten an apple and a candy bar each. If the hurricane was coming anywhere near here, the car probably wasn't the smartest place to be, especially with trees lining their side of the road. He could already feel the gusts rocking the car. The wind would only get stronger.

"Instead of me getting help from that house—assuming someone's even home—I think we should all go there. Stick together."

"And do what exactly?" Eden said.

"Find somewhere safer than this car."

Wallace said, "I want to go home. Can't we just walk there?"

"It's far—maybe six miles—so we'd be walking in the dark with the storm getting worse. We don't even have a flashlight." Jude craned his neck, taking in the way the trees were bending, like they were bowing. "If this keeps up, trees will start coming down." It sounded like he knew what he was doing, but in truth he was talking it through. If his useless car hadn't broken down, he'd have been able to help rescue the whole family, but as it was, he'd have to do his best to keep Eden and Roy and Wallace safe. He could try to reach the house himself, run all the way, but that would mean leaving Eden and the twins, and right now they were all sitting ducks.

"Let's go now," he said. "We'll take the food and anything else that might be useful."

"We should've stayed in town," Eden said, bitterly.

Jude leaned across the seat and whispered in her ear, "I need you to back me up. Could be a damn long night."

She gave a quick nod, grabbed her bag, and scooted toward him. "I'm getting out your side so I don't have to push the door against the wind. Wallace, go out Roy's side, okay?"

Five minutes later they were hurrying down the road. Jude carried most of the supplies, and the twins held tight to Eden's hands. The rain sliced sideways, and the wind pressed on their right, pushing them into the road, not that there was any traffic. A mailbox was planted at the drive, the name *Hatch* in the reflective stick-on letters. The name rang a bell, and maybe that was why the place had stuck in Jude's mind. A girl—Leslie or Layla or Linda. His friends had made fun of her name. Lacy, that was it. Lacy Hatch. God, why did parents do that?

"Down here." Jude waved them on. They turned to face into the wind and had to keep their heads down. Jude led, creating a small slip-stream behind him for the others.

Eden spotted a trailer home in a clearing on their left. "What about that?"

Jude shook his head, using his arm to block the driving rain from his face. "We need a real house. It's not much farther."

When the boys spotted the brick rancher, they let go of Eden and sprinted to the narrow porch. Jude and Eden caught up with them, and they crowded into the small space, relieved to be out of the rain. An old red Toyota truck stood in the parking area to the side. It might have been there for years, unused, or it might be someone's regular ride. Around here it was hard to tell.

Eden rang the doorbell and pushed the hair away from her forehead. "I wouldn't let us in."

When no one answered, Jude jogged around the back of the house, knocked on the back door, figuring someone might not have heard the doorbell over the rain. Nothing. He tried the door. Locked. The windows were either too high to see in through or were covered with blinds. His frustration rose. *Could we get a break here?* On his way back to the porch, he checked the truck on the off chance the keys were in it. No such luck.

"They aren't home." Jude opened the screen door and pushed on the latch. Locked. If he hadn't brought the twins and Eden with him, they'd be safe at home, all together inside the house.

"So now what?" Roy asked.

Jude realized what he had to do. "We don't have much choice. We could go to another house, and it could be empty, too. Maybe no one lives here at all." It could be true. Lacy was grown, after all. Wallace and Roy frowned at him, wondering what he was getting at. "I'm going to break in."

"What?" Wallace shouted. "We could go to jail!"

"I don't think so. If someone broke into our house to be safe from a storm, would that be a good thing or a bad thing?" The wind shifted, and the rain beat against their legs. A plastic table shuffled upside down across the drive, then got tangled in some briars. Jude looked at Eden, inviting her to back him up. She nodded once. "Okay, so that's what we're doing."

Jude ran to the shed he'd seen in the back and scrounged around until he found a piece of rebar and a block of wood. He spotted a grungy towel and grabbed that, too. Outside, he scanned the area around the house. The owners had cleared all the big trees except one. The wind would have to blow from the north to bring it down on the house, and right now it wasn't doing that. So far, so good. As he crossed the lawn again, he noticed it wasn't soggy like at their house, and remembered about the threat of flooding. This house might flood and it might not, but it seemed to be on fairly high ground, and the river was nowhere in sight.

Jude smashed the window in the back door with the rebar, scraping the sides of the pane to knock off the shards. He reached in, threw the small dead bolt, and turned the knob to release the button. How easy was that? Didn't even need the block of wood, whatever he'd thought that was for. He stepped in, pushed the glass to one side with his foot, and went to let his brothers and sister in. The wind shrieked through the hole in the back door. He'd have to figure out how to cover it.

Roy and Wallace crept in slowly, like they were expecting a German shepherd to rip out their throats or a cop to throw them against a wall.

"It's okay." Jude was amped up from breaking in but kept his voice mellow to calm them. "Just don't go to the kitchen at the back. There's glass."

Eden followed them in, shutting and bolting the door behind her. Her hair dripped on the linoleum. She flicked on the switch by the door and stared hopefully at the light over her head. She tried the other switch. Nothing. "Damn."

"Can you find some towels?" Jude said. "I need to clean up the glass, cover that window."

Roy and Wallace stood in the center of the living room, wet and shaking, though it wasn't cold. "I still want to go home," Wallace said.

Jude put his arms around them and pulled them into a bear hug. "Yeah, me, too. But it's too dangerous to try right now." He let them go and rubbed Roy's arms to warm him, then Wallace's. "For now, you're safe here with me."

Eden handed out towels, and Jude gave her a hug, too. "It'll be okay."

"I hate when people say that."

He smiled, feeling like it really might be okay, then went to clean up the glass. If he could find a flashlight, he would try to reach the house. There might still be time. Even a warning about what was to come was better than nothing.

CHAPTER FORTY-THREE

Verity

Ship's Log: USS *Nepenthe*
Date: Friday, July 25, 1980
Time: 2015h
Weather: 84°F, Rain
Winds: 30–40 kn (guessing) SE
CO: Lt. Commander V. Vergennes

Verity woke up in the bow berth. Rain drummed hard overhead. The hatch at the top of the stairs was open, but barely any light fell from the wheelhouse. She'd come down right after dinner because Cyrus and Nellie couldn't keep their eyes open. No one ever got a good night's sleep anymore, so she didn't mind weird bedtimes. Apparently she was tired, too, since she'd conked out without realizing she'd even shut her eyes.

Cyrus and Nellie were curled up together beside her. Verity scooted to the end of the mattress and squirmed up through the narrow stairwell. She was too big for this boat in too many ways.

"Hey," Spider said from the captain's chair.

"What time is it?"

Harper bent over her weather notebook at the desk. "Twenty-twenty, Captain."

Verity peered out the windows on each side, but there wasn't much to see with the rain and the failing light. "How long has it been raining?"

"Started at about eighteen hundred hours, sir," Harper said.

"What about Jude and Eden and the twins?"

"No sign of them, sir. They might be in the house."

This worried Verity, both the idea that her siblings might have come home and not come out to the ship, and that they might not have come home at all. She always knew where everyone was; it was part of being the captain, and since their mother had died, it was part of being the oldest girl. She might not have wanted this role—heck, she'd tried hard to get away from it—but now that she had it, she was bound and determined to see it through. If three of her crew were with Jude, she'd have to trust they were okay.

A gust of wind threw a sheet of water against the window behind Spider, startling Verity out of her reverie. Spider tilted his head toward the house. "Think we should go in?"

"I can think of arguments on both sides."

Spider and Harper exchanged a look that said they'd already covered this. Spider said, "I'm fine here. We can go in later if it gets hairy." He lifted a heavy-duty flashlight from the dash. "This works, and there's another one there." He pointed to the holder below the seat.

Verity nodded. "And we have the supplies we need?"

"Plenty of food," Harper said. "And I doubt water will be a problem."

Verity smiled. "Okay. I don't want to wake Nellie and Cyrus if I don't have to. If you guys get sleepy, join them. I'm good for now."

She took the seat across from Harper, who went back to her notebook. Verity was content to sit in silence, not counting the noise of the storm. She considered again whether they should go inside and decided that their father would come and get them if they were in any sort of danger. This was a boat, after all; being wet was its nature.

She picked up a deck of cards and held them aloft. "Hearts, anyone?"

~

By ten thirty, Harper was yawning every few minutes. She finished her hand—another win for her—and got up from the table. "I'm going to check the barometer one more time, then curl up with the littles." Spider had to get up to make room for her to go by.

Harper whistled low. "Twenty-eight point nine. It just keeps falling."

"I wonder how much rain we've gotten." Spider slid past Harper and stared out the door leading to the deck, listening to the groaning of the pines over the hiss and howl of the wind. "It's impossible to tell from in here, in the dark. Maybe I should go and check."

"Check where?" Verity said. She didn't like the idea of any of them wandering out in this weather.

"Just down the gangway. The ship's batteries are on board. I could turn on some lights. Or use a flashlight. I think I know my way." He smiled at this. How many times had they all come and gone from the ship?

"Okay," Verity said. "But be careful."

He grabbed a flashlight, slipped on the slicker hanging on the wall, and pushed open the door. The wind tore it from his grasp, sending a spray of rain into the wheelhouse. "Whoa!" He stepped out, snatched the door back, shut it hard.

Harper let out a startled cry. Verity wiped the water from her face and checked the door latch, worried what a wind like that might do next. She and Harper watched the flashlight come on, the beam directed toward the gangway. Spider crouched low and sidled down, the beam jumping back and forth, then steadying when he hit the ground. Verity and Harper moved to the front of the wheelhouse, peering over the bow. Spider swung the beam back and forth, lighting up rain and more rain. The house was invisible. About a third of the way across, he stopped.

A sharp gust shoved against the ship, and it swayed a little. Verity was confused at first because during all the time she had pretended to be at sea, she had imagined the ship carried by the rising and falling water. Now it had actually moved, and it scared the crap out of her. Her thoughts were broken by a loud groan, a tree moaning above the rush of the wind. A thunderclap made her jump. Harper grabbed her arm.

The beam from Spider's flashlight swung upward, and in the instant before it swung away, Verity could make out a huge dark shape. The thunder rolled, growling, and she realized it wasn't thunder. A tree was breaking. She felt it in her bones.

The flashlight beam jumped and wavered. Spider was running. The light blinded them at the window as he came up the gangway. Verity rushed to open the door, but he was already there. He opened it only enough to slide inside.

"Did you see that?" His eyes were huge, and he was breathing hard.

"A big tree fell!" Verity looked him over, but he seemed fine. The tightness in her chest eased a little. "Thank God it missed you." Harper was hanging on Verity's arm, squeezing so tight it hurt. Poor kid was scared to death. Verity put her hand on her sister's cheek. "It's okay, Harper. He's fine."

Spider threw back the hood of the slicker, turned off the flashlight. "Even before the tree came down, I wouldn't have been able to get to the house. It's completely flooded."

"How deep?" Whenever it rained hard, the low spot between the house and the ship held a couple of inches of water. The driveway flooded, too.

"I wasn't even halfway, and it was over my ankles." He stared out the window into the dark. "It's still coming down hard."

Verity tried to imagine how deep it was in the low spot, but her temples were throbbing, and she couldn't think.

Harper's voice rose in panic. "So if Daddy wanted to come get us, he couldn't? Or Jude? And we can't get to the house?"

Spider said, "It's too wild out there to try. I don't know exactly where the tree fell, and I don't want to go out there again and find out." He took off the slicker and kicked his soaking-wet Keds off his feet. "Looks like we're staying right here."

Verity slid into the captain's chair and tried to focus. There had to be something she could do. It was her ship. "Let's make sure everything that we need is in here and won't get blown away."

"Like what?" Harper asked.

"Drinking water, food, the medical kit. We only have two flashlights, but maybe there are extra batteries somewhere." The inventory helped clear her mind and steel her determination to keep them all safe.

"I doubt it." Spider pointed in the direction of the stern. "But the ship's batteries ought to work, if we really need them for the on-board lights—or the horn."

"I could go out and get life jackets, at least for Cyrus and Nellie."

Spider shook his head. "You shouldn't risk going out there, not all the way to the stern, in the dark. If we have to leave the ship, then yeah."

Verity nodded. "Once it's light, we can figure it out."

Cyrus peered up at them from the stairwell. Nellie was behind him, rubbing her eyes with one hand and holding Vermin with the other. That guinea pig had a habit of appearing out of nowhere.

"It's wet down here," Cyrus said. "And also loud."

Verity frowned. Water coming in through the hull? Or leaking down from the bow? Either way, it wasn't good.

"I'll take a look," Spider said. He lifted Cyrus and Nellie out of the stairwell and ducked past them.

Verity lifted the seat opposite Harper and saw the medical kit was right where it was supposed to be. She checked the food locker beside the door: a loaf of bread, half a packet of Oreos, a jar of peanut butter, and three apples. Plenty. She slipped back to the captain's chair and made sure the flashlight was secure in its holder. Spider had the other one.

Nellie had climbed on the seat beside Harper and was staring out the window. She couldn't see the storm, but like the rest of them, she could hear the wind howling. "I don't like this," she said. "Maybe it's like in the Bible."

"You mean Noah and the ark?" Harper said, always the first to get the zigzagging logic of the little kids.

"Yes. It rained for forty hundred days. You don't need to say nights because days have them already. And all the animals came, but only two of each." She lifted Vermin so they were nose to nose. "You're single but it's okay. You're with me."

Verity smiled but also saw how scared they all were: Nellie with her thumb back in her mouth, clutching Vermin to her, Cyrus kneeling on the other seat, staring into the darkness with a deep frown, and Harper looking like she might cry.

Spider came up from belowdecks. "I'm guessing it's leaking through the hull, but not too fast."

"Thanks, Spider." Verity breathed out. She'd done everything she could to prepare for the storm, and now she needed to mind her siblings' hearts as well as their bodies, as her mother would. Verity couldn't do what she wanted most—return their mother to them—but she could give them the parts of their mother that lived inside her. Verity was afraid she would fall short, that she would give away her entire self and not make up for what they all had lost. Even with the storm raging outside, scaring the crap out of her, she'd give everything to make sure they didn't lose more.

"Sailors, remember that whatever happens, we've got each other. We know how to work together, how to do our part." She looked at each of them in turn. "I'm proud to serve as your captain, and I love you all so much."

Cyrus reached for her, and she hugged him, then kissed Nellie on the top of her head, and Harper. When she turned to Spider, he was ready with his hand up. "High five, Captain." She could tell he was rattled from having gone out in the storm and was being brave, holding it together, just like she was. After she smacked her hand against his, she squeezed it and told him with her eyes how proud she was of him. He nodded, his eyes wet.

Message received.

CHAPTER FORTY-FOUR

JUDE

Jude found a piece of plywood in the shed to cover up the broken window but couldn't find a hammer or any other tools anywhere. Mr. Hatch must've taken them with him. He'd have to figure something else out or leave it open. The wind wasn't driving the rain inside, at least for now.

Back in the house, Eden was kneeling in front of the twins, who stood there in their underpants. She had a pile of T-shirts on her lap and held one up. "Come on, guys. I know they're ginormous, but it's either these or a pink lady one with kissing teddy bears." Roy stuck his arms in the air, and Wallace did the same. Eden put the shirts on and stood. "You can keep your soggy underpants on or take them off. Up to you."

"I'm hungry," Roy said.

"In a minute." Eden tossed a T-shirt to Jude. "The guy's pants will swim on you."

"I'm fine."

"Phone's dead, by the way."

"Some poles must've come down." He went to the window, wishing he could see farther than the drive, wishing he could see all the way to the house on the island and know what was happening.

Eden came over and must've seen something in his face. "What? Spit it out."

"I'm just worried about everyone else. I wish there was a way to tell them what we know about the storm." If he ran all the way, he could be back here in, what, three hours? What, exactly, would he be able to do there? If he could cross the bridge, get to the house, what then?

"Me, too," Eden said, her voice quiet.

Jude realized his job was to reassure them, not add to their worries. "But they're in a house, just like we are, so that's great."

"Or a ship," Wallace said.

"Right, but they can go to the house. And Dad's there." Roy and Wallace looked up at him with faces so earnest, Jude's throat cinched shut. They wanted to believe their father would do all the right things, that he would be there for everyone they'd left behind. It was like trying to believe in Santa Claus after seeing wrapped presents in a closet on Christmas Eve. There was no point in making them feel worse, no matter how little faith Jude had in his father's ability to handle anything at the moment. "Dad's there, and Verity, too, your captain."

The twins nodded.

Eden said, "I'll see if there's something to eat other than candy bars."

"Thanks, Eden. I'm going to hunt for a flashlight and batteries." He turned to Roy and Wallace. "You two can help, okay? Don't make a mess. Search like spies would."

As Jude searched the kitchen cabinets, sheets of rain crashed like surf against the front windows of the house, a deafening thrum backed up by the howling of the wind in the trees. He wanted to be here for Eden, for the twins, to keep them safe. But he couldn't let go of also wanting to help the others, for little Nellie and Cyrus, whom he'd only recently gotten to know—and love—and for Harper, who would be acting big and feeling small, and, yes, for Spider, whose resistance to Jude was a pain in the ass, but understandable, even admirable. The kid thought he was avenging Verity by holding a grudge against Jude for what happened all those years ago. The truth was, standing in a stranger's house, responsible for three of his siblings, Jude knew that the one he most wanted to protect was the one who was probably in charge of four siblings herself. Maybe he couldn't get to Verity, not without endangering Eden and Roy and Wallace, so he wouldn't go, but in his heart of hearts, that was what he wanted.

~

Jude woke, disoriented. The Day-Glo hands on his watch said it was nearly five o'clock. He hadn't slept more than an hour at a time, waking to make sure the house hadn't flooded or the roof hadn't blown off, like he might've slept through that. Eden was awake about half the time, too, but they didn't talk much, not wanting to rouse Roy and Wallace. They were all huddled on the floor between the living room and the kitchen, lying on blankets and pillows, having decided it was smart to stay away from the windows.

The wind had died down. Jude could still hear it, but it wasn't as intense as it had been all night. Sounded like the rain had eased up, too. Thank God. He got to his feet, put on his shoes, and checked the house for flooding. He scanned out the windows for downed wires or trees leaning over the house.

Squatting down, he gave Eden a gentle nudge. "Hey." Her eyes opened halfway. "Everything's fine."

She rose on her elbow and glanced at the twins. "What's up, then?"

"The storm's died down, and the house is dry. I checked out the windows, and there's no danger of a tree coming down now. You guys are totally safe."

She was waking up and could see what he was working up to. "How long will you be?"

"An hour to get there, an hour to get back if I can't get the truck out. Maybe a little time there to make sure everyone's good." He put a hand on Eden's shoulder. "I promise I'll be back as soon as I can. I wouldn't leave you guys if I thought you needed me here." He felt the promise in his heart and hoped she would know he meant to keep it.

"Okay. I'll tell the boys what you said when they wake up." She lay down. "Thanks, Jude."

"No problemo." He picked up the flashlight he'd found in the truck last night and went outside, closing the door softly behind him.

~

The air was heavy and smelled of pine and something else flinty, like crushed stone. He pointed the flashlight on the ground in front of him and picked his way over the boughs, shingles, and other junk littering the yard. He was curious to see what had happened to the house but didn't want to wake up the boys by pointing the flashlight that way. Instead, he made his way down the drive. The wind was still strong, maybe thirty, thirty-five miles an hour, and a warm rain fell. He kept his guard up, though, swinging the beam up into nearby trees in case branches were dangling, and watching his step. A chill crept up his spine, and he answered by walking faster.

Out at the road, the river was all the way up to the far shoulder. He'd never seen it that high. Just beyond his car, a utility pole had snapped in half, the wires drooping and swaying. He moved to the middle of the road and broke into a jog. He passed another downed power line and more broken branches and fallen trees than he could count, but no people. Not even any abandoned cars. The darkness began to lift, and where he caught glimpses of the river, it wasn't where it used to be.

He remembered what the woman in the store said about the tide and the full moon and figured the water levels might not have peaked yet.

Jude turned off River Road and onto their drive, his heart pounding as much from anxiety and fear as from exertion. His legs burned but he ignored it. What had been outlines of the trees resolved into the trees themselves as the sun rose. He turned off the flashlight just as the bridge came into view—really just the middle of it. The rest was underwater, part of a murky, sloshing soup that was usually marsh. He waded through the shallow water on his side of the bridge and onto the crest. The bottom rail of the gate was submerged; at least that told him he could navigate that far. Beyond there, the road was wet but visible, at least as far as the corner.

He climbed over the gate and ran down the drive. When he got to the corner, he stopped dead in his tracks. The whole yard was flooded, making it look like both the house and the boat were floating. A huge tree had fallen between them, its trunk partly underwater. The flooded area included most of the parking area; his father's truck had water halfway up the tires. The storm had torn off some of the roof, not just shingles, but the whole roof, exposing the inside. Sections of tar paper flapped in the wind, and debris littered the ground and the water surrounding the house. Between the garage and the house, though, grass poked out of the water, and in front of the garage was dry ground. Jude waded into the parking area, trying to catch sight of movement on the boat behind the wheelhouse windows, but there wasn't enough light yet.

"Hey! Hey!" he yelled, waving his arms, but he was too far away to be seen and probably couldn't be heard over the wind.

Jude skirted the pond of the parking area and approached the front porch from the left. He was within a few yards of the house when a figure came barreling around from the side. He jumped back.

It took him a beat to recognize his father, who was covered head to toe in mud. He held a shovel in front of him, the blade above his shoulder, and the look his eyes, bright whites staring out of the dirt-covered face, struck fear in Jude's heart.

"What are you doing here?" his father shouted.

Jude backed up. "I . . . I—"

"I've been working all night. With no one to help me!" His words were self-pitying, but he didn't lower the shovel.

Jude's heart thudded in his chest, but he kept his voice as even as he could. "What are you digging, Dad?"

He motioned with the shovel to the side of the house. "The water was coming up. It's still coming up!"

Jude gave him a wide berth and ventured forward. To the left of the row of peonies was a huge pile of dirt. "Dad. What have you done?"

"Can't you see?" He threw out his hand toward the flooded back-yard, the standing water a few yards from the peonies. "She was going to drown! No one was here to help me save her." His shoulders fell.

Jude's hands went cold. He went up to the hole, but he couldn't make himself look in. A sluice of ice water slipped down his spine. He turned to his father. "Dad, this isn't right."

He thrust the shovel in the air like a spear. "What do you know?"

"Dad." Jude stepped closer. "Please give me the shovel."

"The hell I will!" He gripped it tighter, jerked his head toward the hole. "I got the dirt out, but I can't lift the box. I got it in there, they *made* me put her in there, but now she has to come out."

Jude blinked hard. His father couldn't mean it. "You can't do that." Jude took a step closer. "If you just give me the shovel, I can help you. I can help you put everything back to normal."

"Normal?" His father brought the shovel down, blade first. Maybe he just meant to plant it there, make a point, but Jude didn't have time to think it through. He leaped to the side and grabbed the shaft, jerking it toward him. His father held on to the handle. They wrestled with it, both gasping, grunting. Jude's feet slid on the wet earth, and he let go of the shovel with one hand.

"Let go!" His father yanked hard, wresting the shovel away.

Jude's feet went out from under him, and he slid sideways. He threw his arms out, clawed at the dirt to stop his momentum. His legs swung over the hole, pitching him forward, and he tumbled in. What he saw as he fell didn't register, not completely, but enough for a dagger of fear to slice through him. His left hand, then his shoulder hit something solid with an edge. He cried out as he landed, face-first, and recoiled immediately, pushing off with his right hand, his good hand.

The casket was open. His father had opened it to get his mother out, to save her from the water. Jude was face to face with her, but it was dark down there, and in the shadow of the house, and he caught only a glimpse—gray skin wet from the rain, hair plastered across her face, cheekbones too sharp—before he shut his eyes tight and scrambled to his knees. Horrified that he was kneeling on his mother's body, he screamed, but his throat was cinched tight and no sound came out. He braced his hands on the open lid and wedged his feet in between the casket and the earthen walls. He glanced at his mother's body just long enough to reassure himself that no part of her had escaped the box and slammed the lid shut.

Panic rose inside him. Jude scanned the grave's edge for his father, but there was only dull sky and distant trees, broken tops catching the weak morning light. He climbed on top of the casket and used the makeshift steps his father had carved into the wall to get the hell out of there.

Alone, Jude sat in the dirt and caught his breath. After a minute or two, the terrifying sight of his mother faded, and he remembered why he had come, to find his brothers and sisters, to help them. He got to his feet and staggered around to the front of the house, keeping to the drier ground.

His father had waded out to his truck and was digging behind the seats in search of something. Jude's instincts told him his siblings were not in the house. He'd last seen them on the boat, and if they'd seen anything of what their father was doing, they'd have stayed put. Jude continued to round the house, the water ankle deep, then rising nearly to his knees.

The ship stood where it always had been, but it seemed to tremble in the lake of water surrounding it. Was his mind playing tricks? He blinked hard. Verity was standing on the deck next to the wheelhouse. The canopy had disappeared overnight.

"Verity! Verity!" He waved his arms and waded in farther. He looked around, tried to judge the water's depth, remember the contour of the yard, then looked back to the boat. A profile inside the wheel-house: Spider. Jude called out again. "Verity!"

Verity heard him and waved. "Watch out! It's deep!"

Behind him, Jude heard his father shout something about the kids and the ship. His tone was filled with anger and desperation, but the exact words were lost. With or without his father, Jude had to figure out how to get his brothers and sisters off that boat.

His thoughts spun. As he stood there in the water, helpless, the boat tilted, the far side dipping sharply, the near side's hull rising out of the water. High-pitched screams flew into the air as the boat tilted more, an impossible degree, then, just as suddenly, righted itself.

Fear stopped his heart when it dawned on him that the props had failed, washed away. First one side, then the other. The boat was float-ing. It wasn't simply that the yard had flooded; the river beyond the boat had risen above its banks. The flooded yard *was* the river. On the strength of the storm, and with the thrust of a high tide and the pull of a full moon, the river had come for the boat.

Jude's blood turned to ice. A gust of wind gathered behind him, rushing in his ears. It raced past the house, rippling the surface of the water, the river, bending the boughs of the fallen tree, and carried the boat away.

CHAPTER FORTY-FIVE

VERITY

At first light, Verity emerged from the wheelhouse and inched her way to the rail to assess the situation. She had dozed off at some point and her mouth was dry, her mind fogged. The wind, still fierce, buffeted her, and she grasped the rail tighter. As she squinted to see through the rain, movement on the driveway caught her eye. Jude was waving and calling her name. Relief washed over her, and she prayed he had a plan to get them off the ship.

A jolt threw her backward. She landed on her backside and slid into the locker with her left hip, covering her head with an arm to protect it. Had a tree fallen and knocked the ship? From inside the wheelhouse came screams, and fear struck her heart.

The ship tilted the other way, and she slid to port, slamming her shoulder into the locker. She tried to brace herself for more rocking, but the deck was two inches deep in water, and there was nothing to hold on to. The ship leveled, and she gingerly got to her feet, staying in a squat and crabbing over to the door. Her brothers and sisters were talking, yelling. Someone was crying.

Verity's stomach lurched. In her periphery she saw the world moving past. It wasn't possible.

Holding on to the door handle, she pulled herself upright. The ship was moving.

She yanked open the door. Nellie and Cyrus were piled on top of each other on the floor. Spider was untangling them, saying, "It's okay, it's okay," over and over. Harper was pulling herself out of the stairwell. Her lip was bleeding. They all looked up as Verity entered.

"We're moving!"

"What?" Spider craned his neck to see out the window while cradling Nellie.

"We got knocked off the props! We're floating!"

Spider stood, pressing Cyrus to his legs, and stared out the forward window. "Holy crap!"

Harper climbed onto the desk seat, looked outside, and screamed. Not once, but again and again.

"Stop it, Harper!" Verity ordered. Her thoughts flew and she struggled to pin them down, come up with a plan, anything. A dark thought filtered out of the chaos: if they were moving, they could hit something. "Harper, pick up Nellie, put her in that seat, and sit next to her so she doesn't get thrown around."

Spider pointed out the window. The trees were farther apart here, the river laid out before them, frothy and enraged. "The wind is pushing us out. Any farther and the current will pick us up." He stared at Verity, his eyes wide with fear. As if she might have a solution.

The wind gathered from off portside, a rushing sound like a train approaching.

"Hold on to something!" Verity shouted as the ship rocked to starboard.

The ship picked up speed, more than a push from the wind. The river current was sweeping them along. Verity reached for Cyrus, who was crouched at her feet. A hard jolt from underneath near the bow sent her careening backward, and she collided with the door. It sprang open, and she stumbled out. Her feet tangled beneath her, and she went down. The back of her head hit the engine housing. Flashes of light exploded behind her eyes, and a wave of nausea roiled through her. She turned onto her side, thinking she would throw up, gasping at the shooting pain at the back of her skull. She reached a hand to it. It came back bloody, and in an instant was rinsed clean by the driving rain.

She had to get back inside the wheelhouse. She had to get control of the ship. She crawled across the deck, swaying as the ship rocked. The door was wide open. Harper was in her seat, one arm braced against the wall and the other encasing Nellie. Spider was getting to his feet beside them. Verity made it to the door. Spider grasped her arms, helped her up.

Verity twisted around to close the door, and Spider saw the back of her head. "You're bleeding bad!"

Verity barely heard him over the muffled roar in her ears. She scanned the deck, frantic, then pushed Spider aside, searching the small space in which they all stood, looking past Harper into the stairwell, all the while knowing she would not find what she was looking for. "Cyrus."

"Where is he?" Spider said behind her.

Verity pushed off the doorframe and lunged to the starboard side, planting her feet wide and gripping the railing with all her strength. He had to have fallen off this side. She scanned the surface of the muddy water, back, back, back. An arm lifted, then dropped.

"There!" Verity waved, her heart racing, desperate to let Cyrus know she'd seen him.

Spider appeared beside her. "What're we going to do? We have to get him." He set his jaw. "I'll swim to him. I'll take the doughnut."

"No. Too dangerous." She swept her hand at the water. "Look at all the crap in there." An idea came to her, and she didn't waste time thinking it through. "Spider, start the boat."

"What?"

"We've got the batteries. Start the boat." Spider was frozen. She grabbed his arm and shook him. "Start the boat, and that's an order. We're going to go get him."

Spider hurried into the captain's chair, Verity behind him. She stopped beside Harper, who must've understood what had happened, because her mouth hung open in shock. "Just hang on to Nellie. That's your job." Harper nodded.

"Warming the plugs," Spider said. His fingers trembled on the ignition switch for a long moment while he waited. "Okay, okay. Now, I think." He turned the switch, and the engine roared to life. "Good. That's good."

"Get it moving, sailor," Verity said with more authority and confidence than she felt. He'd never driven a boat and neither had she. It was all theoretical, but theory was going to have to be enough.

Spider moved the transmission lever to forward and eased the throttle up. The ship moved forward, cutting through the water instead of being buffeted by it.

"Slow is fine, Spider." Verity pointed to starboard, to the open river. "Let's get away from the trees and come around that way."

"Okay, okay," Spider said, chewing his lips as he steered. The rain had let up for a while, but now it was coming down hard. He squinted through the window. "I can't see. I'm losing my bearings." His voice was thin, strained, his knuckles white on the wheel.

"Turn around, Spider—a one-eighty!" Verity said.

Spider pointed at the top of the instrument panel. "The compass!" He turned the wheel, eyeing the compass, and the boat swung in a neat arc.

"Great," Verity said. "I'll help direct you from outside. If I say stop, I mean it. Cut the engine." She hurried to the deck, leaving the door open so Spider could hear her, and took the doughnut off the hook on the wall. If it hadn't been in a sheltered spot, it'd have blown away. She tied the free end to the railing, her hands shaking.

The water was rough, and Verity was terrified they'd taken too long. Cyrus could swim, but he was small and would have a hard time not swallowing water. Her heart ached at the thought of losing her brother. As Spider closed the arc and headed against the current, Verity held tight to the railing with her free hand.

She spotted Cyrus. He was holding on to a log, but it was barely keeping him afloat. If only she'd taken the risk and retrieved the life jackets last night. She shook off the regret; she had to focus. "Keep on this course, Spider! Almost there!" They were close enough now that she could see his hair plastered to his head, and his brave expression, which was about to give way to wailing and tears.

"We're here, Cyrus!" She held the doughnut aloft, her arm shaking. With the ship this close, Cyrus would be in worse danger if they didn't maneuver perfectly. "Spider! Just a little closer. A little more. Stop!"

The ship stopped, the engine idling. But they were drifting away from Cyrus.

The current. She'd forgotten. "Spider! Forward, slow! Really slow!" Cyrus was several yards from the boat. "Okay, Cyrus. Here it comes!"

Verity tossed the doughnut and whispered a prayer as it flew through the air. It landed a few feet in front of him. He didn't wait for an order. He splashed forward and grabbed the doughnut. Verity's heart lifted.

She reeled him in, the rain beating down on her, the rope rough in her hands. Cyrus stared at her face the whole time, like it was a beacon. A lump lodged in her throat. She pulled harder, hand over hand. The doughnut touched the hull.

"Don't let go." Verity tied off the rope, yanked to make sure it was secure. "Spider," she shouted over her shoulder, "keep it steady now!" She knelt on the locker, leaned over the gunwale, and grasped her brother's outstretched arm. She pulled him up a bit, and he grabbed her shirt. She scooped her other arm around his torso and, using her back and her legs, hoisted him up and over the gunwale. He collapsed against her. She sank back on her heels and held him so close she could feel his heart beating a million times a minute.

"Okay, Spider! Turn it around!" Verity didn't dare stand. She was dizzy, and her head was pounding. And what if they hit something again? "Cyrus, we need to get inside the wheelhouse. Can you crawl for me?" He shook his head and tightened his grip on her. Verity marshaled her remaining strength and dragged Cyrus inch by inch across the deck until her back rested on the wall beside the door. She reached up, threw the door open.

"Cyrus!" Harper shouted, tears in her voice.

Cyrus left Verity's arms and crawled over the threshold.

They're safe, Verity thought in the moment before the world went dark. *They're all safe.*

CHAPTER FORTY-SIX

SPIDER

The engine sputtered and died. No mystery why: they'd run out of fuel. Spider wished he'd bought more than two cans when he'd gone into town with Jude, but how could he have known they'd actually need it? More diesel was beside the point anyway since he had no clue where they ought to go. Now the tide and the current would decide for them. He cussed himself out. Some navigator.

Verity needed a hospital. She'd been out cold for a few minutes right after rescuing Cyrus, then really drowsy. How long had it been? Maybe twenty minutes, thirty? Spider's heart was beating too fast, and his mind was a blur, so it might've been a lot longer. He'd torn up his T-shirt and bandaged her head as best he could, but she needed a doctor.

Spider switched off the engine and got up. His legs felt wobbly, and he steadied himself against the wall.

Harper was still at the table, Cyrus on one side, Nellie on the other. Cyrus hadn't said a word since he'd been pulled out of the water. Harper looked up at Spider with eyes so frightened he got a lump in his throat.

"We're out of fuel," he told her.

She turned to the window, and he followed her gaze. They weren't in the middle of the river, where the current was probably strongest, and they weren't near the edge, either—or what was the new edge—so they were away from the trees. Rain was hammering down, but the wind had died some.

"Now what?" Harper said.

He was about to say he didn't know, but that was lame. "We're going to figure it out, Harper." Just saying it made him feel better, even with his sister lying on the floor. He could see her chest moving with her breath, so that was a relief. He turned back to Harper. "We need to get help, get someone's attention."

She thought a minute. "Will the horn work?"

The horn. Of course she remembered it—he'd scared the crap out of her with it. "It runs off the battery, so yeah. Great idea." He got back in the chair. "SOS. Three short, three long, three short."

"Cover your ears," Harper said to Nellie and Cyrus.

Spider blasted out the sequence, waited a few minutes, then repeated it. "I'll do it again in a little while." He scanned the river for boats, people on the banks, but the visibility was lousy. He twisted toward where he thought the house was, and wondered what his father was doing, and what had happened to Jude and Eden and the twins. For the first time it occurred to him that they might be hurt or stranded—or worse.

Spider shook his head to get rid of the negative thinking. He had enough problems right here without creating ones that might not exist. He called to his siblings, "I'm going to signal again! Cover your ears!" As he pushed the button, sending out the sequence, the word *signal* triggered a dim memory from years ago, when he and his father had sorted through the boat lockers.

Spider jumped out of the chair, ducked into the stairwell, and sidled down the steps, landing at the bottom in a foot of water.

"Crap!" They'd taken on a lot of water, and he had no idea how much was too much.

"What's wrong?" Harper said.

"Nothing. I just forgot it was wet down here." No point in worrying about that now. He unlatched a small cabinet high on the wall to the right of the stairs. His father had told him to put the signal flares in there so the little kids couldn't reach them. With any luck, they'd still work. He pulled out the clear plastic case and went upstairs to show it to his siblings. "Bingo," he said, proud of himself for remembering them.

"What's a bingo?" Nellie asked.

"They're flares, kind of like fireworks. Just watch." He opened the box on the captain's seat and read the directions, then read them again to make sure he had it right. He put three cartridges into one pocket and the aluminum cylinder in the other and stashed the box. He headed for the door, stepping carefully around Verity, who moaned with her eyes closed.

I'm getting you help, Captain. Hang in there.

Spider went out and positioned himself facing the wind. He pulled out the cylinder, made sure the safety clip was in place, and slid a cartridge into it. He screwed on the cap, his hands shaking. Wetting his lips, he pointed the flare straight up and flipped the safety clip off the firing plunger. Spider held his breath as he pulled the plunger out, then released it. It snapped back, and with a bang, the flare shot out. It rocketed up and up, then exploded in a red burst, arcing just beneath the cloud cover, burning bright.

Someone had to see it. They just had to. Spider turned to see Harper and Nellie and Cyrus craning their necks to see the explosion, mouths open. He checked the ship's clock. In ten minutes, he'd launch another one.

He'd done it. He'd signaled for help. He and Verity had rescued Cyrus, and now, with any luck, he'd sent the signal that would save them all.

CHAPTER
FORTY-SEVEN

JUDE

Jude stood helpless as the USS *Nepenthe* floated away. He shouted for his father, who gave up rummaging in his truck and stood well behind Jude and off to the side, as if Jude were the scary one.

"What in God's name—" his father said.

Jude couldn't see exactly what was happening on the boat because of the trees and the distance and the rain, but there was no mistaking the sound of a diesel engine starting up.

"They're turning around," Jude said, mostly to himself. "If it's running, maybe they can go somewhere? A dock?" He half turned, hoping his father would engage, but he just stood rooted there, covered in mud, staring at the spot in the river where five of his children were on a boat that hadn't been in the water in more than fifteen years. Jude approached him, keeping his eye on the boat. If nothing else, he needed his father's truck and the keys to the gate—that was, if the truck would make it over the bridge. Any other plan would take too long.

"Dad," Jude said when he got within a yard of him. "Let's take the truck, see if we can get to a phone. A phone is all we need." His father glanced at him with a look he might give a stranger who'd asked him for money, then continued to stare out at the river. "Dad!" Jude needed his attention but didn't want to set him off. He couldn't risk his father throwing the keys to the gate into the river or something equally unbelievable, like attacking him.

The boat's engine cut. The silence of it made Jude's stomach twist. He started devising other plans that didn't include his father, like running back up the road, past the Hatches', just running until he found someone. Or tackling his father and taking his keys, assuming they were on him, and bashing the truck straight through the gate.

A bright-red light soared from the boat into the air. It took Jude a second to realize it was a flare. He watched openmouthed until it went out. "You see that, Dad? You see that?" His dad didn't say a damn thing. He'd walked away, was going to the house, like walking out of a movie he didn't like. Unbelievable.

Anger rose in Jude, and it felt just like that flare. He ran after his father, splashing water everywhere, and pulled the front door out of his father's hands. Stood blocking his way. The rage inside him was building like a fever under his skin. He needed to get help, and his goddamn crazy father was not going to stop him. "The keys, Dad. If you aren't going to do anything, fine. Stay here. Just give me the damn keys."

He just stared back, his eyes flat, dead.

Jude grabbed his father's collar, shook him. His father was strong, stronger than Jude, but in that moment it didn't matter. Jude wasn't backing down, not for anything. "Give me the keys!"

He shook Jude off, backed up a step, dug in his pocket. He dangled the keys and dropped them into Jude's hand. His father crumpled then, sagging through the shoulders. His face screwed up tight with pain, like someone had stuck a knife in his back. "I'm sorry. I just couldn't leave her." He turned away, leaned against the door, covered his head with his arms.

Jude left him there, waded out toward the truck, a bitter taste in his mouth. His mother must've been a larger force than he'd ever given her credit for to be able to make a man like that seem mostly normal. It made Jude think that there were probably lots of crazy, miserable people roaming around, barely kept in check by someone who cared enough to keep the charade going. Or maybe it wasn't a charade. Maybe his father really had been a better person, a halfway decent one, when Jude's mother was around, and now he'd come unglued.

He climbed in the cab, shut the door, and prayed the truck would start. He turned the key in the ignition, and the starter churned away, didn't catch. He waited a minute, his right foot hammering on the floor, then tried again. Same thing. Damn. He looked over at his mother's station wagon, but as low as it was, there was no way it would start when the truck wouldn't. Jude tried it one more time. Nothing.

He popped the hood, got out, and vowed that if he got this truck going, just long enough to get help, he'd devote his life to becoming the best damn auto mechanic in Virginia. His hands shaking, Jude jiggled and checked wires and belts and plugs and God knew what, the rain running down his face, his back, his frustration with himself and with his father clouding his ability to think through what might be wrong with the truck.

He slammed the hood closed and stared out at the boat, bobbing like a bath toy, imagining how scared they all must be feeling, how they must be hoping someone would rescue them. If only he were out there with them.

His father was slogging through the water toward him. Was he actually going to help?

Jude waved his arm to hurry him up. "I can't start it!"

His father came up to him, a little life in his eyes. "It's a diesel. You need to warm up the glow plugs first." He pointed inside the truck at the dash. "Push that knob in and wait a minute or two and do it again. They're weak."

Jude climbed in, did as his father said, keeping watch on the boat while he counted a minute, then two. He switched on the ignition. It fired right up. Jude rolled down the window. His father looked half-destroyed and half-pleading, like Jude could save him but it might not be worth it. Jude was so used to his father dismissing him, ragging on him, ignoring him, that the idea that Jude could help the man never occurred to him. "Dad." He choked on the word.

Out on the river, the growl of a boat engine. A larger boat was coming up alongside the *Nepenthe*. Jude couldn't believe his eyes.

He pointed to it excitedly. "Is that a rescue boat?" With any luck it was the coast guard, but any working boat with adults on it would do.

His father squinted, pursed his lips, then finally nodded. Relief surged through Jude. He reached out and put a gentle hand on his father's arm. "Let's find out where they're taking them, okay? I'll bet you've got some idea."

His father nodded again and went around to the passenger side, the first sign that maybe his mind was clearing, that he knew he wasn't fit to drive, and that he wanted to come with Jude, who would lead him back to his children.

Jude drove slowly through the flooded area. His father kept an eye on the boats in the side mirror, and when they got to the gate, he took the keys from Jude and opened it himself. The water had gone down a little; the tide was going out.

Jude pulled into the Hatches', pointing out his disabled car on the shoulder, explaining how he'd broken in through the back of the house. His father didn't respond. Jude stopped the truck and got out, went straight up the walk, anxious to see Eden and the boys.

The front door flew open, and the twins came rushing out, Eden behind them.

"You're here! You came back!" the boys sang, throwing their arms around Jude, immune to the rain.

Jude pulled them closer. His little brothers. "Good to see you rascals." He smiled at Eden, who waited her turn with tears in her eyes. She looked exhausted but otherwise in one piece. Together they turned to their father, who stood by the fender of the truck with his hands deep in his pockets.

Roy let go of Jude first and ran over to their father, then stopped short, his arms awkward at his sides. "Hi, Daddy."

Their father dropped to his knees, pulled Roy to him, and buried his face against the boy's neck. Wallace came over, and their father pulled him in, too. Their father's shoulders heaved up and down. He was sobbing.

It was hard to watch. Crying was better than being a zombie, though, and Jude hoped it meant his dad was tipping toward normal. The family needed him. Jude needed him, dammit.

"Everyone in the truck," Jude said. "I'll explain on the way."

Eden had kept the twins busy putting the house back the way they'd found it, minus a broken pane and a couple of T-shirts. They closed the front door and piled in the truck, Roy and Wallace in the rear seats and Eden in the middle up front. With all of them damp, the windshield fogged up, and Jude cracked the windows.

Their dad waited for Jude to swing the truck around, then pointed south. "A couple of private marinas are nearer, but if it was the coast guard—and it looked like that to me—they'd go to the training camp. It's got a sturdy dock, and they'd know all the ins and outs. If we see a store or another place, we ought to call down there."

It was more than he'd said to Jude in weeks. "Sounds good."

Their father stole a glance at the boys, like he was reminding himself of who they were. Jude concentrated on the road, steering carefully around the downed branches, keeping an eye on the power lines, reminding himself he had half his family right there with him. The weight of it swung against him again and again—what he had, what he might have lost, what he might still lose—but he held on to the steering wheel and didn't allow it to show. In a corner of his mind, he wondered, given the enormity of the feelings he struggled to contain, how he'd managed to do without his family for so long.

CHAPTER FORTY-EIGHT

CYRUS

Spider was stomping mad the coast guard men wouldn't let him ride in the ambulance with Verity. They had white uniforms like they were in the navy, and one of them told Spider for the fortieth time: "There isn't room."

Cyrus couldn't see inside the ambulance because it was still raining cats and dogs, and they were all huddled indoors.

"Which hospital is she going to?" Spider asked in his mad voice. He'd done such a good job with the ship and getting everyone rescued that maybe he'd graduated to adult now. If you asked Cyrus, he'd earned it.

"Walter Reed in Gloucester."

"That's near our house," Harper said, because she knew everything.

They piled into a little bus with some other people to go to a shelter, which made Cyrus think of a place for stray dogs, but it turned out to be the high school where Verity and Eden went. The driver said to go to the gym, but Cyrus was beat. No way could he do any exercise now. The gym had beds and tables with food and water, so he was wrong about that, too. The people there gave them clean clothes, but Nellie wouldn't change.

She had her thumb in her mouth the whole time and stuck to Harper like a barnacle. A nice lady cleaned up Harper's lip and told her she was brave, and some other lady came and gave Spider some papers and a pen.

"You have to do homework?" Cyrus asked him. "I thought it was still summer."

"They want information for people who might be looking for us."

At first Cyrus thought their mom would be looking for them. Then he remembered, and his stomach fell into a hole. It happened all the time, thinking Mommy was there, that he had both parents like he was supposed to. "You mean people like Daddy?"

"Right," Spider said. "Or anyone."

Harper was lying on a bed with Nellie. "Like Jude."

"Yeah." Spider stopped writing and chewed the end of the pen. "Like Jude."

"You think they're looking for us?" Cyrus asked.

"Sure they are," Harper said. "If you were older and had a car and could drive, wouldn't you look for your brothers and sisters?"

Cyrus nodded. Jude and Eden and the twins had been gone all night. Who knew where they were and what had happened to them, especially with that car of Jude's. Cyrus used to automatically think things would turn out fine, but after the ship actually sailed off for real and he went man overboard and had to not drown for ages and ages, well, he was just happy that Spider and Harper and Nellie were there with him, and that Verity was in the hospital, where the doctors could take care of her. That seemed like a lot for right now.

"I hope they're all okay," Cyrus said, pulling a blanket around himself. "Even Roy."

~

Cyrus fell asleep without meaning to, and when he woke up, his father was right there, sitting on the end of the bed like he'd meant to read

Cyrus a story, which made his heart hurt, the way he wished it were true. His father had on a bright-white T-shirt, and his hands were clean, but his pants were muddy, and there were globs of dirt in his hair.

"Hi, Daddy."

"Hey there, Cyrus." His voice was quiet, and his eyes were red but not angry red. He reached out his arms, and Cyrus climbed into them without thinking about it. "I'm sorry you had such a scare, I really am." He brushed the hair out of Cyrus's eyes. "What a swimmer you are, huh?"

Cyrus felt proud. He looked around for his brothers and sisters.

Eden was lying on a bed with Harper and Nellie in the middle. She lifted her head and smiled. "Hey, Cy."

Spider walked up holding a tray piled with sandwiches. "Welcome back." He grabbed one and saluted with it, then took a huge bite.

Cyrus sat up, and before he knew it, Roy and Wallace had yanked him away, shaking him and clapping him on the back, but not as hard as they did when they were trying to rile him up. This was more like a hug broken up into pieces.

Roy slung an arm around Cyrus's shoulder. "Heard you went into the drink, sailor."

Wallace said, "Man, that must've been cool. Wish I'd seen it."

Cyrus asked, "Where were you guys?"

"Jude smashed his way into this house after his car broke down," Roy said.

Cyrus wriggled free of his brothers. "Where's Jude?"

"At the hospital with Verity," his father said. "I'm headed there soon, but I wanted to make sure everyone here was okay first." He kept looking at each of them, like he was counting them but kept losing track, the way Nellie did with number salad.

"We're okay, Dad," Spider said, handing out sandwiches. He seemed taller than before, but that was impossible.

Their father went over to Spider and put one hand on Spider's shoulder and the other on the back of his neck. They stood there for forever, and Cyrus got a lumpy throat. Their father touched his forehead against Spider's. "Thank you, son."

He let go. Spider's face was red but also happy. Their father said to Cyrus, "Be back as soon as I can. Rest up, okay?"

Cyrus nodded and lay down again. It'd been a long day. The crew of the USS *Nepenthe* had survived the Bermuda Triangle and a real live hurricane. He'd have drowned if Verity and Spider hadn't saved him, and now his father was being a father again. Cyrus watched him walk away and got a little of that floaty, syrupy feeling in his chest he used to have when he was near his mother. He might never feel it as strong as he used to, but at least she hadn't taken all of it with her to heaven.

CHAPTER
FORTY-NINE

JUDE

Jude had been waiting in the emergency room for two hours. Two hours to beat himself up about having done a lousy job of taking care of his family—Verity, mainly, but also the other kids on the ship with her, who shouldn't have been out there in the middle of a hurricane, and also his father, who went from harsh dad to zombie to crazy person, and should've had help, serious help, long before he tried to pull his dead wife out of the ground.

He sat on the linoleum floor, his back against the wall. All the seats were taken when he got there, and he didn't care enough to move when one freed up. His shirt was torn, his jeans streaked with dirt, his sneakers so caked in mud they could be white or black, take your pick. His throat was raw from lack of sleep, and his heart was beating fast, too fast. The floor was tracked with slick mud, and the smell of stale water and fear hung in the air. The rain wouldn't stop. It ran down the windows, catching dots of light from outside, white headlights of idling cars, amber overhead lights, the blue and red from the police car at the curb, dots of light blinking and running together on the glass.

The windows themselves seemed liquid, like they were flowing into the flooded parking lot and bringing the whole hospital with them, and all the buildings, all the houses, everyone and everything going under.

Two hours was a long time, so Jude made the most of it. He watched the rain streaming down the windows and moved on to older regrets, blaming himself for not doing enough for his mother, for being someone else she had to worry about instead of someone who made what turned out to be the last days of her life better, sweeter. He couldn't do anything with his regrets about his mother, couldn't rewind the five years they'd been apart, but he promised himself that if Verity pulled through, he'd make it up to her. The promise was lodged front and center in his mind; he wouldn't be a coward one day more. Anger and ego, Jude had learned, would become monsters if you fed them. And the ones you promised to keep safe were left to survive by virtue of their bravery, or drown.

Jude vowed to deal with his dad, too. Because that was part of it. Everyone in the family was part of it.

"Vergennes?" a nurse standing in front of the reception desk called out. "Family for Verity Vergennes?"

Jude jumped to his feet and wove through the crowd, trying to read the nurse's expression for the kind of news he was facing. "That's me. I'm her brother."

The nurse was broad shouldered and graying. She gave Jude a sharp nod. "The doctor didn't have to call for a craniectomy to relieve the pressure, so that's good news. And she's awake. Follow me." She pushed through the double doors, down the central corridor, through more doors, talking as they went. "You can't visit long, and don't expect much from her, but she's doing all right. The doctor will tell you more."

"Is he there now?"

The nurse paused at a door that looked like all the others. "He was a minute ago, but he has to be everywhere on a night like this."

The number of machines surrounding Verity's hospital bed made Jude's breath catch. Her head was bandaged, and she lay on her side, to not put pressure on the wound, he guessed. Her eyes were closed.

"You can talk to her, touch her gently," the nurse said as she checked the monitors.

Jude squatted beside the bed, put a tentative hand on Verity's shoulder. She seemed so fragile. "Hey there."

Her eyes opened. They were bloodshot. "Hey," she croaked.

He smiled to reassure her. "Everyone's fine." He thought about their father but decided to keep it simple. "Everyone's at the shelter, and they're just fine."

Her face relaxed a little.

"Does it hurt?" he asked.

"Not bad."

The nurse said, "We can't give her pain meds right now, but I expect she's got a terrible headache and is being stoic."

"Sounds right," Jude said. She'd had to endure a lot, not just during the hurricane, but for years as the oldest kid at home, picking up his slack. He'd pushed his guilt aside, blaming his father for making it impossible for him to come home. But it was his willingness to put himself before his sister in the aftermath of the attack that was the real problem. He was ashamed of himself.

Jude took Verity's hand, the one without a needle in it, and held it in both of his. It was warm but barely, and his chest tightened. "I'm so sorry, Verity. I'm so sorry about everything." She kept her eyes on him, and he felt her willing him to continue. "I'm going to do everything I can to make it up to you. I promise." He kissed the back of her hand. Verity closed her eyes.

"That's plenty for now, son," the nurse said. "Are you going back to the waiting room?"

"Yes, I am."

"I'll come get you in a bit, after she's rested." She looked him over, like she hadn't really seen him until then. "You probably need to call your people, tell them she's doing all right. I expect you don't have a pocketful of quarters on you. Ask up front, and they'll make change for you, assuming the phone line's been repaired."

"Thanks."

Jude got two dollars in quarters. The line of people waiting to use the phone told him it was working. He didn't drink coffee, but he got a cup from the vending machine anyway and drained it before the taste got to him, burning his tongue in the bargain. To stop himself from worrying about Verity, he focused on how his other sibs were safe at the shelter and on the idea that even if his father had a relapse or whatever, there were people around to help. After twenty minutes of waiting, it was his turn. He dialed Uncle Henry's home phone, the best bet for a Saturday.

When Uncle Henry picked up and found out it was Jude, he let out a huge breath. "Lord, it's good to hear your voice. I've been waiting by the phone since last night. What's going on? Is everyone okay?"

Jude had been rehearsing what to say. "The kids and my dad are all at the shelter, except Verity. She injured her head, but they told me she'll probably be fine."

"Shame about Verity. You at Walter Reed?"

"Yes, sir." He glanced over his shoulder. A couple was waiting for the phone. "I have to make this short, but I'm hoping you can help me."

"I'll try, Jude. You know I will."

"My father lost it last night. He's been rocky since my mother died, but I'm not sure he should be in charge of anything right now."

"Okay, I'm listening."

"Part of the roof came off the house, so the upstairs is damaged anyway. I'm guessing we can't move back in, not soon." Homeless, that's what they were, and he felt both proud and nervous knowing the fix was down to him. "I need to find us a place."

"Everything's a mess right now because of the storm, but FEMA will be coming in, I'm sure about that." Uncle Henry paused. "I don't know what I can do about your father, though. If I say go right, he goes left. But if all of you want to squeeze in here, we can try."

Jude imagined his family crammed into his uncle's one-bedroom duplex. He had to do better. "Nice of you to offer, but we'll need more room."

"Listen here," Uncle Henry said. "Your aunt Faith called me this morning wanting to know if I'd heard from any of you. I can call her for you."

Aunt Faith, his mom's sister in Roseville, where Aunt Sarah and Uncle Bo lived, too, and their mother, Jude's grandmother. An idea bloomed in his mind. "That's okay, I'll do it."

"All right, then. You take care, and look after that sister of yours."

"Will do." Jude swallowed hard. It was one thing he was certain of.

~

It was dark out when the nurse found him slumped against the wall and woke him. She led him to Verity's room again, saying she was awake and stronger. They reached the room, and the nurse pointed to an easy chair in the corner.

"Might as well use that. And I'll bring you a sandwich. Some volunteers dropped off two trays full."

"Thank you. That's so nice of you."

"Just part of the job." She smiled to let him know it wasn't really.

Verity was sitting up partway and smiled when she saw him. It was the best thing that had happened all day. "You look awful," she said.

"Been a day." He picked up a glass of water from the tray angled over the bed. "Want some of this?" She nodded. He sat on the edge of the bed and held the glass for her as she sipped. He thought about telling her about his call with Aunt Faith. He'd floated the idea of the family staying with their grandmother for a while—she was alone in the huge family house—and Faith had been encouraging. But Jude needed to talk to his dad, so he decided to wait to tell Verity. She was going to need a while to recuperate—he had no idea how long—and that included not putting the world on her shoulders.

Verity leaned back on the pillows. "Any news from Dad? Is everyone still all right?"

"He's coming over once they're settled. I'm sure they're fine. The shelter is in the high school, did I tell you that?"

"No. What happened to you and Eden and the twins last night?"

He told her the story, a short version, skipping the part about their dad trying to rescue their mom's body from the flooding and going after Jude with the shovel. He'd tell her eventually, but not now. He had something more important to say.

"Before, the first time I was in here, I apologized to you, but I wasn't sure you heard me."

She fiddled with the edge of the sheet. "I heard."

"Well, I want to say what for." He took a deep breath and let it out. As many times as he'd done this in his mind, it was never this hard. But seeing Verity lying there, waiting for him to make things right, gave him the courage he'd never found before. "That night, when Nellie was born, I shouldn't have been drinking. Dad and Mom left us in charge of the kids, and I made a terrible mistake." He glanced down at his hands, trembling in his lap. He looked Verity in the eye. "All this time I couldn't face it. I made it about butting heads with Dad, and then I got used to that story, and it seemed impossible to back down, to come home, to apologize." His nose stung and he blinked hard. The words tumbled out. "But the thing is, you *are* one of the kids. I should've been looking out for you. I was always supposed to do that. Always." He let the tears fall. "I'm so sorry, Verity. I'm sorry I couldn't admit it. The longer I stayed away, the more ashamed I felt and the harder it was to face. I'm just so sorry."

Verity reached over and brushed the tears off one cheek, then the other. "It's okay."

Jude held her hands. His breath caught in his chest. "I'm going to take care of you now. You and that head of yours."

"Okay." She leaned back against the pillow, her eyelids heavy.

"You can go to sleep. I'm right here."

She nodded and yawned. She closed her eyes, and her breaths lengthened. In a few minutes, she was asleep, still holding her brother's hand.

~

Once Verity was fast asleep, Jude went to the lobby to try to phone his dad at the high school. It was weird he hadn't shown up, and Jude hoped it didn't mean something had happened. He passed by the front doors on the way to the phone, weaving through the crowd, and there was his father, standing under the overhang, pacing. Behind him rain was running off the roof like a waterfall. Jude pushed through the doors.

His father saw him, rushed over. "Is she all right?" He seemed worried but not frantic or strange.

"Yeah, the doctor said they have to watch her, but she'll be okay. She's sleeping now." Jude pointed to the lobby. "Why are you out here?"

His father studied his feet. "Restraining order. I sure wish I could see her."

"I'd forgotten about that." At least he had a logical reason. "Maybe I could talk to them and they'd make an exception."

His father nodded. "You could try. But just knowing she's okay is plenty." Jude sensed he was building up to something, but struggling with it, like Jude had with Verity. "Your brothers and sisters are doing fine. Tired, but fine."

"That's good." Jude waited.

After a long moment, his father looked him in the eye. "I know I haven't been much of a father since your mother died. I know I've been worse than no father at all." His voice was halting. Jude could feel how it cost him to admit it, and he felt sorry for him. "But thinking how I could've lost any of you kids today, well, it pulled me right out of myself." He put his hands over his face, overcome.

"Dad," Jude said, not knowing what to say.

His father squared his shoulders, returned his gaze to Jude. "I know you and I have a lot of patching up to do, and it'll take time, but for right now I owe you some gratitude." He reached out his hand. "Thank you for looking after Eden and the boys, and for getting me away from the house when you did."

Jude shook his father's hand, felt the strength and warmth of it. "You're welcome, sir."

CHAPTER FIFTY

SPIDER

Spider slid his dad's lunch cooler behind the passenger seat and climbed into the cab. His dad was tightening the straps over the truck bed, making sure the wind couldn't pull off the tarp covering their stuff. The bed wasn't that full; since they didn't know exactly what their living situation would be in Roseville, his father told them they shouldn't take much. The storm had made some decisions for them. Spider thought he'd have cared more about his stuff—his models, his posters, his favorite sweatshirts and baseball hats—but none of it mattered, at least not as much as other things, like Verity recovering from hitting her head and his dad becoming a dad again.

Spider's gaze fell on the freshly dug area to the left of the house, the spot that had been his mom's grave. Someone had gone over it with a backhoe, probably the funeral-home people. His father had told the older kids the coffin had to be removed because of the flooding, and since they were leaving town, the funeral director had suggested cremating the remains, "so you can be flexible." Their father accepted that, like he'd been accepting a lot of things recently. When he told the little kids the family was moving to Roseville, Cyrus asked what would happen to their mother. Their father showed them the box that held the ashes.

"Mommy-to-go," Nellie said, which made them all laugh for the first time in ages.

His dad got in. "All set?"

"Yeah, sure." Spider stared at the house, memorizing it. The roof had been boarded up, but otherwise it looked pretty much the same. The shed lay in a heap where it'd been flattened by the storm, and there was debris all over the place. The boat wasn't there. Before it sank, some folks across the river pulled it to their dock. They found Vermin in the captain's chair and went to the trouble of getting her back to Nellie, who was the only one not surprised she'd survived.

His dad rested his forearms on the steering wheel and joined Spider in studying the house. "It was a fine house. Probably could've convinced the feds to let us stay even without putting it up on stilts."

Spider nodded. "It's not the same without the boat, though."

"No. No, it isn't." He turned to Spider, really looked at him. "I've been meaning to tell you that what you did on the boat during the storm, driving it, sending up signals, well, I'm really proud of you."

"You already told me, Dad."

"I know, I know. I just want to make sure you heard me."

"Okay." Spider didn't mind him repeating it, not even a little.

His father went back to staring at the house. "We need to make some changes. That's why we're leaving." He rubbed his chin, glanced over at Spider. "What am I saying? I need to make some changes, and your mother's family is generous enough to help me do that."

"It's nice of them, for sure."

He nodded. "Never thought that with nine children I'd be saying we needed more family, but here we are." He sat there a minute longer, then started the truck. They went down the drive and over the bridge. Neither of them turned for one last look.

They didn't talk much as they made their way to Richmond, then on toward Lynchburg. Twice his dad pointed out interesting cars, and Spider asked his father what he knew about the Richmond canals: not much. The silence didn't bother Spider. He didn't want to talk about what leaving Mobjack meant to him or how he felt about moving to a new town, going to a new school. He wouldn't know what to say. How could he know how he felt about leaving until he'd gone? Or about the new house or town or school until he'd experienced it? He'd been a baby the one and only time he'd been to Roseville. Jude had been ten, Verity almost six, Eden two. After that trip their dad said if they went again, they'd have to tie some kids to the roof. All Spider knew was that Roseville was a smallish town near Asheville, his grandmother's house was right on Main Street, and lots of his mother's family lived nearby. Whatever happened there, however it turned out, he'd find a way to deal with it. The last few months he'd dealt with some tough stuff, and he'd come through okay. Better, even.

Spider watched the cars and trucks passing the other way, the drivers out on errands or going to work or driving away from an argument or maybe moving to another town, like him. He realized today might become an important day later in his life, the way the death of his mother might hurt more in years to come, more than it did right then, in some moment when he needed her. There was just no way to predict how much something would weigh in your life, what would come to be important. When Spider had taken apart the ship's compass, how could he have known he would use it to help rescue his brother? Life wasn't a straight line, and no one could see around corners.

After his mother died, his father had come unglued. Spider didn't blame him, though it was hard on everyone, including him. Like it or not, he and his dad were similar, both confused about the size of their feelings and lousy at handling them. They preferred to see the world as made up of things that could be taken apart and fixed, not of people whom you could love and lose. His father had opened up to one person, and when she disappeared forever, he couldn't handle it. How could you blame someone for that?

"The park's a few miles ahead," his dad said.

"Great. Because I'm starving."

Spider couldn't decide whether, for guys like him and his father, it might be better never to find someone special than to risk losing them. There was no point in fretting over it too much, though, because it wasn't something anyone could control.

~

Jude and their dad had made two plans for moving day: one for good weather and one for rain. The day was sunny and not that sticky for August, so the three vehicles would meet at a park in Farmville, about halfway through the six-hour trip. Verity was recovering from her head injury and wasn't allowed to drive, so Uncle Henry and Jude were the other drivers. Nellie, Cyrus, Harper, and Eden rode with their uncle in the station wagon, and Verity and the twins rode with Jude in the Nova, which their father had worked on so it was "more or less reliable," as he put it.

By the time Spider and his father arrived in the truck, the others had already set up the picnic on a table. The little kids were racing around as if they'd been caged for months. It was great to see them cutting loose, laughing.

"Hey," Jude said as Spider came up to the table.

"Hey." He nodded at Eden and Verity. "Hiya."

Jude pointed to the food. "The Vergennes Deli is serving ham, cheese, and ham-and-cheese sandwiches today."

"Ham and cheese for me."

"Two?" Jude asked, grinning.

"Yeah, thanks." Spider climbed onto the seat next to Eden, giving her a friendly nudge. "Harper keep you guys entertained?"

She rolled her eyes. "If that's what we're calling it."

For a while there, Spider had worried Eden would put up a big stink about moving away from Mobjack. She put up a little stink when she was first told it was a done deal, complaining about not being able to live without her friends. Over the next few days, Jude had talked her down, convincing her that they wouldn't be uprooting the whole family unless they had to, and that it would be worth it if they were all together and happier. Hearing Jude make the case shifted Spider's attitude toward his brother, that and how Jude was pitching in like crazy and making sure Verity rested like she was supposed to. He was acting like a big brother, and Spider could see Jude really cared about them, all of them.

Jude handed him a plate with his sandwiches. "There you go. Drinks in the cooler."

Spider said, "You got something yet?"

"Not yet."

"I can grab one for you."

"Pepsi's good."

Spider dug out two Pepsis and handed one to Jude. He felt Eden watching them, monitoring how they were getting along. He realized then how his attitude wasn't just his business, how in a family they were linked together. Spider had had his reasons, but what good had it done anyone, himself included, to hold on to his grudge with Jude? It dawned on him that it had always been more about him and his father anyway.

Spider popped the top on the soda can and glanced around at his brothers and sisters, eating, talking, roughhousing. His dad was at the next table with Harper, their heads nearly touching as they bent over a map. Spider lifted his soda to Jude. "To road-tripping."

Jude laughed and touched his can to Spider's. "To road-tripping."

CHAPTER FIFTY-ONE

HARPER

Harper stood in the doorway of her grandmother's house in the same navy dress she'd worn to her mother's service at the church in White Marsh. Her feet didn't want to move.

Grandma Jean took her handbag from the table by the door and looked past Harper at Spider, the twins, Cyrus, and Nellie waiting on the front porch. "We'd best be going before those little ones find trouble and dirt."

"Yes, ma'am."

Today was her mother's second service. Her father said she didn't have to go, but of course he wanted her to. He said the town wanted to honor the Maeve Bradley they'd known, and to welcome her family. "It's more of a celebration," he explained. In the month since the storm, her father was more like he used to be, paying attention, back in charge, but with a softer touch. Harper didn't want to disappoint him, or Grandma, whose house they'd taken over two weeks ago like a swarm of bees. Grandma said the house was meant for a big family, not one shriveled-up old woman. She was a trouper.

Grandma Jean gave her a closer look. "Not sure about it, are you, Harper dear?"

"No, ma'am." Harper fiddled with the belt of her dress. "Hard to be reminded is all."

Before they moved to Roseville, the easiest way for Harper to remember her mother was to look at photos or straight in the mirror. Now Maeve Bradley was everywhere. Grandma Jean had her daughter's hazel eyes (or the other way around, in actual fact). Uncle Bo had the same long fingers and the same way of looking up into the corner of a room when he was thinking hard. Aunt Sarah had the same wavy brown hair as Harper and her mom, and the same nose. She talked a lot, so maybe that was something that skipped straight to Harper. Harper had studied the photographs hung on the walls and standing on tables in her grandmother's house, tracing features and attitudes through the family. It was hard, though, because a photo wasn't the same as a person. Eden and Verity had the exact same giggle; you'd never see that inside a frame.

It wasn't that Harper was trying to forget her mother, but she didn't want to go running toward the hurt of remembering, either. She wanted someone to take the hurt away, like her mother did when she kissed her bruises and scrapes. She wanted to be a little kid again so she could forget faster. Everything that had happened since her mother got sick made her realize she wasn't in a hurry to grow up after all, that eleven really was eleven, and sometimes closer to ten.

Her grandmother took her hand. "I'll be right here with you. We all will." Harper let herself be led onto the porch and down the walk, feeling small but less scared.

They walked to the community center, which was just a few blocks away like everything else. The rest of the family had gone early to set up, whatever that meant. When they got there, people were milling around outside in clumps, and pretty much everyone turned to stare at them with cautious, sad smiles. Harper wished she'd stayed home.

The center was one big room, and lots of people were already sitting in the rows of folding chairs. Eden and Verity and their father were on a small stage, talking to Uncle Bo, Aunt Sarah, and some younger people Harper didn't know. Jude was over by the food tables with a bunch of ladies who were all smiling at him and touching his arm.

Cyrus tugged her hand. "Harper, is that you?"

She followed his pointing finger to a table crammed with photographs. She moved closer, not sure what she was seeing. The large black-and-white one facing them was her, except she'd never once had her hair ironed out and flipped up at the ends. She realized it was actually her mom as a girl, and it weirded her out, like her mom had handed Harper her life to do over again. What was that called? Reincarnation?

A loud voice yanked her back to reality. "Aren't you the spitting image of your mama!"

Harper came face to face with a hunched-over old lady with eyeglasses on a chain who looked like a raccoon. The lady was grinning at Harper, so Harper grinned back. "I guess I am."

"I'm Mrs. Hooper. I taught sixth grade here for years, had your mother in my class." She grabbed Harper's wrist with a cool, bony hand. "I'm so sorry for your loss, dear."

"Thank you," Harper said. She'd heard this a million times at the first service and knew that was all she had to say.

"Are these little ones your brother and sister?"

Cyrus and Nellie were going from one photograph to another, picking out their mother, and saying, "There's Mommy," again and again. People were stopping to watch, shaking their heads, and saying, "Oh my," and, "What a shame."

"Yes, ma'am," Harper said to Mrs. Hooper, and thought she ought to do something about Cyrus and Nellie, that they shouldn't be doing that. Or was it okay? This service was so much more confusing than the last one because here no one knew them, but they all knew their mother.

Spider came up to her. Roy and Wallace were crowded up behind him, like they were afraid of getting stranded. "We should go sit."

Spider led them to an empty group of chairs at the front, and the rest of their family came to sit, one by one, until they were all there. Harper felt better with the strangers behind her, and Nellie and Eden on either side, and her father directly in front, sitting between Grandma Jean and Verity. Uncle Bo stood in front and welcomed everyone, said a few things about their mom, and then Aunt Faith did the same. Someone who was a high school friend told a funny story about her and their mom getting lost in Asheville, and how their mom had talked a stranger into bringing them home, and how the friend had ended up marrying the stranger. Harper didn't get the point of it, but she didn't listen too closely. She was waiting for Eden, who was going to sing. Eden was so brave it made the three years between them seem more like twenty.

There was a poem, and then Eden got to her feet, scooted out to the aisle and up to the front. She was wearing a sleeveless yellow dress with white piping on the collar and armholes. It fit close to her waist, then poofed out. Harper wondered where she'd gotten it—a thrift store maybe? Eden's hair was held back from her face with a skinny white headband. The whole outfit made her look younger than she was, but more sophisticated, too, like it was her favorite dress, the one she always wore when she sang in front of people.

Harper held her breath. She knew what Eden was going to sing. Her mother had told them a hundred times it was her favorite song because it had made their father fall in love with her. If he overheard her say it, he'd claim the song had nothing to do with it, and their mother would just smile at him. She hardly ever sang it, but she hummed the melody so often it was a part of her, like her wedding ring.

Eden took her place, and everyone went quiet, quieter than it ever was in church. Eden took a deep breath and sang out the first notes, so clear, so pure, it almost hurt.

"Oh, Danny boy, the pipes, the pipes are calling
From glen to glen and down the mountainside"

She sang it slowly, like it was pouring out of her, just liquid feeling.

"The summer's gone, and all the roses falling
It's you, it's you must go and I must bide."

Harper's throat grew tight, and she blinked back tears. She had no idea how Eden could be strong enough to sing up there like that and not fall apart. Maybe the singing was the feelings, the way of letting them go. Maybe that's why Eden cared so much and got mad easier than the rest of them. Her feelings were huge.

"But come ye back"

Eden's voice soared to the roof and out the open windows, not by singing loud, but by singing sweet and true. Tears ran down Harper's face, and her love for her sister exploded in her chest, and it didn't stop there because all around her was her family, whom she loved just as much and just as true. She realized every single person in there was part of it, was behind her and her exploding love, that they'd come there because of her mother, sure, but also because of Grandma Jean, who lived in the middle of their town, and because of Uncle Bo, and because of the aunts and their families, and because of the Bradleys who weren't there at all. Harper felt the people of Roseville, the old teacher, the high school friend, and all the ones she didn't know anything about—she felt them behind her, and it was Eden who was binding them all together in their mother's name, with their mother's song.

Harper looked at Spider on the other side of Eden's empty seat. His face was wet, and when he turned to her, he gave her a smile, and she was 100 percent sure he had the same feeling inside him that she did. They all did.

"It's I'll be there, in sunshine or in shadow
Oh, Danny boy, Oh, Danny boy"

"I'm sorry for your loss," was what everyone said, and it made sense because the person, in this case her mom, wasn't coming back. But Harper realized the loss wasn't actually the size she thought it was. It was still gigantic and dark and sharp; there was no getting around that. Starting today, though, the loss of her mother wasn't something she carried alone. Eden had sung the loss out into Roseville, and when it echoed off the hills, it came back as love.

CHAPTER FIFTY-TWO

Verity

On a Sunday in the middle of November, Verity was on her bed with her calculus book open in front of her. Math had always made sense to her. If you understood one idea well, then adding the next one on top of it was no big deal, but if you went forward before you were ready, the whole thing collapsed. She'd always been a careful person, never dipping her whole leg in the water if a toe would do, so mastering one concept before moving on came naturally to her. Chemistry and physics rewarded the same patience, but she'd have to wait to take those. Two classes were all she had this semester at the community college, freshman English being the other.

She'd just about finished the problem set when her dad peeked his head around the door. "Should I come back later?"

"No, it's fine."

He sat on Eden's bed and smiled at her. "I've been looking at our money situation. Business has been good, good enough, anyway, so you can add another class next semester if you want."

Vergennes Service Center had been in business for over two months. The only auto shop in town had gone up for sale when the owner had a stroke, and her father had gotten a good deal on it. He wasn't licensed for auto repair, but there were plenty of lawn mowers, weed whackers, washing machines, and other tools and appliances that needed fixing. Uncle Bo had gone in on the shop with her father. He was sick of working in the factory and was already partway to getting his mechanic's license. Verity had never seen her father happier to go to work in the morning. Being his own boss suited him. He'd never had the opportunity, or never created it.

"That's awesome, Dad, but are you sure?"

"I'm sure."

"Because I'm not in any hurry. And what about the extra time away?" Three classes was almost full time.

"We've got it covered."

"What about Jude? He's already taking two classes, too." The guitar lessons Jude gave paid for most of his tuition, but classes and studying took time.

He nodded. "How about that? Two in college. Your mother would be so proud of both of you." He rubbed his chin. "In point of fact, for next year I'd like you to take a look at Radnor University in Blacksburg."

Verity stared at him. "Radnor? That's over an hour away."

"We've got plenty of vehicles." He got up, laid a gentle hand on her shoulder. "It's your turn, Verity. We'll make it work."

She threw her arms around him. "I'm so happy. Thank you."

It was her turn. Finally.

~

Verity parked the station wagon in the parking lot of the admissions building, an old Victorian house painted pale green and white. She'd gotten a little lost trying to find it and had only five minutes before the campus tour started. She hurried into the building, pulling her jacket closed against the cold. The admissions officer she'd spoken to on the phone had suggested she visit before finals week to get a more representative feel of campus life. Verity had almost responded by saying she was interested in only the classes, not campus life, but stopped herself. What did she really know about what she wanted? The whole point was to open doors, not run past them.

The tour guide was a senior biology major from Orlando, Florida. "Still not used to the weather," he joked, tugging on the fur-lined hood of his parka. He walked backward and smiled the entire time he talked, both of which impressed Verity. Judging from their clothes and their attitudes, some of the students in the tour were more like Verity than the ones at Halliwell had been. Radnor wasn't a liberal arts college; it had a nursing school, a business school, and an arts school. Verity was hopeful she'd blend right in.

If she had to decide then and there, she'd choose nursing, but if the past was any indication, she might change her mind next week, so she listened to everything the tour guide said. She imagined herself walking into the business school, standing over a bench in the chemistry lab, or being a student teacher at the campus preschool. The parents on the tour asked most of the questions, which almost always embarrassed their kid, and Verity was glad it was just her.

After a swing through the sports center, the guide led them into the student union. The main corridor was crowded with people mostly heading in the opposite direction. "End of lunch," the guide shouted over his shoulder. They followed him single file until they arrived at a central hall domed with glass.

The guide pointed out the offices around the perimeter. "There's peer counseling; the *Banner*, the student newspaper; the campus events center; ROTC and NROTC; Lend a Hand, the community outreach program . . ."

Verity tuned out the rest. A young woman came out of the ROTC office dressed in navy whites. She stopped near Verity to talk for a minute with another student wearing regular clothes, and Verity overheard them arranging to meet later. Verity didn't know much about ROTC, only that it paid for college if you agreed to go into the military afterward. What she did know was that she could see herself as that young woman as clearly as if she herself were dressed in whites right this minute.

As soon as the tour ended, Verity went back to the student union, screwed up her courage, and walked straight into the ROTC office.

A man in uniform, maybe forty years old, looked up with a serious expression when she approached the counter. "How can I help you?"

"My name is Verity Vergennes, sir. If you have time, I have lots of questions."

~

Verity arrived home just as everyone was sitting down to eat. Jude and Eden had made dinner—it was their turn. Verity greeted her brothers and sisters with smiles and hugs and sat down at her place to the right of her father, bursting to tell him what she'd learned. She was used to sharing her father with her siblings, but today, just today, she wished she didn't have to. Her father supervised the passing of dishes on his end of the table, and Jude took care of the other end, serving their grandmother first. At long last the only noise was the clatter of forks.

"Verity," her father said, "how'd the tour go?"

"Radnor's great," Verity said. "I could see myself going there." Her father nodded, but he didn't say anything, maybe sensing she had more to say, which she most certainly did. "They have ROTC there, and NROTC, too. Did you know that?"

"I didn't." His fork stopped halfway to his mouth.

"What's ROTC?" Harper asked.

Verity said, "It's a program where you go to college, but also get military training. The NROTC is for the navy and marines." The table hushed as now Spider and Eden also looked her way. "They pay for college, and then you agree to a few years of service."

Her father said, "I had no idea you were interested in that."

"You're going to college to be a soldier?" Harper said. "That's freaky."

Verity took a sip of her milk and rearranged her speech in her mind for the forty-seventh time. "I never thought about it before. I saw the ROTC office, and after the tour I went in to talk to them. I sat down with the officer in charge of the program at Radnor, and he explained it to me. He asked me about my grades and what I knew about the military."

Roy's eyebrows shot up. "Did you tell him you're already the captain of a ship?"

"And that you were in charge of a search and rescue?" Cyrus asked.

Verity smiled at them. "Actually, I did, but maybe not exactly like that." She turned to her father. "I told him you'd been in the navy, and that we'd all learned about discipline and order from you."

"And being responsible and accountable," Nellie said.

"Yes. That, too."

Their father leaned forward. "That's all fine, Verity, but what did he say?"

"He said that with my grades and SAT scores, and with my personal story, I'd be a shoo-in."

"What's a shoo-in?" Nellie asked.

"A superstar," Eden said.

"That's very encouraging," her father said. "You obviously need to think about it, make sure it's what you want."

"Sure," Verity said. "But then he said that considering my scores and everything, I should aim higher."

Her father blinked at her. She smiled at him, a big, open smile.

"Dad, everybody, I'm going to apply to Annapolis."

~

Time sped up after that decision, as if once Verity had settled on the direction her life would take, the wind gathered behind her. She finished the fall semester at Wyethville Community College and registered for two more classes for the spring: physics and Spanish. The credits wouldn't transfer—the naval college was four years no matter what—but she could keep preparing anyway.

The biggest hurdle was a physical one; she had to pass the same fitness test all military recruits did. She'd never been into sports, unless you counted hoisting children, but if she wanted to become an officer, she had to get into shape. She scheduled something every day—push-ups and sit-ups, calisthenics, and the worst, running—and wrote down exactly what she accomplished so she could see her progress in black and white. It was slow, especially the running part. At first she worried that her siblings would make fun of her, but they never did. When she ran around the backyard, Cyrus ran alongside her and quit before she did, calling her "a running monster." Nellie did jumping jacks with her, and Harper timed her shuttle runs. After three months, Verity ventured out onto the streets for her runs, and Spider jogged with her. He'd taken up cross-country.

"I'm way too slow for you," she said.

"Nah, I'm not supposed to run hard all the time."

She didn't know if that was true, but she appreciated the company. Running was boring.

One warm March day Verity was lying on the grass trying to catch her breath after a two-mile run. Two miles!

Eden came out with a glass of water. "Are you gonna drink this, or should I pour it on your head?"

Verity took it from her. "Thanks."

"You need new clothes, I think."

Smaller was what she meant. Verity was amazed how kind Eden had become. Maybe she'd always had it in her, but now that the family was healed, or healing, she let it show.

"I guess, although with any luck I'll be in uniform most of the time."

Eden waved her hand. "But not all the time. I know some places."

A year ago Verity would've said no. "You're right. I can pull off my jeans without unbuttoning them."

"Convenient." They both laughed.

Eden lay down beside her. The sun had real warmth in it for the first time this year, and it made Verity feel hopeful that better things were unfolding not just for her, but for all of them. One of the photos that survived the flooding of the house in Mobjack was of the crew in uniform in front of the USS *Nepenthe*, taken right before Jude left, before Nellie was born. The photo was on a wall in their grandmother's living room now, and Verity often looked at it, holding on to the feeling she'd had then of security, of things being as they should be, of her place in her family, which was then her world.

She thought of the photo now, and saw the lettering of the ship's name, its meaning growing large in her mind like a banner. A potion to take away pain, to erase what had broken your heart. When she'd looked up the meaning of *Nepenthe*, Verity hadn't known that grief would come for her and her family, that it would fell them like a tree. But she knew it now and also knew that without the ship, she and her siblings might not have survived their grief, not because of some special potion but because of their common purpose, built on love and carried through time.

Time and love. That was the antidote to grief.

The thought of going away left a hollow in Verity's heart, but it was a feeling she could bear and even feel grateful for. Serving her family in a crisis had given her the strength to leave them; that was the irony of it. If her mother hadn't gotten sick and died, Verity doubted she would've gone to Halliwell; she hadn't been ready. She'd needed to stand tall within her family, to guide their ship during the roughest storms in order to leave them behind. Now that they were safe, with their father at the helm, and Jude on board, Verity could set sail on a course of her own making.

"I'm going to miss you, Eden," Verity said.

Eden turned to her and smiled. "I'll miss you, too."

CHAPTER
FIFTY-THREE

JUDE

Jude scanned the roommate notices on the bulletin board outside the college cafeteria. July wasn't the best time to look for housing, but it was better than waiting until September, when the competition got stiffer. He was also eager to be settled somewhere before the fall semester started. At his father's urging, he'd signed up for three classes. Jude worried that with Verity leaving for Annapolis at the end of the month, his father would be overwhelmed, but he'd insisted. Jude figured he could always drop a class if it came to that.

Most of the listings were in Wyethville or north of there, and even the best of them sounded basic. He couldn't afford much but didn't want to end up in a dump. After more than a year of cooking, cleaning, and organizing for his brothers and sisters, he had standards.

> Housemate wanted (Colson's Bridge). The place: sunny, your own room w/ closet, shared bath (it's not the Hilton), decent kitchen, parking. Me: reasonable, friendly, but with ugly bathrobe. You: not a douche.

He laughed out loud and tore off one of the tabs. *"Charlie 555-3435."* Colson's Bridge was perfect, halfway between school and Roseville. Jude found a phone booth, called the number. A guy answered.

"Hi, can I speak to Charlie, please?"

"Not right now, but if you're calling about the room, you can come over any time after three."

Jude paused, wondering if this guy lived there, too. He'd hoped for just one housemate to keep things simple. Maybe this guy was moving out, but Jude didn't want to ask a bunch of questions over the phone. "I'll be there about four, if that's okay."

"Charlie'll be here." He gave Jude the address and directions.

~

The house was two streets back from the Colson's Bridge main street, which wasn't exactly Fifth Avenue. All the houses on the street were similar, wood but on stone bases, with deep porches and intricate carvings along the roofline. Jude didn't know much about architecture, but these seemed older and definitely nicer than the low brick houses that were everywhere.

He parked, climbed the steps, and knocked on the door. The porch had two plastic chairs, a small glass-topped table, and a few potted plants that weren't dead. The doormat was clean and newish. Promising.

The door opened, and a young woman about his age stood smiling at him, a half-eaten apple in her hand. The first things he noticed, aside from the smile, were her freckles. They reminded him of Wallace. Her hair was reddish brown and thick and hung loose over her shoulders. She wore a pair of faded overalls over a tank top and nothing on her feet.

She waved him in. "Jude, hi, c'mon in."

"Hi. Thanks." He followed her in, looking around for another person.

She caught his gaze. "It's just me. I'm Charlie."

"Oh, okay." He regrouped. "So the guy who answered the phone—"

"Is Pete, who's moving out. Moved out, I ought to say. Left right after you called. He landed a job in Raleigh, which is great for him but too bad for me. You know . . ." She gestured at him.

"New housemate."

"Correct."

"Hopefully not a douche."

"Correct."

She smiled again, and it caught him in the chest. He ignored the feeling because it was too random. Charlie led him through the house, pointing out obvious things, like people do when they show a house. She ended the tour with the empty bedroom.

"This is it. Walls, a floor, a ceiling, two windows, the works."

"It's great. Especially the walls."

Another smile. If she did that again, he might have to sit down. He concentrated on the place, whether it was right for him. It was better than anything he'd seen, better than he had any right to expect for the price.

"Is the landlord okay to deal with?" he asked.

"Mostly. He's a stickler for getting the rent on time."

"I'm never late with rent." It was true but sounded incredibly dorky.

"Good to hear. But he only gets on my case about it because he's my dad." She started walking out, then smiled over her shoulder. "You want something to drink, shoot the shit on the porch?"

"You betcha." *You betcha?* What was wrong with him?

She got them ice waters, and they settled into the chairs.

Jude asked, "Do you go to college in Wytheville?"

She nodded. "I'm majoring in psychology, hoping to go into counseling, probably with kids. What about you?"

"Music. I give guitar and piano lessons now, which is fine, but I'm thinking of becoming a music teacher, like in a school." Whenever he said it, it sounded strange to him. He couldn't imagine himself walking into a school, having kids call him Mr. Vergennes, being in charge of lessons, the school band, the whole shebang. It seemed so adult.

"That's cool. And you obviously agree with me that kids are awesome."

He'd been staring out at the street at nothing much, but Charlie's comment made him look at her. "Yeah, I do." This was where he logically would tell her about his enormous family. It was always awkward. People wanted a reason for it. "I've got eight siblings. I'm the oldest." He waited for her eyebrows to go up, prayed she didn't make the Waltons joke.

She tilted her head. "I've got four, and I'm the youngest, but I want to hear about yours first."

He told her about his brothers and sisters, and about his mother, and his father, about the hurricane and moving to Roseville. He hadn't planned on talking so much, but she kept asking questions, and shared pieces of herself along the way. The sun slid toward the horizon.

Charlie got up, picked up their glasses. Jude figured it was time for him to go. She probably had plans anyway.

"You hungry?" she said. "I'd offer you something from the fridge, but you'd have to take antibiotics first. There's a crappy burger place just up the street. Anything else is a drive."

He smiled. "Crappy burgers it is."

"On the way we can take down the room-for-rent notices I plastered all over town." She caught herself, and her cheeks flushed. "That is, if you think you like the place."

He scratched his head. "Oh, I don't know . . ."

Charlie's face fell, but then she broke out into a grin that made Jude dizzy. "Hilarious," she said. "Simply hilarious. Just for that, you're buying."

~

Jude took Verity's bag from her and swung it into the back seat of the station wagon. It couldn't have been more than forty degrees, and a light rain was sifting down, but everyone was huddled around Verity taking turns getting one last hug before she headed back to Annapolis. Their dad was there, all the kids of course, plus Grandma, Aunt Sarah and Aunt Faith with their husbands, and Uncle Bo. Any longer, and Jude would have to break the speed limit to get her to her bus on time.

Grandma Jean pulled Verity close, then pressed a foil packet into her hands. "A couple of turkey sandwiches for the bus, with cranberry sauce the way you like it."

"Thanks, Grandma. Your Thanksgiving turkey is the absolute best. Our mother always said so." Verity bent to kiss Nellie, who was wearing Verity's white naval cap. Verity put the cap on her own head. "Don't get any bigger before Christmas."

"I'd rather grow than stay short my whole life."

That made everyone smile, and Verity used the distraction to back away and get into the car. Their father closed the door for her and leaned his arm on top of the car. "You call if you need anything, Captain." He'd taken to calling her that since she had been accepted into the academy.

"Will do, Dad."

He leaned in to kiss her cheek. That sort of show of affection was recent, like he was trying out a new language, or relearning an old one. He took more time with the smaller kids, too, reading to them, or talking with them about school or friends. He even closed the shop sometimes if one of the kids had something special. It made Jude feel better about not being around as much, even though he was just down the road and ready to pitch in whenever. Right now, everyone was getting most of what they needed, and it seemed they would all be okay. Jude knew for a fact that his brothers and sisters missed their mother in one way or another every single day. He'd talked it out with his older sibs more than once, and together they'd reasoned that with some luck and with time to trust the world again, they all could become happy, solidly happy. The same might be true for their father, too, and that thought settled Jude, making him realize how much he loved him.

Jude started the car, and Verity waved out the open window as they pulled away. They crossed the town limits, and Verity rolled up the window and wiped at her eyes.

"Only a month until Christmas," Jude said.

She let out a long breath. "It's so hard to leave again." She was quiet a minute, switching gears. "I haven't had a chance to tell you how much I like Charlie."

"Yeah?" Charlie was a regular visitor, but yesterday was the first time she'd met Verity. Jude had been shy about telling his family his housemate was also his girlfriend, worried that it might break the spell, that she might change somehow if he shared her with his family. It had been a dumb thing to worry about. Charlie was Charlie, and everyone loved her.

"Yeah. You are kind of dense, Jude, but even you can see how special she is, and how she's nuts about you."

Jude grinned at his sister. "Go figure, right?"

She ignored the bait. "The two of you light up the room. Hopeful, that's what it is."

He was touched by that and fell silent. The rain came down harder, and he turned on the wipers.

"You know," Verity said, "I used to think hope was something you had because you didn't have what you really wanted. Kind of a consolation prize." She took off her cap, smoothed her hair, and put the cap back on. "I didn't think you could make anything out of it because it was too weak."

He wasn't sure where this was going, but her thoughtfulness made him curious. It was the same with Charlie, who was good at careful thinking. Jude admired that. "And now what do you think?"

She twisted on the seat so she faced him. "That hope's more important than what you actually have in your hand. You can lose what you have, but there's always more to hope for."

He swallowed hard. "You're talking about Mom."

"Sure," she said softly. "But not only her. We almost lost you, too."

Jude turned into the lot behind the bus station, a huge lump in his throat. He put the car in park and reached for his sister, drawing her close and accidentally knocking off her cap. She laughed, and the sound warmed him. They stayed like that for a moment; then he let go.

"You'll miss the bus." He got out, retrieved her bag, and came around the front of the car to give it to her. "Call us later so we know you got there."

"Will do." She moved off and waved to him. "See you at Christmas."

He watched her go, thinking of how different they were. Never a sailor and certainly not a captain, Jude had to leave in order to return and see the worth in caring for his family, something Verity had always known. By coming back, Jude made it possible to say goodbye to his sister like this, as a loving brother, and to leave home himself in the same way that she was, the only good way to leave home—with blessings and with hope.

AUTHOR'S NOTE

My inspiration for this story came from an episode from the radio show *This American Life*, entitled "The Land of Make Believe." Act One was about the Seinfels family of fourteen, whose father, Jim, constructed an elaborate wooden gunboat in their suburban Chicago backyard. I was immediately enthralled and used the concept as a jumping-off point for *The Family Ship*. Both Jim Seinfels and Arthur Vergennes served in the navy and believed the order and discipline of navy life would be good for their children and that the ship would entertain them. As far as I know, that is the only parallel; the sole source of the rest of my story was my imagination.

I adapted the recipe for number salad from the wonderful children's cookbook *Pretend Soup and Other Real Recipes* by Mollie Katzen and Ann Henderson.

ACKNOWLEDGMENTS

This is my sixth novel, and my agent, Maria Carvainis, has been steering my career with a steady hand during the entire journey. I'm grateful for her thoughtful guidance and unflinching support. Thanks also to her right hand, Martha Guzman.

Many thanks to my editor Chris Werner for his insight, intelligence, and kindness. I'm fortunate indeed to have my books in the care of Lake Union, and I want to thank everyone who helped bring this story to readers, including Jacqueline Smith, Gabriella Dumpit, Nicole Burns-Ascue, Hannah Buehler, and the talented art department. Special thanks to Tiffany Yates Martin for her incisive edits delivered with humor and grace.

Thanks to Karyn Cassello and Michael Renner for schooling me on data management and security, and to Julie Valerie for a map of Chesapeake shipwrecks, including a merchant vessel named *Nepenthe*, which sank in 1929.

I wouldn't want this job without my writer friends. So, Kate Moretti, Heather Webb, Holly Robinson, Kelly Harms, and Aimie Runyan, this is your fault.

While writing this book I received support and friendship from all over the place: my daughters, Rebecca and Rachel Frank, the Tall Poppy Writers, friends who loved me before I became a writer, and, of course, my readers. I heard and appreciated every kind word, every welcome distraction, and every joke, especially the bad ones. Thank you.

Richard Gill is always my first reader because he's closest, and because he's nice. He wants more fabulous meals, after all. Joking aside, he reads first because no one can be proud of me the way he can. I love you, corona buddy.

BOOK CLUB QUESTIONS

1. For the Vergennes family, the ship is much more than a playhouse. How did it seem to you in the initial chapters? How did the role and the significance of the ship change as the story progressed?

2. In large families it is almost inevitable that the older children will have to pitch in to care for their younger siblings. Is this fair? What are the advantages and drawbacks of large families, and is your perspective colored by the size of your own family?

3. Not surprisingly, the assault Verity suffered had lasting effects. Which stood out to you? Do you think the fallout from the assault would've been different for her if Jude had shown remorse earlier? Was it a good decision by Arthur and Maeve not to involve the police? Might that have changed how Verity coped with it?

4. Birth order and personality are two main factors in sibling dynamics. The middle child is typically the "forgotten" one, and Harper feels her position keenly. But Spider is also a middle child eager to be noticed, by his father in particular. How do Harper and Spider each deal with their anonymity, and what do they learn about themselves by the end of the story?

5. Arthur's love for Maeve was fierce. Is it possible to love someone too much? How did you feel about their relationship? In the wake of Maeve's death, what did Arthur learn?

6. What did you think of Eden? Outside of the context of the Vergennes family, would she seem like a normal teenager? How did her bond with Jude provide a springboard to both trouble and healing?

7. The story takes place forty years ago. Has parenting changed significantly since then? What sorts of challenges do you think the Vergennes family would face if the same events occurred now (e.g., Verity's school choices, the mandatory family time, and the relative social isolation)?

8. Jude had difficulty apologizing to Verity for his role in what happened to her. Did you empathize with him on this? How did interpersonal dynamics interfere with the ability of the family to heal from this traumatic event?

9. In a sense, Verity and Jude had opposite journeys in this story. Verity had to prove to herself she was strong and independent before she could embrace leaving home, while Jude had to return home and regain his sense of belonging before he could venture out again. What role did their parents play in fostering either independence or loyalty to the family in Jude and Verity? In your own life, how do you resolve the balance between individual needs and collective ones?

10. At the end of the story, Jude is on his way to becoming a music teacher and Verity a naval officer. What occupations or fields do you see the other children pursuing?

ABOUT THE AUTHOR

Photo © 2017 Tamara Hattersley Photography

Sonja Yoerg is the Amazon Charts and *Washington Post* bestselling author of the novels *Stories We Never Told, True Places, All the Best People, The Middle of Somewhere*, and *House Broken*. Sonja grew up in Stowe, Vermont, where she financed her college education by waitressing at the Trapp Family Lodge. She went on to earn a PhD in biological psychology from the University of California, Berkeley, and wrote a nonfiction book about animal intelligence, *Clever as a Fox*, before deciding it was more fun to make things up. Sonja lives with her husband in the Blue Ridge Mountains of Virginia. For more information, visit www.sonjayoerg.com.